For Jim

Acknowledgements

Thanks to my family who have supported and encouraged me without fail; my patient friends who have endured the anti-social tendencies of a writer; and my publisher who believes in me. For information and inspiration thanks to *Liverpool Wondrous Place – music from Cavern to Cream* by Paul Du Noyer and *Greenham Common: Women at the Wire* by Barbara Harford and Sarah Hopkins, and special thanks to all the fragile people who inspired me with their stories.

Our humanity rests upon a series of learned behaviours, woven together into patterns that are infinitely fragile and never directly inherited.'

Margaret Mead, Anthropologist (1901–1978)

PROLOGUE

July 2003

The light was hopeful. Julia Swann moved along the bow of the Royal Daffodil, taking in the intensifying scene: a forest of red, white and yellow cranes soaring above the skyline, jutting at inelegant angles over warehouses; tower blocks; two cathedrals, like prehistoric creatures emerging from extinction, bellowing into the evening skies. She read them as a good sign; this was a city rising to meet the challenge of a new millennium. Even the ferry was in collusion, slicing mercilessly through tea-brown waters to carry her to her purpose.

The sun, which had scorched the day, was now low, turning the city pink and casting a spotlight over the surprising grandeur of the Three Graces: the Cunard Building where travellers had once waited with great expectation to purchase transatlantic tickets; the Port of Liverpool Building, inspired by Italian Renaissance palaces, and, most striking of all, the Liver Building, stretching up into gull-startled skies, standing steady under an impossible cornucopia of turrets and domes. Perched at the very top of this colossus, balancing one on each of its arms, she saw the legendary Liver Birds, wings stretched ready for flight, one facing out to sea the other towards the city. She had heard it said that if the Liver Birds ever fly away, Liverpool will cease to exist. She imagined that these unclassifiable creatures, neither Cormorant nor Eagle, had strained at their ropes more than once since they'd been hoisted to the top of Britain's first skyscraper a century earlier. They had certainly seen a few sights in their time: from bombs to Beatniks; doomed transatlantic passenger ships to the gaunt faces of dockers. Nevertheless they had stayed, unable to resist the will of a determined people; or perhaps out of loyalty to a city that, at the very least, is never dull.

As the ferry reached the granite lip of the waterfront, serenaded by the swoop and cry of gulls, it seemed to Julia that she had travelled much further than the small wedge of the Wirral Peninsula – lying barely a mile across a bronze scimitar of water. With the first step on dry land, a thousand voices lured her into the blushing streets. The voices whispered of rebellious politicians and political poets; they promised to reveal their secrets. But more persistent for Julia than the call of the city was the cry from within herself. It had always been with her, growing louder with every passing year, until it had become almost unbearable in its intensity, rising to a deafening wail, a primal scream, and she could resist it no more.

CHAPTER 1

November 1983

People don't walk in straight lines. This thought returned to Beth Swann over and over again that day; she even found herself whispering the words until they became a nagging motif; an insane soliloquy. She was staring out of her third floor office window at the dark figures weaving their way through Williamson Square. What strange creatures, she thought; backs hunched against the winter wind, some walking purposefully, only swerving to avoid collision with other strange creatures; some turning on the spot, eyes raised towards street signs with brows drawn into puzzlement. The wind lifted hats and teased strands of loose hair; it tore at several stray pages of the *Liverpool Echo*, whipping them into a frenzied dance around dark columns of legs.

Beth had once read that when running from danger, we have a tendency to turn left, eventually returning to our own starting point. We don't walk in straight lines; we make patterns – curves, zigzags, messy diagonals, great flourishes, tight circles – and each line in the pattern is fragile and mutable; it can easily be shattered, or be sent careering off course. She wondered if, at the end of our lives, we could see the patterns we've made and what they would tell us about the sort of person we have been, the kind of life we have lived.

It was on this same day in November 1983 that a single sperm battered its way into one of Beth's last frail eggs. All morning she'd visualised the sperm's journey, hoping that its route would be straight and determined so that it could accomplish its mission before being swept, defeated, from the hostile environment of the cervical canal. Unconsciously, her hand dropped to her abdomen and she tore her eyes away from the scene in the square, back to the work on her desk.

She shuffled a pile of papers and randomly selected one sheet, covered in messy scrawl, and placed it on a stand in front of her. From another pile she lifted a virgin piece of A4 and slid it expertly into the typewriter so that the top was perfectly in line. She stared at the blank sheet for several minutes, thinking about her life and how it had turned out. She whispered a barely audible 'Gosh!' as reality finally bit.

Not only the reality of what she'd done but the fact that not one single person in the office, or in her life for that matter, knew that on the previous lunchtime, rather than cut diagonally across the square to Sayers where she usually sat alone in the functional caferia eating an egg and cress sandwich with a cup of strong tea, she'd made a great sweeping curve in the opposite direction. Nor did they know that she'd popped into a clinic, a hunched, grey building, where the sperm of an anonymous donor had been injected high into her vagina using a large syringe. The procedure had caused mild discomfort and some embarrassment but Beth was able to shut her mind off from what was happening down below and focus on six, dull strip-lights set in a yellowing ceiling. After only a ten-minute rest she slipped off the bed to make room for the next customer.

She still had time to pop into Sayers for a sandwich on the way back to the office. She sat all afternoon, legs crossed, imagining the sperm swimming with all their might up her fallopian tubes; she had chosen an athlete from the discrepant list of donors to give the sperm the best chance of success. Now she just had to wait.

After work, Beth waited outside a flaking red telephone box, stamping and shuffling against the wind; her home telephone was on the blink, yet again. Once inside the narrow cubicle she took shallow breaths so as not to inhale the smells of ash and urine and last night's curry and chips. She allowed the phone to ring fifteen times before placing it back in its cradle. She felt the need to tell someone what she'd done and Jack was the only person she thought would understand. She felt mildly annoyed that he didn't answer, imagining he was out with some new woman, gallivanting under the bright lights of London where he'd moved six months earlier.

She left the phone box and jumped on an 86 bus, climbing to the top deck and claiming the front seat. As they moved away from the city centre she leant her head against the window, absently taking in the scene and was overcome with weariness. For the first time Beth noticed the shabbiness of her city; it was as if something had shifted in her so that she could stand back, look at things anew. In the 60's Liverpool had been the apple of England's eye, but the media, which had once loved and courted her, simply could not get enough of her, now painted her as a slag, a thief, a scallywag. This angered Beth; she knew the reputation was largely undeserved, although she did know there were things wrong with her city, very wrong. She thought again of her father's words – she'd been thinking about her parents a lot lately – and one of his oft repeated mantras in her childhood, 'Hamburg managed to get back on its feet after the war, why not Liverpool; it's still a bloody bomb site.' She'd dismissed his words as the moans of the older generation but now, years later, Beth felt that Liverpool had indeed had its day. The docks were practically dead, the music scene was limping towards the brighter lights of Manchester and the population was in exodus. Last year at least two more cinemas had closed down, including the Futurist on Lime Street, one of Beth's favourites and the scene of her first kiss with Jack.

She jumped off the bus on Smithdown Road, pulled her black trench coat around her and bent her head into the wind as she made the short walk to Brookdale Road, where she was renting a small Victorian terrace until she could afford to buy again. She felt a sense of relief as she shut the front door against the night and breathed in familiar smells: an underlying odour of damp and hints of other people's habits living under layers of wallpaper. While she'd hated these smells when she first moved in and had made every effort to remove them with bleach and lemon air freshener, it had proved impossible. Now she subconsciously found the smells comforting.

Once inside, Beth hung up her scarf and coat and kicked off a sturdy pair of brown brogues. She turned the kitchen radio to BBC4 and was greeted by the mild voices of upper middle England. She pulled courgettes and onions, tinned tomatoes and rice from various cupboards and without much thought prepared one of her standard menus – a rotating mix of vegetables, stir-fried and spooned onto a steaming bed of either rice or pasta, along with sharp, tomatoey sauces sprinkled with dried herbs. While Beth loved food she found the daily preparation of meals a burden. Jack had been the better cook and it was at meal times that Beth was reminded most fiercely of his absence. She grabbed a bottle of red wine and then remembered she shouldn't drink. She felt disappointed, realising it was the wine that made the food palatable.

After eating, she turned off the radio and retired to the sitting room where she turned on the TV. She felt a pressing need to switch off from life. I might be pregnant; I might be pregnant. The thought was persistent and she didn't want to think anymore. Unfortunately it was a bad TV night and she became tired of getting up and down to change channel on her dying black and white portable.

After an hour, she switched it off and looked to her album collection for distraction. She filed through Joan Baez, Carole

King and Joni Mitchell but was wary of exposing herself to the beautiful cries of wounded women. She hovered over Dylan but finally succumbed to Badfinger. That morning she'd heard on the radio that one of the band members, Tom Evans, had been found hanging in his garden. She was shaken by the news. She'd had a thing for Tom Evans since first seeing him at the Cavern in 1966 and news of his death evoked all sorts of complex emotions in her. He hadn't even left a suicide note, the least you would expect from someone who wrote the haunting lyrics of *Without You*. It seemed a strange coincidence that Tom Evans had ended his life on the day of the insemination. Despite considering herself to be a rational person, Beth allowed her mind to dwell on this thought, imagining there might be some serendipity in it.

'Stupid woman,' she immediately reproached herself, 'What's got into you?" But it was too late; these quixotic daydreams had already led her to thoughts of Jack. She was surprised to find herself crying. 'Oh Jack,' she said aloud. 'What ever happened to us?"

CHAPTER 2

In the beginning there was neither male nor female, only a 'round' creature with four arms, four legs and two faces looking different ways but joined at the top to make a single head. There were three 'sexes,' if we can call them so, of these creatures: the double male, double female and the male-female; the first derived from the sun, the second from the earth and the third from the moon, which is at once a 'luminary' and an 'earth.' But as yet there was no sexual love and no sexual generation. The race procreated itself by a literal fertilisation of the soil. These creatures were as masterful as they were strong and threatened to storm heaven... As a measure of safety Zeus split them longitudinally down the middle and reconstructed them so that their method of propagation should henceforth be sexual. Since then man is only half a complete creature and each half goes about with a passionate longing to find its complement and coalesce with it again. This longing for reunion with the lost half of one's original self is what we call 'love' and until it is satisfied none of us can find happiness... if we continue in irreligion it is to be feared that Zeus may split us again, and leave us to hop on one leg, with one arm and half a face.
(Plato's Symposium c 385 BC)

"I still miss Beth." Jack Berry felt the oddness of telling his story to a stranger. "She's part of my life, always will be."

"So why do you think you left her?"

"She couldn't accept all that I am. God that sounds pretentious, doesn't it?"

The therapist didn't rise to the question.

"And what are you, Jack?"

Jack had to think for a minute.

"I'm not sure. I don't know if I'm a product of nature or nurture."

"Perhaps we can come back to that." the therapist nodded slowly. "Where did you meet?"

Jack wasn't sure if Cassandra was being over-curious or if her question had some significance.

"I believe first meetings are important," she said, as if reading his mind, "They tell us a great deal."

Jack wasn't sure what she meant but this was their second session and he was confident she knew her stuff.

He said, "At the Cavern Club in Liverpool. It was 1970."

Cassandra's eyes widened and Jack thought she slid forward slightly on her seat so that her voluminous dress slipped a little further up her calves. It was a nice dress, though a bit flowery for his liking; he guessed Laura Ashley.

"The Cavern!" Cassandra's face suddenly looked young and eager. Jack imagined her youth had been spent largely in the pursuit of knowledge and a good career; as a result she'd become a rather serious and sensible person. Perhaps she was living her life vicariously through the compelling and slightly sordid lives of her clients.

Jack said "I got the nights wrong."

"What do you mean?"

"I wanted to see Wishbone Ash but they'd played on the Monday. I think I have a habit of missing boats." Jack let out a short laugh. "Instead I went on the Thursday. I remember the date because Beth likes...liked to remember the anniversary of our first meeting. 5th February 1970. Anyway, one of Beth's favourite bands was playing; she was infatuated with the bass player. She told me later I reminded her of him." Jack smiled at the thought of this girlish trait in the otherwise very grown-up Beth. "I was only seventeen."

"And Beth?"

"Beth was twenty-four."

"So, quite a big age gap?"

"I guess so, but it didn't seem to matter at the time."

Another flush of interest was sparked in Cassandra, who had a keen interest in why we choose our partners.

"And what attracted you to Beth?"

"She reminded me of my mother." Jack wished he hadn't said this; he was only playing into Cassandra's hands and her obsession with all things Freudian. In fact, he'd never thought about it before, but he suddenly realised it contained some truth.

Cassandra nodded, her eyes skating upwards, left, towards the ceiling, as if remembering something, or putting two and two together. She has nice eyes, thought Jack, even if her face is a little plain. It was curiosity that made her eyes so attractive.

"Beth was a backslidden Mod," Jack continued. "At that time the Cavern was split into two – basement and ground level. You had to walk through all these growling Mods to get to the hippy scene in the basement, really weird. I saw this woman who stood still for me in the crowd: warm eyes, warm smile. She looked… safe. She had silky blond hair and lovely brown eyes. I offered to buy her a drink. Elizabeth Swann. Such a beautiful name; it kind of flies off the tongue. But she hated the name Elizabeth, and I think she preferred to be a duckling rather than a swan." Jack chuckled at his own joke. "She was just such a lovely, genuine person. I felt instantly at home with her."

"At home, that's an interesting way of putting it."

"I suppose I just felt comfortable with her. She was very accepting."

"Of you or of everything?"

Jack paused before answering. It was a good question. He

realised this was part of the problem. He'd married Beth because she was accepting of him; he'd divorced her because she was accepting of everything. She didn't challenge him, but neither did she embrace all that he was; it was a passive thing, her acceptance.

"Both. She was the most grounded person I'd ever met. I proposed to her a year later. Or rather we agreed to get married. She doesn't really like all that proposal stuff. 'Archaic sexist twaddle' she called it."

"Did she know then about your...preferences?" A blush momentarily brightened Cassandra's face. Jack wondered if she'd be able to deal with his story.

"I told her before we married."

"Immediately before or some time before?" Jack sensed personal judgement slip into Cassie's question and he realised the impossibility of finding an impartial listener.

"Two weeks after we were engaged," he said, without compromise and then, trying to balance the statement in his favour, he added. "I was only nineteen. You can be really selfish at that age, can't you? I thought she could love me enough to accept it. I suppose it was slightly better than waiting until afterwards. That would have been less fair."

Cassandra didn't look convinced. "How did Beth respond?"

"She laughed at first. I'm not sure if she found the idea funny or if she just didn't believe me."

"Or perhaps it made her feel uneasy."

Jack thought it probably made Cassie feel uneasy. "Perhaps. Anyway, I tried to convince her I would change... for her. And I meant it.'

"Didn't she ask any questions?"

"No, nothing, she just kissed me as if I'd told her I had an incurable illness and she wanted me to know she'd always be there. I feel guilty now thinking about it, but I did genuinely believe I could overcome my... perversion, as I saw it back then, with the help of Beth's love."

"But you couldn't."

"No. I couldn't."

*

Jack decided to make the long walk home from the leafy reaches of Highgate, with its babble of psychoanalysts, to the shabby grandeur of Stoke Newington with its underworld of artists and dropouts. Jack knew where he belonged, but it was still nice to travel up to the elegant sweep of Cholmeley Park once a week, to get fixed. The walk gave him time to think about the session and shake off some of the sadness that often accompanied the slow raking up of the past. At the same time he knew the painful process was somehow essential to his wellbeing.

It was a cool evening and the dark, moonless sky wrapped itself tenderly around the city. He walked along Hornsey Lane and over the elaborate cast iron arch, with its dramatic drop down to Archway Road, where Jack knew many people had over the years ended their lives. The therapy obviously hadn't worked for them.

He stopped to admire the view across London, looking southeast over the city and the river to the wasteland running eight miles east of Tower Bridge, the Isle of Dogs and London Docklands. There's nothing sadder, thought Jack, than an area once so vital lying waste. He continued to weave through streets that became significantly less affluent as he dropped down to Finsbury Park. He cut through Clissold Park to Church Street and was relieved to finally reach a deep blue door in Carysfort Road, the place he'd called home for the past six months. He momentarily wished he wasn't living in a shared house, but then he thought of Maddie and his heart responded.

CHAPTER 3

Certain points in life mark a dramatic change in direction, thought Beth, as she pulled weeds from the allotment skirting the edge of Sefton Park; a juncture after which it is impossible to say what the alternative would have been. She shook the weeds hard so that the good, rich soil fell back to the earth, then she threw the intruders into a large green bucket. She realised she'd had several of these points over the years; some of her own making and some beyond her control. She thought back to her childhood when she'd often had the sense of being carried along by events rather than influencing them. As a post-war baby she'd frequently been reminded by her elders that she didn't know she'd been born. She'd grown up on Scotland Road, known affectionately by locals as 'Scottie Road', where Lancashire met Italy met Ireland met Wales, met Scotland, met Poland; where Catholic met Protestant, church met pub, pawn shop met wash house and poverty met poverty, met poverty.

They'd been right to an extent, thought Beth, as she removed a large stone from the soil and placed it with several others on the path; as a child she hadn't been aware that her life was impoverished – there was little else to compare it to. It hadn't mattered whether she'd played on the beaches of the Riviera or the rubble of a bombsite, as long as she played and as long as she was loved. She'd always felt loved, but then she'd never had to try very hard; she'd been a lovable child: pretty, compliant, unchallenging and happy in her own company. Perhaps this was because she was an avid reader – the Lending Library on Scottie Road had been one of her favourite haunts. Rainy days were spent at home, sprawled on the rag-rug by the fire, her face buried in a book. She remembered, on occasion, emerging from a childish fantasy world to see her mother standing by the door watching with an expression unreadable to a child.

It was only in recent years, and not long before her mother's death, that Beth found an unexpected and delightful intimacy with her. They'd chatted like old friends and on one occasion Mary had confessed to Beth that she'd always felt guilty about not producing another child until Beth was too old to really benefit. The seven-year gap between Beth and her younger sister, Maria, was much longer than Mr and Mrs Swann had planned. "Not because I failed as wife or Catholic," her mother told her emphatically, "I rarely denied your father his conjugal rights and he never withdrew too soon; even though he was a Protestant." They'd both giggled at this. She went on to tell Beth she'd desperately wanted a big family, within reason – not the ten or twelve ragged-child families littering the neighbourhood – maybe four or five, a respectable number. But neither God nor nature complied with their wishes and after Maria arrived like an angel of hope in response to much prayer to St Jude, the patron saint of desperate causes, no more babies were forthcoming.

"Everyone was suspicious, even my own family." Mary told Beth, "they even doubted the depth of your dad's conversion to the Catholic Faith." Mary's expression was intense as if she was still living the humiliation. "It's only recently I've found out I probably had endometriosis and there was absolutely nothing we could have done about it."

Beth and her mother agreed that in hindsight this had been both a curse and a blessing: the shame of a small family was balanced by the lack of mouths to feed, meaning more food for each mouth. Mr Swann was doing well on the docks; he'd been promoted and was bringing in a decent wage. Soon they were able to move from the tiny back-to-back in Scottie Road, before the bulldozers forced them out to one of the sprawling and under resourced new estates outside the city centre. When Beth was nine and Maria two they moved to the more prosperous reaches of Wavertree. They had a backyard and a parlour and were close to a park. Beth had never experienced so much space and she quickly developed a liking for it. Unlike her mother, she didn't miss the sweaty intimacy of Scottie Road with its constant comings and goings: the knees-up every Saturday night when her parents brought friends and huge jugs of frothing ale back from the pub to continue the party at home, or the racket made by uncles playing banjos, accordions, pianos, harmonicas and old pans for drums, while Beth lay upstairs holding a pillow over her ears and Maria snored gently by her side. She didn't miss the haunting cries of rag and bone men clattering along the cobbles or the incessant chatter of women huddled in courtyards around clothes mangles and washing lines. She didn't miss the overpowering smells of communal Scouse and cabbage and she certainly didn't miss the stink of the poorest families living in overcrowded conditions. Beth found that, like her father, she needed peace and quiet. Wavertree was hardly rural England, but its roads hadn't yet been overrun by cars and the only disturbance was the distant rumble of trams along Smithdown Road.

Encouraged by her father, Beth joined the local Brownie troop, although her mum thought it was all a bit posh. She enjoyed the organised fun and quickly made friends. She obediently and quietly did her good deed each day. However, it was a Protestant organisation and when Brown Owl suggested she attend the local Methodist Church it posed a problem. As a Catholic, she couldn't conceive of attending a Protestant service and so it was politely suggested she leave the troop. Deeply disappointed and with a sense of rejection, she left without protest. Later, she realised that rejection was a stubborn pattern running through her life.

Mrs Swann never quite got used to Wavertree; she missed

Scottie Road and told Beth and Maria endless stories about it. Maria loved her mother's stories and longed to get back to the magical place she was a little too young to remember. Beth didn't want to go back, although she loved the stories softened by her mother's honeyed nostalgia. In fact, looking back, her mother's childhood often seemed more vivid than her own.

Before Beth came along, Mrs Swann had danced every Saturday night at St Sylvester's Social Club. She loved any type of music as long as it had a decent melody but she loved Country & Western most of all. "It came in from the sea," she said, her eyes acquiring a wistful expression, "brought by American sailors like a wave of melancholy crashing over Liverpool before anywhere else." In contrast, Mr Swann was a Jazz man; it was more in keeping with his Protestant reserve than the emotional outpourings of Country & Western, but out of love for his wife he tolerated the regular sing-alongs. Mrs Swann often sang in her thin, sweet voice and even tinkled along on the piano, which they had acquired with their rise in wealth. "If you can play the piano in Liverpool you're never short of a party to go to." It was true; they were invited to a string of rowdy parties that left Beth longing for escape.

Beth gently stamped down the soil and then crouched to make furrows with the trowel in the pleasingly rich, weed-free soil. She dug several deep holes and planted a row of onions. It wasn't the ideal time of year to plant but she'd neglected the allotment since the break up with Jack, followed by the death of her mother earlier in the year. The allotment had become a bit of a nuisance; she'd agreed to look after it for a friend who had gone to India three years earlier to 'find herself' and still hadn't returned. Beth felt she had no choice but to keep it up. She knew this was another fault in her character.

At the age of sixteen and shortly after the death of her father, Beth became involved with Billy, her first boyfriend and a passionate Mod. He was seventeen, although he seemed older. He was tall and gangly with short dirty-blond hair and an acne-ravaged face. He worked reluctantly as a post boy in the same office as Beth. After several weeks of his persistent flirtation, Beth succumbed and agreed to go with him one lunchtime to see the Animals at the Cavern Club. They left the office without telling anyone where they were going and taking Billy's advice Beth took a change of clothes; she soon realised why. As they descended the greasy steps to enter the cellar, Beth felt she was being drawn into something sensual, even slightly sordid. Perhaps it was the residual stench of rotten fruit rising to meet her as she descended into the earth, or the damp running down the walls in steaming black rivulets to form puddles on the floor. She felt she was entering a secret society, an ancient catacomb with primitive symbols painted on the walls, the sort of place she'd read about in books. The warm flesh of eager young people soon filled every inch of space, and any air that was fresh and wholesome was forced out into the world above. The clatter of the band and the screams of frenzied girls crashed off the concave ceiling and walls so that it was difficult to discern any individual sounds. Beth watched in a wonder of horror and delight, certain she was participating in something slightly sinful.

After that Beth went to the Cavern regularly with Billy and his friends, both at lunchtime and in the evenings. She had her hair cut into a sharp bob and bought Mod fashion from the market. The whole gang drove over to New Brighton prom at the weekends, showing off their sharp new fashion as well as their vespers and lambrettas, like preening birds on the promenade. Beth almost felt a sense of belonging – Billy was leader of the gang and took Beth under his wing. Life was never dull with Billy but he was always dreaming of London, where the *real* Mod scene was happening.

In October 1965, nearly two years after their first date, the relationship came to an abrupt end. The Who were playing the

Cavern and there was a great deal of excitement among the Mods. Billy was more uptight than usual and constantly on the move. Beth suspected he'd taken purple hearts, but knew not to ask Billy too many questions. They waited in a long queue that rippled with excitement outside the Cavern.

"Wow, Billy, it's great to be here, isn't it?"

"Don't get pushed around, Beth." Billy pulled Beth by the arm to get her away from the crowds, hurting her far more than the crowd had. Inside, the atmosphere was electric but Beth felt she was wilting in the oppressive heat. Billy pulled her around to different spots, hoping to get a better view of his idols until eventually she protested, "I'm going upstairs for a bit of fresh air."

"Silly cow!" he said when she returned. "You don't walk out on The Who. You're a fake Mod you are; I've always thought it." His eyes were wide, his jaw clenched and Beth felt afraid of him. She realised in that moment she didn't like him. The problem was, she couldn't think of a way out of the relationship; she was Billy's girl and you didn't rock Billy's boat.

But fate took its own course. After the gig a fight broke out on Matthew Street. Beth watched, terrified, as Billy kicked a man's head in; she heard the crack of bone; she saw hatred in Billy's eyes mixed with a glistening pleasure. She shook from head to toe and was sick in the gutter. Police and ambulance arrived, but Billy ran. The man he'd kicked was in a critical state.

Beth didn't see him again, although she heard through the grapevine that he was hiding in London. To her relief she also found out some time later that the man he'd brutalised made a full recovery.

After Billy left Beth felt enormous release; she could finally be herself again. But with the loss of Billy also came the loss of Billy's friends, who had never quite become her own. Beth had a miserable Christmas and New Year, retreating once again into books. However, at the end of January 1966, she felt ready to venture out once more. She re-visited the Cavern with Joyce, her one remaining friend, and it was there that Beth's eyes first fell upon Tom Evans. He instantly became the prototype for her ideal man – dark gipsy good looks, a gently sculpted face; the complete antithesis of Billy. Beth watched, spellbound by the movement of his long fingers over the strings, the heartbreaking soar of his vocals and his total abandonment to the music. Her heart pounded, her loins turned to water and she swallowed the desire to scream. After that Beth went to see him whenever she could, following his changing career through music magazines. On 5th February 1970, Badfinger played at the Cavern and it was at this gig that Beth met Jack.

Beth stood up and stretched her arms high to loosen the tight knots in her back. She shook the soil from her clothes, packed up her gardening tools and locked them in the small shed on the allotment. She noticed a line of ants marching with military precision across the path. Perhaps it was time to take some positive action.

CHAPTER 4

"Stoke Newington's an up and coming area," Ayesha said over dinner in her clear voice that retained only a whispering memory of India's lilt. Her dense, black hair, further thickened and curled by a fashion perm, swayed gently like a large cloud about her face. "You can see it if you look around."

Terms like Yuppie had recently hit the headlines and there seemed to be a frenzy of money spending and property buying. But Stoke Newington didn't look up and coming to Jack. It was full of squats, dilapidated bed-sits and arty types.

"You have to know the signs," said Mike.

"Yes," said Ayesha, "they're subtle, but they're there."

"Like what?" asked Jack.

"Well, look at trends in other areas, like Islington, which is also a run down area but starting to come up, as are the house prices."

"Well it doesn't really affect me," said Jack, "I'm kind of out of the game when it comes to home ownership. Not that I'm particularly bothered at the moment. It's nice to be free of it for a while."

"Well don't get too complacent, my dear," Ayesha wagged a long finger at Jack. "Property is the future you know."

Mike and Ayesha were something of an anomaly to Jack: a mixed race English, Asian couple, early twenties, passionately into Jamaican Ska and Reggae; talented musicians. At the weekends they played in local pubs and bars; they talked of riffs and chords, rhythms and rhymes and dabbled in cannabis and cocaine. During the week they dressed in suits with padded shoulders, travelled to Kensington High Street and worked in an Estate Agent's office where they talked about sales and profit margins, the market economy and mortgages. They were a dichotomy, hovering between two worlds: part-time hippie, part-time yuppie. But Jack was as enthralled by his housemates as he was by his new life in London. It was the daily encounter with anomaly that convinced him he'd made the right decision in moving to the capital.

Jack arrived in London with the distinct sense he was escaping; running away in order to find something. He'd made the decision quickly and acted on it, to everyone's surprise, not least of all Beth's. He felt some guilt but knew it was the only way. Life was just too painful for him in Liverpool. He still loved Beth, although he wasn't in love with her and he didn't want to drift back into a relationship, which he suspected she might easily agree to.

He told Beth he was leaving Liverpool over coffee one rainy Saturday afternoon in a café on Hope Street. Her eyes turned glassy but the tears didn't flow. He suspected she'd cried them all out when he'd ended their marriage several months earlier. He often thought, if he'd been of a previous generation, he would never have left Beth; there had been no particular reason to do so. He valued her steadiness and reliability; she was good company; they'd still had sex occasionally. But it no longer felt right and there were no children involved, although Jack wasn't sure if this would have made a difference to his decision. They remained good friends, meeting up once a week to go to the theatre or cinema and he would miss that, but it wasn't reason enough to stay.

He arrived at Euston Station with two small bags and the address of a hostel near Kings Cross. The first few weeks had been hard, but he'd never been tempted to return to Liverpool. At times he felt shocked that he'd fallen so far in the world, sharing digs at the grand age of thirty-one with young travellers and drop-outs; leaving behind a wife, a car and a nice semi in South Liverpool.

He was offered a job as a computer programmer with Hackney Council, the same job he'd been doing for the past two years in Liverpool. He spent a week looking for a place to stay and due to financial constraints settled for a shared house in Stoke Newington. It was a large house on Carysfort Road, in a gentle sweep of Victorian terraces emerging opposite Clissold Park. The size and solid structure of the houses hinted at their grand origins, although many of them had now fallen into disrepair. Even from the outside they were intriguing, with slight variations in style from house to house. Rising to four levels, with basements and attics, a variety of bay windows and a hotchpotch of skylights and dormer windows added at different periods in the life of the houses. The particular house he was soon to call home was even more intriguing inside than out. He'd been expecting shabby, lodger-land digs, like the many others he'd seen and rejected over the past weeks. In contrast this was an amazingly bright house, flooded with light from unexpected quarters and with an unusual combination of old and modern style. Several large paintings hung on walls and looked to be original. Jack couldn't take it all in immediately; he'd never seen anything quite like it. He was shown around by a small, crop-haired woman called Pat who was abrupt and anxious and wore a mishmash of baggy clothes over a squat frame. She asked him a series of, he thought, peculiar questions and he found it difficult to equate the bold, artistic splendour of the interior with this rather depressed looking soul. The room he was shown was small, but he didn't hesitate to say yes.

Jack moved in the next day and his spirits were instantly lifted. Over the following week he met all the residents of the house, including Mike and Ayesha, who had lived there for a year, and Pat who surprised him by leaving a vase of sweet peas in his room. It turned out Pat was in her late-forties and described herself as a 'Small-Garden Designer', something Jack had never heard of before. He laughed at first, thinking she was talking about her own diminutive stature but, with a frown, she explained it was about maximising the tiny amount of outside space that was all most people had in London. She was building up the business at the weekends, while remaining employed as a care worker with elderly people during the week.

Pat had a daughter, Kate, also living in the house. Kate was sixteen going on seventeen and had just started college. She wanted to go into advertising and make lots of money. Pat looked embarrassed when Kate talked like this; her daughter's materialistic attitude obviously grated against her own values. Jack thought Kate was a sweet girl, dying to start her life and not afraid to tell everyone how much she wanted to leave 'this hippy dippy place' for a sunny modern flat of her own. Kate frequently used American jargon, making her mother raise her eyebrows and tut. She attended aerobics in Islington twice a week and wore a pink Lycra leotard with matching woollen leg-warmers. She had blond hair, made blonder by bleach and cut short and spiky, with a long side fringe falling over her heavily made-up eyes.

Jack didn't meet Greg immediately. Pat told him, with some derision, that Greg had a "very full life" and wasn't often at home. Greg had the whole basement room to himself, was in his mid-twenties and described himself as an 'interior designer', another job title Jack had only vaguely come across. However, he was working in a bank, until his business 'really took off.' Greg also described himself as gay and had a partner, Dave, who visited the house regularly. Greg was good to have around. Apart from being, true to his name, a gregarious character, his partner Dave, a more reserved personality, was a chef and loved to test out new recipes on the household.

It soon became apparent to Jack that Greg and Pat had a long-standing personality clash. However, there was a loose and unexpected harmony in the household, with each tenant being united by the desire to develop an artistic interest of some description. Jack himself had discovered a talent for sculpting in school and still occasionally dabbled in it, although largely in secret. He harboured a fading hope that he would one day have a real go.

Everyone in the household was also united by Maddie, who was away when Jack arrived. It was only after a week that Jack realised Maddie was in fact the owner and she was in some way important to all of the tenants. It didn't take long when she returned for Jack to realise why. It was clear she held the loose strings together and brought unity. People noticeably brightened when she was around, like restless children when their mother comes home. It dawned on Jack that this wasn't just a house with a landlord and disconnected tenants; it was more of a community. In consequence, he realised it was no accident he was living there; he had in fact been carefully selected. He hadn't chosen the house, as he'd naively assumed, the house had chosen him.

CHAPTER 5

Beth felt a small unfurling of panic in her chest. Her usually tame emotions were rebelling along with her expanding belly and she felt acutely just how alone she'd become. Following the break-up with Jack she'd experienced a confusing mix of anger and relief. On the one hand she felt she'd wasted years of her life on a man who never really loved her enough. On the other she felt the sad truth that she'd never had enough about her to keep him and relief she didn't have to try any more. Perhaps that's why she'd lost him, she thought, this worrying tendency to resignation.

Immediately after his departure, she forced herself to join various clubs and societies venturing out on cold evenings to pottery and French classes. She also found herself reacting to the growing nuclear threat and Thatcher's acquisition of huge quantities of cruise missiles, and so she joined CND. Beth had grown up in a political climate; her father had been a union man, quietly fighting for the rights of dockers and as a child she'd been inspired by Bessie Braddock, or 'Battling Bessie', the first female president of Liverpool's Trades Council.

One Saturday afternoon, not long after the sperm clinic, Beth was hovering on the edge of a CND rally when she met a group of women who swept her up into their company. They were highly political, intelligent and, Beth soon realised, much more extreme in their views than her. They assumed she shared their political passions; they interpreted Beth's quietness as determination and her vague anger about Jack as a general anger about the oppression of women by men. They were women with grievances, but they shared a camaraderie and sisterhood that Beth desperately needed at the time. So, Beth dropped the classes, for which she she had no aptitude, and took to politics instead.

However, she was moderate at heart and preferred quiet protest, while her new friends aligned themselves with the growing might of Militant. In late November, not long after the pregnancy had been confirmed, two friends from the group, Sasha and Mandy, came to visit her at home. This was unusual in itself as the group usually met in the Flying Picket, talking passionately over pints and peanuts. The women had an earnest look on their faces and their bodies were set in a determined stance as if ready for battle. Beth liked Sasha; she was a highly intelligent woman, Cambridge-educated and with a dry sense of humour, saving her from over earnestness. Mandy, her partner, was much tougher, less likable. Beth had gleaned over time that Mandy was a damaged person – damaged by life, by childhood experience, by a series of men. Beth had seen her drunk on more than one occasion, dangerously, despairingly drunk. Once she had lain on the pavement face down, sobbing and cursing as if the world was just too heavy for her to bear. Sasha had patiently crouched beside her, counselled her, stroked her hair, despite the bitter abuse Mandy levelled back at her, until she convinced Mandy to rise and stumble home.

"We've got a proposition," Mandy said before they even sat down.

"Cup of tea?" Beth offered.

"Lovely," said Sasha, smiling broadly, although seemingly a little strained.

"Anything stronger?" Mandy looked around the room, her eyes narrowing.

"I've only got red wine."

"That'll do." Mandy dropped down hard onto the sofa so that

the habitat cushions flew up on either side of her. She lifted one DM-booted foot onto her opposite knee and hooked her thumbs into the red braces holding up huge, grey-flannel trousers.

Beth brought in drinks on a flowery tray and placed it on a stripped-pine coffee table. She moved over to the stereo and lowered a Joni Mitchell record onto the turntable. Beth associated Joni Mitchell with Mandy, who despite her tough appearance had the voice of an angel and sang haunting songs by female artists in a bar on Smithdown Rd.

"We're going to Greenham Common. Are you coming?" Mandy asked in a challenging tone. She quickly downed the glass of wine and then, without asking, poured another. She rolled a cigarette from a metal tobacco tin, reminding Beth of one her father had once owned. Beth didn't want anyone to smoke inside the house, especially now she was pregnant and any strong smell set off her sickness, but she decided not to bother with a confrontation. Nobody yet knew she was pregnant; it was Beth's gloriously terrifying secret.

Sasha laughed, but not at Mandy. She laid her hand on Mandy's knee in a non-threatening manner. "I'll give Beth a bit of background first and then she can decide, hey?"

Beth felt herself grow hot inside and a wave of morning sickness – which hit her at any time of day – coursed through her body. She controlled it.

"Mandy and I have been following the events at Greenham common..."Sasha began.

Mandy interrupted. "Yeah when the press have bothered to cover it rather than cover it up."

"Anyway," Sasha continued, "a mate of ours, Fiona, has been there from the start. Fi was part of the 'Women for Life on Earth' march from Cardiff to Greenham in '81, she helped set up the camp and was arrested after dying symbolically with seventy-five other women outside the London Stock exchange in '82. This year she climbed the fence to dance on the cruise Missile silos.

She's cool."

Mandy sat forward and held the glass of wine at a precarious angle; there was an intense glint in her eyes. "Fiona said if you're at the wire around the base you can feel the evil, see all the preparations for nuclear war."

Beth suspected Mandy was as much excited by the prospect of a fight as by the cause.

"In August she was part of the die-in for Nagasaki day..." Sasha continued.

"Yeah, all the women painted their profiles on the road, like dead bodies," said Mandy. "She's taken fencing down, been arrested four times, had several beatings by the Pigs. Anyway, today she called us and said the first missile-carrying transporters have just arrived at Greenham."

"On 11th December they're doing this huge thing with mirrors," said Sasha. "They want to get at least fifty thousand women to encircle the base and reflect the evil back at itself."

"We all should go." Mandy pointed jaggedly into the air and began what sounded like a rehearsed speech, "Cruise is a symbol of nuclear terror, male domination and imperialistic exploitation. Even the oppressive labels dividing women in our male dominated society are coming down, lesbian and hetero, black and white; we're all having dialogue at last. We're all one, fighting against patriarchy. It's men who determine how our world resources are used." Mandy started to pace the floor, still clutching the glass like a hand-grenade she was prepared to throw.

As if sensing Beth's hesitation, Sasha added an imploring note to her voice. "Beth, you already know that women make up half the population, do two thirds of its work but only get one tenth of its income and less than one-hundredth of its assets. Our stolen wages subsidise the world military economy. We have absolutely no economic power."

Beth had a growing sense that Sasha was trying to prove to

Mandy she was wrong about Beth's apathy.

"And that's why," Mandy continued, "last year Britain spent over eleven million on armaments while eighteen million of the world's children died of starvation."

"I know that, but..." Beth attempted.

"Unlike male society where we compete for everything, instead of working for the good of all." Mandy now hovered above Beth, legs planted wide apart, wine glass held high like a torch, "At Greenham Common they function without hierarchy. For generations we've stored up our rage towards men – fathers, bosses... husbands." Mandy nodded pointedly at Beth. "All the relationships that make us feel powerless. Now we need to start from scratch with women. But we're going to peace instead of war. It's a women's revolution, a resistance."

"We need to build a positive image of ourselves in a way that isn't so much anti-men as pro-women." Sasha tempered Mandy's rage with soft tones.

By now Beth's head was spinning with the barrage of information. They were telling her nothing new, or anything with which she didn't already agree. However, she was growing increasingly anxious by what her own response must be. She knew the news of her pregnancy would cause confusion among the women and that their views of her decision to use a sperm donor would vary. They'd had a discussion about it recently, following a news item on the subject. One or two of the women, including Mandy, expressed their revulsion at having any contact, no matter how perfunctory, with male sperm; others said they could just about do it if the end result was guaranteed to be female. Sasha had argued that surely using a sperm donor was the ultimate act of feminism, at which point the debate had turned savage. This had put Beth off the idea of sharing her news with them until absolutely necessary.

"But what about living conditions at the camp?" Beth felt feeble for raising something so pedestrian. Mandy looked baffled by the inane question.

"Yes it's a challenge, Beth," said Sasha, "but Fiona said it's also an adventure. Yes, it's hard in winter, but not impossible. They've built warm, comfortable homes called benders; you can build one in an afternoon. Supporters from outside are always sending food and firewood to keep them going –"

"Maybe I could do that!' Beth attempted with a sudden flash of enthusiasm. I could send stuff from the allotment..."

"It's not the same as being there." Now there was anger in Mandy's voice. Beth shrank in the face of it.

"Look," she caved in, "I might come to the mirror thingy on 11th December, just to see, before I commit."

Sasha smiled, her body relaxing into the sofa. But Mandy was still puzzled. She leaned over Beth, her boots making deep indents in the rug. Beth caught a whiff of alcohol, stronger than wine, on her breath.

"Why can't you just commit, now."

Beth looked to Sasha for support.

"No that's great, Beth," said Sasha, looking up at Mandy imploringly. "It's a good start."

CHAPTER 6

At six am on 11th December Beth and ten other women, including Sasha and Mandy, boarded a battered blue mini-bus outside the Union Centre on Hardman Street, to travel to the US airbase at Greenham Common. Mandy was at the wheel, smoking a roll up, her elbow sticking out of the open window despite the sharply cool air of an unmerciful winter's morning. Beth felt half dead, although no-one except Sasha commented on her paleness; they were already firing themselves up for the fray. They drank strong coffee from flasks and ate warm toast wrapped in foil while singing protest songs.

The sun rose at eight as they were leaving the M5 at Gloucester and the sense of excitement increased as the Cotswolds opened up before them like the promise of a new world. They arrived in Newbury at nine and were welcomed onto the main camp by Fiona.

"Hey sisters!" She hugged Sasha warmly and Mandy less so. "Glad you brought peace reinforcements." She smiled broadly at all of them. Beth was aware of her own clean-cut appearance. Fiona was browned by the elements; her fingernails were short and dirty and her straw-blond hair was tied in a tatty knot on top of her head. She wore a pair of faded blue dungarees, carelessly rolled up above black DMs.

"How about some tea to warm you up?"

All the women nodded enthusiastically. They sat or squatted in and around Fiona's bender, warming themselves on a communal fire and sipping surprisingly good tea. The benders were makeshift structures made up of a hotchpotch of ready-made tents with extensions of bamboo and branches covered in plastic and tarpaulin, giving a refugee feel to the camp. Some of the women used pallets under sleeping bags while others had various mattress substitutes. The women had a few modern luxuries such as deckchairs, cushions, Calor gas stoves, cooking utensils and plastic washing up bowls. There was a variety of musical instruments strewn inside and out of the benders.

Beth was shocked by the miles of harsh, wire fencing surrounding, what Fi explained, had once been common land covered in golden gorse and teeming with wildlife. Now the area was flat and laid with grey concrete. However, outside the wire there were still plenty of trees providing beauty as well as shelter from cold winds. There was a strong scent of grass and damp earth that had the pleasing effect of relieving Beth's sickness. Fiona took a lead in explaining the plan and answering any questions from the new arrivals.

"Same time last year we had over thirty thousand women to embrace the base," she said, sitting on her haunches and sipping tea, while balancing a cigarette between her fingers. "It was amazing. My God, it was a massive thing, but we did it and it was a huge success. We're expecting more this year and we've added the mirror idea. We also had telephone lines set up in London and Newbury for all the enquiries. You wouldn't believe how many women asked if they could bring their husbands along. We had to keep telling them this is a women's action. Why do we always have to fight for the right to organise for ourselves?"

There were nods and noises of assent from women in the circle.

"The energy of the women was amazing; we felt it could dissolve the evil from the camp, lock in the horrors of war. All the women decorated that wire fence," Fi nodded towards the offending structure, "with balloons and rags, wool and twine, photographs and baby clothes."

Beth's hand automatically fell over her womb; she disguised the movement with a quick rub as if removing a speck of dirt from her clothes. "Tell me, what was it like... the march and being the first women here?"

"The march was amazing, Beth. We sent out these fliers. On one side was written '*Why are we walking 120 miles from a nuclear weapons factory in Cardiff to a site for cruise missiles in Berkshire?*' on the back was a picture of a baby born dead and deformed, a victim of radiation from Hiroshima."

A shiver ran down Beth's spine.

"For most of us it was a radical thing to even take ten days out of our normal lives," said Fiona. "None of us knew what would grow out of it."

"Anyway, now that you've started warming up, do you want a tour?"

Fiona stood up in one graceful movement and they all followed. The camp was made up of an array of tipis, tents and benders as well as fairly primitive toilet blocks and showers, which Fiona explained had been donated by a woman's group.

Fiona led them to a Porto Cabin. Inside, there was a long table littered with leaflets, badges and posters advertising upcoming events. One wall was covered with messages of support from women all over the world. A stack of materials, which Beth assumed was for making banners, filled one corner while several balls of wool were piled high in another. Beth had seen pictures on the news of the Greenham women making large webs out of wool. It had become one of the most poignant symbols of the interconnectedness of women.

"This is the office," said Fiona. Loads of people have donated stuff ranging from typewriters to offers of hot baths in their homes. We invite speakers to a public meeting here every Sunday."

They left the Porto Cabin and Fi led them to a tall Poplar Tree.

"This is the tree house. In May, last year they tried to evict us; we climbed up there. They tore it down and dragged us out, damaging the tree and hurting some of us in the process."

They continued their stroll through the camp observing women going about their daily routines. Beth noticed a few young children running about, but she couldn't help feeling it wasn't a fit place for a baby.

"In June last year we did a 'Die in' at Hyde Park," said Fiona, "Reagan was due to visit at Thatcher's request and we couldn't let it go unmarked. We met in Jubilee gardens…"

"Bloody early," said one of the women, Angie.

"We just lay in the road, really still," said Fiona

"I was scared I'd be run over by a car," said Angie, "or worse still be jabbed by an irate office worker with one of those pointy umbrellas."

"One of the biggest events so far was on August 9th, Nagasaki day. We planned to get into the base. I was terrified about it; there was a threat of fourteen years in prison for breaching security. We got in and sat round in a circle holding hands. We didn't even get arrested, just escorted out."

"We then raided our heads for an even better idea to attract attention and we came up with the 'Surround the Base' idea. We worked out we needed at least ten thousand women to completely surround the base." Fiona led them back to the office where they sat in a circle making banners and weaving webs. More women were arriving all the time in vans and cars, sometimes on foot or by bicycle.

It happened spontaneously. No shouts or orders, no whistles, but at some point women stood up and linked hands around the camp. Hymns and folk songs echoed around the wire like hypnotic spells breaking the curse of nuclear arms, rising up above the camp to form a web. Some women planted flower seeds around the circumference of the fence. All held up mirrors to reflect the evil images of war back into the camp.

"Take a good look at yourselves, war mongers," some of the women shouted. Others cried, "Peace." Some just lifted their faces to the winter skies, silent tears streaming down cheeks pink with cold. Beth found her own eyes spontaneously streaming with tears; for a moment she glimpsed the possibility that love could really stop war and the destruction of the planet; she felt a rare certainty that this was right, that she could live here, bring a child into the world among all this love and purpose. What was the future for her child if she didn't take action? Beth lifted her mirror high, feeling a sudden energy infuse her body and mind. She was growing a life and she had to make sure the world was safe for that life.

Then the violence began. Police came in vans, dragging women by the hair, throwing them in the mud or into the back of the vehicles. Beth was astounded and scared; despite knowing this might happen the reality was beyond anything she had experienced. She tried to run away, but the mud clung to her boots making it difficult to move, like in a bad dream. There were women all around her, some standing up to the force of the police, some cowering before it. Then she saw Mandy fighting with all her might. She was battering a police woman, using her fists like a real fighter, as well as her booted feet, while swearing and cursing. Beth was shocked but stood rooted to the spot unable to leave the scene.

Another police officer came to the policewoman's aid and together they threw Mandy off, but not before she'd done some serious damage to the policewoman's face. Blood dripped from her nose and her eyes was already swelling into an unrecognisable mess. They ran after her, cursing. Mandy went lurching across the ground, still swearing and blind with fury. She fell into Beth, catching her between the ribs with an elbow and then stumbled on, unaware of the collision.

Beth felt winded and scared. She hobbled back to Fiona's

bender in agony, clutching her ribs, with the shouts and screams of women echoing all around. She took off her muddied boots outside the bender and then curled up on the lumpy mattress fully clothed, her right hand resting over her womb. It was a long time before she stopped shaking and much longer again until she fell into an uneasy sleep.

She was up at six am vomiting violently among the trees. She knew with certainty she couldn't stay here. It was the wrong time, or she was the wrong person; she wasn't sure which, but she longed for the warmth and security of her own home. She felt disappointed in herself, but it wasn't that she didn't care; she just didn't care enough to put herself, or her unborn child, at risk. She poured fresh water into the kettle and lit the stove.

"Wow what a day." Sasha stretched from the tent an hour later. It was obvious she'd slept well and looked totally at home in this Armageddon.

"Are you OK Beth? I came looking for you last night and I found you here, dead to the world?"

"Yeah, I was tired."

"Let's get some more tea brewing, shall we?" She re-filled the dented tin kettle, and placed it back on the stove. "So simple, hey."

Mandy soon emerged from another tent; her face grey. Beth was surprised, firstly that she'd escaped arrest and secondly that she didn't appear to have a mark on her. Mandy sat down heavily on the plastic sheet and rolled a cigarette in silence.

"Hey sisters!" Fiona appeared a few minutes later, clutching a towel and soap. "Great, you've got the tea on. There's bread hiding out somewhere; I'm starving."

Gradually other women joined them, some carrying wood, some food and drink. They discussed the events of the previous day in jubilant tones.

"I've just heard there were over fifty thousand women here yesterday," said Fi, "twenty thousand more than last year. A few women have ended up in hospital, though, after the police got hold of them."

"Shit!" said Sasha. "I actually had quite a good chat with one policeman; he almost seemed to sympathise with what we're trying to do."

"A lot of good talking's going to do." Mandy grunted. "They're incapable of understanding anything; thick as pigshit, the pigs."

A vivid picture was playing in Beth's mind: Mandy laying into the policewoman, hatred in her face. Beth studied Sasha's face. She was attractive, beautiful at times. Her pale, luminous skin, bare of makeup was striking and her dark lashes framed jade-green eyes. There was so much intelligence in those eyes and, what was the word Beth was searching for…compassion. Yes, there was genuine compassion. Was it the compassion that kept her with Mandy, or was it fear? There had been rumours that Mandy had hit Sasha on more than one occasion, usually when drunk. Sasha had excused it with, "She's not in her right mind," or, "She's had a hard life."

"So who's staying?" Fiona finally asked the question Beth had been dreading. She looked around, smiling, as if she couldn't imagine anyone wanting to leave this haven of female love.

"Yeah definitely," said Sasha and Mandy in unison. A couple of the other women nodded vigorously.

"I'm even more convinced after last night," said another woman, through a mouthful of bread.

"How about you, Beth?" Mandy looked at her pointedly, the others turned.

"Er… yesterday was brilliant, so worthwhile; I'm really glad I came…but no. I'm not staying."

"Why not?" Mandy wouldn't make any concessions.

"It's just not the right time for me." Beth felt feeble. She was growing hot inside.

"It's the right bloody time for the world, woman. What are you going to do, wait until the planet's been obliterated? Will that be the right time?"

"I'm sure Beth's got her reasons, Mands." Sasha spoke gently and laid her hand on Mandy's thigh.

"Yes," Fiona nodded, "We've each got to make our own decision."

"Everyone's got a bloody reason not to act." Mandy pushed Sasha's hand away and looked pointedly at Beth, "It's just apathy."

The words hit the target and they stung. At last Beth felt the rise of anger. "It's not apathy… I'm pregnant." She couldn't have anticipated the silence that fell or the look of horror in Mandy's eyes.

"How?" Sasha looked wounded as well as shocked, and Beth could see her sharp mind trying to work it all out. Jack had left over eight months ago and it was clear she was only in the very early stages of pregnancy. She hadn't mentioned a new man in her life.

"I used a sperm donor." Beth reddened.

"Why the hell did you do that?" asked Mandy.

"Because I wanted a baby, of course," she said with sarcasm. She'd had enough of Mandy's bullying.

"Yeah, so you can conform to society's expectations. Like you keep contact with Jack, despite what he did to you."

"But I didn't say he did –"

"Despite the fact he's an oppressor. You're a traitor." Mandy awkwardly rose from her seated position and stormed off, cigarette ash flying through the air like shrapnel.

Beth began to cry. Sasha hung her head in obvious embarrassment.

Fiona patted Beth's back. "Don't take it too much to heart, hun. She's just angry."

"I didn't realise she disliked me so much."

"She doesn't dislike you." Sasha lifted her head. "She just doesn't… understand you." Beth was sure she was about to say trust rather than understand, but she guessed both amounted to the same thing.

Not all of the group were as harsh as Mandy but it was becoming increasingly obvious she had little in common with most of them outside of the anger that bound them together. In truth, when Beth found out she was pregnant, her anger, which had only ever been moderate, crumbled away like plaster from a damp wall, leaving her true self-exposed beneath – dispassionate and quiet. Once again, she felt like a fake. She had nothing left to say.

The less committed drove back to Liverpool silenced by shame. Beth huddled for warmth beneath a damp blanket at the back of the bus. They said awkward goodbyes as she slipped out on Smithdown Road. Beth felt deflated as she entered the darkness of the house. Her ribs hurt even more than on the previous day and she felt nauseous. She knew that once again she had lost not one, but a whole group of friends.

CHAPTER 7

December 1983

At first, Jack had been shocked by Maddie's beauty. She had a broad face and clear, green eyes, reminding him of marbles he'd played with as a boy. Her flaxen hair contrasted with smooth, honey-brown skin. She might have appeared cool if it wasn't for the ripeness of her lips and the smile habitually playing around her eyes. Her mouth looked as if it always held a question waiting to be asked. Jack felt the stirring of his heart but he quickly stilled it. He had already made the decision to seek out a therapist and try, once and for all, to understand the inner workings of his mind. He knew it was not the right time to be falling in love.

He decided to stay in London for Christmas and was glad to have a reason not to visit his father in Liverpool. He was weary of trying year after year to force conversation and jollity from a desperate situation, knowing they would eventually give in to the opiate of television. Jack's sisters Maggie and Agnes had given up inviting him for Christmas years ago.

"He just complains about the noise the kids make," said Agnes. "He prefers to dwell in his own misery."

For years Jack and Beth had invited Dan to spend Christmas with them but as soon as their dinner plates were clean he would demand to be taken home.

"It's as if he can't bear to be away from the house where Mum died," Jack once commented to his sisters.

"He should have appreciated Mum when she was alive," said Agnes. "Instead of treating her like crap. Does he think she's going to come tappin' on the window like the ghost of bloody Cathy?" However, Jack felt sorry for his dad, understanding how easy it was to heap misery and regret upon your own life.

Two weeks before Christmas, Maddie invited Jack up to her flat for "a drink" and to "make a proposal," she said, with a tantalising smile. He'd never seen her apartment before, it was a mystery to him, a place at the top of the house where she disappeared to at night or when wanting to be alone.

After dinner Jack walked tentatively up the stairs to the third floor, clutching a bottle of Rioja and feeling surprisingly nervous. It was as clear as possible that he and Maddie were just friends. However, it was only as he made the ascent to her rooms that he realised they'd rarely been alone together for more than an hour in the seven months he'd lived in the house. He knew he was crossing some sort of line by accepting the offer of drinks in the hallowed space at the top of the stairs, but he didn't know what the line was and this made him uneasy. He also knew that what he felt for Maddie was more than friendship: he thought about her constantly, always wondering what her opinion would be on any subject. He fantasised about being alone with her, kissing her, making love to her. He was falling… had fallen in love. He had no idea if she felt the same.

Jack was concerned that, given the right circumstances, he would spill out his life story to Maddie. He was confessional by nature and Maddie was easy to be honest with, but he feared a confession would dramatically alter his friendship with her as well as jeopardise his place in the house. Jack felt instinctively that Maddie was accepting, non-judgemental, in fact probably more so than any other person he'd met, but he didn't want mere acceptance, he wanted love and that required a different level of acceptance altogether. He decided that it wasn't the right time to tell Maddie about himself and therefore it wasn't the right time to start a relationship with her; or anyone else for that matter.

Jack was shaking as he reached Maddie's door, his knuckles white around the neck of the bottle. He was close to turning back but was driven on by a need to see her. The door was deep red and sturdy, marking a true separation between Maddie's flat and the rest of the house. He knocked timidly. Maddie's face was flushed, accentuated by a red dress, not a dissimilar shade to the door. He was suddenly aware of how young she looked – only twenty-six and six years younger than him. It wasn't a particularly big age gap but the barrier dividing the decade suddenly seemed significant. What had he known at twenty-six? What had he been able to hear? He was thrown, startled by her appearance. Her hair was loose rather than tied in the usual knot on top of her head. This made her beauty appear wild, untamed and harder to resist – he hadn't been prepared. There was a thin sheen of red gloss across her lips and he hadn't seen that dress before. It was a plain wrap-over with a plunging V-neck, showing a modest slice of cleavage. It looked like silk. However, she was bare-footed as if shoes might be one step too far.

"Welcome to my abode," she said a little self-consciously and waved him in with a dramatic sweep of her arm, coinciding with Jack shoving the Rioja towards her. This resulted in her knocking the bottle out of his hand. Fortunately it landed on a rug, saving it and the evening from a disastrous end. They both laughed.

"God this is so weird," said Maddie when the Rioja was safely in her hands. "It's like we've only just met," Jack agreed, grateful for Maddie's acknowledgment of the strangeness.

"Wow!' Jack looked around the flat, which had been renovated to create a large, open-plan space. Two bedrooms had become a twenty-six foot kitchen and sitting area, with a separate bedroom and bathroom. It was similar in style to the rest of the house, but Maddie's personal belongings gave the flat an air of intimacy and femininity. There was a large and diverse collection of books in two alcoves and a decent record collection. Photographs were exhibited on various surfaces including one of a petite woman with the same broad face and blond hair as Maddie. Jack assumed it was her mother. There were other people too; part of Maddie's life Jack knew nothing about, including several young men, who already felt like a threat to Jack.

As in the rest of the house the floors were stripped-wood, covered with richly coloured rugs. Jack hadn't lived anywhere with bare floorboards until he'd moved into this house. He'd grown up with cold linoleum underfoot. Wooden floors were what lay beneath, dusty and grey. The focal point of the living room was a small fireplace, lit and crackling and decorated with holly. A small Christmas tree sparkled in one corner and Jack was surprised to spot one of his sculptures next to a vase of Christmas lilies on the mantelpiece. He'd carved it out of a scrap of wood one evening and flippantly handed it to Maddie.

The scent was different up here; it was purely feminine. Jack breathed in deeply as Maddie poured the wine.

"This is really beautiful," he said

"Thanks, I like it. Sit down."

Tom Waits growled from the stereo.

"I'm really lucky, I suppose, that I had money to do it up."

Jack already knew Maddie had been left some money following her mother's sudden death. "It's a great way to use it, by creating something so beautiful."

"That's partly what I wanted to talk to you about, Jack."

He felt his body stiffen. "Oh yes."

"Don't look so worried." She laughed. "I'm not going to tell you off."

"Sorry, I'm just a little nervous."

"Don't be. It's just that I need a sculptor and, Mr Berry, I do believe you are one."

"No, no... I just mess around."

"Jack, I've seen a couple of your things. You're good."

"I'm not a proper sculptor Maddie; I just do it compulsively, with whatever I lay my hands on... wood, clay, paper clips."

"What the hell's a proper sculptor? You mean you don't get paid for it. Anyway, the Vortex is putting on an exhibition of local artists in February and I just wondered if you wanted to do a piece for that?"

"Cripes, I don't know… I hadn't even thought."

"Ok, well do think. I'd really like you to do one… for me. This is my first chance to organise an exhibition and I need artists. You can use the gallery to create your piece if you like; I know you don't have much space in your room."

"Yes," said Jack, feeling a thrill not unlike jumping off a high board. "Yes, I'll do it." Maddie pouted her lips at the same time as smiling, in the peculiar way she often did when she was pleased.

"So tell me how you came to Carysfort Road?" he asked to stop himself falling towards those lips.

"Well, it was my parents' house; I was brought up here. I guess I wanted to make it beautiful as a tribute to my mother."

"Was your mum born in London?"

"No, she moved to London from Oslo in the fifties, to work as an au pair. She met my dad soon after she arrived; he's Scottish and a skilled builder. They bought this house at a snip, with the intention of taking in lodgers to bring in extra income. They didn't do much to it really. People didn't bother so much back then, did they? A good clean and a new lick of paint and it was ready."

"It must have been weird living with lodgers."

"We lived up here, on the third floor; my dad fitted a kitchen and bathroom so we were completely self-contained. I got used to passing this straggle of lodgers on my way to school each day, but I liked it; it was interesting; all the lonely people."

"Do you mind me asking about your dad? You never talk about him." Jack was still trying to quell his rebellious nerves. He was aware of digging deeper than ever before, scraping diamonds. She answered with an easy, almost flippant, composure; her voice clear, subtly laced with Scandinavian accent.

"Dad left when I was five; he just walked out one day and we never saw him again. So it was just me and Mum."

"That's very sad," Jack marvelled at her cool. "And who did you inherit your artistic flair from?"

"Probably my dad, although he didn't ever fully use it; I suppose it came through in his building work. He was known in the trade as a perfectionist."

"Like someone else I know."

"That's my Scandinavian side too; my mum would unpick a whole dress and start again if it wasn't right… she was a seamstress," Maddie added.

"Oh, I see. I thought she just had a strange habit of pulling clothes apart."

Maddie laughed. It threw Jack off balance.

"So where did the South American thing come in?" Maddie had once mentioned that she'd spent some time in Nicaragua.

"Let me just turn the record over." Maddie rose from the sofa and walked towards the record player. Jack watched and envied her feline curves, the gentle slope of her back falling into the exquisite mound of her bottom. Every movement stretched and made art of the red silk dress. With the unfolding of each limb; with every tilt of the head; each rise and bend of an arm, there was a sculpture waiting to come into being. She flipped the record over; even this was the action of an artist – in one, seamless movement she slipped gleaming, black vinyl over steel, so that it sank effortlessly into place. Finally she moved the needled-arm across and placed it so carefully at the edge of the album; she returned, unselfconsciously, to the sofa, bending supple legs beneath her and falling back into the cushions. She picked up the thread of the conversation.

"I finished my degree in Art and Politics and then decided I wanted to do some voluntary work abroad. I was fascinated by South American politics and art, so when I saw a job, teaching English in Nicaragua, it seemed the obvious place to go. I love the work of Armando Morales."

"I don't know him."

"Oh you have to see his work." Maddie's eyes lifted to the ceiling in an expression of ecstasy. "His voluptuous fruits evoke the softness of human skin and his sensual nudes evoke the lushness of fruit. I used to study his paintings for hours, learning from his skill with oils. I also love Hugo Palma; he uses such magical forms and earthy colours. I felt really inspired in Nicaragua. I would have stayed longer but I got the news that my mother had been involved in a car accident. I flew straight home and arrived just hours before she died."

"Oh God, Maddie, that's awful."

"You know, Jack, 'Love' was the last word she spoke as she held my hand." Maddie lifted her eyes to meet Jack's. "None of us knew whether she'd been about to start a sentence with that word, or whether it was all she could manage from 'I love you.' It was funny; there was so much speculation among family members. I became obsessed with that word; I felt it was somehow important. At the end of one very long night, just as the dawn came, I realised the word had been a command; the command to love. From that day forward I've repeated that word to myself every day. I've written it; painted it and tried to do it. It sounds very corny but I kind of feel it's my purpose; to love, but I don't think it's a sweet or soppy thing; I think it's a deeply challenging, sometimes heartbreaking force and never passive."

"You have a remarkable way of describing things, Maddie."

"I have a strange linguistic heritage, remember." Maddie laughed.

"But it must have been difficult staying here... after your mum's death."

"Not really. I love this house and I could see great potential for it. I didn't do anything to it for weeks, except give all the lodgers their notice; I wanted the place to myself. I used to wander through the rooms; some of them I'd never even seen before. I wanted to get a sense of the way they looked at different moments in the day: the character; the shadows in the corners; the various features and how they caught the light. I sketched my vision for the house, but I didn't have a clue how I would explain it to anyone else. Then one day I was working in the Vortex Gallery when Greg walked in."

"Oh, I wondered how you two met; it's like you've been friends for ever."

"That's how it feels at times. He came in for a coffee and to have a browse. He came over to me and said, "I love that piece," pointing to one of my paintings out of a whole heap of other artist's. I said, "Thanks, that's mine. I like it too." Greg was amused by my lack of modesty, but I feel kind of detached from my work once it's finished. Anyway, we got chatting and he told me he was 'an interior designer in the making'. He said he was working in a bank, 'Until people wake up and realise they need me.' I asked him if I could be his first customer."

"You're both so sharp it's a wonder you don't cut each other." Jack realised he felt some jealousy at the easy intimacy shared by Greg and Maddie.

"When Greg saw this place and my rough plans for it, he was beside himself with glee; he wanted to start the project straight away. I had inherited some money from my mum, but I realised it wouldn't be enough to accomplish my vision. Greg offered to do the work at a minimal cost if he could live here rent-free for a year. He said he'd soon be, 'out on his arse' after a row with his landlord. It seemed a perfect arrangement.

It was amazing, Jack. The minute we ripped partition walls down and threw carpets into a skip the house seemed to breathe again. Greg made some suggestions; he had a vision that seemed to go beyond the norms of the day and I was happy to let him do his thing. He introduced me to the idea of mixing traditional with modern including that glass wall at the back of the house to allow light to flood in; it was radical. He said he hated Victoriana and I do too so we agreed on that. I wanted plain, white walls so I could hang paintings and I wanted to incorporate some of my Scandinavian heritage into the decor. I've never lived in Norway but when my mum took me to visit aunts and uncles I was really impressed by the clean lines and lack of clutter. It took about nine months for the house to be re-born and then people started to move in."

"When I moved in I got the impression everyone had been… hand-picked for the house. So how come you let Pat select me?"

"You make it sound like some social experiment." Maddie gave a wry smile, "I needed a holiday; I was exhausted. I also needed a replacement for this awful tenant, Derek, who lived here for a while. He turned out to be a megalomaniac. Pat agreed to find a replacement while I was away."

"What is it with Pat?" asked Jack, "She fawns over you like she'd happily do whatever you asked."

"Pat was in a bad way when she came looking for rooms here. She was very grateful I gave her and Kate a chance. They'd looked at hundreds of places before they found us and Pat was at breaking point. She's a very loyal friend. Anyway, when I got back from Andalucía I found you reading at the kitchen table. You looked so vulnerable with your head bent over a book."

"Vulnerable?"

"There's something about the back of a man's neck when he's off guard; it's very vulnerable… and very sexy." Maddie's smile was teasing. "More wine?"

Jack had a sudden and strong compulsion to tell Maddie everything about himself, in one lethal outpouring. He held out his glass. "Oh… er… there's something I wanted to ask you," he stammered.

"Go ahead."

"I'm worried about Beth." Jack hadn't intended to raise the subject of Beth tonight but it was preferable to spilling out other things. Beth had been on his mind since she'd called a few weeks earlier to announce the pregnancy. She sounded lonely and uncertain.

"Why?" Maddie's smooth brow creased.

"She's pregnant."

"Oh, I see." Maddie's voice was flat and tight.

"She used a sperm donor." Jack quickly added. "I think it was an act of desperation."

"Oh, I see." Now there was curiosity in her eyes. "Doesn't she have support in Liverpool?

"Not really. Her mother died recently and her sister is occupied with her own family. She doesn't seem to have many friends at the moment."

"Oh, that's awful." Maddie's compassion visibly ousted less noble sentiments.

"I just wondered if you would mind me inviting her to stay for a few days over Christmas. She can have my bed; I'll sleep on the floor. She'll probably say no, but I'd like to ask."

"Of course; she's welcome."

After that the evening had fallen flat. Maddie seemed less transparent and certainly less playful than earlier in the evening, and an unwelcome, stilted atmosphere materialised between them. Jack left earlier than planned and lay on his bed, mulling over the change that had occurred in Maddie; trying to make sense of it. In a state of emotional turmoil he resolved not to spend too much time alone with Maddie again; at least until he had sorted himself out.

CHAPTER 8

Looking back, Jack believed that one of the most significant moments in his life had occurred at the age of eight, when he'd buried himself in a mountain of his sister's dresses and for ten wonderful minutes was lost in a sea of silk and taffeta. He remembered the sensation of floating in an exotic bouquet of cheap perfume and sweet, musty sweat made by dancing and kissing and running for the bus. The moment imprinted itself on Jack's still malleable brain, coursed through his synapses and became fixed in his memory as one of the safest and happiest moments of his life.

Jack's sister, Agnes, was much older than him. At sixteen she was a pretty, fluttery girl with lots of friends and suitors and lovely things to do that kept her away from home and left her unaware of the dark undercurrent that dragged and tossed Jack about. Agnes was also a messy girl: piles of clothes lay abandoned on every surface; her room was an Aladdin's cave of powders and perfumes and a rainbow of lipsticks shaped into lopsided mounds by her small, soft mouth. She had shared the room with Margaret, their older sister, but when Margaret left home to get married Agnes's belongings easily expanded to fill the vacuum.

The events leading to Jack's 'moment' were not overly dramatic, but they were significant. Indoors Jack lived in the uneasy shadow of his parents' marriage while outdoors he was faced with the hostile streets of a poor neighbourhood, where gangs vied for power and boys had to fight or fall. Every week he cycled to the cinema with his older cousin, Philip who, at twelve, seemed very grown up. But today they weren't just going to the usual Saturday morning matinee at the Rialto, where a gaggle of boys and girls, clutching jam jars for entrance currency, screamed over talent contests; made a riot of noise, drowning out the Lone Ranger and Flash Gordon; scrapped in the aisles; tossed ice cream tub lids into the projector light to make them sparkle and pestered usherettes for ice-cream and zoom lollies. Today was special; it was Jack's eighth birthday and his Dad had given him extra money to see a real film at the Odeon and to buy ice cream and coke. He and Philip were going to the afternoon matinee of *The Alamo*. Jack had been waiting with restless anticipation all week; he loved John Wayne. The posters alone were thrilling with the Alamo jutting its ravaged remains into the brooding Texan sky, surrounded by a mass of men, guns waving in the air, ready to defend their land.

Jack and Philip locked their bikes up to a lamppost outside the cinema and entered the dark, popcorn and boy-scented interior. From the start Jack was absorbed in the action, sitting forward on his seat, hardly aware of his surroundings. The final magnificent scene left Jack and Philip full of bravado and when they spilled back into the sunlight with the crowds, their bikes had miraculously turned into horses, tied up outside the Alamo, saddled and ready to ride. They whooped their way home. Philip waved goodbye two streets before Jack's, while Jack cut along the alleyway, slicing through the middle of the terrace, running behind the crumbling two-up-two-down's with their stinking outside toilets. As he approached home, Jack's bravado rapidly evaporating: his father had been in a dark mood all morning, sullen and critical while his mother had looked small and defeated; she'd had a distant look in her eyes as she'd cleared away the breakfast dishes.

As Jack reached the middle of the alley a gang of older boys appeared at the other end; the low early evening sun blinded him and turned the boys into menacing silhouettes, blocking his escape like the baddies in cowboy films. Jack squinted into the sun and froze, not recognising the boys from his own street and sensing that they were hostile.

Jack turned to make for the nearest escape route, trying to mount his bike but in his panic he wheeled over a large lump of stray coal, causing his bike to wobble and almost topple over. He hopped awkwardly along on one leg, scraping his shins against the rusted pedal and chain guard, desperately trying to beat the baddies.

The shouts of the boys grew closer. "Get the bike!" He sensed their nearness, their cruel breath, their musty testosterone. Before he knew it he was lying on the cobbles, a mound of dog-dirt twelve inches from his face, his bike gone. All he could think was how angry his father would be. Jack ran home through the ever-open back door and straight up the stairs. He instinctively headed for his sister's room to find comfort from her, but she was out. Instead he leapt beneath her laundry.

After that Jack made occasional journeys to his sister's bedroom when she was out and when he was feeling particularly vulnerable. Over the years he progressed from lying among her clothes, content with just feeling their softness and breathing in the female scents, to slipping various items on over his clothes. As he became more confident still he removed his own clothes and slipped on Agnes's so that they lay right next to his skin.

This is how his mother found him one day when she returned from shopping. Jack had fallen asleep on Agnes's bed wearing her pale, yellow slip. He awoke startled to see his mother's face above him. It wasn't an angry face, but, worse, there was horror and disappointment in her eyes. Jack had always been her special boy, her little boy blue; now he had let her down. She told him calmly to get dressed and never to enter Agnes's room again. She made no further reference to what had happened.

It was soon after this that two major events took place: Agnes married and removed all of her clothes and possessions to her new home; and a few months later Jack's mother died from a vicious cancer. Jack had just turned twelve. He was left stunned. He had a strong sense that he'd brought this tragedy upon himself by his perversity and he couldn't forget that look in his mother's eyes. With sisters and mother gone, Jack was left alone with his bereft father. One night, in a state of bitter grief, his father burned all his dead wife's clothes in the back yard while Jack looked at the scene from his bedroom window. Mr Berry fed the flames of the fire, as well as his own internal rage, with a bottle of cheap whisky, while howling mournful songs of lost love into the endless blackness of the sky. Jack watched this ritual, horrified. At times, in certain lights, his father's face looked almost demonic. Afterwards, the house became threateningly male – stuffy, dirty uncared for – with nothing soft or feminine left and not a thread of female clothing in which Jack could find comfort.

Puberty hit Jack like a runaway train tossing him into the air to land in an unrecognisable jumble on the floor. He was a prisoner of this early imprinting, which had formed a pattern in his mind he was compelled to repeat, over and over again.

*

"Is there anything in particular you wanted to bring this week?" Cassie looked fresh and summery in a nouveau-Edwardian dress.

"Probably just prefer to carry on with the story. It's kind of making sense of things for me."

"Ok, well last time you talked about your first sensual experience and how it was linked to the softness of your sister's clothes. I was interested to hear about your adolescence and how you coped after your mother's death...when you were twelve?""

"Yes twelve. I guess I on some level I felt I was to blame in some way for my mum's death."

"You mean what she discovered about you in some way led to her death."

"I suppose so."

"Magical thinking."

"What do you mean?"

"At certain stages of development children experience what's called 'magical thinking'. They believe they are omnipotent, what they do affects things in some global way. It happens when we're very young and sometimes again in adolescence. It always stays with us to some extent.'"

That's how it felt, like my perverted behaviour had caused my mum and dad's unhappiness and finally my mum's death."

"Do you still feel that?"

"Logically no; her cancer was there way before she found me in Agnes's knickers; I discovered that from my sisters years later. For months Mum didn't tell anyone she had cancer. She only told my dad and the girls towards the end. But I can't escape my childhood beliefs."

A small silence fell between them and Jack wondered what had been imprinted on Cassie's brain in her early years. He could only imagine sunny rooms smelling of beeswax and home baking with contented parents nurturing their cherished child towards her dreams.

"Well maybe you'd like to continue with the story," Cassandra hurriedly interjected, perhaps sensing curiosity brewing in Jack. It was a definite no, no to indulge a patient's curiosity about the therapist, a shift in the therapeutic relationship.

"You ended last time by saying you felt a sense of ennui, or despair, even suicidal ideations at times. How did it get to that point?"

"Well, my mum's death coincided with my move to an all-boys' secondary school. I remember feeling really scared on my first day after leaving the relative paradise of primary school. It was one of the roughest schools in Liverpool and by an accident of birth I was the youngest in my class. Some of my classmates were inches taller than me and eager to prove themselves. I suppose smaller boys were a good way to test out their strength."

"Did you have friends?"

"One or two but I felt mainly detached from other boys at school and spent a lot of time in a defensive posture, waiting for the thump in the back, the gang outside the school gates."

"You talk a lot about the threat of boys, their cruelty and aggression. What was your view of girls at that age?"

"I think I was jealous of girls. They seemed to live by different rules."

"How do you mean?"

"There was something more inclusive about girls, the way they played, the way they talked. Of course I didn't think like that at the time but now I have this image of girls as lilies in the wind, gently leaning and swaying towards each other in gentle communion. This was a stark contrast to what I saw as the separateness… the loneliness of boys. I feel sorry for boys and what they don't have, what they have to prove. I remember feeling I wanted to have that sense of belonging girls seem to take for granted; sharing secrets, laughing. I know it's a rosy picture and not the whole story, but this is what stuck with me. At times I really hated what boys represent and I hated being in a single sex school."

"How did you manage this… bleakness?"

"I made this connection with my art teacher, Mr Symonds. He picked up that I had a natural talent; in fact he discovered it – I had no idea. Mr Symonds loved sculpture. He talked about the likes of Rodin, Henry Moore and Robert Adams and about his summer trips to London art galleries or the Louvre in Paris. He made these places sound mysterious and exciting, although they seemed about as inaccessible to me as the locations in Western films. But it gave me aspiration, something beyond my misery. Mr Symonds introduced us to some of the basic tools and techniques of sculpture. He taught us about the moulding and modulating of various materials, stone shaping and metal casting. For the first time in months I felt totally absorbed in something other than my troubles. He always encouraged me and said I had talent. No one had ever said that before and it made me want to do well, for him.

"At the end of term My Symonds enticed us with pictures of the works of great sculptors, ancient and modern, and he described the new skills we would learn in the next school term. I couldn't wait; it made the thought of returning to school bearable after the long summer holiday. But Mr Symonds didn't turn up for the next lesson. I only learned weeks later that he'd dropped dead of a heart attack, appropriately in the Louvre in Paris.

"'We won't be replacing him,' was all they said. They didn't bother explaining why. I guessed it was because art wasn't seen as that important."

"It must have been confusing to be a child in this adult word where things aren't explained. Did you tell anyone how you felt?"

"God no! I found no way to protest or to make my views heard. I didn't even think to try. I don't even remember mentioning it to my dad; he probably thought art was a sissy subject anyway."

"Did that lead you to despair?"

"It didn't help, but I was still fighting with my desire to wear girls' clothes and there was no way for me to express it. I felt so guilty that I repressed it for ages. I buried myself in music instead. I listened to records obsessively and, almost without realising it, I made figures out of whatever materials I could get my hands onto – plasticine, mud, wire. I didn't believe I could ever be an artist, of course. I thought my window had closed when Mr Symonds popped his clogs. By fourteen, I was feeling miserable most of the time. I saw myself as a freak, always locked in my room listening to scratched vinyl on a crap record player. My dad thought I was a freak too. His generation didn't really allow for teenage angst, you just grew up and got on with it. I seriously considered suicide for the first time when I was fifteen."

"What stopped you?"

Jack thought about this for a few seconds. "I suppose it was a coincidental meeting at a cousin's wedding. Typical wedding, I suppose: kids running everywhere; curled up ham sandwiches, crap music. I was fifteen and it was 1969. I was thinking that life must have more to offer than this. I sneaked out to have a smoke and escape the terrible music for a few minutes and bumped into a cousin, who was about the same age as me. We were talking about how weird it was that we'd never met before, even though we were related. I'd never had much to do with my dad's family; they were all a bit odd, according to my mum's side of the family.

He invited me to Calderstones Park the next day for a smoke and to chill out with his mates. I discovered this whole new scene going on. Calderstones Park was only a couple of miles from our house, but it was a different world. That's what Liverpool was like then, still is I guess: territorial. I felt like I was walking into forbidden territory. I remember it was a gorgeous day and these middle class kids were doing what I'd always wanted to do – living the hippy dream."

Cassandra nodded but didn't interject.

"I escaped there as often as possible after that. We sat in these gorgeous gardens in a haze of cannabis smoke, listening to Deep Purple and Pink Floyd on portable cassette players."

"Why do you think you fitted in there more than in your own neighbourhood?"

"I guess I was too soft for my own neighbourhood. I was wrong in some way and I couldn't grow a tough skin; though I did try. I even got into a few fights and stuck the boot in a couple of times, but I always hated what I'd done. It's like I was born with the outer layer missing."

"Did this new crowd accept you?"

"They did once Gloria Harding accepted me." Jack laughed. "I lost my virginity to Gloria Harding." He still had a vivid memory of his patchouli-scented goddess, wrapped in swirling flower-print fabrics. They'd made love in daisy-littered parks and on beige, shag-pile carpets in her parents' lounge.

"She thought I was cute. I was relieved to know I wasn't gay; although my dad was convinced I was. In hindsight gay might have been easier. God, Gloria's family had rooms in their house they didn't even use; these pristine rooms smelling of furniture polish and fresh flowers. I thought it was amazing."

"What did these rooms symbolise for you, Jack?"

"Wealth... luxury; they were just sitting there waiting for something nice to happen in them; so unnecessary but so beautiful."

"Did you resent this wealth?"

"No, not at all. It's just how it was, but I did aspire to it, in the same way I aspired to see the world, to travel. I aspired to one day have a room with no other purpose than just to be there, to use as I pleased."

"So what was it that attracted you to Gloria?"

There she went again, those first meetings, first attractions. "I suppose it was the poshness, the unavailability. But then she went to France with her parents before leaving to study. I knew I didn't have her for very long."

"And perhaps you'd learned from an early age that good things and good people don't stay around for very long?"

"Yes. I had."

"What else attracted you to Gloria?"

"I liked her underwear," Jack laughed, still not sure how Cassie would receive his candour. He noticed a quick, double blink of her eyes. Despite her prudish exterior Cassie seemed open-minded and he had begun to enjoy their sessions; it was a relief to talk so unreservedly with someone. It was one of the myths of the working classes, Jack often thought, that middle class people are easily shocked. In reality people of his own class were generally much more conservative.

"Although Gloria was a little too fond of hippy-cotton," he added. "I preferred the silky stuff girls of my sister's class tended to wear."

"So what did Gloria come to represent for you?"

"I guess she became a prototype for the sort of woman I would like to be with." Jack laughed again and paused for dramatic effect. "…As well as the sort of woman I would like to be." He was still testing Cassie out, seeing what she could hear. A slight smile tugged at one corner of her mouth.

"So what happened to Gloria?"

"As predicted she didn't stay around for long. She returned from the exotic reaches of the Riviera, bronzed and sophisticated and looking much older than sixteen. I didn't even try to rekindle the relationship; I just stood back and watched her slip easily into the world of 6th form college, while I was left behind."

"So, what did you do?"

"Things were really bad at home. I didn't do very well in my exams, even though I had brains. I remember the Moon landing at the end of July and feeling that the world was a much bigger place than I knew; that I was only seeing a tiny piece of all that was out there. I ran away to the Isle of Wight Festival at the end of August and spent my sixteenth birthday crossing the Solent on a ferry. It was easy to get in without tickets – I just climbed the fence. But when I got into the festival I realised I needed a tent. I'd heard there were these big marquis to sleep in but they were all full so I had to make my own with plastic sheets and tree branches. I used the rest of my dosh to buy an Inca-type blanket these hippies were selling; it was bloody freezing at night. I didn't eat much and had to scavenge for food.

"It was the year before the big one with Hendrix, but it was bigger than anything I'd ever experienced. In '68 there had only been ten thousand people at the festival, when I went there were a hundred-and-fifty-thousand. I couldn't believe it. Psychedelia had really kicked in and even bands associated with Mod culture like The Who and Pretty Things had gone psychedelic, never mind Dylan and Free.... Sorry, you don't need to know all this."

Cassie smiled. "This time is yours, Jack, to use as you like. So what was the festival experience like for you?"

"It was like finding heaven; like discovering a new city of people just like me. Life was at last making sense. I was listening to this band, Blodwyn Pig; they were singing a song called *Dear Jill*, when suddenly this gorgeous girl just throws her arms around me and says "Guess what? My name's Jill." We spent the weekend together. I moved into her tent and shared her food. She was at the festival with some girlfriends all off their heads on dope. She was older than me, about seventeen and very well developed. She had this long brown hair that she could sit on. She liked to curl it around my neck as we made love, very kinky. She was from London and more extreme than Gloria, more edgy. She talked about really living the hippy dream: free love, drugs and all that; she made it all seem possible.

"I remember one day we saw this couple kissing in a mass of soap foam in front of the crowd. This reporter asked the girl where she came from and she said spontaneously, 'Nowhere.' Jill just sighed, 'It's all so beautiful.' Everything was beautiful to Jill. She didn't seem shocked by anything. For me it was like I was being given these little messages of hope.

"Everything was building up to Dylan. He came on late and only did a short set; it was magical. Jill and I danced together like real lovers and I thought that at last life had started; a new life where anything was possible. But then the crowd got upset because Dylan's set was cut short – they wanted more. This guy, the compere came on and said, 'You are the blessed generation. You are the body beautiful.' Probably to placate us all, but I took these words to heart. It was probably the acid, but it was like he was speaking to me personally; it was another message. I felt liberated. All the oppression, the stagnation, the self-loathing seemed to evaporate.

"I confessed to Jill that night about my liking for women's underwear. God, I hate those words." Jack's eyes returned to Cassandra's. "They don't tell you anything about the layers of pain and self-disgust that went before; they just class me as a common pervert in the eyes of the world. Anyway, I imagined me and Jill together forever, living the hippy dream. Instead she called me a freak, told me to piss off. She laughed in this really cruel way; kicked me out of her tent. So much for hippy love, hey? Suddenly I felt very cold and alone. You know, I don't even think her name was Jill. It was Mary or Joyce or something."

"That must have shaken your view of the world."

"I guess it did. I came down from the drugs and went home. I felt totally disillusioned at first, although I gradually realised I'd been to a fantastic event and had an amazing experience. But it felt like the 60s was over and I'd missed the heartbeat of the decade, like I seemed to miss the best of everything. My dad hit me for the first and only time when I got home, 'You stink of beer and shit,' he said. He left a bloody big bruise on my face. I can see now he'd been worried sick about me, but I couldn't see it then; I thought he was just a bully who didn't understand me.

"Then I started an apprenticeship in Plessey's. I was a bit more daring after the Isle of Wight; I grew my hair long and my flares got wider. But it was out of kilt with the skinheads in the neighbourhood and at work. My long hair and flared jeans, flapping around my Gola pumps, were like a red flag to the big black boots of the skinheads. I regularly took a beating. I was living dangerously: heavily into acid-fuelled music and off my head on LSD most weekends. I was having suicidal fantasies again." Jack could feel his heartbeat increase as he re-lived the events of times past. He wasn't sure how much deeper he wanted to go. "Then I was saved by Beth."

"Women seem to play an important role in saving you from serious consequences. Do you think this is true?" Cassie's look was intent.

Jack laughed. "Sounds like one of those exam questions. Discuss." Jack couldn't resist teasing Cassie; she took her role so seriously. She looked embarrassed and Jack felt sorry for his flippancy. "I hadn't really thought about it but now you mention it, I suppose I did elevate women; I think in most ways women are superior to men."

"Yes." Cassie seemed to mull this over for a while. "But Jack, you've jumped forward in time to Beth, though you didn't meet her until the following year. Are you avoiding telling me what happened in-between?" Jack was silent.

"You say you were having suicidal fantasies again but you don't say much about what took you there. Apart from the desire to wear women's underwear it sounds as if you were going through what many young people go through at that age. What was different for you?"

Jack wasn't sure if he was ready to tell Cassie what happened next. He felt safe and to some extent accepted by her, if this could be said of a therapist. In reality his compulsions and his despair had cranked up to a new level after the Isle of Wight and he still felt a deep shame about it.

"I need to think about that one."

CHAPTER 9

When Beth received the invitation from Jack to go to London for Christmas her first response was to turn it down. She couldn't think of anything worse than spending Christmas in a strange house with strangers. But following the expedition to Greenham Common she'd been suffering a sense of desolation the likes of which she had never before experienced; it flattened and grounded her. She not only felt she was useless and had nothing to offer the world but also that she'd made the biggest mistake of her life in using a sperm donor; that it had been an irresponsible and despicable thing to do. Her mind was swimming in dark waters and she struggled to eat or sleep. She might have taken refuge at her sister's, but Maria and Mark had booked a family holiday in Florida for Christmas. The final straw came when the boiler packed in and the landlord didn't seem in a rush to get it fixed.

Beth travelled from Lime Street Station on Christmas Eve and was met by Jack at Euston.

"You look knackered," said Jack, simultaneously taking Beth's bag and hugging her.

"Thanks," said Beth, "that makes me feel great." She realised how much she'd missed physical contact with a man.

"Sorry love, but it's not surprising in your condition."

They jumped on a bus to Stoke Newington, catching up on superficial news while Jack pointed out various sights en route. Beth had no desire to talk about the pregnancy just yet, although she knew Jack would raise the subject soon enough.

Beth's heart rate increased as they made the short walk from the bus stop to Carysfort Road. She was anxious about meeting new people and she was particularly anxious about meeting Maddie, who she'd heard so much about. She'd already guessed from her telephone conversations with Jack that he was falling for Maddie, even though he didn't admit or even seem aware of it himself. His voice softened as he said her name and he managed to divert every conversation towards her. Maddie sounded strong and decisive; the sort of woman Beth wished she could be. She felt mild jealousy; not because she wanted to be with Jack, she had pretty much let go of that idea, but she didn't know if she could bear to watch a love blossom before her eyes, when she felt so unloved and so unlovely.

"You'll meet everyone this evening. Apparently Christmas Eve at Carysfort Road is a tradition that everyone must be part of."

"Or what?" Beth laughed

"Or you have Maddie to answer to." Jack raised an eyebrow, "Only joking. I get the impression no-one would miss it for the world."

"And what about tomorrow?"

"Unfortunately everyone will be away tomorrow visiting family or friends, even Maddie. We'll have the place to ourselves. Sorry, you'll have to put up with my company all day."

Beth felt a surge of relief course through her tired limbs. That was manageable. If she could get through the gathering tonight then she could just slob around with Jack all day tomorrow and not have to make any effort at all.

"I'll manage somehow. I've brought a bag of goodies for us to enjoy."

As Jack opened the front door Beth was greeted by a warm hallway decorated with fresh holly and the scent of home baking. Strains of music were coming from somewhere above them in the cavernous interior.

"That's Kate playing her pop music," said Jack, "She cranks it up until someone shouts, but she's a good kid really."

"The house looks amazing."

"It's pretty cool. Let me take your coat and I'll show you where everything is." They moved through to the kitchen where a woman was peeling potatoes. Beth's first thought was that this was Maddie and she felt a strange mix of shock and relief.

"Pat meet Beth," said Jack. "Pat's daughter is the one playing the music upstairs."

"Yeah, sorry about that." Pat made a small nod towards Beth and then continued with her peeling.

"As you can see this is the kitchen." Jack filled the kettle with water and flicked on the switch. "I'll show you the rest of the house."

Beth was glad to leave the kitchen; she was feeling negative vibes from Pat and in her current state of mind assumed it was about her.

Jack showed Beth the ground floor and then led her to his room.

"You're in my bed and if you don't mind I'll kip on the floor next to you."

"God I feel guilty kicking you out of your own bed."

"No worries; you know I can sleep anywhere and you need it more than me in your condition…"

"That woman… Pat, she seemed a bit cool." Beth clumsily changed the subject.

"Oh she's like that with nearly everyone, except Maddie – she thinks the sun shines out of her backside. It's a running joke. She's OK when you get to know her though, just a bit suspicious. Anyway, I'll leave you to freshen up. A cup of tea will be waiting for you downstairs."

Beth was alone. It was odd to see Jack in such a small room in a shared house. She felt the sadness of all they had lost in the divorce. The room was fairly minimal except for a large stack of LP's on the floor, a stereo, a few books and a couple of Jack's sculptures dropped almost carelessly on various surfaces. Beth wasn't sure she liked Jack's sculptures. She didn't really understand them and they all looked a bit tortured to her. Perhaps they were an accurate reflection of Jack's soul and that made her feel uncomfortable – she'd never gotten close to it.

Beth stretched out on Jack's narrow bed and found herself burying her face in his pillow. It was rich with his scent, still familiar and comforting, yet no longer hers. She sat up quickly, to release herself from the sadness descending on her, but she was overcome with a wave of dizziness. She bent her head towards her knees and then stood up slowly, straightened her large cable-knit jumper, which covered her already expanding hips, bottom and belly. She went to the bathroom, washed her face, cleaned her teeth and pulled a brush through her short, silky hair, which she'd noticed was thinning a little. She looked briefly in the bathroom mirror, not wanting to focus on her irretrievably sagging face. She rubbed her cheeks vigorously as her mother had once shown her, to give a natural flush, and then she went down to the kitchen.

Pat was still peeling things.

"Oh sorry, I thought Jack would be here…'

"How long are you staying?" Pat's tone was hostile.

Beth was thrown, "Only for a couple of days."

"Maddie will be in soon; she's buying stuff for tonight. She always makes Christmas Eve special. In fact she usually does Christmas dinner here but she's decided to go away this year."

Beth felt it was somehow her fault that Maddie was going away. She didn't know how to respond and stood in silence for a few seconds, waiting for Pat to elaborate.

"Jack's next door."

"Oh… thanks." Beth left the kitchen feeling she was being dismissed. She was forming the distinct impression that she was somehow a threat – not something she was used to. She knew it must have something to do with Maddie. She started to regret her decision to come to London. Why on earth hadn't Jack thought about the dynamics in the household when he'd invited her to stay? She felt a deep weariness take hold of her, body and soul.

She found Jack building a fire in the lounge, crouched down and looking very much at home by the hearth. A small strip of his back was revealed between jeans and t-shirt. He had a good back, slim and strong.

"Your tea's there." He nodded towards a nest of table. "Sit down and make yourself at home."

"Do you mind if I take my tea upstairs and have a couple of hours sleep before tonight? I'm feeling bloody exhausted."

Jack turned and scrutinised Beth's face. He frowned.

"Of course, love. Are you OK?"

"Yes, yes. It's just the journey and everything. Give me a shout in a couple of hours." Beth was already moving towards the door, longing for the darkness of the bedroom, the oblivion of sleep.

When she woke the room had turned from grey to black. She fumbled for the bedside lamp, groggy and disorientated. She could hear music and voices coming from a distance. She imagined a house full of happy, smiling people, except for Pat who was growling like a dog at anyone who went near the precious Maddie. Perhaps if she just stayed in bed they'd all forget about her; she could go down in the morning when everyone had left. There was a knock on the door and then Jack's voice.

"It's me. Are you decent?" He had always used that phrase.

"Yes."

Jack pushed open the door and carried a steaming mug to her bedside. "It's fresh coffee from one of those percolator thingies. It'll bring you round."

"Ooh very posh; it smells lovely. I'm feeling a bit out of it."

"Well people are starting to arrive and the champagne is

flowing so don't take too long in case you miss it."

"I won't. I'll just have a quick shower and pull something on."

"OK love." Jack kissed her on the head; she could hardly bear it. His eyes were bright with concern and it made her want to weep with self-pity.

"OK, get out so I can start getting ready." She put on a bright, efficient tone.

Beth felt better after the coffee and a shower. She slapped on a minimal amount of makeup and then pulled on a black jersey dress over black leggings. She slipped on a pair of wine-coloured suede ankle boots and tied a scarf in a matching colour around her neck. It'll have to do, she muttered into the mirror.

She walked slowly down the stairs carrying two empty mugs and trying to calm the furious beating of her heart. She went to the kitchen and, to her dismay, bumped into a woman carrying a plate of mini-quiches. It could only have been Maddie. Her face was serious with concentration, framed by indecently blond hair. Beth waited for a cool smile, a starched welcome, but suddenly the ice-maiden face was inflamed with a radiant smile that reached and illuminated her eyes.

"Oh, you must be Beth, I'm Maddie. Welcome."

"Oh hello; thank you so much for having me here." Beth placed the cups in the sink.

"Don't bother washing them now." Maddie came closer and Beth could smell a subtle perfume. "Don't worry about that lot in there, they'll make you welcome. I think Jack is playing with the fire again. You know what men are like with their fires." She spoke in a light, conspiratorial tone, making Beth feel both calmed and cheered. She followed Maddie into the living room, relieved that she didn't announce her arrival. Instead Maddie walked over to a table where she placed the plate of food down and immediately became engaged in conversation with one of the guests. Beth walked over to Jack.

"Can't you leave that fire alone?"

"No, it needs me. Wow. You look great Beth. That sleep did you good." Jack stood up and kissed Beth on the cheek. "Champagne?"

"Oh go on; just one. I'll be on the lemonade for the rest of the night."

Beth feigned interest in the crackling flames while Jack fetched a drink. He soon returned with two glasses. As they sipped at the champagne and chatted, Beth allowed her eyes at last to browse the room. It was indeed the picture of Christmas cheer with a tall Norway Spruce in one corner, tastefully decorated with white lights and large pine cones. There was fresh holly and mistletoe over the fireplace, bowls overflowing with fresh fruit and dried dates, and the smell of spiced wine along with other Christmas fare. Beth recognised Ella Fitzgerald on the stereo. There were about fifteen people in the room and Beth's first impression was they were London types: tall, fashionable, self-assured. She was sure they'd all have interesting jobs, interesting things to say. She quickly identified Mike and Ayesha and the young, ambitious Kate. She completely understood Jack's reasons for moving to London; it was a better place for him, a bigger place in every sense of the word.

She wished she could stay by the fire observing the action and chatting about inconsequential things with Jack, but already a tall man with thick, sandy-blond hair was walking towards them, smiling.

"Is this the Beth we've heard so much about?" He bent to kiss her on the cheek.

"Beth, this is Greg. He lives in the basement."

"Oh, Jack, you make me sound like some subterranean creature; though I am quite partial to dark, hidden places." Greg threw his head back and laughed loudly. Beth could see he had a big personality that would compensate for her reserve.

"So what do you make of our humble abode, Beth?" Greg swept his arm around the room.

"Hardly humble," said Beth, "and very lovely. Jack tells me you created it."

"Oh oh." Greg pulled exaggerated faces. "I really wouldn't want anyone to know that."

"Sure," said Jack, "You're so modest Greg."

"Is he bragging again?" another man walked over, smaller than Greg and with Mediterranean looks. Attractive, thought Beth, but in a less obvious way than Greg. He nodded towards Beth as he joined them. "The house was mostly Maddie's idea."

"Oh darling," said Greg, "you always have to bring me down to earth, don't you."

"Hi, I'm Dave, Greg's partner, as you might have guessed." Dave leant towards Beth and kissed her on one cheek. She wasn't used to so much kissing.

Beth was happy to listen as the banter between the three men continued. She realised she'd largely lost the art of conversation, except for the intense, political kind that she'd had with her female friends. This talk seemed light, almost frivolous; she could picture Mandy's disapproving glare. Beth realised how desperately she needed some lightness in her life; she was far too serious and gloomy. She needed to laugh, to chatter, to have some fun. Her eyes fell on Maddie who was laughing with a female friend across the room. The two women touched each other's arms frequently and talked in intimate tones. Beth longed for a good friendship with a woman. She'd hoped Sasha would become a friend but she'd blown that possibility in Greenham.

Maddie left the friend and walked towards the door. With a sudden surge of courage Beth excused herself and followed. Maddie went into the large kitchen where a few people were drinking and chatting.

"Can I help with anything?" Beth asked.

Maddie looked around. "Oh, you can take out another plate of salmon; they're ravenous beasts in there."

"You have a beautiful house."

"Thanks. I think so." Maddie gave Beth her full attention; she placed the tray back on the work surface. Her eyes seemed to scrutinise.

"And how are you Beth? I've heard the first weeks of pregnancy can be very tough."

Beth was taken aback by Maddie's directness.

"Oh, I'm OK. Just tired…and sick all the time."

"Well I'm sure Jack will take care of you while you're here. He's very good at that."

"Yes, he is." Beth had a sudden longing to say to Maddie, "Jack doesn't love me, he loves you; the way is clear." But these words were impossible to her; it was the sort of thing people said in films, not in real life. She found it difficult to read Maddie's face. The friendliness seemed genuine, but did she also see the dark cloud of jealousy? It was impossible to tell. She couldn't help but like Maddie and she could see why Jack would be attracted to her: She was strong and self-assured, never mind beautiful; he needed someone like that.

When Beth went down to breakfast the following morning, after a fitful night's sleep, Maddie had already left. Jack was making scrambled egg in the kitchen with the radio turned up loud and Pat was rummaging around gathering things for her journey. Intermittently Pat ran to the bottom of the stairs and shouted loudly for Kate to get up. She hardly acknowledged Beth. Greg and Dave were the last to leave. They were going to Greg's mother for Christmas dinner and seemed reluctant to start the journey. Greg muttered and flapped while Dave tried to calm him down.

It was midday before Beth was alone with Jack and a lovely hush fell across the house. She felt the muscles of her neck and shoulders relax.

"I'm going to put the turkey in now," said Jack, "and then I thought we could have a walk before we eat. It's a lovely day."

"A turkey seems a bit extravagant just for the two of us," said Beth, as they walked along Church Street in the weak winter sun.

"Don't worry, Dave will probably rustle up some magnificent feast with all the leftovers."

"Of course," said Beth. She paused. "It's a very... special household, isn't it?" She realised she felt some resentment that Jack had found this colourful, almost too perfect world, with the goddess-like Maddie weaving her magic over it all, while she was alone in her grey little universe.

"It is special, but it isn't as perfect as it seems," said Jack. "There are often tensions and fall outs. Maddie can be a bit controlling at times; she wants everything to be perfect, like last night."

"She's a lovely woman, Jack. She obviously makes the whole thing work."

A flush widened over Jack's neck.

"Jack, it's obvious you like her."

He turned, surprise on his face. "Well... yes, I do like her, but just as a friend."

"I don't think that's the complete truth. You don't have to worry about admitting it to me you know. I can cope."

"OK, perhaps I feel more for her than friendship, but even if she feels the same about me, which I don't think she does, nothing can happen right now."

"Why not?"

"This is Abney Cemetery," Jack announced, as they climbed some steps up to an iron gate. "There are lots of famous people buried here."

Beth took in the trees, the tangle of undergrowth, a host of rejoicing angels and crumbling graves.

"Very atmospheric; it's like something from a horror story. So why not?"

"Why not what?"

"Why not you and Maddie."

"Oh. It's just not the right time, Beth."

"Why not?"

"Well, you and I haven't long divorced."

"Come on, Jack, that was ages ago."

Jack stopped by the figure of an angel, one hand raised to heaven as if to escape the tangle of ivy slowly engulfing her; he ran his hand over one small, marble foot. "I'm scared of telling Maddie about me, Beth. What if she can't handle it?"

"I see."

"When I came to London it was with the intention of sorting myself out; trying to understand my compulsion." Jack laughed. "I never thought I'd go to a therapist. It seems so American, but it's really helped."

"In what way?" Beth felt unusually brave.

"I think I imagined it could be a cure; that I would somehow come out of it normal. But the more I go the more I realise it's not about cure, it's about acceptance. This is the way I am, Beth; I can't be different and I don't think I want to be."

Jack looked into Beth's eyes. A guilty heat infused her body. "I was never very good at understanding that was I? I'm sorry."

"Oh, Beth, don't be sorry. You did your best, more than you should have had to. But that's just it. If I ever have another relationship I want… I need it to be with someone who can fully accept me and I realise not only is that a very selfish thing to want but it might be totally impossible. Why should any woman want to be with an old trannie?"

"You're not so old." They both laughed.

"Maddie's a bit scary at times," Jack grinned, "but she has more tolerance and compassion than anyone I know," he paused, "but Beth, you know it isn't easy to be tolerant when you have to live with something day after day; I really don't know if Maddie would be able to deal with it."

Beth took Jack's hand; its size and shape were so familiar to her as well as the warmth that seemed constant, no matter what the outside temperature. "Look Jack, it's none of my business, but I strongly suspect if anyone can deal with your peculiarities, she can. There. I've said enough. It's your life."

The sun was already dipping low and the cold growing intense by the time they returned to Carysfort Road. The evocative smell of cooking turkey filled the house.

"I'll baste if you peel." They soon fell into the easy partnership of long-married couples, moving around each other like accomplished dancers. Jack, as always, turned on the radio and they found themselves singing along to Christmas melodies, interspersed with recollection of the past, forever sewn into the shared part of their lives. It crossed both of their minds at various points that it seemed ridiculous for two people to be so at ease with one another, so compatible in many ways, yet not together.

"You always were a good cook," said Beth as they finished dinner.

"I see you haven't lost your appetite," said Jack,

"It's come back with a vengeance. I've hardly eaten for weeks."

"Beth, I have to ask you about the pregnancy. I know you'd rather I didn't."

Beth stared at her empty plate, smeared with gravy. She felt bloated and just wanted to lie down and watch rubbish on TV. She was tired of thinking about the baby and felt irritated with Jack for bringing the subject up now.

"What do you want to know?"

"I want to know why you used a sperm donor."

"Because there was no other bloody way of getting pregnant. I wasn't going to wait for the Angel Gabriel to appear, was I?"

"OK, no need for sarcasm. I'm… I'm just concerned."

"What are you concerned about? I'm fine."

"Beth, how will you manage on your own?"

"Thousands of women manage on their own every day, whether they want to or not." Beth couldn't control the bitterness in her voice, which surprised her with its resurgence. "What makes you think I won't manage?"

"I'm not saying you wont manage, I just think it will be difficult."

"Yes, it will be difficult, but I'll do it. Don't worry about me, this is my life not yours."

Jack sighed. "Beth I'm so sorry for everything. I feel I drove you to this."

"I don't want your guilt and pity Jack. I made the decision and I'll live with it."

"But that doesn't reassure me, Beth. It sounds as if you regret it already. And have you thought about the future. What about in eight years or eighteen years' time? How will you explain things to the child?"

"Explain what?"

"That you don't know who the father is, that he can never be found."

"I'll just tell the truth, Jack. Lots of children don't know their father. They just have to get on with it." Beth didn't like the tone of her own voice and the defensiveness that had crept in.

"OK, love. You're right, it is your life; it's none of my business."

Beth sat back in the chair, trying to ease the pain in her belly. There was no point in falling out with Jack. She desperately needed to talk to someone, to share her fears. After all it wasn't just her life; she felt the truth of this acutely.

"If you want to know, Jack, I'm bloody terrified." Against her will long suppressed tears flooded out. "I wish I'd never done it; I regret it every day. I have bloody awful nightmares about giving birth to half a child, deformed and looking absolutely nothing like me." Beth could feel a wobble of hysteria in her chest; she breathed deeply, trying to control it but she grew unnaturally hot and started to hyperventilate.

"OK, OK." Jack stood up; he looked scared.

"Come next door and sit down. I'll bring you some water." Beth was grateful to move into the relative coolness of the living room. Lifeless grey and white ash from last night's fire was piled high in the hearth. She lay flat on the sofa and accepted the water from Jack.

"Don't get angry with me," he spoke tentatively while kneeling beside her, "but is it too late to… do anything about it?"

"I couldn't Jack. It would feel wrong."

"More wrong than what you feel now?"

Beth thought for a few seconds, testing out her feelings. The idea of an abortion was abhorrent to her. She nodded. "In my rare moments of sanity I can still feel excited about having a baby. I already feel connected to it in some way. It's mainly during the night that the bad thoughts come."

"Look Beth, why don't you think about moving to London? There's not much for you in Liverpool anymore. You could stay here until you find your feet. I could help you with a flat."

"Oh Jack, you are lovely," Beth smiled and stroked his sculpted face, "but it isn't realistic. I can't depend on you forever; we have to move on from one another. Most couples who divorce don't ever see each other again unless they have to."

"But we're not most couples, Beth. I value your friendship. We're grown-ups now; why shouldn't we be friends?"

"Well perhaps you're more grown up than me; perhaps this is harder for me to handle." Beth found Jack's eyes. She saw realisation dawn in his.

"God, I'm so bloody insensitive. I didn't know."

Beth took Jack's hand. She wanted to stroke his hair, tangle her fingers in the curls as she used to but it felt like forbidden territory.

"I've accepted we shouldn't be together Jack, really I have, but it doesn't mean I've stopped caring for you. This has been lovely, but I couldn't live here all the time and watch you fall in love with someone else. Anyway, my hormones are all over the place at the moment and I don't trust my feelings. Let's just keep it the way it is for now, shall we?"

Beth wasn't due to catch her train home until Boxing Day evening and after brunch and a brief walk in the park, Beth suggested they "chill out" to an afternoon movie. She didn't want to talk about anything heavy, especially not the past; it seemed all that could be said had been said – they experienced an unexpected closeness; important things had been voiced; important fears aired and now they could just relax. They stretched out on the sofa, as they used to, with Jack behind, his arm draped across Beth's shoulder.

"So have you thought of any names?" Jack couldn't resist asking when the film had finished.

"A few."

"Go on, tell me."

"Well, I know I want something modern and fresh."

"So not Elizabeth or Jack then?" He squeezed her side playfully.

"Well the names that keep coming to me are Julian for a boy…"

"After John Lennon's son?"

"Yes. Or Julia for a girl."

"Oh, I love that name; after our song?"

"It wasn't our song, Jack, but yes after that song."

"*Sunlight bright upon my pillow, lighter than an eiderdown…* It was our song!'

"No, our song was *Love Grows*, Edison Lighthouse. How soon you forget."

"*Will she let the Weeping Willow, wind his branches round*. OK, it was one of our songs. You don't just have to have one song, you know. Sing it with me."

Beth laughed. “I can’t sing.” But she sang anyway. “*Julia dream, dreamboat queen, queen of all my dreams.*

“*Every night I turn the light down…*”

*

When Maddie returned she found Jack and Beth lying side by side on the sofa. Jack’s hand was resting over the indiscernible bump of Beth’s pregnancy.

“I’m going to have a bath,” she said from the doorway. “See you later.”

Jack and Beth turned quickly, a shared laugh changing to shock and then embarrassment on their faces. Before she turned Jack noticed a look in Maddie’s eyes he had never seen before.

CHAPTER 10

To Beth's surprise Sasha did keep in touch, the only one of the group who did. She made the trip between the camp and Liverpool once a month to collect contributions from supporters. She first called on Beth in February, with a sheepish smile on her face. She didn't need to say she was sorry for not defending Beth that day at Greenham. Beth was forgiving. She was happy to see Sasha and knew all too well what a powerful pressure a group can exert. She noted how much easier it was to relax in Sasha's company without Mandy's intimidating presence. They chatted about the cause but also about books, music and life generally.

Throughout spring and summer, Beth made sure she had boxes of produce from the allotment ready for Sasha's visits, as well as blankets and clothes, soap and shampoo. Sasha was always appreciative. Between every visit Beth's belly expanded, along with her acute anxiety. She had no idea how she would get through the birth, never mind care for a child on her own.

In the onerous heat of the last day of August, Beth thought she would melt; that she would never be cool again. At least she'd finished work and now all she had to do was wait. But she had too much time to think as she sat alone in the confines of her home, sash windows wide open, a creaking fan doing little to cool her glowing skin, and a jug of iced water by her side. She put down her book, eyes tired after several hours of reading, and rested her hand on her belly and sang a lullaby, as much to calm herself as the baby.

Since Christmas and her chat with Jack, Beth had been thinking of names almost obsessively; in an odd way it was a distraction from thinking about the actual baby. She knew she didn't want a traditional Catholic name like the succession of Elizabeth's and Mary's', James' and Johns' that had trickled through her family for generations like holy water. She still had memories of her grandparents' house littered with plastic statues from Lourdes and pictures of Jesus with his heart bleeding over every bed in the house. She wanted something new, modern and, if it was a girl, which she secretly hoped it would be, then Julia was the name she wanted. It reminded Beth of jewels and light; a welcome departure from the dusty layers of Catholic tradition.

The anxiety returned as it always did, forcing its way through every thought and activity, invading her dreams and disturbing her sleep. Sometimes it wasn't even specific to the baby – it was a vague, floating thing; a nebulous sense of doom about the future, about the state of the world. She wondered how it might have been had she and Jack been doing this together. Since her visit, Jack had continued to phone on a regular basis, ignoring her feeble suggestion that they break the tie. She was glad; she needed his friendship. Despite their conversation, he had still not made a move with Maddie. He was nearing the end of his therapy and he confided in Beth that he was considering telling Maddie everything; when he found 'the right moment'. Beth wondered how Maddie would handle the information. She remembered the moment Jack told her the truth about himself, two weeks after they were engaged.

"There's something wrong with me Beth. I should have told you sooner." She remembered the lurch in her stomach, the dryness in her mouth, the sense that the beautiful, soft rug was about to be pulled from under her feet. A hundred possibilities coursed through her mind, but not the thing he actually told her. They had been sitting in the park, like any other couple in love. They had a blanket and sandwiches and some cider. She was wearing a long, Indian cotton skirt and a broderie anglais top. He looked so worried that she wanted to comfort him.

"What love, what is it?"

Jack bowed his head and his neck reddened at the back and sides. She could see he was struggling.

"Tell me Jack, it doesn't matter what it is, just tell me. It'll be OK." She remembered how in love she'd been with him then.

He lifted his head but still couldn't look her in the eyes.

"I-I like to wear… silky underwear."

Beth had laughed involuntarily. It didn't make sense. At first it seemed like a joke, Jack was a bit of a joker. It seemed to be the least of the horrifying things he could have told her. But what was he telling her exactly? Jack must have seen the confusion in her face and clarified his statement.

"I like to wear women's underwear."

"Oh." Beth's voice was small. The meaning of the words began to sink in. But she was a rationalist. She took hold of Jack's words, compacted them, rolled them into a tight ball and closed her mind around them. What she concluded was that Jack liked to play sexy games occasionally. It was the 70s after all; she could manage that. If not, she would tell him she wasn't interested. One of the women in work – a rather posh woman – had told them, after a great deal of Martini at the Christmas do, about a 'wife swap' party she'd been to in Woolton. They'd all laughed hysterically at the idea, all been pleased at how liberated they were. It was surely manageable.

"I'm so sorry love. I should have told you. I promise I'll stop."

This was even better; he would stop for her. It didn't need to be a problem at all.

"OK love." Beth stroked his thick, dark hair; the hair she loved; her very own Tom Evans. "We'll be OK." The rest of the picnic was a little bit strained but that night they saw a new film, Erich Segal's *Love Story*, at the Futurist and everything was forgotten.

It was three years after they were married that Beth came home early from visiting Maria on the Wirral and found Jack watching the football, wearing silk cami-knickers. It was the final minutes of a Liverpool game and Jack was screaming at the TV over a bad decision by the referee. The sight was incongruous: her football loving Jack, shouting obscenities at the TV in silk knickers. She felt the urge to laugh again, but her sense of betrayal was stronger. Jack jumped, guilty as a cat. He turned the TV off and covered himself with a cushion.

"We need to talk."

Beth knew they must. She removed her coat and flung it over a chair.

"I've tried to stop, I promise. But I can't."

Beth wanted to shout, but it wasn't her style. She could see the edge of the underwear as they spoke, the contrast of the stretched silk against his muscular legs.

"Why is it so difficult, Jack?"

"It's a compulsion, Beth. It's so strong I can't fight it… I'm not sure if I want to anymore." Beth accepted on an intellectual level what Jack was saying, but something shifted in her, a very subtle thing, almost imperceptible. She loved him still, there was no doubt about that, but she no longer fully trusted or respected him. He wasn't quite the person she'd thought he was. She didn't feel the same when they made love. She recognised her conditioning in this; she recognised that, despite her claims of feminism and liberalism, she wanted a man to be a man and all she was conditioned to believe that meant. No matter how much she tried she could only see Jack's compulsion as a flaw in his manhood and conversely a negative reflection on her womanhood. She felt she wasn't woman enough for Jack and that his love for her wasn't big enough to make him stop.

"It isn't whether you're enough for me," Jack reassured her. "It's whether I'm enough for myself." Beth didn't really understand what this meant but she accepted the gist of it.

They reached an agreement that Jack could dress as often as he liked when she was out, but not when she was in. And in this way they got back to some normality. Most of the time Beth didn't even think about Jack's peculiarity and she ignored the stash of silky items in a plastic bag on his side of their bed. This is how they jogged along for the next few years, with Beth largely happy but disappointed and Jack largely happy but frustrated. They put off having a family for various reasons but neither of them talked of the real reason.

Beth felt a twinge in her abdomen and her thoughts flew again to the birth: it was like a wide-mouthed monster waiting to swallow her; she had no idea how to approach it. How had she allowed herself to become so isolated? Maria had offered support of sorts, but she always seemed too busy looking after her own family to have time for anything else. She said she'd be there at the birth, as long as she could get a child minder, but that wasn't very reassuring.

Beth's thoughts were broken by a ring at the bell.

"Wow, you're twice the size as last time I saw you." Sasha beamed.

"I know; I feel like I'm bursting at the seams."

"You look well on it though. How long to go?"

"A week; I can't wait to get it over with."

"And who's going to be with you at the birth?" The concern in Sasha's voice mirrored Beth's fears.

"Hopefully my sister, if she can get child minders. If not, I'm on my own."

"Oh God, Beth, you can't do it on your own. You just can't."

"I'll be fine." Beth felt like weeping on her friend's shoulder but feared she wouldn't be able to stop. "Anyway, how are you? You look pale."

Sasha's eyes brimmed with tears. "I've had a bit of a tough time. Mandy and I split up last month."

"God, I'm sorry, Sash." Beth's immediate feeling was one of relief.

"It was for the best. I'd taken enough beatings from her."

"My God Sasha!"

"It's been going on for a long time. She's a troubled woman."

"She might be troubled, Sash, but it's no excuse." Beth felt anger burning in her chest.

"I know, I know, but she's had an awful life."

"Sasha! Would you be saying that if she was a man?"

"No, but..."

"Surely it's the same thing."

"No, it's not. Male aggression is about power. It's different."

"Yeah, yeah I understand the whole power thing, Sash, but you know as well as I do that it doesn't mean women can't oppress other women or even men; they can and they do and we shouldn't excuse it."

"I know. That's why I left her, but I still feel crap."

"But why...?"

"She self-harmed; big style. Her arms and stomach are like a bloody road map. She's done it loads of times before, but this was more serious. She spent three days in hospital."

"God, I'm sorry."

Sasha blushed. "It didn't help that she caught me snogging Fiona."

Beth laughed "You and Fiona?"

"Yeah, what's wrong with that?"

"Nothing, I really like Fi. How did it happen?"

"We sort of had a fling at University but the time wasn't right. We've realised over the past months that we still have feelings for each other. It was the only time we kissed, honest, but Mandy, as you know, was never far from my side. She's a very jealous woman... she was mad jealous about you."

"Me, but I'm not a lesbian."

"You're a woman, Beth, that's threat enough for Mandy. That's why she picked on you. She knew I liked you."

To her annoyance Beth reddened and said too quickly, "So what are you going to do now? The camp is a bit cosy for both of you, isn't it?"

"To be honest, I don't think Mandy will stay around. She isn't greatly liked by the other women; it's a peace camp remember and Mandy didn't always get that concept. She doesn't think we go far enough in our protest."

The image of Mandy brutalising the police woman resurfaced but Beth didn't bother telling Sasha, she had no doubt the relationship was over.

They drank iced lemonade while Sasha recounted stories about the camp. She always saved up amusing anecdotes to entertain Beth, but what really amused her was Sasha's inability to tell a funny story without crumbling into laughter.

"Do you know the DHSS came to visit us saying we had to register for work? Now we're all signed up for bloody part-time jobs in Newbury." The last part of the sentence was disrupted by Sasha's laughter. "And then the police tried to evict us again. They took our precious Portaloos in case we tried to camp in them." Sasha threw her head back and roared. "Can you imagine us trying to set up camp in a bloody Portaloo?"

Beth dissolved into hysterical laughter at the spectacle of Sasha's red, crumpled face and at the images she painted with her stories. Neither could talk for several minutes; it was a much needed release for them both. Then Beth felt the first grinding pains of labour.

CHAPTER 11

September 1984

"It's a girl!" Jack announced to everyone in the kitchen. "Beth's had a little girl; she was born at ten minutes past midnight. Her name's Julia."

"Julia, how lovely," said Maddie who was slicing deep red tomatoes for one of her summer salads. She didn't look up.

"Great," said Greg, who had just returned from a fortnight in Corfu. He was reading *The Guardian* magazine, feet up on a stool, muscles glowing in the slant of sun pouring through the kitchen windows, like some lazy Greek god. Kate was singing along to Cyndi Lauper on the radio. "Neat," she said between verses. A Pineapple Studios bag was flung over one shoulder and she shimmered in pink Lycra and leg warmers.

"Don't be too late home," said Pat, examining troughs of Basil on the windowsill. She didn't comment on Jack's news.

By the time Jack had finished his coffee and was washing his cup at the sink, only Maddie and Pat remained in the kitchen. Maddie was engrossed in the salad while Pat tended her herbs.

"See you later," he shouted

Maddie looked up. "Off to see the witch doctor?"

"Yeah, hope she can cure me today."

"I think it will take a bit longer." Maddie smiled.

"Hey, watch it you." Jack splashed her with water from the sink. Pat looked hopefully at their reflections in the window.

Jack and Maddie had resumed their playful banter, but Maddie was reserved and spent more time alone in her flat than usual, or painting at the studio. Jack pondered on this as he made his way to Highgate, in the still-strong light of 1st September 1984. The air was breathtakingly clear and without the usual haze hanging over London's skyline everything looked sharply focused. It was as if all the pollution had been sucked out of the sky by a giant vacuum cleaner. He took a different route to Cassandra's house today, avoiding main roads as well as, he realised, this particular therapy session. He felt it was going to be the most difficult so far.

There had been several long gaps between sessions over the months, sometimes due to either his or Cassandra's holiday plans but mainly due to his conscious or subconscious avoidance of the painful wounds these sessions opened up in him. To a lesser degree he feared Cassandra's rejection, horror, loss of respect, although he knew this was a ridiculous thing to feel about a therapist.

The streets leading up to Cassie's house had a much more suburban feel than those of Hackney and a gentle breeze played with leaves, now making their slow turn into autumn, as well as rows of washing on garden lines. It reminded him of a day sixteen years earlier. He should have been at work but he'd had just about enough of restless skinheads venting their anger on him, solely for the crime of self-expression in his choice of clothes and hair style. The dreams of the Isle of Wight had quickly faded into the grime of Liverpool's streets and he'd returned to a state of despair. All over the weekend he'd been filled with an almost overwhelming desire that both scared and delighted him. Everything made him think of sex, from the budding of late summer plants in the parks to the insouciance of young girls, nylon-clad legs gliding one against the other beneath daring mini skirts or floaty hippy dresses. On Saturday he'd sauntered into town to browse in music shops. He couldn't help glancing at Lewis's window display on the way past to be confronted by models in seductive mini-dresses. He was confused between the desire to make love to a girl wearing such clothes and the desire to wear them himself. By Monday morning he felt he was going to burst; he was struck by the startling energy of the day. Everything vibrated with life; it was almost too painful to witness. The razor-edged light carved through grime and energised tired streets. Jack knew he couldn't go to work, not today. He couldn't face the cruelty of young men and so he phoned in sick.

He cut through Sefton Park to exit on Aigburth Vale, a far more affluent area than his own and somewhere he was not likely to be known. Jack ventured down tree-lined streets passing neat pebble-dashed semis. His heart pounded like a trapped animal but he was driven on by the heat in his groin and a deep, unnameable desire. He hadn't set out to complete a mission but the further he walked the more overwhelming and seductive the idea became. Unlike his own neighbourhood, these houses had gardens and it was a good day for washing. A breeze ruffled dad's shirts, baby's bibs and mum's under garments. Jack was agitated, both scared and excited. Without allowing himself to reason he climbed a fence and tore like a rabbit across the lawn to the washing line, ripping off the first woman's garment he could lay his hands on and stuffing it into his canvas work bag. The garment was a seductive pink genie beckoning to him as he made his way home across the park; but he resisted it. Clouds were gathering. The genie tantalised him but he didn't summon it from his bag until he was home and up the stairs to his room. The house was empty. He put a Bob Dylan single on his record player. The clouds were thickening and the sunlight battled with darkness, forcing its way through chinks in the clouds, creating a silvery ambience in his bedroom.

Lay, Lady, Lay …..

Jack removed the under garment from his bag and for the first time had a good look at it. It was an underslip, pink polyester with a satin finish. It had spaghetti straps and there was a slit up one side decorated with lace and three little rosebuds. The pattern was repeated around the low neckline. The slip had thin patches in places and had obviously seen better days. Perhaps it had been part of a wedding trousseau but was now tired and frayed along with the bride who had become a mother. In the strange, thundery light the slip had a magical, luminous quality. Jack removed his rough work clothes and underwear so that he stood naked. Blue and yellow flecked linoleum felt cold beneath his bare feet.

Lay across my big brass bed….

Trembling, Jack put the slip over his head. He could smell fresh air and washing powder all around him. It filled him with joy, reminded him of something he'd lost. He smoothed the slip down over his body, feeling his growing hardness, incongruous beneath the soft fabric. He only had a tiny mirror in his room and he tried to position it so that he could see himself, but he could only see small slices of pink against his skin. It was probably a good thing. The slip belonged to a large woman and hung like a pink tent over Jack's still boyish frame. But in his imagination he looked beautiful, like Elizabeth Taylor.

It was only years later that Jack realised he'd been a beautiful boy. He saw in photographs that his eyes were dark and fluid; he had cheekbones women would die for; his skin had been soft and pale in contrast to the dark brown hair, framing his face in a wild mane. His lips were almost disgracefully full as if ready to burst with forbidden passion, his body soft and not yet submitted to the brute force of masculinity. He'd been fortunate to reach the minefield of adolescence at the same time that artists like Jim Morrison and James Taylor had broken onto the scene making his androgynous looks acceptably fashionable.

Stay, lady, stay…

Stay with your man awhile…

He closed his eyes and swayed gently to the music, shutting out the drabness of his bedroom, the drabness of his life.

...his clothes are dirty, but his hands are clean.

And you are the best thing that he's ever seen…

He climbed on top of the yellow candlewick bedspread, draped over his narrow single-bed, eyes closed, long lashes kissing his cheeks. He allowed his hands to move slowly over his whole body, caressing himself; seducing the girl within.

Stay lady stay,

Stay with your man awhile…

Unable to bear the exquisite pressure anymore he lifted the slip; thunder rolled; he held his penis in one hand.

Why wait any longer for the world to begin

You can have your cake and eat it too…

The movement of his hand grew faster. He felt the pleasure of immediacy, of relinquishment…

Stay lady stay,

While the night is still ahead

Release came quickly like a dam burst; his masculinity spilling out over satin, over yellow candlewick, over skin.

I long to see you in the morning light

His exhilaration melted into a few minutes of perfect contentment. Then she was gone.

I long to reach for you in the night…

The guilt struck him like a large man's fist; he was flooded with self-loathing. The record had finished but continued to turn, hissing out empty white noise. He tore the slip off, scrunched it as small as possible and wrapped it in pages of the *Liverpool Echo*. He shoved it to the bottom of the bin. The rain came, battering the window; thunder growled its disgust. Jack climbed beneath the bedclothes and cried for a very long time.

It was several weeks before he ventured out to Aigburth again and only when the thought of having soft and feminine fabric against his skin had become a persecutory obsession, making his life a daily misery. The relief was again good but the self-disgust soon overwhelmed it and he was left in a dark and dangerous place for several days. He was less terrified the third and fourth time and almost blasé by the fifth. It was then that he got caught. He didn't take as much care as usual and didn't notice the man of the household pruning roses in one corner of the garden. The man chased him as he ran towards the fence, clutching silk knickers in his hand. He was halfway over the fence when the man grabbed his legs and dragged him to the ground. He held Jack down while his wife called the police. He called him a filthy pervert over and over again until Jack felt battered by the words.

*

Jack saw the small flicker of change in Cassie's expression as he finished this part of his story. It was one thing for a child, a vulnerable young boy, to find comfort in soft items of clothing, but a different thing altogether for a young man to steal from washing lines, to masturbate over silk lingerie. She recovered herself quickly, a true professional, but Jack saw the hesitation.

In reality Cassie was shocked but not repulsed by Jack's story. She liked Jack very much. In fact she'd had fantasies of her own about him. She liked beautiful men and Jack was certainly beautiful, with startling eyes and thick, dark hair. But it wasn't just his looks; it was his honesty, his openness. You'd think this was something she was used to as a therapist, but it was rare to see honesty to the level Jack displayed. It was as if he tore his skin off every time he sat before her. This did something to Cassie, deep in her loins. She wasn't sure if it was a sexual or a maternal feeling. She had begun to look forward to Jack's appointments more than any other. Cassie allowed Jack to meander in the sessions, unconsciously wanting them to continue longer than necessary. He seemed dangerous, like a wild Heathcliff confined in her small neat room. There was this intriguing contradiction to him; it was almost as if the masculine was a mask and his female persona shone through from time to time. Yet, in other ways, he was so masculine: the way he teased her; his physical presence; his strong arms. She felt excited by his sexual ambiguity.

"Do you understand any of this?" Jack asked, clutching at Cassie's professionalism. "My compulsion to cross-dress…this drive."

"A little." Cassie boldly met his eyes. In fact, since meeting Jack she had spent several hours in the British Library researching the subject. "There isn't a great deal written on the subject and there doesn't seem to be any conclusive reason why people cross-dress; psychiatrists have tried to understand it for years. Someone called Magnus Hirschfield coined the phrase 'transvestite' last century but it was treated as a deviance back then."

"Still is." Jack gave a wry smile.

"You could argue that we all live on a continuum and the idea of male and female is a fairly complex thing. Apparently, in some tribes, there are several genders people can choose to live by."

"Did good old Freud have anything to say on the matter?"

"He doesn't say much but his theories tend to be psychosexual, about absent fathers and the like."

"What a surprise." They both laughed.

"More recent theories are from biological determinists who talk about hormonal or genetic factors."

"I see."

"So what happened…after your arrest?"

"I was charged with theft, but because of the circumstances they sent me to a psychiatrist rather than a remand centre. He recommended aversion therapy. Each week he sat me in this gloomy room in a leather chair. I was strapped with electrodes and shocks were sent through my body. I had to stare at these ridiculous pictures of hairy men in women's underwear and respond appropriately. Of course I wasn't turned on by the pictures; I fancied girls. My need to dress as a girl was not really understood back then. They probably thought I was a latent homosexual. I ended up doing what I thought the psychiatrist wanted just to get through the sessions. The aversion therapy didn't help; it was like Nazi torture and really humiliating. Those bloody electric shocks." Jack spoke quickly, jaggedly, without pause. "I don't think Dad had a clue what went on in the sessions and he never asked. He was deeply ashamed of what I'd done and very rejecting; he couldn't even look at me. Not that I blame him; I felt like I was the worst pervert in the world. That Sid Barratt song, *Arnold Layne*, was out at the time and I totally took it to heart. I don't know if you've heard it? *Arnold Layne had a strange hobby, collecting clothes, moonshine washing line. They suit him fine… Now he's caught – a nasty sort of person. They gave him time, doors bang – chain gang…* It seemed to be about me. I really didn't see myself as a pervert but I felt I must be and I imagined that's how everyone else saw me. I would go home after the therapy, straight to my room and sculpt these really tortured shapes out of whatever materials I could get my hands on. I've only recently binned them; they were too shocking. I thought about death a lot. I thought about being with my mum.

"Did you do anything about it this time?"

"Yes." Jack came back to the present. His eyes searched for Cassie's eyes and found them there, ready to meet his.

"Why is it men choose such aggressive ways to end their lives?" Jack shook his head from side to side. "Women take pills and slip into a quiet sleep; or they slit their wrists in a hot bath until their life slowly ebbs into the water. Men jump from buildings and smash into a bloody mess on the ground so that someone has to clean it up; they jump under trains causing delay for everyone; or hang themselves from ceiling lights so they are found swinging by the wife or kids. They say women are drama queens; nothing compared to men. But then they say men are more likely to succeed. There's no chance of turning back once you've jumped from a ten storey building, is there?" Jack smiled.

"How did you do it, Jack?"

"Pills and alcohol; I don't think I really wanted to die; I just wanted things to get better. Anyway, Dad came straight home from work instead of going to the pub as usual. I suppose in that sense you could say I escaped death.

"'You stupid bastard,' he said. I was shocked; he didn't often swear. He called the ambulance and I had my stomach pumped. The doctor said I was lucky. When I came home from the hospital Dad didn't mention it again. It kind of made it a non-event. No one had witnessed it so it hadn't really happen. I felt freaked out by that."

Jack started to shake uncontrollably and then sob. It was the first time he'd talked about his suicide attempt to anyone. He'd had no opportunity in the hospital; they'd just drained his stomach and sent him home, while his father had ignored it, hiding the horror from family and friends. Jack realised for the first time how things might have ended. He felt drained of words, scraped clean. He sat for a few minutes; shaking and sobbing in his chair. He didn't want to be sobbing in front of Cassie, it was unfair, but there was nothing else he could do; a brutal exorcism was taking place and it was beyond his control. He sat exhausted in the aftermath.

Cassie didn't know what to do either, not in the face of such naked grief. To her horror she felt the heat of tears sting her eyes. She blinked furiously trying to stop them, biting her lip to bring herself back to professionalism.

"And then you met Beth." It was the wrong thing to say. She shouldn't be leading the client away from the place he was in. She felt angry with herself.

Jack blew his nose and coughed. "Yes. Then I met Beth." he spoke softly, his voice still cracked with emotion.

"Did you tell Beth about your suicide attempt?"

"It's the one thing I've never told her... or anyone else, until now."

"Why?"

"I didn't want her to feel responsible for my welfare, or have the worry of it hanging over her head for the rest of our lives. I remember when I was very young hearing my parents talk about one of our neighbours who'd attempted suicide. He'd tried to hang himself but pulled the ceiling down instead. 'Poor Elsie.' My mother kept saying, 'She hasn't had a minute's peace for years worrying if he's going to try it again, selfish sod.' Those words stuck with me.

"Anyway, as soon as I'd made the attempt I felt an amazing certainty that I didn't want to die and was pretty sure I would never try it again."

"Pretty sure?"

"You never know what might happen in your life, do you? I suppose it's our final act of control. You see I felt totally out of control. People just don't understand the absolute drive, the compulsion. They think you can just choose to stop. Perhaps you can if you're really strong but I couldn't. I also knew I couldn't keep stealing washing from lines; it wasn't safe and it was very self-destructive. The aversion therapy didn't help – it just made me feel like a freak and I still had powerful compulsions that wouldn't go away. Beth was a strongly calming influence. I didn't do the washing line thing again. I felt safe with her, but I knew the worm would surface again one day."

"Did you tell her about stealing underwear?"

"Yes, eventually. She swallowed it like a bad prawn at a dinner party, too polite to spit it out. I guess I was surprised by her initial acceptance, but I also suspected she didn't fully understand. She was fairly naïve back then. I knew I should explain properly, tell her what it meant to me, this overpowering compulsion, how hard it would be to stop. But I didn't.

Things were good between us for three or four years. We loved each other and I managed to suppress most of my urges. But then they began to resurface, which I suppose was predictable. The desire to dress again became very strong and I bought the odd thing in secret. I went through this awful cycle of buying stuff and then feeling an overwhelming guilt, which led to this purging ritual when I threw everything in the bin; I'd resist the compulsion for a while until it became too strong and the cycle began all over again. One Saturday Beth found me wearing silky underwear. The look on her face! Shock, horror, embarrassment, disappointment… it was awful."

"Like your mother all over again?"

Jack nodded. "Beth wasn't as open with me after that, the love in her eyes seemed… clouded, and her love-making was slightly hesitant. I tried to explain how important it was to me. She eventually agreed I could dress when she was out but never when she was in. She said she'd prefer not to discuss it again. I was happy I could dress without the guilt of deceit, but what I really wanted was to dress with Beth, to sit with her in the evening in silky clothes. I wanted her to know it wasn't about sex. I felt incredibly relaxed and happy; it was as if all the stress of life left me. For a time this new arrangement seemed to work. But it wasn't enough. That was probably the beginning of the end of our marriage, although it took six more years to finally die."

"Out of interest," said Cassie at the end of the session, "have you continued to sculpt?"

"Only a little," said Jack. "I guess I've given up on that dream. What's the line by that American poet? *Men at forty, learn to close softly, the doors to rooms they will not be, coming back to*."

"But I thought you were only thirty-two." Cassie smiled.

"You're right; I am," said Jack.

Jack left the therapy room feeling lighter than he could ever remember. He jogged back to Stoke Newington with joy overflowing in his heart. It was the first time he'd told anyone everything about himself and the relief of the unburdening was better than any drug he'd tried. The fact Cassie hadn't kicked him out of the therapy room or looked disgusted gave him great hope. He marked this day as the beginning of new life: both for baby Julia and for himself.

Maddie caught him off-guard when he arrived home. Or rather they caught each other off guard. She was alone in the kitchen reading a book. When she looked up her expression was sad. She quickly put on a bright face.

"Oh, you scared me!"

"Why aren't you at the festival with the others?" asked Jack.

"I did go for an hour but it's so hot. I was wilting. Greg got sloshed on red wine and was arguing with Pat. Dave was trying to pacify them. I thought it was time to come home."

"Wise move."

"How was the session?"

"Good; very good."

"You look different. Happy."

"I am."

"Wine?" Maddie held up a bottle of Sauvignon Blanc, still opaque with condensation from the fridge.

"Yeah, go on. I think I only need one more session, to tie off loose ends. It feels like the right time to stop."

"Oh. That's quite a decision."

"It is, but it's the right one. I'm as fixed as I'll ever be. I don't want to be a therapy addict."

Maddie looked concerned. "I remember after my mum died I saw a bereavement counsellor. Friends only want to hear about your loss for a few weeks then they want you to move on. The counsellor was the only one who kept listening. All I'm saying is make sure you're ready before you stop."

"I can see that, Mads, but my sessions aren't really about loss in the same way yours were. I can't get any more from them; it's all down to me now."

"Oh," said Maddie. "I'm sorry, I made assumptions."

Jack caught the look of surprise on Maddie's face; he felt a surge of love for her that stole his breath away. He knew the moment had come. He felt brave; he felt that today he could take the consequences of even Maddie's rejection. He poured them both another glass of wine.

"Can I tell you something?"

CHAPTER 12

On Christmas day; Jack's second Christmas in Carysfort Road, he returned from a walk in Clissold Park to an unusually quiet house. After the customary Christmas Eve soiree, Greg had caught an early morning flight with Dave to Barcelona while Pat and Kate had gone to stay with relatives in south London. Mike and Ayesha had finally moved out at the beginning of December. Maddie hadn't yet found a new tenant to take their room but had vowed to do so after Christmas.

"Jack, can you help me?"

His heart still thrilled at the sound of Maddie's voice with its short, lilting Scandinavian vowels. It was now three months since he'd confided in her and she'd reacted in the way he'd hoped: with love and acceptance. She hadn't shied away from the subject; she'd asked a few, sensible questions, with no sign of horror or disgust. Yet still Jack was unsure of her feelings. It was as if they were locked in a cycle of hope and doubt that neither of them could break. Jack concluded that while Maddie was accepting of his condition and would never waver in her friendship, it might not be something she wanted to deal with in a romantic relationship.

In his final therapy session, Jack had told Cassandra about his feelings for Maddie and how relieved he'd been by her reaction. He thought Cassie's face closed down a little. At the end of the session she wished him well and agreed no further therapy was necessary. It was only on his way home it dawned on Jack that

Cassie's feelings for him had strayed beyond the therapeutic boundaries. He felt bad for Cassie, but it gave him hope that someone who knew every sordid detail of his life could still have romantic feelings towards him. He decided he must throw caution to the wind and confess his feelings to Maddie, even if it meant expulsion from the house.

Maddie's voice sounded distant and he guessed she was on the third floor in her flat. He climbed the stairs and found the front door wide open.

"Maddie?"

"Come in Jack, I'm up here."

He entered tentatively. He was surprised to see sturdy wooden stairs folded out from an attic door.

"I need help with this."

Jack felt instantly protective. "Coming," he called, "Just wait until I get up there." He climbed the narrow stairs. The light in the attic was so bright that he couldn't see a thing and he had to shade his eyes with one hand while pulling himself up the stairs with the other.

"God, that's bright. I can't see anything."

"It's ok, you're safe now."

Jack stood in the centre of the attic. It was a large room covering the whole length and width of the house. It had rough, wooden floors and stark white walls. There was very little in the room except a large trestle table, a straight-backed chair, a green winged-chair and a tailor's dummy. There was no sign that the room was currently being used except for a vase of lilies standing on the table.

"My God! What a room… I didn't know you had this."

"I don't use it. It was my mother's sewing room. I was only allowed up here for a special treat. I used to sit in that chair." Maddie pointed to the faded, green-winged chair in one corner. "I watched my mother for hours; she was an excellent couture and made good money from her work. This room always smelled the same; it still does: raw wood, fresh fabric and a hint of my mother's floral perfume. I haven't been able to change anything, and I can't paint in here – it's too crowded with memories – but I feel so guilty about the wasted space."

"It's an amazing room," said Jack, "just doing nothing."

"Happy Christmas!"

Jack didn't understand. He looked to Maddie, trying to read her enigmatic face; then he looked at the flowers. It didn't make sense.

"The flowers…?" He pointed vaguely at them.

"The room, you moose."

"No!" Jack couldn't take it in. He looked around him again, then to Maddie, waiting for her face to crack into mischief, but it didn't.

Maddie, seeing his confusion, took both of his hands between hers and spoke softly.

"Jack," she said his name as if to a lost child. "I am giving you this room as a gift. It is yours to use as you want – to sculpt or just to sit and stare at the walls, whatever you like."

He still couldn't believe what he was hearing, although he could already see all the possibilities this room had to offer. He heard the question Cassie had asked him months earlier, "What did these rooms symbolise for you, Jack?" This room meant the opportunity to sculpt. Not the tiny stunted figures he created in his boxy room, but the grander visions inside his head. Finally, Jack focused his eyes on Maddie's and he saw it there; unmistakably, unchangeably; irrefutably: love. Without thinking he pulled her towards him and kissed her, feeling his whole life narrowing into its purpose. Maddie pulled away and with a sickening plunge Jack was back in the mire of doubt.

"I'm sorry," Maddie stammered, "I've done this all wrong; this room… I didn't want anything in return."

Jack was horrified; he felt the blood drain from him; how could he have been so mistaken? "I'm so sorry… I thought... Oh my God I was wrong."

"No, no, Jack, you were right; but I have to tell you something first. It could make all the difference in the world. Sit down."

For the first time Jack saw shocking vulnerability in Maddie's eyes. He sat down heavily in the straight-backed chair, while Maddie sat at some distance in the other chair.

Without hesitation and in a steady, strangely formal voice, Maddie began to speak. "I've had quite a few boyfriends since the age of fourteen, but the only really serious one was Daniel. We were in love all through my final year at University."

Jack flinched. "You don't have to tell me this."

"But I do. Just listen. He ended the relationship, quite coldly, and it was partly this that led me to accept the teaching job in Nicaragua. The other reason is more difficult to talk about.

"My brother, Fredrik, was born two years after me. He was soon diagnosed with a severe form of Duchenne Muscular Dystrophy, a devastating muscle wasting disease. My father couldn't cope with a disabled child and he left the house one night, when Fredrik was three, saying he was going to the pub. He never returned. Fred died from the disease a year later."

Jack didn't speak; he drew his hand to his mouth. He overcame the desire to go to her, stop her words with a kiss; tell her nothing she could say mattered.

"Doctors told us my mother was a carrier of the disease. They said I was also a carrier, although I had no symptoms. There was a fifty per cent chance I would pass it on to a male child." Maddie looked, fleetingly, at Jack, as if afraid to meet his eye for fear of what she might see. Jack maintained a steady look. She continued.

"When I went to university I got involved in this philosophy and ethics group; we had these amazing debates about all sorts of stuff and my views were constantly being challenged. In one meeting we talked about the decision to bring children into the world. I can't remember much except it got very heated and someone said that having children was not a right but a responsibility and therefore not everyone should have them. It struck me like a hammer blow. I realised in a single moment that I had to make a choice never to have children. I couldn't risk passing the disease to my child. It was devastating. I suppose up until that point I hadn't allowed myself to think about it, or I'd just hoped it would somehow all work out. By then I had started to see Daniel. I knew I should tell him straight away but I didn't. I was already infatuated and I was afraid to lose him. I only told him when he suggested we get engaged after our final exams. He just crumpled. Then he got angry; then he disappeared for days; he finally returned and ended the relationship." Maddie's head dropped. She took a deep breath and looked up, holding his eyes in her unfaltering gaze.

"Jack, I love you and I want you; I have from the first moment I saw you."

Jack could now hardly see the details of her face; she was a ghost. The sun had moved away from the skylight, leaving them in the flat, grey light of mid winter. A chill descended on the room. He waited.

"Jack, what I want from you is that you don't make any decisions until after Christmas. This is something you really need to think about. I've had years to come to terms with it; I won't change my mind on this, Jack. But you; you have to imagine yourself five years down the line; ten years; twenty years. Think about never going to sports days or parents' evenings; never watching your children open presents around a tree. Imagine never seeing your son or daughter graduate; never having the joy of being a grandfather. Think of all that and more before you say another word to me about it."

Jack sat paralysed; he couldn't have spoken even if Maddie hadn't ordered him to silence. He wasn't sure if he ever wanted to talk or move again.

*

Jack managed to find a hotel on Boxing Day; it was nearer Oxford than London but seemed stranded somewhere between the city and a rural idyll. It was without character or charm and the bedroom was purely functional. It suited Jack's mood. He had come here to think and that was all. Eating, sleeping, daily ablutions, all were perfunctory; they were just pauses between his thoughts.

But thinking wasn't as easy as it sounded and no matter how hard he tried to focus, his mind went wandering on its own path. Eventually he jogged down to reception and asked for paper and pen. The receptionist obliged with polite disinterest. He went to the bar, ordered a single malt and then returned to his room. Sipping the whisky he scribbled down every thought that came to him in a manic outpouring, hoping he could achieve what he'd set out to. The problem was, no matter how hard he tried to focus, his legion of thoughts kept marching back to just one dominant thought.

He wrote down all the things Maddie had asked him to think about and more; deliberately painting a Victorian ideal of family life, only to desecrate the image and rob himself of the possibility, over and over again. He tried as hard as he could to cast himself forward five years, ten years, twenty years, imagining himself bereft of all of the things he'd described. But he couldn't feel the required grief. All he could see when he looked into the future, whether a day, a year or forty years hence, was a picture of himself and Maddie, together. Perhaps he lacked the necessary imagination to feel the agony of a childless life; perhaps it would hit him at some point in the future and only then tear open his heart – he knew this is what Maddie feared – but all he could imagine in the here and now, and it seemed vivid enough to him, was his need to be with Maddie under any circumstances, and the delicious certainty that she would be all he ever needed. He pushed his few things into a hold-all and checked out of the hotel.

CHAPTER 13

The Liver Building stood hard and incongruously ornate against the wasteland of the docks, like a wedding cake resting in the lap of an abandoned bride, thought Beth.

On this colourless January day the water looked impenetrable and unable to sustain life. The sky met the horizon like a sheet of seamless steel, plunging into the grey mass of river and a shoreline of dying industries and crumbling warehouses. It was in this moment of bitter winds and bleak skies, while cradling the tiny Julia in her arms, that Beth made the decision to leave Liverpool.

She had made this crossing many times as a child. It had been wildly exciting to sail on the Royal Iris, feel the salty wind in her face. She remembered the swoop and cry of gulls accompanying their arrival, the honk of the ferry's horn as they drew closer to New Brighton, the squelch of tyres on the dockside as they came to land. It was always summer and always hot and she spent glorious days with her mum and Maria playing on ice-cream coloured sands; screaming on the fairground; riding on donkeys and letting out gleeful giggles at the archaic brutalities of Punch & Judy. She remembered the pleasure of smuggling sand from the distant and exotic beaches of New Brighton back home to Liverpool – in her hair, between her toes, on her sun-scorched skin. It would be straight in the bath for Beth and Maria once home, but not before Beth rescued a little sand from her pumps to store in her secret jam jar along with a collection of shells and unusual pebbles.

Beth loved New Brighton with its wide roads and open landscapes. On the rare occasions Dad had a day off and drove them through the Mersey tunnel in his shiny Morris Minor, they even ventured to the ancient expanse of Thurstaston Common where they played for hours on Thor's Rock. She loved being in the real countryside and vowed to live there one day. She would buy a house surrounded by heather and yellow gorse; a sandy path littered with pebbles and shells would lead to her front door.

However, on this particularly dead January day Beth was on her way home from the Wirral where they'd spent Christmas and New Year with Maria, her husband Mark and their two children. It had been a pleasant stay, especially the time spent alone with her sister, but far too long and Beth felt enormous relief when she left the pristine, mock Tudor house to catch the ferry home. Maria was conservative in every sense of the word: she'd married at twenty-five and now had two lovely, wispy-haired children and a nice house on a new estate, decorated with fussy Victorian prints and dark-wood dado rails. A large mock-Adam's fireplace overwhelmed the low-ceilinged living room and the kitchen glinted with all the mod-cons. Beth felt their differences markedly, especially now she was a single mother. Maria could barely disguise her disapproval. She remained a staunch Catholic and couldn't get her mind around the idea of a fatherless baby, as if it was somehow the antithesis of the Virgin birth. Beth didn't take to Mark, with his overpowering aftershave and obsession with money. The feeling seemed mutual. He expressed his disdain for Beth's lifestyle with barbed humour that largely went unnoticed by Maria. He criticised her "hippy-dippy politics," and her bohemian life in Liverpool – that dangerous Sodom controlled by militants and miscreants. It made Beth's visits wearying. Maria seemed to bow to his every whim, treating him like some overgrown child. Beth often wondered what had happened to the girl who loved to dance and sing.

After a week of lying empty, Beth's house felt colder and damper than ever. The boiler was spluttering and there were only two electric rings working on the hob. As she lay on the sofa, breastfeeding Julia, she felt a merciless fatigue and wondered how she could have ever considered raising a baby alone. It was a miracle Sasha had been around when she'd gone into labour. She'd flown into action, calling a taxi, grabbing Beth's overnight bag, alerting Maria. She stayed with Beth throughout the long labour, holding her hand, talking her through the pain. Maria arrived just as Julia was placed in Beth's arms. Since then, Sasha had become a good friend and a kind of non-religious godmother to Julia, but she had now settled in the South of England with Fiona, and Beth saw her infrequently.

Beth put Julia down for the night and poured herself a large glass of wine. She turned on the radio. More than once Beth had considered moving to the Wirral to be closer to her sister. Maria had even encouraged it – "You need to get out of that dump; it isn't good for a baby." But Beth knew it wouldn't work. The psychological barrier of the river made the relationship manageable. Beth also knew that neither did she want her child's future to be in a decaying city with only a sad and lonely mother for company. When Jack called soon after Julia's birth and suggested they move to Carysfort Road, "Until you find your feet," Beth had laughed. Typical Jack, she thought, magnanimous but naïve. He imagined they could all live together as one big happy family. But, increasingly, Jack's offer was beginning to sound like a good idea; the only good idea.

She wasn't concerned about Jack and Maddie: despite mild post-natal depression, the depth of love Beth felt for Julia was way beyond anything she'd expected. It blew her mind and filled every part of her that mattered. It erased the longing for Jack, or for any relationship for the time being. Before the birth Beth had worried her love might be too thin, that it wouldn't stretch very far without tearing; but she'd proved herself wrong. When she held Julia for the first time she knew what if felt like, this opening up of the heart like a Jasmine flower in water; this excruciating expansion of emotions.

Beth scrutinised the kitchen: everything looked shabby. The house needed some serious money spending on it and she knew that the landlord wasn't prepared to spend a penny more than was absolutely necessary. Besides, she needed to start thinking about buying a place of her own with the money sitting idle from the sale of the marital home. She pulled Wednesday's *Guardian* across the kitchen table. She'd had a moment of unusual clarity while crossing the river that morning. She knew she needed a change of environment and possibly even a change of career, for her own sake as well as Julia's; she'd been wearing this threadbare life for too long. She took a red pen and boldly circled social work jobs in London.

PART II

CHAPTER 14

August 2002

The sun flooded the kitchen, invigorating the velvet-blue of a bunch of Iris arranged loosely in a clear glass vase. It highlighted the rich grain of the light-oak table top on which they stood; set a sparkle to two dozen wine glasses standing in rows on a deep green work surface, and exposed the lustre of a head of dark, chestnut hair. Julia loved the kitchen in the mornings; it was the largest room in an otherwise boxy flat, attracting light through its large, modern windows. Each day during the long summer holidays Julia went to the kitchen after her mum left for work and performed the same rituals: she made a cafetiere of coffee; warmed a cup of semi-skimmed milk in the microwave and whipped it into a mass of white foam with a hand frother. She cut two thick slices of bread and spread them with butter and marmalade; she plunged the coffee and poured it into the frothing milk. She sat at the kitchen table and listened to the radio while sending text messages to friends, perhaps arranging to meet later for a picnic in Clissold Park. After breakfast, she checked emails and then practiced scales and chords on her keyboards before going out.

That morning, an unusual amount of excitement accompanied her ritual. It was two days before her eighteenth birthday. Today there would be non-stop planning and activity leading up to her party the following evening. A hundred text messages would fly through the ether: making and confirming arrangements, planning strategies for the party, which would have many agendas other than the celebration of Julia's coming of age. It would be a vehicle to kick start hesitant romances, a time to experiment, a time to gossip about who wants, needs, desires or is growing to hate, whom. As the eldest in her year Julia was the first to reach the magic gate into adulthood and in this, like most things, she willingly took the lead, relishing the role of torchbearer.

The party was to take place at Carysfort Road. The house was big enough for Julia and her friends to have space and privacy while allowing the old crowd to enjoy their own soiree and keep a casual eye on proceedings. Julia did consider having the party at a club but some of their group, particularly the boys, could not yet pass for eighteen. Besides, all of Julia's friends thought Jack and Maddie's place, as well as Jack and Maddie, was cool.

Maddie and Beth agreed to prepare enough food for forty while Jack and Greg would give the party a kick-start with crates of beer, wine and soft drinks. On Sunday, her actual birthday, Julia had chosen to go to a Lucian Freud exhibition at the Tate Modern with her mum, Jack and Maddie, followed by dinner at her favourite restaurant. She felt that life was brimming with all sorts of possibilities. She would be back in school on Monday for her final year in the sixth form; after that she had plans.

Julia turned up the radio to hear a single from a new band, The Libertines; she had recently seen them at a gig with her boyfriend, Jamie. At that moment the post dropped noisily onto the laminate floor in the hallway. Julia jumped up, the child still strong in her. She gathered a very large pile of mail into her arms and took it back into the kitchen. She placed bills and other correspondence she didn't have to worry about in one pile and envelopes addressed to her in another. There were several multi-coloured packages, which she knew were birthday cards and she was confident there would be many more over the next couple of days. She decided to save their opening until her actual birthday.

There was also a large A4 manila envelope, enticingly bulky, with a Liverpool frank mark on the front. She felt as excited about this as about her birthday cards. She tore open the pre-stick flap and pulled out a glossy brochure with the words LIPA (Liverpool Institute of Performing Arts) written across a collage of pictures of Liverpool. Julia smoothed her hand over the surface of the prospectus and then automatically lifted it to her nose to breathe in the scent of fresh cardboard and ink, as if she could smell the salt waters of the Mersey and the acrid city air. She poured a second cup of coffee and read through the prospectus.

Half an hour later, Julia pulled on a pair of converse trainers, a black hoodie and absently brushed her long hair, before venturing out onto Church Street. It was a warm day with no whisper of autumn yet in the air. She crossed over the road so that she could walk alongside the park. She passed St Mary's Old Church on her left with its straggle of ancient gravestones. St Mary's new Church stood opposite, looking almost modern in comparison, yet still a century-and-a-half-old. She passed the library and entered Spence Bakery, with its burnt orange exterior. The smell of coffee beans and fresh bread was instant. This was one of her favourite places on Church Street, although not where she usually met friends. It was really only a bakery with a coffee machine and a few chairs, but she felt it was her own, secret place.

She took the window seat, where she could see everyone who passed by. A soprano sax played mellow Jazz. She ordered a latte and a slice of cherry cake and bought a loaf of bread to take home. She settled with *The Guardian* Magazine, left by someone else. A man sat in one corner dressed all in black except for a canary yellow tie; he wore a black Homburg hat and looked like he was waiting for his stage call at the Vortex. An elderly woman sat at another table wearing too much makeup on what must have once been a striking face. Raven black hair drained the colour from her skin; Julia thought she looked like a vampire.

After fifteen minutes Jamie blustered in, instantly shattering the ambience.

"Sorry I'm late," he said cheerfully. Vampire lady looked up, disapproval in her impossibly black eyes. Julia resisted the urge to put her finger to her lips; she was acutely aware of atmosphere and hated to disturb a good one. She smiled at Jamie and spoke softly, hoping to draw him into the mellow mood.

"Don't worry," she said, "it's cool."

Jamie, largely insensitive to ambience, continued to bluster. He'd misjudged the weather and removed a heavy zip-up hoodie to reveal a long-sleeved t-shirt beneath. He'd obviously been running to get there and two ever-present pink patches on his faintly freckled cheeks flared bright red.

"Shit, I couldn't get away from the studio. Mac was going on and on, 'Just one more take.' I said, 'shit, man, it's done, finished, lets get out of here.'" Jamie bent down to kiss Julia; she met him with her cheek. She was wishing they'd agreed to meet somewhere nosier, where Jamie was less conspicuous. She sensed annoyance from Mr Homburg.

"Do you fancy a walk?" Julia asked. Jamie looked confused.

"Er... don't you want to stay here?"

"It's just such a lovely day, I feel like a walk."

"OK, cool. I'll grab a cold drink from a shop; I'm boiling over."

They walked along Church Street with Jamie holding Julia's hand a little too tightly. He chatted about his morning at the studio in Soho. They stopped at a newsagent's to grab icy cokes from the fridge and continued their walk, past the Red Lion and the Daniel Defoe.

"Let's go in here," Julia pulled Jamie up the steps into the coolness of Abney Cemetery.

"God, you're a weird chick." He liked to use these dated

expressions, talking out of one side of his mouth. Julia used to find it amusing.

“It’s not weird,” she felt irritated, “It’s where we’ll all end up; you’d better get used to it.” She didn’t like the way she talked to Jamie these days; it wasn’t natural to her. She’d once been beguiled by his boyish carelessness but now she felt somehow responsible for him and it was a burden. They’d been dating for five months but Julia felt she’d matured significantly in those months, outgrowing Jamie by miles. Now he was trying too hard, fooling around like a manic clown; it was painful to them both.

“Look Jamie…” She pulled him around so that he was facing her; he looked very young. He had smooth skin like a girl and in the sunlight she could see wispy hairs on his chin. His blond hair was thick and tousled; his blue-green eyes eager. He was lovely. “I want a bit of space at my party tomorrow…”

“What d’ya mean, I always give you space.” She saw his defences rise and a blush darkened his skin.

“I just mean I want to have fun, talk to lots of people; I don’t want us to be all lovey-dovey in the corner.”

“Fine. I don’t either.”

“Good.”

Awkwardness creaked between them as they walked amid moss-ravaged gravestones and the overhanging branches of Willow and Swamp Cyprus, Silver Birch and Oak. The cemetery was a magical mass of overgrowth and undergrowth. Julia loved it here and often came alone to walk among ancient trees and wild flowers, Japanese knot-weed and blackberry brambles. A kaleidoscope of butterflies, seldom found anywhere else in London, gathered in abundance here. Gravestones were slowly sinking into the earth; some already lost, while others were bravely fighting back. Stony arms forced their way up to escape the dense foliage, waving for attention; severed marble heads peered with unseeing eyes from among the tangle. Above it all the angels hovered in celestial superiority. Even so, ivy and bindweed climbed their torsos, crept about their necks and trapped their wings. One day, thought Julia, nature will win.

She imagined her own gravestone with an ominous blank: daughter of whom, Elizabeth Swann and a single anonymous sperm? She often thought about writing a grave enscription for herself, hiding it in a box to be discovered at her death; something about who she really was. But what could she say about herself at this point? Not yet eighteen, hardly any life lived and not even sure who she was.

"I've decided to go to Liverpool to do a BA in music." The words spilled out of her mouth as if convincing herself this is what she must do. Jamie's head jerked around.

"Liverpool! Why the hell Liverpool?"

"Why not?"

"Well… surely the best stuff's in London. I don't see why you'd want to leave."

"There is life outside of London, you know." There was sarcasm in her voice. "It's one of the best music courses in the country and… it's different."

Jamie was silent as he stared at the pale, oval beauty of her face, the fluid treacle of her eyes hardening before him. He felt her slipping further away. He knew he was only hanging by a thread anyway; there was nothing he could say.

When Beth returned from work at three, Julia was home, curled up on a chair reading Madam Bovary. Beth felt harassed. There was so much going on in the office at the moment. Social work had changed dramatically since her first tangle with it sixteen years earlier.

"God, I can't do this job for much longer; it's a young person's game. Roll on retirement." Beth threw her bag down on the table.

"Poor thing! Do you want a coffee?" Julia gave her mum a hug. Beth flopped down on a chair. "I'd prefer tea thanks; I've been drinking coffee all day."

"Have the kids been giving you a hard time?"

"It's not the kids; it's the bloody social workers. I don't know what they teach them at college anymore… sorry, love, enough about work. How are preparations going?"

"Great. I've been buying stuff for tonight. I got these brilliant balloons on Church Street; really cool, black, purple and silver."

"I got some stuff too on the way home," said Beth enjoying her daughter's enthusiasm. "Party poppers and a few more snacks."

"Ta. Oh, I met Jamie earlier. He's getting way too intense. I hope he's not going to cling to me at the party; I just want to have fun."

"He's just crazy about you, love. He can't help it."

"He's a bit immature though Mum… Oh, by the way, look at this." Julia jumped up and grabbed the LIPA prospectus; she plonked it down in front of her mum.

The smile abandoned Beth's face. "I really can't understand it, love. Why Liverpool…?"

That question again. "I told you, it's one of the best music courses in the country."

"I'm sure there must be equally good courses in London… or Brighton; anywhere other than Liverpool."

"Well, I don't think so. This course suits me best. It's all the stuff I'm interested in."

"If I thought that was your only reason for going…"

"Look Mum, Liverpool is part of my heritage. You're always doing that social work speak about heritage and identity, but you don't want me to know about mine." Julia jumped up again and fiddled with buttons on the microwave.

"You know it's impossible to find your biological father, don't you? That's the whole point of anonymous donors."

"Don't you think I know that?" Julia looked pale and wounded; her voice was thick with emotion. "Anyway, I've got stuff to do." She left the kitchen, her back stiff against her mother.

Beth remained, trembling, at the table. She examined the

brochure with its pictures of a bright new Liverpool: the Liver Buildings, Liverpool by night – looking more like New York. She opened it and read: *LIPA is located between the two landmarks of the Gothic Anglican Cathedral and the modern Catholic Cathedral*. Religion and football that's all it's got to offer, thought Beth, and both of them cause nothing but trouble. *Liverpool is a vibrant and culturally rich city…* She remembered the deadness of the early '80s… *offering LIPA students a fantastic choice of arts and entertainment opportunities… great for nightlife…stunning architecture for film locations…more museums and art galleries than any other city outside London*. Well, why not stay in London then? Liverpool doesn't have anything to offer that London hasn't got ten times over. Beth felt agitated. She snapped shut the prospectus, stood up and popped two slices of bread in the toaster.

She felt she'd reached the inevitable moment, the moment she'd been dreading for eighteen years. She had once naively imagined that when Julia reached eighteen she would awaken from some fairytale sleep, fully aware and demanding to know about her father. In reality, eighteen marked only a legal transition into adulthood and what Beth hadn't been prepared for was that Julia would be brimming with curiosity and endless questions from almost the moment she could talk. The questions had only become more sophisticated and persistent with each passing year.

Beth had always tried to answer truthfully and at first Julia seemed to accept her mother's story. In Julia's vivid imagination her father was a prince, a knight or a pop star who would one day return to claim his daughter. In the meantime, Julia seemed happy to adopt other men as father, including Greg and Dave, but notably Jack, who she loved dearly. Julia was a happy and vivacious child, loving and easily loved and Beth felt enormous relief that she'd so far successfully negotiated her way through the tangled forest of parenthood.

However, on Julia's twelfth birthday it was as if a switch was turned on – she asked more searching questions about Beth's decision to use a sperm donor and tried to find out everything she could about her biological father. Beth told her all she knew and felt wrung out by the questions and by the poverty of information she had to give her daughter. Soon a new tone entered Julia's questions; it was accusatory. At sixteen, she finally broached the dreaded subject of searching for her father, wondering whether it had ever been done, whether it was possible and how could one go about it.

The difference now at eighteen, thought Beth, was that not only would Julia soon fly the nest, but she would be flying into a brave new world, unrecognisable from the world of eighteen years before. With the explosion of the internet, there were seemingly endless opportunities to search for information, to find things out. Beth felt bewildered by it all, while Julia took to it like a… a mouse to a mouse mat.

The toast popped up, too well done for Beth's liking; Julia had adjusted the setting. She absently buttered it and sat at the table, her eyes unwillingly magnetised by the colourful prospectus. She chided herself for ever thinking that using an anonymous donor would mean half of Julia's genetic make-up would be insignificant. Eighteen years ago, Beth had believed largely in nurture; she imagined that, as the main guiding influence in her life, Julia would be mostly like her – quiet, largely content, unassuming. She now realised she couldn't have been more wrong.

CHAPTER 15

"It was like having everyone that matters to me in the whole world, together in one place," said Julia, with an expansive gesture, over dinner; although she couldn't help but think of the one person who hadn't been there. Julia didn't share this shadowed thought with anyone; she didn't want to upset her mum again and, besides, she'd asked all the questions she could ask about her biological father, now the journey was hers to make alone.

The weekend celebrations were coming to an end with an intimate meal for those Julia considered to be family. Each person there felt a measure of pride that they had been responsible in some way for Julia's blossoming into the young woman who now shimmered, apple-cheeked and glossy haired, before them.

"It was a great party," Jack grinned. "I certainly enjoyed it."

"A little too much," said Maddie, "judging from the state of you this morning."

"Yeah, great bit of dancing, Jack." Julia laughed,

"Dad dancing," said Greg, "but brilliant all the same.

"What do you mean 'dad dancing'? I out danced most of the young lot."

"That's true," said Beth, "although maybe they just knew when to call it a night."

Carysfort Road had been festooned with balloons, streamers and lanterns and it was warm enough to throw open French windows leading to the garden, where more lanterns were dotted about. The evening began with strict partition between the young and not so young but ended – largely due to the process of intoxication – with the happy intermingling of the two groups.

At midnight Julia had extracted herself from Jamie who, unbounded by too much alcohol, had abandoned his promise not to cling to her. She found Greg and Dave in the garden. At forty-two Greg looked much younger than his years and Julia considered him to be impeccably trendy. Dave had always been more relaxed about his appearance and, though still attractive, had developed middle-age spread and had shaved his head to disguise thinning.

"So how's Soho?" Julia asked, waving a glass of champagne in the air. She felt exquisitely tipsy.

"We've been there ten years this month, you know," said Greg. "We love it, Jules; it's like being in the centre of the universe. There's so much going on it's a wonder we ever get to bed."

"It's a wonder we ever get out of bed with your sex drive," said Dave. "Julia, you look gorgeous."

"Yes, you do," agreed Greg, "It hardly seems any time since we were bouncing you up and down on our knees and now you're like a proper woman."

Julia laughed raucously. "Not too proper I hope,"

"Oh, by the way, did we tell you we're thinking of adopting," said Greg, clapping his hands together.

"No. That's brilliant. But will they allow a pair of old fags like you to adopt?"

"Hey, less of the old," said Greg, thumping Julia on the arm.

"Of course," said Dave, "If we choose the right borough. We're going to an information evening next week."

"That's brilliant. I think you'd make great parents. Keep me informed."

"We will. Anyway what's going on with you, birthday girl?"

"I'm applying to do a music BA in Liverpool."

"Why would you want to go to a tiny place like Liverpool?"

asked Greg.

"God, don't you start; you southerners are all so prejudiced."

"Aren't you a southerner?"

"I was born in Liverpool."

"Has this got anything to do with your invisible dad?" asked Dave.

"No," Julia jumped into defensiveness, "Well maybe. I don't know. Of course I'd like to know more about him, but I think I'm pretty realistic about my chances of finding anything out."

Greg looked unusually serious. "Just don't let it take over your life, Jules. Blood relatives aren't all they're cracked up to be; I should know."

"I'm not looking for a dad," said Julia, aware as she said it that this wasn't completely true. "It's more about knowing who I am; it's like half the story's missing."

"We don't always have to know everything about everything."

"I know, Greg, but if you adopt wouldn't you want your kids to know about their parents?"

"Of course we would; but what I'm trying to say is, and it probably sounds really gay and corny, sometimes what we're looking for is right on our doorstep."

"Uggh, yes that does sound gay and corny," said Dave. "Look Julia, at the end of the day nothing we say will change anything. You just have to do what you have to do and I'm sure you'll sparkle…" Dave gave Greg a sharp dig in the ribs. "Just like this present."

"Ow," said Greg, retrieving a large parcel from the lounge, wrapped in purple tissue paper. "Happy Birthday!"

Julia tore it open to find a glittering, purple keyboard case inside.

"God, where did you find that; it's gorgeous?"

"His choice, not mine," said Dave.

"We'll never lose you in Liverpool with that," said Greg, throwing his arms round Julia.

Beth was enjoying a moment alone, sipping white wine on a little bench in the garden, watching Julia in animated conversation with Greg and Dave. After a few minutes Jack joined her. "How's it going?"

"Well thanks." Beth made room on the bench.

"You sound a bit flat?"

"Well, there are big changes around the corner." She nodded towards Julia, "And you know I don't like change. I'm so proud of her but…"

"But…?"

"Well, she can't get this Liverpool fixation out of her mind. Has she talked to you about it?"

"Yes she has, a little."

This didn't surprise Beth. "And what do you think?"

"I kind of think she's going to do her own thing whatever anyone says. What's your worry?"

"She's been talking a lot about her biological father and I can't answer her questions. I just have this nagging worry that she's going to Liverpool to find him. It scares the hell out of me. The idea of the pain she might have to go through… the disappointment, the rejection."

Jack's expression changed to concern. "Has she said that's why she's going?"

"No. But she isn't a good liar. And why else would she go to Liverpool?"

"Well, it's where she was born, her Aunty Maria lives there and it is one of the best popular music courses in the country; isn't that reason enough? Liverpool's changed a lot since we lived there you know, love."

Beth smiled. Jack always managed to be both positive and rational. "I guess so."

"Anyway, isn't it supposed to be impossible to trace sperm donors?"

"You'd think so, but the world has changed. Anyway, the clinic

I used was… well a bit dodgy…"

"Oh Beth!"

"I know, I know, but I was desperate and it was cheap and it was the only place I could find that would treat single women of my age."

Jack took hold of Beth's hand. "I'm so sorry love."

"Don't apologise, Jack. I don't regret it; look at her." Their eyes fell on Julia who was now dancing with Greg.

"She's beautiful." Jack smiled.

"She's also very bright and determined. If anyone can find someone who doesn't want to be found, it's Julia."

"The intransigence of youth, hey."

"I can't remember feeling so bloody invincible at that age," said Beth.

"Me neither, but as you said, it's a different world now. Maybe it's a journey she has to make, no matter how painful."

"God Jack, I didn't know parenthood would be so agonising."

"I can imagine."

Beth flinched, "I'm sorry; I know it's been difficult for you and Maddie at times."

"No worries; we're fine."

"Can I just ask you one more question and I really want you to be honest with me."

"Go on."

"I remember you being quite disapproving of me using a sperm donor all those years ago. Do you think I did the wrong thing?"

Jack didn't answer immediately; he took a long slug of Stella from his bottle. "Look Beth, I felt at the time you did it out of desperation and I admit I was worried, but I've never judged you for it. The modern world gives us so many choices; it's hard not to take them."

Beth felt grateful. "I suppose I didn't think enough about the consequences at the time; I just thought it would all work out, somehow."

"I think you've done the very best you can. Look at the evidence in front of you."

Beth nodded, desperately trying to hold back dogged tears; this wasn't a night for tears. "Thanks Jack."

"Now I'm going to find Maddie; I haven't seen her all evening."

Beth remained on the bench and studied her daughter who seemed as complex and iridescent as a rainbow. She could hardly believe she'd produced this marvellous creature, now standing on the edge of everything and ready to fly. Had she looked as magnificent to her own mother at eighteen? Beth remembered herself as hunched and unsure, going through life muttering and apologising, while Julia made an entrance, glided, glittered. Beth didn't like to think that the best of Julia might have come from her incorporeal father: the long, athletic legs, the talent for music, the creative imagination. But when she looked at her daughter, her dark hair tumbling in curls down her slender neck, eyes intensely bright, she didn't see much of herself. Perhaps around the nose and lips, the parts of her Jack had once praised, and in her love of books.

Beth felt an odd mix of pride that she'd brought such beauty into the world and fear of what beauty can mean. She remembered reading that too much beauty in one's child can be disturbing; like genius, it's better off in other people's children. Despite Jack's reassurances Beth felt that all those years ago she'd made an ignoble choice to fill a gap in her own life and in doing so had inadvertently created a void in her daughter's soul. She had a sense of foreboding that wouldn't go away, as if something awful was about to happen. She knew all she could do was stand and watch with the trembling anticipation of Dr Frankenstein.

CHAPTER 16

She said, "I am summoning Venus Castina, who understands the yearnings of feminine souls trapped in male bodies." She created him in her own image and pronounced him good. She named him Anna and he was glad.

It was two years into their relationship that Maddie's suggested they venture out to Oxford Street to buy the clothes and accessories necessary for transformation. Like guilty, giggling school children they pulled dresses and skirts, blouses and scarves from rails, in a variety of sizes and styles. And then, loaded with bags, they ran from the shop to allow suppressed laughter to explode onto the street

At home, Maddie cast a spell with dinner and candlelight, soft music and two large glasses of wine. She then stripped him and shaved him, softened him and bathed him, and so began the ritual transformation.

Jack sat semi-naked, trembling on an upright chair, hair pulled from his face by Maddie's silk stocking; he was at her mercy, his face a smooth canvas for her artwork. With terrifying purpose she pulled brushes and sponges, cotton wool and cold metal implements from a large bag; she applied lotions and potions, unction and balms, layer upon layer; first a curious, green cream, "it will tone down the redness in your skin," and then foundation, "to even you out," followed by powders and pencils, more powders for cheeks and eyes, "you're lucky, you've got amazing cheekbones and your eyelashes, wow, they're like healthy, young spiders."

"You're a witch Maddie. Is this what you do to yourself?"

"Me, no, a bit of mascara and a swipe of lip gloss is all I need, but you, my dear, will need much more than that."

Next came layers of clothes to slim and shape, improve and disguise: silky undergarments beneath flattering dresses, complemented by well-chosen accessories and a spray of seductive perfume.

"I feel like a Victorian; how do women go through all this?"

"It's a secret you have to learn."

The transformation was only complete with the crowning glory, silky brown tresses, teased and tugged by Maddie until just right.

They were silent: stunned.

"She has to have a name." Maddie eventually spoke in a cracked voice, "she deserves a name of her own."

"You name me; you created me."

Maddie took her time, looking intently at her woman-man. Jack didn't dissolve before her because he saw wonder, not the disgust he had feared, in her eyes.

"Anna. You're Anna."

In spring 1992 Jack went out dressed for the first time. They booked into a hotel in the Marais District of Paris. During the day they were conventional tourists, visiting Notre Dame and the Pompidou Centre; drinking coffee on the Left bank and strolling though the Tuileries Garden. They visited the Louvre where Jack insisted they see Mona Lisa again, although Maddie wasn't impressed by her. It was the first 'famous' painting Jack had seen on his first trip to Paris in 1986 and he'd had an epiphany.

"It was like seeing all the women I've ever loved – my mother, sisters, Gloria, Jill, Beth, You and Anna, all merged into one."

With the fall of night Jack made his transformation into Anna.

They strolled through the tangled lanes of the Marais district, shaky and stumbling beneath Van Gough skies. Jack clung to Maddie's arm, afraid to fall from precarious heels. Maddie conquered a crashing heart, fearing cruelty or humiliation, but no one batted an eyelid; or at least not that they noticed, and Anna walked tall, growing into herself, becoming all that she was and would be.

With the bright expanse of the attic room at his disposal Jack's sculptures became bolder and more accomplished. Occasionally he sculpted en femme and felt a subtle shift take place within him that seemed more than just about a change of clothes. He was conscious of the relaxation of his whole body and spirit; the dissolution of a hard shell. He noticed his sculptures were different. It wasn't that they became more feminine but they tended to be less geometric, less pained; less aggressive.

However, while sculpting was a creative outlet for Jack, he had never believed he was a naturally gifted artist like Maddie and he didn't have any great hopes or even desires for commercial success. It had taken a little while longer for Jack to discover his true talent. Like many people in the 1980s and 90s Jack had fallen into computers as a way of earning a living but he soon grew tired of them and when he saw an advert for a peripatetic computer teacher in Hackney he applied for the job and got it.

He found he had skill for imparting information as well as for gaining the respect of young people. However, it wasn't until later that Jack found his true calling when an art teacher in one of the schools left under a cloud of controversy and just before final exams. There was protest from pupils and parents, but it was impossible to find another art teacher at such short notice. It was then that Jack came clean to the school Head about his interest in art and sculpture. In a move that Jack later saw as the serendipitous closing of a circle, he became the permanent art teacher at the school, deriving great satisfaction from helping inner city kids to discover hidden talent. Jack believed teaching was his gift, while sculpting had largely been a creative outlet for his suppressed desire to cross-dress.

Jack and Maddie flopped side by side on the sofa, exhausted after a hectic weekend of Julia's eighteenth birthday celebrations. It was midnight and the moon was small and bright outside the window, casting a blue sheen on the long strip of slate roofs opposite. They talked about the weekend and about the Lucian Freud exhibition they had visited with Julia that day.

A small silence fell between them and then Jack coughed.

"Do you think I should tell Julia about me?"

"Why would you feel a need to tell Julia?" Only a slight frown gave away Maddie's concern.

"It feels disingenuous not to. I think of her as a daughter, you know, and she's an adult now."

"It could dramatically change things between you. Perhaps you need to think about it a bit more."

They had discussed this more than once over the years and Maddie always cautioned Jack, saying that not everyone would have the capacity to accept his disclosure and that he would have to prepare for a shift in relationships, or even the loss of some. Jack had experienced this 'shift' briefly in a moment of carelessness in the early days of living at Carysfort Road. He often wore a silk slip to bed but was careful to have a man's dressing gown to hand. However, one morning he awoke at three am and in a state of half-sleep stumbled into the kitchen for a glass of water. What he didn't realise was he'd been woken by Greg returning from a club. Greg found Jack in the kitchen in a black silk negligee.

"For God's sake Jack, what are you doing?" There was horror in Greg's eyes.

"God I'm sorry; I thought everyone was asleep." He felt his face colour and resisted the urge to run.

"Obviously!" Greg walked away. "I'm going to bed."

Jack didn't sleep again that night, worrying about the aftermath of his carelessness. It was in the days before Maddie knew anything and he was terrified of blowing it with her. He was disappointed that Greg had reacted in this way and he realised again how far his behaviour was outside most people's comfort zone.

Greg and Jack avoided talking about the incident for several weeks and engaged in an embarrassed dance around each other. Jack felt a growing resentment towards Greg, believing that, as a gay man, he should at least try to understand.

Then, one evening when Jack was watching TV alone, Greg came in and sat beside him.

"Sorry mate, it was just so unexpected. I'm a bit of a prude at times."

"That's OK," said Jack, "It must have been a shock."

"You can say that again, but I still should have talked to you sooner. I've been embarrassed about my reaction rather than about what I saw. I talked to Dave about it – only Dave honest – and he called me a prude and bigot and all the names under the sun. I'm sorry. I don't fully understand, but I don't judge, and it really doesn't make any difference to our friendship. I guess I'm quite a straight-gay man; if you know what I mean."

"Yes I do. I'm quite a straight-straight man, actually."

"At least you've got good taste; I really couldn't have coped if I'd found you wearing some god awful frilly number."

"Look, Greg, I don't understand this shit, myself. That's why I'm seeing a therapist."

Greg looked uncertain, as if he wasn't sure he wanted to be drawn into this discussion. He stood up, walked over to the French windows and pushed them open. He pulled a cigarette from a pocket, lit it and stood, lean and elegant in the doorway, blowing smoke into the night. He turned to Jack.

"Have you had any contact with other people… like you?"

"No. I've never really thought about it."

"Well the only advice I can give you from my own experience is that there's nothing worse than feeling like you're the only freak out there. Find other people, talk, do some research into what it's all about. Believe me, it lessens the horror."

"Horror, that's a strong word."

"Look, I've had the benefit of coming out during the gay revolution. Before that… well I don't really want to talk about it. I'm lucky, I'm part of a movement. Take my advice, Jack, the world won't change of its own accord; you've got to force it to. Use tears, humour, high kicks, whatever you can, but don't do it alone."

Jack thought a lot about Greg's advice and eventually he did make links with others. He talked to people in America and Denmark; people across the globe. He read as much as he could find, until he came to a definition of himself that was neither rigid nor intractable.

"OK, I'll think about it some more," said Jack. "I just don't want to tell her on my death bed."

'That's a bit dramatic, isn't it?" Maddie rose from the sofa, took Jack's hand and led him into the bedroom. Jack sat on the bed and pulled Maddie onto his lap. "In my experience life is dramatic, Mads, and pretty unpredictable, so let's make the most of it while we can, hey?"

CHAPTER 17

July 2003

Beth was alone when Maddie called with a loose bunch of wild flowers cradled in her arms. The evening was flushed and dusty and the sounds of Stoke Newington seemed intimately close in the still air. It had been a difficult eight months for Beth since Julia's eighteenth birthday. Against her wishes, Julia had applied to LIPA and, as predicted, she did well in her exams and was offered a place. She'd left early in the month for Liverpool after they'd had an unusually fierce row.

As always Beth was pleased to see Maddie; they'd become good friends over the years, even though they described their relationship as 'chalk and cheese'. They felt at ease in each other's company and, of course, they had Jack in common.

"How are you doing?" Maddie kissed Beth once on the cheek and handed her the roughly arranged flowers.

"Oh they're lovely," said Beth, "I'm doing OK." She felt her eyes soften with tears; she quickly recovered herself. "Cup of tea?"

"Do you have anything cold and alcoholic? This hot weather makes me go all Mediterranean."

The women sat together sipping white wine in Beth's tiny garden. Beth noticed how beautiful Maddie looked; her skin still smooth and firm, framed by soft, platinum hair, which gleamed in the gentle evening light. When she looked in the mirror these days Beth only saw a tired, puffy face staring back.

"Your veggies are coming on well," said Maddie, admiring rows of green beans and courgettes.

"Yes, it's been a good year though the heat is taking its toll."

"Beth, I'm sorry you've been having a difficult time," Maddie came to the point of her visit quickly, "It must be hard when your only child flies the nest."

"You know, I think I would have coped under normal circumstances. I'm happy for her to be stepping out into the world; I know she's ready for it. It's just... well the row was awful. We both said things we shouldn't have said and I'm really scared of losing her."

Maddie leaned over and touched Beth's leg. "Oh Beth, you will never lose her, it's impossible. She loves you so much."

"I know she loves me, Maddie, but she's such a strong character and I feel so weak at times. What if she finds her biological father? What if he's so enticing, so amazing that she... oh I know it's stupid."

"If, in the unlikely event she does find him, it doesn't mean she'll have to choose between you, does it? She just needs to find out who she is. I know I had a strong urge to find out more about my Scandinavian roots at Julia's age but it didn't make me want to run to Norway."

"I'm sure you're right. It must be my Catholic guilt; I just can't stop thinking what goes around comes around; that one day, I will be punished in some way. How ridiculous, and I call myself an atheist!"

"Old habits die hard, hey? Look, can't you chat to her on the phone, try to at least make up after the row?"

"She called last night from my sister's but the conversation didn't go well. I hate telephones; we misunderstood each other and ended up going over old ground. If anything it feels worse."

"Oh dear, perhaps you need to give her a bit of time then."

"Yes, that's what I've decided to do; let her settle."

"So what about you, Beth, do you have any plans for yourself?"

This question startled Beth. She'd given little time to planning her own future. "Oh, perhaps I'll do a bit of travelling when I retire. I'd love to see more of Europe, especially Italy; I've always had a thing for Italy." Beth hadn't eaten much all day and the wine quickly intoxicated her. She didn't mind; it felt nice. It loosened her thoughts and her tongue, drawing out the girlish side of her character.

"That sounds great, but what about now?" Maddie persisted.

"I think I'm tired of London; it's just such a wearing city: Fantastic if you're young, but at my age… the same goes for the job. If I'm honest, Maddie, I just want a quiet life."

"And what does that mean… a quiet life?" Maddie scrutinised Beth's face with her keen eyes, demanding honesty. Beth gathered together the thoughts and reflections that had been scattered about her mind for several weeks.

"Well, I've been thinking about it a lot recently. Looking back I realise I've been drawn into adventures over and over again, almost against my will." Beth laughed, embarrassed by her confession. "The Mod scene in the 60's, Greenham Common and even the endless music festivals and parties since I've been in London. It's always someone else's idea and I just go along with it."

"I'm sorry Beth," said Maddie, "We probably have been a bit pushy at times. Jack thinks you'll become a recluse if we don't drag you out to things."

"He's probably right. I've needed to be pushed, I really have. It's like, despite myself, I've had an exciting life. I just seem to attract these big people who lead me by the hand into their own adventures. Do you remember that eccentric actor chap I got in with years ago when Julia was about eight?" Beth's eyes sparkled at the memory.

"Yes, yes I do. How did that happen?"

“He just fell madly, irrationally in love with me. I didn’t give him any encouragement he just decided to woo me. It was quite flattering at first, but unfortunately I didn’t feel the same. When he kissed me, yuk, it was horrible. I used to find all these creative ways to avoid it. The poor man was too thick-skinned to pick up on my revulsion.”

“Why didn’t you just end it? I couldn’t understand it at the time.”

“That’s my bloody problem, Maddie, I get into things and I can’t get out of them. I’m hopeless.” Beth laughed with unrestraint; Maddie joined in, throwing her head back with glee. When they calmed down Beth continued, still with humour in her eyes. “Maddie, I just want an ordinary life; a quiet life. I always had this dream of a detached house in the country with roses around the door; old fashioned and dull, I know and it seems unlikely now. Anyway how about you? Any plans to move?”

“No, I’m a city chick through and through; I can’t imagine living anywhere else… Paris maybe or Barcelona, but nowhere else in Britain. I think London suits Jack better too. It’s a… bigger place for him.”

“Yes, that’s what I thought when he first moved here.” Beth took a gulp of wine; her heart accelerated. There was something she’d longed to talk to Maddie about for years but had never had the courage to. “Look Maddie tell me to shut up if I’m being intrusive, but I’ve always wondered…what has it been like for you…you know with Jack?” Beth was astonished by her own boldness.

“You mean his cross-dressing?”

Beth reddened and nodded. She noticed there was no hesitation or embarrassment in Maddie’s response. She might as well have been discussing the European Union.

“When he first told me I just thought, OK, that’s fine. I didn’t feel shocked or repelled; I just saw it as another aspect of the man I loved. Men in our society are only allowed a small spectrum of emotion, aren't they?"

"I guess so, but I found it difficult to move that far along the spectrum. More wine?" Beth refilled their glasses.

"Well, I guess at first I didn't equate Jack's cross-dressing with him being a transvestite. I don't think Jack did back then either. I saw it as a need he had to wear soft clothing, to relax into his feminine persona. I found it perfectly understandable; partly I suppose because I've never felt completely feminine. I enjoy being female but I don't always relate to aspects of what is defined as female behaviour, while I often do relate to what is described as male behaviour. I guess I've always seen sexuality as a spectrum rather than a polarised thing."

"Intellectually I understand what you're saying, Maddie, and I agree, but I always found it difficult to translate to my heart. I suppose it was just too close to home with Jack."

"It's easy to be accepting when it's someone else's struggle. I think I realised that my relationship with Jack would always be more intense and complicated than the average relationship and it would definitely require more energy. But I knew cross-dressing was essential to Jack, to his wellbeing, and that if I loved him I couldn't ask him to stop. I didn't want to ask him to stop, although at times, I have to be honest, I have wished the bloody thing would just go away."

"Really!' Beth felt some relief that Maddie wasn't quite as magnanimous as she often appeared.

"Oh yes, as we get older I think we tend to move more to the centre, to a place of comfort; which is why it's young people who should push boundaries."

"You know I always worried that Jack would want to take things further, that it wouldn't be enough. I knew I would find it really difficult to cope if he asked me to accept more than I already had."

"Well, after we'd been together for about two years, I guessed Jack wanted to dress completely en femme, but was probably too scared to ask; so I suggested it. At first I think I saw it as a kind of sexy, dressing-up game. I've always loved dressing up – carnivals, masked balls; any excuse. But I wasn't prepared for the transformation. The man I loved changed before my eyes. I swear he even smelt differently. I felt this weird protectiveness towards him."

"Maddie, you are so much braver than me; I don't know how you could do it."

"It really freaked me out actually. It didn't feel like a game, it felt like an archaeological dig, an unveiling. It was like seeing all of him at once, and how many people can you say that of? Beth, I've never felt so responsible for someone else's happiness."

"So, how did you go about it, what did you do? I'm sorry I'm being so nosey."

"No, it's good to talk about it actually. We decided to make an occasion of it. We were both really nervous. It's incredibly difficult to put make-up on someone else, you know, never mind a man." Beth and Maddie giggled. "My hand was shaking ridiculously. I kind of felt Jack was my canvas and he was the most important work I'd ever been commissioned to do. After makeup he got dressed, trying on all the stuff until we got exactly the right thing. He's lucky, he's so slender; he didn't look bad at all; having said that we couldn't stop giggling at the sheer absurdity of it all."

"Oh my God." Beth drew her hands to her mouth. "How did you deal with it?"

"Well, the transformation was unbelievable and I think we were both shocked by it."

"Don't you ever question yourself?" asked Beth. "It made me feel somehow… less than a woman or not woman enough."

"I did have a few worries at first that he might actually want to be a woman, make the full transition but he reassured me he had no desire to take hormones or have the operation and I believe him. I know some people might ask what kind of a woman would stay with a transvestite; perhaps I was a suppressed lesbian or had really low self-esteem? But I couldn't conjure up fears and anxieties that just didn't exist for me. Perhaps I'm a bit odd, but it's not how I feel."

Beth drained the wine bottle into their glasses. The sun was now low like a benevolent orange lantern, singeing the tops of roofs and trees. Blackbird song swelled the air with almost unbearable sweetness. She felt a sudden nostalgia for the things she'd lost, for the things she'd never had.

CHAPTER 18

The weeks leading up to Julia's arrival into Liverpool had been some of the most difficult of her life. For the first time she'd had a serious row with her mother, leaving them both reeling and wounded. Julia knew she'd said some cruel, unnecessary things, which she was regretting painfully, but she'd been unable to say sorry. It was guilt that drove her up north several months before the start of her college course.

Initially she stayed with Aunt Maria on the Wirral but she soon found life in the household stifling. After three days she decided to travel by ferry to Liverpool and find a hostel, until she could move into halls of residence.

Following her initial elation at arriving into Liverpool from the vantage point of the ferry, Julia felt a shift into disappointment. Her weariness, following a terse telephone conversation with her mother, combined with the colourless intermission between sunset and true night, left Julia feeling despondent. At the Pier Head she climbed into the sticky heat of a black cab, which crawled along the Dock Road like a beetle in the heat. It turned into Upper Parliament Street and then Grove Street. Everything seemed too quiet and listless after the constant throb of London.

"You a student love?" the cab driver asked in a guttural accent that sounded closer to Scandinavian than English.

"Yes, I am."

"You won't be staying around for long then, will you? They all get their degrees then bugger off home." He laughed as if he'd told a joke.

They arrived in Falkner Square where grand Georgian houses graced a large square, reminding her of some of the elegant squares in London. But the area looked run down and the once great houses were converted into bedsits or hostels. However, there were some signs of regeneration with scaffolding and skips marking the start of a new era.

The hostel catered for travellers and was basic but clean. Julia was shown to a bunk, a plain wooden structure, one of eight in the female dorm, all with starched white sheets and yellow duvets. She threw her backpack onto a top bunk and then, clutching a book, she ventured into the kitchen. It was a large but cosy room with an unlit wood-burning stove and a quarry-tiled floor. Several people were sitting around a rough wooden table in the centre of the room, eating and chatting; others preparing evening meals. She could make out accents from all parts of the globe. French windows were flung wide open onto a small, high-walled yard where a colourful array of people were sprawling and smoking and chatting in the balmy warmth of the summer night.

Nobody took much notice of Julia and she felt lost. She suddenly missed her friends, most of whom had accepted places at London universities, or not too far from home. They had tried to persuade her to stay in London but she couldn't be persuaded. She had a greater mission, which now seemed improbable if not impossible. She longed to hear her mum's voice; her mobile phone was close at hand in her pocket; but she resisted using it. She was suddenly aware of how sheltered her life had been. She studied the faces of the other guests who all looked older than her and much more worldly wise. She imagined they had travelled extensively and knew how to get by.

After an hour of sitting alone, pretending to read, she became aware of a man standing above her.

"Do you want to share vodka?" he asked, with a heavy accent. He held up a clear bottle that she didn't recognise. It had a curvaceous neck and the word ‘Wodka’ written in small letters with the word ‘Wyborowa’ written in larger letters beneath. The bottle was misted from being in the freezer. The man leaned over slightly, bottle and glass poised in his hands. Julia could smell mild sweat, which wasn’t unpleasant and something else, like freshly baked bread. He was older than her, she guessed by several years.

“I don’t have anything to mix it with,” Julia apologised, “I haven’t had a chance to buy supplies yet.”

“I have some orange juice, if that will do?”

He took a carton of orange from the communal fridge and splashed it into the vodka and then without invitation sat next to her on the floor.

“So, don’t tell me,” he said. “You are travelling the world after finishing your degree to try to... *find yourself*.”

“Nooo.” she says indignantly, “I’ve come from London… to study, and I don’t want to find myself.”

“No, of course not.” He seemed to mock her but his face broke into an open smile and he offered his hand.

“Tomasz,” he said. His hand was warm and dry like flour. “And yours?”

“Julia.”

“And what are you studying, Julia?”

“A BA in music at LIPA.

“What’s your instrument?

“Keyboards.”

“Very sexy’

“That’s a bit of a stereotype, isn’t it?”

“Is it? I guess so.” He tilted back his head to drain the vodka and she had chance to study his face. He was both good looking and unusual; rugged was the word that came to mind, with fine lines around his eyes, emphasised by a light tan. His face was angular, with a strong jaw line and an expressive mouth, inquisitive blue eyes and a day’s growth of stubble.

"So when does the course start?

"Not 'till October."

"OK, so why are you here in July and why stay in this place?" He looked around, implying she looked out of place in the shabby environment.

"You ask a lot of questions, Tomasz."

"Do I?"

They both laughed at this.

"Well, I kind of have connections in Liverpool... family connections," said Julia.

"That sounds mysterious; like the mafia or something."

"No, my mum is from Liverpool... and my father." She felt the thrill of self-reinvention. She saw a further question form on Tomasz lips.

"I haven't been to Liverpool since I was very young," she explained "and then only to visit my grandparents... but they're both dead now. I can't remember anything about Liverpool at all. I'm staying here because I can't move into halls until late September and I can't afford anything else..." She knew she was rambling, telling Tomasz things she didn't need to tell him but his keen eyes had the rare quality of a listener. "My aunt lives on the Wirral, but I hardly ever see her...my mum kind of avoids Liverpool, so the Wirral might as well be a thousand miles away. I didn't really realise how close it was until I came here today on the ferry..."

"Well there's a lot of stuff there," he interrupted, "but I won't bombard you with more questions... yet."

Tomasz's familiarity didn't make Julia uncomfortable; she already liked him. He was nothing like Jamie or any of the other men she'd known before.

"So where do you come from and what are you doing in Liverpool?" She sipped the vodka, relieved for the focus to shift to Tomasz.

"I'm from Poland. I grew up in Gdansk, although I left at

eighteen to go to University in Warsaw. I'm a writer. I've been here for two-years. I suppose I came here to see what all the fuss is about, but I too have special connections with Liverpool."

"What?" Julia's eyes brightened.

"Politics, music and Football."

"Music I can understand," she said, "but what is it about men and football?"

"Now who's doing the stereotyping?" Tomasz wagged a finger at her. He poured more vodka for himself and then waved the bottle in the air. "If you want a stereotype, what is it about you Brits and this habit of diluting good vodka?"

"I don't know. Perhaps we want the effect without the taste. But then, you're from the land of vodka aren't you. It's in your blood."

"It is my blood, darling! Did you know," Tomasz leaned towards her conspiratorially; he spoke softly as if telling her an outrageous secret. "The absolutely perfect percentage for vodka is 38% a standard set by Alexander III of Russia in 1894. Any less it is too watery, any more it burns. The distillation process was kept a secret for centuries. You see, alcohol could only reach 14% by natural fermentation. Now we can produce 95.6% alcohol with no taste or smell. Vodka literally means little water, 'woda' and was first used in the middle-ages as a medicine to increase fertility and lust."

"God, I'd better not drink any more then."

"Wyborowa is my favourite vodka. It literally means 'ex-quisite.' It should be drunk very, very cold and very, very straight. Try it?" The bottle hovered above her.

"OK." She held up her glass.

"Nie, nie. I'll get you a clean one. He jumped up giving Julia further opportunity to observe. She noticed his arms were muscular and the hairs on his forearms golden. His hair was short, thick and sandy blond, sticking out at odd angles. He was tall but not overly so; she guessed about five-eleven. He was wearing blue jeans and a t-shirt with an abstract design on the front. As he reached for another glass Julia noticed his shapely bottom. She felt a small thrill at the sight of this strange, foreign man pouring her a drink.

He sat down and handed her the glass. "Now you should really drink it in one go, followed by a morsel of food to hold the alcohol? But I want you to sip slowly, notice the smell, flavour, the burn on your tongue and the aftertaste."

Julia did as he said. "It's quite…creamy…and maybe…nutty."

"Yes, you've got it!"

"So you're a writer Tomasz. What do you write?"

"Crime fiction."

"And why Liverpool?"

"I like it. It has a similar history, similar population to Gdansk. Similar troubles too. It was once a great shipping port; it's unpretentious. There is also a good history of murder here; many dark alleyways and a big, dirty river." Tomasz looked at his watch. "I must go. I have to get to work." He jumped up and placed the vodka back in the freezer.

Julia felt disappointed; she was enjoying their conversation.

"But," he added, "I want to take you on a walk soon."

"A walk?"

"Yes, a walk of this city. I want to introduce you to her again."

Julia felt she should be offended by Tomasz's presumptuousness, but she enjoyed the irony of his proposal. It was only when he'd left that she looked at her watch and realised it was already midnight.

She didn't sleep well that night; apart from the sticky heat, from the age of seven she'd lived in the quiet environment created by her mother. The contrast of a dorm room with all the comings and goings was disturbing. However, in the morning Julia felt a fluttery excitement and alertness. It was her first morning in a new city; she felt she was on the edge of something. She had breakfast alone, only sharing polite exchanges with the other residents but she couldn't help looking out for Tomasz.

She left the hostel soon after breakfast for her first glimpse of Liverpool by day. She threw herself into her new existence with élan. It was a pavement scorched day in the hottest summer on record. The trees were choking on the heat and the grass in the parks had wilted brown. The sense of gloom she'd felt the previous evening had now flown and she fully enjoyed the sensation of being alone in an unknown city. She realised she'd never been in this situation; she'd always had a short thread connecting her to loved ones.

At first, she felt directionless, not knowing how to approach this city without the simplicity of the tube, burrowing beneath the roads. After some time she found herself on Wood Street, a narrow cobbled strip, which she learned from one bartender had once been home to sugar warehouses, but was now bursting with trendy bars and cafés. She climbed steps down into a basement bar called Modo and was surprised, after having received several negative responses, to be offered three shifts of bar work a week. The manager, an efficient black woman who introduced herself as Susan, told Julia she was lucky. A permanent member of staff had just let her down. Julia agreed to start that Friday evening. She felt elated by her success and treated herself to a coffee on Bold Street where she stayed reading for a couple of hours.

As she made her way back to the hostel Julia found herself sinking back into the malaise of the previous evening. It seemed that once the light drained from the city, so did her optimism. Whatever adventures the daytime brought, dusk was imprinted in childhood as the time to return home to bright lights and familiar cooking smells. She felt tearful and again questioned her decision to come to Liverpool. However, as she entered the hostel she was greeted by chattering voices, the clink of plates and glasses, music, and the smell of frying onions and garlic. Her spirits immediately lifted; it brought back memories of Carysfort Road and the buzz of the community. She dumped her daypack on the bunk and carried a plastic bag of provisions into the kitchen, from where the melee was emanating. As she imagined, people were in the full flight of preparing evening meals, sitting around the large table eating, or sprawled outside in the walled yard with bottles of beer. There were one or two nods of acknowledgment as she came in. Then she saw Tomasz, sitting alone by the window, cleaning his plate with a large chunk of white bread and unselfconsciously cramming the sauce-soaked portion into his mouth. He looked up as if sensing her presence and tried to smile through the bread. Julia wished she'd bothered to have a quick look in the mirror to check her hair. She gave a small wave and then walked to a free strip of work surface, emptied the contents of the shopping bag and began to chop onions. After a few minutes Tomasz joined her, washing his plate quickly and efficiently, drying it and placing it back in the cupboard.

"So you are only eighteen?" He asked, as if there had been no gap between their first meeting and now.

"I'm nineteen in six weeks. I was the oldest in my class." She realised this remark sounded childish.

"Oh well, you're ancient then."

"Piss off." Julia could feel herself blush; she kept her head down, feigning unusual interest in the progress of the onions magically turning from opaque to translucent in the pan. She was cooking a pasta dish and Tomasz couldn't stop himself from offering advice, "It is better to heat the pan before you put in the oil… for more flavour crush the garlic rather than chop."

"How old are you, then?"

"Me, I'm twenty-seven."

"OK, old man, what about this walk? If you can manage it, that is."

"Old man, hey? I'll show you how to walk through the night, young girl."

Tomasz joined her as she sat down to eat. He asked her about her home in Stoke Newington. She told him how the hostel brought back memories of Carysfort Road and how she'd missed it when she moved into a modern flat with her mum at the age of seven. She told him about Jack and Maddie and then she found herself telling Tomasz about the attic room and how she loved to watch Jack sculpt in the shaft of light pouring in from the roof. She told him the story of how Maddie had given Jack the room as a gift; the story had now become legendary among friends and she held onto it as the most romantic act she could imagine.

"I think rooms are symbolic of many things," said Tomasz. "I was born in a really grim government owned apartment block in Gdansk. The policy back then was that you rented rooms rather than whole apartments. Since my family couldn't afford the whole apartment we weren't allowed to use one of the rooms. It was kept locked. My brother and I spent the first ten years of our lives wondering what was behind that door. We grew up with an idea of what was forbidden rather than what was permitted."

The unfamiliar intonations of Tomasz's voice intrigued Julia and she longed for him to continue.

"How old is your brother?"

"Jakob was the same age as me; we were twins, but he died when we were kids."

"Oh..."

"Do you fancy a game of chess?"

"I can't play, but I'm happy to learn." Julia thought better than to dig deeper, although she couldn't shake Tomasz's words from her mind. She cleared her dishes while Tomasz set up the board and they settled down to play. Julia had bought a bottle of Vodka and she shared it with Tomasz, although he reprimanded her, saying she was a student and shouldn't be wasting her money. He explained the rules of the game and between moves he told her about his work as a security guard, how mind-numbingly boring it would be if he didn't use the time to write his stories and how ignorant and rude his boss was.

"So apart from our terrible habit of diluting good vodka, and people being generally rude, what else do you think is wrong with this country?" Julia asked, moving a pawn.

"I wouldn't use the word wrong, necessarily, but I can give you my observations, as an outsider. But remember I have chosen to live here because your country offers more, at the moment, than mine can."

"Oh yes and when things improve in Poland, you'll bugger off back home."

"Very possibly; and you would do the same in reverse."

"OK, so give me your observations of England."

Tomasz moved a knight. "Well, for a start I think you treat your dogs like children and your children like dogs."

Julia let out a yelp. "How rude!' she slapped his arm.

"I just mean things are a bit...what's that word... skewed. I had a girlfriend here who let her dog sleep with her every night. I couldn't believe it. I left her for that reason. I don't want to share my lover with a stinking dog."

"OK that's true, but we don't treat our children like dogs. If anything I think children are over indulged here." Julia moved a rook.

"Yes. Like your dogs." Tomasz laughed at his conundrum. "It's hard to explain. Children here are on the one hand grossly cosseted and over-protected. Everything is about children, yet nothing. It is a sentimental love. Everywhere there are new playgrounds for children; even in your pubs and restaurants you have play areas; it's so bizarre. Children even have self-contained bedrooms with computers and TVs. Yet all of this seems to be about getting rid of children, in the safest possible way."

"Well, what do you do in Poland?"

"We talk to our children; they eat with us; they are expected to be part of the conversation, not squirming on the floor or running off to play. They sit with us at the dinner table at night while we share stories about our day."

"Yes. I noticed that in France. Children stay up late but they're so well behaved, sitting around the table in restaurants. Parents don't seem to jump to their every demand."

"Exactly! I think it is the same in many places. I think children grow up happier, more rounded. I think many of your children are unhappy. *In the precarious jaw of parenting, children swing*."

"What's that?"

"Nothing; I just think parents play a dangerous game with their offspring; they are creating monsters of the future."

"You might be right about that. What else don't you like?"

"I don't want to offend you. It is your country. I can criticise Poland without mercy, but if a foreigner does it, well that's a different matter."

"No, go on. I'm interested to hear."

"Well, I think it is strange that your society seems to be built around the minority; the criminals and anti-social people."

"Explain!'

Tomasz moved his queen. "You have more CCTV cameras then any other European country and your politicians are trying to introduce ID cards. Everything seems to be about protecting yourselves from some enemy out there."

"But isn't that the case?"

"I don't know, is it? I don't see terrorists or criminals running about on every street corner, though you would think there were by the amount of fear in the air. I just think it's strange that your landscape is being designed around the few rather than the majority. Why not put more effort into changing the few and creating the society you want for yourselves?"

"Well, we don't have a lot of say in that. That's the government…"

"The government, the government," Tomasz's voice increased in volume and his face took on the serious expression of the previous evening, "everything is the government's fault. You have a vote don't you? It reminds me of Poland under the communists, but worse because you have the freedom to change things and you don't bother."

Julia wasn't sure how to respond; she felt her ignorance keenly. As a child her mum had told her stories about Greenham Common and her flirtation with politics in the eighties but Julia had found no interest in politics or protest.

"I'm sorry," Tomasz said, seeing her confusion. "I get a bit heated about certain subjects. It's checkmate and I have to go." Once again Tomasz disappeared into the mysterious inkiness of the night.

CHAPTER 19

Modo was a trendy establishment set in a dimly-lit basement, with state of the art furnishings and a long, curved, blond bar. On Fridays it was popular with office workers who came en masse in suits, eager to relinquish the responsibilities of the week. They drank liberally on empty stomachs and were quickly intoxicated.

One of the bar staff had called in sick leaving only two of them, plus Susan, to quench the thirsty mob. Julia had made it clear to Susan that she had never previously worked in a bar. Susan had replied curtly that she would have to learn on the job as no one had time to train her. After several fraught hours Julia wondered if Susan regretted hiring her. She became irritated when Julia was slow or gave the wrong change to customers. By the end of the evening Julia felt defeated and considered quitting before Susan sacked her anyway. However, she was surprised when, as she left at two in the morning, Susan said, "Well done, see you tomorrow."

Julia felt baffled by Susan's ambivalence. She was used to being liked and was upset by her inability to please. She struggled to fall asleep that night in the narrow bunk, despite her exhaustion, and found herself fixating on the rhythmic breathing of her roommates. It seemed to get louder, building to a crescendo, until it was like waves crashing around her.

The following morning Julia got up late and was surprised at how much her legs ached. After a hurried breakfast she walked into town to loosen up before returning to Modo for the lunchtime shift. When she arrived Susan was already busy stacking glasses, placing ashtrays on tables and scraping chairs into order with quick, efficient movements. She didn't acknowledge Julia who stood, strangely paralysed by the woman's brusqueness. Julia noticed Susan's long, braided hair; clear, honey-black skin and strong bone structure. The slimness of her nose and lightness of her skin-tone suggested mixed heritage. She wore tight jeans, emphasising a high, round bottom, and a blouse with a burnt orange and olive-green leaf pattern that complimented her colouring. Julia found it difficult to determine her age, as she did with many African-Caribbean women who often looked younger than their years; she guessed anywhere between twenty-eight and thirty-five. Susan's top rode up her back as she stretched across tables, revealing a slim waist. Her fingers were heavy with gold rings and a gold chain hung around her neck. The braids separated and fell around her shoulders, occasionally into her face and Susan swept them back with a brisk flick of her hand. Julia had once had her hair braided at Glastonbury. She remembered their weight, how they felt when she moved her head from side to side and the relief of finally taking them out to free her hair again.

Just as Julia made the decision to take initiative Susan spoke: "Don't just stand there, girl, put the spills on the bar."

"Sorry, the spills?"

Susan blew out what seemed to be an exasperated breath. "The things that collect beer spills; they're in the back."

Julia took several minutes to find the spill trays and then placed them carefully along the bar. "It was busy last night," she attempted.

"Always is." Susan continued to work without a sideways glance.

People began to drift in for lunchtime drinks and Julia was relieved to be occupied. It was relatively quiet and she had chance to get to grips with the art of pulling a pint, pouring measures, pricing, and eventually she even managed a few pleasantries with customers. She observed the Liverpool style: the jokes; the harsh words with soft centres; the innuendos and play on words. It was a different verbal culture to the one she was used to and at times it seemed abrasive, though rarely offensive. She was reminded of her mum and Jack; this was their heritage; it was also her own.

By the end of the lunch shift Susan still seemed a closed book to Julia but she felt she'd proved herself and she returned that evening ready to take on the challenge. It was a different crowd, less office worker, more weekend reveller and several men made passes at her. She was both amused and baffled by this, not being used to such overt flirtation. In London mating was generally a more subtle undertaking, with furtive glances and covert signals. By the end of the night she understood it was a game and she even began to enjoy it.

It was on the night bus home the thought struck Julia that Susan reminded her of an old school friend, Carla. Julia and Carla had been inseparable in their primary school in Hackney, a multicultural establishment where children from many ethnic and cultural backgrounds simply got on with the business of playing together. It was only as they moved into secondary school and tribal divisions, based on gender, class and academic ability, emerged that the children became attentive to their differences, using acerbic adolescent humour to highlight them.

Julia had loved going back to Carla's home after school to be greeted by the smells of Caribbean cuisine, fleshy matriarchal chatter and colourful, pictorial reminders of Africa's heat. This contrasted greatly to the serene, more subtle milieu of Julia's own home where her mum, an unwilling cook, repeated the same spiceless recipes each week, until Julia was old enough to add her own more adventurous dishes to the menu.

Carla was a physically mature girl and, like Julia, academically bright. They were known affectionately by teachers as the terrible twins and they competed for top marks in every subject. However, when they made the transition to secondary school they were placed in different classrooms and everything changed. Cliques formed, friendships became more intense and new alliances were made. Carla grew closer to a group of black girls in her own class and was less interested in her old friends. Julia missed Carla's friendship and felt snubbed by her. It seemed to her Carla had developed a hard exterior that wouldn't allow closeness, although Julia felt humiliated by her efforts. Despite being popular throughout her school years, this early rejection never quite left her.

In adolescence Julia became obsessed by the idea of identity and felt a measure of jealousy towards people and cultures that, unlike her, seemed certain of theirs. She imagined Susan had already found her identity buried deep in her soul; securely sewn into her being and rooted in the scorched soil of Africa. It was coloured red and orange and yellow and sounded like the seductive beat of African drums.

Susan triggered uncomfortable and contradictory emotions in Julia. She felt flawed by what she perceived to be Susan's coldness but was also moved by a desire to scrape the coldness back, like ice on a windscreen. She felt a strong, irrational need to be liked by her. Julia imagined that Susan's defensiveness was about her experience of racism in a city that, while it boasted multi-culturalism, was inexplicably segregated. However, she couldn't shake off the feeling of discomfort Susan evoked in her and the confusion she felt at Susan's resistance to any attempts to connect.

As the weeks went by, Julia established a routine based around the job at the bar, her explorations of Liverpool, keyboard practice and her time spent at the hostel. It felt like a strange, disconnected life, thrilling in its dissonance. The bar job connected her to Liverpool life but there was no-one among the bar staff, and certainly not Susan, with whom she felt she could become friends. It was only Tomasz who somehow held everything together and, on the occasions when she felt lost and out of her depth, he unknowingly prevented her from running home. She found herself waiting for his appearances and looking forward to their conversations.

CHAPTER 20

"Let's go."

"What, now?" Julia was lying in a patch of sunlight in the hostel common room. She was better at thinking when lying down; it settled her mind and the warmth of the sun on her face gave her a rare quiescence.

"Yes, now! It is your birthday walk."

"My birthday's tomorrow."

"What time were you born?"

"At ten minutes after midnight."

"Then we will walk into your birthday."

Tomasz was enjoying the sight before him; in fact enjoying it too much. He could have looked at Julia for a very long time. She had a magical face that could alter dramatically from wholesome, girl-next-door to ravishing beauty. At the moment she was the latter. The sunlight further exposed her; its uncompromising rays highlighted her youth with its ripe contours, fullness of cheek and softness of arm and breast. He could hardly bare to look. He either had to kiss her or else direct his energy elsewhere. "Come on, let's walk!"

"Ok, in a bit. I like it here at the moment."

Julia was aware of Tomasz's eyes drinking her in and she enjoyed the feeling, but she was also enthralled by the idea of the walk he had talked about for weeks. Unlike most of the men she knew, Tomasz was decisive and it was nice not to have to take the lead for once.

Tomasz jumped up. “OK, I’ll grab a few things and we’ll leave in ten minutes.”

When the sun abandoned her face Julia got up and joined Tomasz in the hallway. He had a rough canvas bag flung over one shoulder.

“So, where are you taking me? They stepped outside into Falkner Square. It was seven o’clock and the sun was low but still hot in an azure sky. It was reported to be the warmest year on record and the evenings were surprisingly balmy, eliciting rare scents from the earth, from the tarmac on the roads, from the trees, the river and even from the bricks and stones. It gave everything an exotic air, reminding people of holidays abroad; warming up the British temperament to only slightly apologetic inhibition.

“Places you’ve never seen.” Tomasz spoke in an exaggerated accent and swept his arms above his head like Svengali, commanding his audience. “I will show you the Liverpool of the past and present; Liverpool of murder and horror; a place of dark seductive secrets and… other things.”

Julia laughed. “You crazy man!” She felt a sudden tenderness towards him. She loved his foreignness as well as his child-like exuberance. He was still a mystery to her but she believed the darkness beneath was contained. Yet there was something dangerous about setting off for a walk though the night with this almost stranger. She could hear her mother’s soft pleas to “be careful.”

They left Falkner Square, passing a woman on the corner in a tiny red skirt. Thin, child-like legs marked with purple bruises fell like anaemic strips into shoes that seemed too high; she was like a girl dressing up in her mother’s heels. Her arms were folded protectively across her body and her hair fell in mousey straggles around her narrow shoulders. She looked like she was in the last place she wanted to be.

When they had moved some way past her Tomasz said, “In Poland we call them prostytutka or some not so nice people call them Kurwa, which is a word used for a multitude of curses and insults."

"How long did it take you to learn English; you're very good."

"Oh I have been absorbing the language for years; mainly through music and detective novels, but I really became fluent when I moved here two years ago."

They cut down Canning Street and passed a dog tearing at the pages of a cheap paperback with wolfish rapacity. One ear was torn; its brown fur was matted and in places patchy.

"What is it eating?" Tomasz went closer to inspect the book. The dog gave him a wary look and sloped away. Tomasz kicked the book over. "My God, it's *Wuthering Heights*; at least it's nutritious, hey?" He laughed.

"Fancy throwing a book away!" said Julia, "especially *Wuthering Heights*; it's one of my favourites."

"Mine too."

"I always wondered why Heathcliff came from Liverpool," said Julia.

"Emily Bronte wrote it at the time thousands of people were leaving Ireland during the potato famine and settling in Liverpool; there was overcrowding and desperate poverty with children like Heathcliff begging in the streets; she must have been aware of it."

"Is there anything you don't know, Tomasz?"

"Yes, the meaning of life." He laughed, wryly. "Most of what I know is useless fact."

They turned into Bedford Street South; it looked as if it had once been a fairly salubrious road but had been carved up, leaving it with a mishmash of stranded buildings from Victorian grandeur to 1970s postmodern functionalism.

"This is the scene of our first murder, known as the 'Positivist Tragedy.'" Tomasz studied Julia's face, trying to gauge her mood. She presented a mildly amused expression. Her full lips were drawn into a pout and the dark curve of her eyebrows rose into cynicism. However, he saw the glimmer of delight badly disguised in her eyes and knew he was hitting the mark.

"Our villain is one William Macdonald, a carpenter and a Marxist. He became interested in Positivism, the philosophical belief of those who attended the Temple of Humanity in Upper Parliament St. It was a philosophy developed by August Compte, who was named the first sociologist. In Positivism the individual's rights are far more important than the rule of any one person, therefore there is no higher power and humanity is at last able to govern itself. Perhaps that is why, on a cool October evening in 1913, Macdonald was able to take matters into his own hands and eradicate the lives of three people, including his own."

Julia wrapped her arms around her torso, feeling a sudden chill as the sun moved behind a tall building, leaving them in shadow.

"It all started when Macdonald became obsessed with another member of the group, Mary Compton, the daughter of the founder of the weekly meeting held in Hope Street. Macdonald was insanely jealous of a young man in the group, Paul Gaze, who had been adopted by Mary Compton when he was orphaned. Macdonald was convinced there was more to this relationship than first appeared.

"On 7th October something snapped in Macdonald and, armed with a gun, he went to the home of Richard Price Roberts, who had introduced him to the Temple of Humanity. He shot him twice, but Roberts survived to tell the tale. Macdonald then moved on to Grove Street, not far from here, where he shot Paul Gaze dead at his lodgings. Finally he came here to the home of Mary Crompton. He shot her in the head, killing her instantly. He then turned the gun on himself."

"Oh God." Julia's eyes scanned the deserted stretch of road as if looking for residual signs of horror. Tomasz let her dwell on the story for a few seconds.

"After these events the Positivists disbanded."

"I'm not surprised."

Tomasz walked on and Julia followed him into Catherine

Street, where there was more in the way of human activity: people taking evening strolls or heading to public houses. They turned right on Catherine Street and stopped outside an unusual church building. A sign told them it was the Church of Philip Neri.

"This church was built after the First World War," said Tomasz, "based on Venetian design and in Byzantine style. Come and look at this." He walked to the left of the church along a brick wall topped with Spanish tiles. There was a barred gate and two barred windows in the wall. On the other side stretched a narrow garden, formal in design, with free-standing pillars, a petal shaped water feature and low trees and shrubs.

"It is *El Jardin della Nuestra Senora*." said Tomasz. "One night, during the blitz, a bomb fell here, on this very spot; it blew out all the windows in the church and left a crater. In the 1950s they laid a Spanish garden."

"It's lovely," said Julia, breathing in the heady summer scents. "Really peaceful. It's sad it's behind bars. I'd love to sit in there."

"Come into the church!" said Tomasz. Julia tentatively followed. It was quiet inside and lit by a host of candles; there was a strong smell of frankincense, which caught in Julia's throat. She hesitated to walk further and hovered by the door.

"You suddenly seem timid, like a little church mouse," said Tomasz.

"I'm not used to wandering around churches. I feel like a trespasser."

"Oh, I practically lived in churches as a teenager; I feel quite at home. Don't you have a religion?"

"Not really. My mum is quite anti-religion, even though she was raised a Catholic; most of her friends are either new-age hippies or humanists. Churches weren't exactly high on our agenda of places to hang out. I guess it's rubbed off on me. Mum even chose my name as an anti-Catholic statement, something 'modern and uncluttered,' she said."

Tomasz gave a sudden laugh. It echoed around the church.

"What?"

"Julia, your name comes from Julius; it was the name of a saint and more than one Pope. I'm afraid your mother inadvertently fell into the Catholic trap."

Julia's mouth fell into horror and then she laughed, clasping her hand over her mouth to stop the noise.

"Poor Mum."

They stepped carefully around the church, speaking in hushed voices; they peered into small chapels and examined friezes and statues decorating the church interior. Despite her reserve Julia felt herself seduced by the unfamiliar liturgical sights and scents."

You know a lot about this place?" she said.

"Well, my grandfather settled in Liverpool after the war. I guess that's another reason for my interest in this city. I never knew him, he died before I was born, but I was told by my parents there was a Polish chaplaincy here for almost twenty years after the war and even a Polish priest. I have a picture of my grandfather taken outside this church in 1955 with a group of people; he looked happy. It's the only photo I have of him. I was so excited when I came here and found the church intact." Tomasz looked at his watch. "Anyway, time to move on, we have a lot to do."

They left the cool interior of the church and were surprised by the languid warmth outside, although the sun was now setting and the sky was turning from azure to a pale, milky blue, streaked with pastel reds.

"Now I will take you to another site, where an altogether different religion is celebrated." Tomasz held Julia's hand and pulled her along with him. They turned right out of Catharine Street and after about fifty metres turned left into Egerton Street.

"And here we will have a little aperitif, before dinner." He waved his hand at an old white pub with a red sign, *Peter Kavannah's*. There was a lantern above the door and stained glass windows. Two men of indeterminate age sat on benches outside the pub clutching pints of Guinness. Inside it seemed as if the pub hadn't been touched for decades. A crusty alligator skin, a bicycle and several old radios hung from the ceiling, along with other discrepant items. The pub seemed designed to model the inside of a galleon ship. Planks of dark stained-wood curved around walls and covered ceilings; cracked leather bench-seats lined the walls. An eclectic bunch of people sat at the bar; Julia imagined them to be Liverpool intellectuals and artists, deep in boozy and enigmatic discussion. A man with a shaved head was sitting on a stool at one end of the bar he nodded to them as they entered.

"Hi Arthur," said Tomasz, nodding back. "That's the barrel man," he informed Julia as he led her into one of the snugs. "He has ears full of gold, a mouth full of silver and a heart full of stories. He can tell you absolutely anything about this pub and its history. OK, one drink only! I don't want you pissed before we even start the walk. I suggest vodka. It will affect you less and you can drink it quicker."

"God, you're a bossy sod; what if I don't want vodka?"

"It is your choice, Julia Swann; have a triple whisky and a Guinness if you prefer."

"OK Vodka… with orange."

"I will make an exception to your watering down good spirits this once. They are connoisseurs of ale rather than vodka here."

Julia noticed a woman sitting alone in the main bar, nursing a pint of half empty beer. Her head was bowed over the shiny copper-topped table as if in prayer or, Julia imagined, eternally staring at her own wretched reflection and wondering how her life had been lost in a pint glass. Loose grey hair fell in greasy tendrils around her hard-bitten face. A grubby woollen hat was perched on her head in defiance of the heat. Her clothes were a mishmash of styles, mostly too big for her small frame. The name Eleanor Rigby sprang into Julia's mind. 'Defiant.' That was one of the adjectives this place conjured up, defiant and haunted. Her eyes fell onto the mural.

"*Pickwick Papers*."

"What?"

"The mural: it's a scene from *Pickwick Papers* with caricatures of old customers and the landlord, Peter Kavannah. It was painted about 1857. Na zdrowie. Cheers." Tomasz slammed his glass into Julia's. "Happy Birthday my Liverpool Lou."

"Your what?"

"It is strange. You know nothing about your heritage, do you?"

"Not much. What I do know is mainly negative."

"Well I'm going to change that tonight."

"Thanks Tomasz. This is a cool birthday present; different, but cool."

"OK. Now tell me one secret about yourself."

Julia hesitated; she looked into Tomasz' eyes. She realised how little she knew him, what a stranger he really was to her. Yet she had the desire to tell him everything; her whole purpose for being in Liverpool and more.

"It doesn't have to be deep or profound; just something."

"Will you do the same?"

"Of course."

"OK. When I was twelve I shoplifted from Woolworths for a dare."

"Shoplifted?" he frowned at this new expression.

"I stole stuff from a shop."

"Naughty! What did you steal?"

"I panicked and just grabbed the first thing I could lay my hands on. It was a card of cheap brass buttons; useless. My friends took the piss out of me for months afterwards. I still have the buttons though. OK, your turn."

"OK. My parents own a bakery. I grew up there. When I was ten I spied my parents making love on the bakery floor."

"Yuk, that's disgusting." Julia instantly regretted her reaction. It seemed immature, predictable and not what she felt.

"I didn't find it disgusting. I was fascinated. My mother had only a yellow skirt on; her breasts were covered in flour. They looked like two soft bread rolls. My dad was completely naked and caked white. They both looked like strange creatures, unearthly. They laughed a lot. I thought they were playing a game. I was just happy to know they loved each other. They were not often happy. Anyway, that is all. I am only telling you one secret; for now. Drink up; we have to move on."

Julia swigged back her drink, still thinking of the scene in the bakery. They stepped outside into the now flat light of dusk; the colour was seeping out of the landscape and a slight chill was creeping into the air. Julia pulled a black cashmere sweater tied around her waist and slipped it over her head.

"Where to now mein guide?"

Tomasz didn't answer. He turned back onto Catharine St and then left along Huskisson St.

Julia gasped. The Anglican Cathedral loomed ahead, jutting its gothic tower into darkening skies. The sight was unexpected and she was momentarily startled. Just as she was thinking this was a small city, it surprised her. Ornate spires, like mediaeval instruments of torture, pierced the skies from the corners of the tower and dramatic arched doorways opened into dark, mysterious interiors. Huge sandstone slabs held the weight of smaller bricks decorated with a large Rose window and several arched openings, all housing magnificent stained-glass.

Julia had the impression that Tomasz had timed her first view of the Cathedral to perfection. The dusk sky was bruised with purples and reds; the sun had set and a full moon was beginning to rise. The Cathedral was almost a silhouette, magnificent and menacing against this backdrop. Hundreds of starlings flew about the tower like black rags dusting the spires.

"Is this the first time you have seen it?"

Julia nodded. She felt ashamed to admit it. She had explored the city centre shops and cafés but hadn't yet bothered with the cultural sights.

"It has been waiting for you to discover it."

They walked around the perimeter of the Cathedral and Tomasz pointed out Gambier Terrace, "Where Stuart Sutcliff lived and John Lennon often visited." Julia found her heart beating fast. There was no-one else about; this was a private exhibition, a closed gallery, with only herself and the curator present; it was one of the most intriguing things that had ever happened to her. They walked down into St James's Park at the side of the Cathedral; it was lower than pavement level giving the Cathedral the appearance of having sunk into the earth to be reclaimed by curling branches and dark tendrils of ivy and vine. The park was scattered at the edges with lichen-dappled gravestones. Tomasz and Julia strolled for a few minutes reading the details on the stones. Many belonged to seafarers lost in storms en route to destinations such as Jamaica, Australia and Pittsburgh. There was a large communal grave listing the names of an inordinate amount of young children, perhaps taken by cholera or other savage diseases of the time.

"I will not bother you with too much information," said Tomasz after several minutes, "except to say that five bodies lie buried beneath the ground here and I want you to think of them as we move to our next destination."

It was almost dark when they left the Cathedral grounds; the graves had merged into a mass of eerie grey mounds beneath the clutching tree branches. They climbed back to the road and walked down Upper Duke Street and across St George Street into Nelson Street. They turned into Grenville Street.

"And thus to the scene of our second murder; known as the Leveson Street Massacre. It created such horror in the area that the name of Leveson Street was changed to Grenville Street South, which is where we now stand.

"In March 1849 a young Irishman by the name of Maurice Gleeson, a ship's carpenter from Limerick, answered an advert in the parlour window of this house placed by the owners Anne Hinrichson and her sea captain husband, advertising a 'room for let'. Captain Hinrichson was away at sea, while his pregnant wife was alone with her two children and the maidservant.

One day an unsuspecting delivery boy called to the house to deliver two jugs, which had been ordered by Mrs Hinrichson. When there was no answer he peered through the window to see the battered bodies of five-year-old Henry and the maidservant, Mary Parr. Police broke into the house and found the bodies of pregnant Ann and her three-year-old son, John. They had all been beaten to death with a poker.

Gleeson washed his bloodied clothes in Toxteth Park and sold a stolen gold watch on London Road. He bought new trousers and boots with the money before visiting a barbershop for a shave. He made enquires about a wig, insisting that his hair was falling out. He also asked about securing a passage to America for three pound. The barber spotted blood on Gleeson's wrists and became suspicious. Gleeson boarded a ferry and spent the night across the water in Birkenhead before returning to Liverpool the following day. He was eventually arrested when arousing further suspicion by trying to sell a second watch. He was taken to the main Bridewell and sentenced to death. He was hanged in Kirkdale Gaol in front of a large crowd. His victims were buried in St James's cemetery, the site next to the Cathedral. The captain returned home to find his family obliterated. Captain Hinrichson later became dock master at Queens Dock; so to our next destination and dinner."

They cut down Cornwallis Street and Blundell Street across to Queens Dock and King's Parade. The moon was rising like a cool slice of pearl. The chill of dusk had now passed and the sky was thick with heat and lavish with stars. They walked a little way north along the river, not passing another soul on the way. They settled on a circular hunk of steel Tomasz informed her was a capstan, used to tie ship ropes. Tomasz took off his bag and pulled out a cloth and various packages. He then pulled a Swiss Army knife from his pocket and flicked open the largest knife.

"My God, you're a genius Tomasz Symansky. I'm starving." Julia unwrapped the various packages to find bread, cheese, roasted vegetables, spicy sausages and hummus, while Tomasz uncorked a bottle of Shiraz and poured a generous measure into thick glass tumblers. They cut slices of cheese and tore hunks of bread and stuffed them into their mouths along with roasted vegetables gleaming in oil and green olives, spitting the olive stones into the darkness of the Mersey, and they washed everything down with wine.

The river seemed purified by the darkness, sleek and oily, with moonlight making patterns on the water. Julia looked across the river to the dark shapes that formed the Wirral waterfront. The smell of the sea reminded her of childhood holidays on the Dorset coast.

"Do you like being close to water?" Julia asked, "It always unsettles me… in a good way."

"Well perhaps because I grew up in Gdansk, I love all the comings and goings of ports: the opportunities for new blood, for intrigue, for disappearances. The sea air carries a sense of incipient disaster."

"If I was of a nervous disposition I could be getting worried by now Tomasz. You seem obsessed by murder. Are you planning to bump me off?"

Tomasz laughed. "What fascinates me is the shit that happens in life; in a single moment, an event can take place that changes things forever. Whether it is something you choose to do or something that happens to you, against your will. I still haven't decided whether it is all random or whether there's a divine pattern for our lives. Have you?"

Julia was thrown by the question. She was a big reader, a promising student; she was able to have an intelligent conversation about many subjects, but the spiritual part of her education was missing; not just from her, she suspected, but from most of her generation. She wondered if with evolution this part of the brain would eventually disappear altogether. She felt this absence in herself as a spartan, grey thing; unformed like a foetus that will never grow. She felt a vague anger towards her mother for being so reasonable, for attempting to leave her mind uncluttered, rather than filling it with wonderful nonsense for her to unclutter in her own time.

"Not really. In a vague way I do believe in something, but I suppose I don't know what there is to believe in."

Tomasz didn't challenge her answer; he looked interested, as if she had said something profound. "OK time to tell me another secret,' he said. "This time something a little bigger; something only one or two other people know."

"You go first this time. It's only fair."

"OK, I will. Tomasz took a large gulp of wine and looked out across the river. Julia studied his profile, which unlike Jamie's, had the strength of manhood in the line of the nose and jaw.

"I started a fire in my family's bakery when I was twelve-years-old."

Julia's eyes widened. "Are you joking? How did you do that?"

"It is easy. I made a flour explosion using a paint tin. Trouble is it exploded next to some aprons and dishcloths and they caught fire. I ran out. Fortunately a passer by heard the explosion and called the fire brigade. I had to admit to it when the police found the paint tin. My dad thrashed me."

"My God, Tomasz, that's serious stuff." Julia wondered again what lay beneath this man's composed exterior. "Why did you do that?"

"I said one secret only. I've told you mine; now yours."

"I don't have many secrets; I guess my life has been pretty straightforward up till now."

"There must be something."

"OK, I snogged this boy when I was still going out with my boyfriend, Jamie. I was drunk. Only my best friend knows about it. I felt crap about it afterwards, but I did enjoy the snog. I think that was the beginning of the end for me and Jamie."

Tomasz smiled. "Have you had many boyfriends?"

"Quite a few, though nothing serious before Jamie. I was part of this gang, we all hung out together and I went out with most of the boys; very incestuous. They were usually only brief relationships, just a couple of months before moving on to the next. Childish stuff I suppose. I was with Jamie for six months and was really into him for the first four months."

Tomasz made no comment but continued to explore Julia's face with his eyes.

"Stop staring at me; you always do that." Julia sensed Tomasz was falling for her, but she didn't want to voice it. She wanted to watch the slow unfolding of his feelings from a distance. She noticed his eyes, soft in the moonlight, the slight parting of his lips. It would be so easy to lean towards him and kiss his foreign mouth; she was sure it would be good; almost certain he wouldn't resist.

The moon was now bright and almost painful to the eye, its light obliterating the stars.

"You've got a fascinating face," Tomasz continued to stare, "so expressive. It's like all your emotions ripple beneath your skin and surface in your eyes. You would make a terrible liar."

"Tell me about it. I never get away with anything."

"Is there something you want to get away with?"

"Hey, same rule applies Tomasz." Julia wagged her finger. "One secret only."

It was nearly ten o'clock when they recommenced their walk north along the riverfront. They passed the relatively new development of the Albert Dock and Tate Gallery, walking at an easy pace, occasionally drifting together and colliding like two boats anchored in a calm sea.

"Thanks for dinner; Tomasz, it was really good." Julia felt it had been magical but she didn't feel she could say this. They were at a precarious place in their friendship; a place when anything, a word, an assumption could knock them off course, send them back into separate orbits. They were both keenly aware of this and neither wanted to disturb the sweet balance of their budding friendship. Julia knew she was attracted to this almost stranger. It felt good to be with someone who seemed as dislocated, as fragile as herself.

She said, "You know, I hardly ever just walk like this. I am always jumping on tubes or buses, meeting friends, listening to my ipod."

"I'm afraid it's the modern world baby. Do you ever get that feeling of being inside a place?"

"What do you mean?"

"Not just walking on the surface of things, really being inside a place. That's how I feel in Liverpool; I feel wrapped up by this city. It's a bit like reading a good book; you suddenly realise you've forgotten that you are reading, you are completely in the story. I feel that with some places."

"You are crazy Tomasz Szymanski."

"Perhaps I am crazy. It's the writer's curse; thinking too much."

They walked in silence for a few seconds.

"I have been thinking a lot about my mum." Julia felt it was her turn to reveal something. "I keep imagining her walking the same streets I'm walking now. It's a bit morbid; it's not like she's dead or anything. It's a bit like when you go to an old castle and imagine all those people who lived or died there, it gives you a strange feeling. I keep getting this weird sensation about the past, as if it's seeping up through the pavements. My mum lived here in the sixties, you know; she went to the Cavern, saw the Beatles and other famous bands. She must have walked along here at some point, though it would have looked different back then."

"Perhaps it's a kind of genetic memory."

"How do you mean?"

"Carl Jung talked about a collective conscious, like we are all plugged into this reservoir of experience of our ancestors. Well, what if memories are passed down from our parents and grandparents, through our genes? They are all stored in our genetic memory bank; if personality traits such as sense of humour can be passed on, why not memories?"

Julia thought of her father, out there somewhere in the night, with all his experiences, thoughts, feelings. He could be living within a mile of where she now walked.

"You look troubled," said Tomasz.

She smiled at his quaint use of English learned through decade-old novels.

"I'm fine. It's just that all this thinking is hurting my brain."

"As I said, you are not a very good liar, Julia Swann. However, we have reached the place of our third murder, so I will let you off the hook… for now. There used to be a public house here called the Black Horse. The landlord, Joe Tyler was also known as the King of the Dock Road and he thought he ruled the roost… is that how you say it?" Julia nodded

"At four am on a freezing January morning in 1870, thirteen-year-old John Peters was caught breaking into the pub. Tyler tied him up and threatened him with a revolver until he confessed who had put him up to it. The boy eventually gave a description, which fitted that of a local caretaker, Bob Woods. The next time Bob Woods entered the pub Tyler and his mob took him into the cellar, tied him up and blindfolded him. They set up a kangaroo court and sentenced him to death. They then carried out a mock execution to put the fear of God into Woods, laying his head across a block and bringing a wet mop down on his neck. The joke went badly wrong – Bob Woods died from fright. The boy admitted to police that he'd given a false description and in fact Bob Woods had been an innocent man. Tyler went on the run and boarded a ship to New York. However, in some weird justice, the ship was lost at sea when hit by an iceberg; all passengers were assumed dead."

"I thought you were going to give me a positive impression of Liverpool."

"I am. Remember the good comes with the bad. Liverpool is always trying to turn rage into beauty, it always has. Now we will head for the centre."

They cut up from the dock road so that the Liver Buildings swept into view. They turned into Water Street where grand embassies and commercial buildings from a more lucrative era lined the roads. Renovation work was in progress everywhere and the area appeared part building site, part ruin. Some of the buildings were still black with soot and age but there were glimpses of extreme architectural beauty and a vision of what Liverpool had once been.

"Although slaves didn't ever pass through the port of Liverpool," said Tomasz, "the money made from slavery furnished these streets."

They cut up Exchange Street and turned right onto Tithebarn Street passing Silkhouse Lane on the left and turning into Hackins Hey on the right.

"And here is Ye Hole in the Wall." Tomasz pointed to a crooked pub. "It's the oldest pub in Liverpool, dating back to 1726. A report sent to your House of Lords two hundred years ago said, 'These are the haunts from which sailors sometimes disappear forever.' It talked of Liverpool's pestilent lanes and alleys putrid with vice and crime."

They continued to weave through small streets and narrow lanes and eventually came to a stop in Cumberland Street outside the Poste House. The pub was a narrow brick building set in a narrow street. "Let's stop here a while. I want to tell you about a really interesting connection to this pub."

"Yeah and we've been walking for three hours."

The pub was quiet and they were able to find a table. Julia was conscious of being watched by several elderly men who seemed part of the pub furniture, as if waiting for tales from foreign visitors; the return of lost sons from the sea.

"Let me get this one." Julia bought the drinks and then they settled in a corner.

"I want to tell you about one of the most notorious murders of the nineteenth century, which has resonated down to the present day. It involved a Liverpool cotton broker, James Maybrick, who frequently drank at this pub. His wife Florence Maybrick was from Alabama, where they met and married in 1881. They returned to England and moved into Battlecrease House in Aigburth. Florence made quite an impression on the social scene in Liverpool and they were often seen out together at grand balls. They appeared to be a happy couple, but not all was as it seemed. They were facing financial difficulties and Florence wasn't happy; she was used to a good lifestyle. Then she discovered that James had been keeping a mistress and five children on a hundred pounds a year for five years."

"Bastard!"

"James was a hypochondriac and was known to take strychnine as well as arsenic, which was believed to be an aphrodisiac. He was probably an addict. Possibly as an act of revenge Florence began an affair of her own with another corn broker, Alfred Brierly. James found out and threatened divorce.

Household staff noticed that Florence had purchased large quantities of fly-paper, which she soaked in water. She said she was extracting arsenic, a common skin remedy at the time. She had an eruption on her face, which she wanted to clear up before the autumn ball. However, when James became ill, suspicions arose among family members and household staff. She was watched closely and was reported to tamper with James's medicine and some meat juice used to build up his strength. Both were analysed but only a small quantity of arsenic was found.

"When James Maybrick died on 11th May 1889 after being ill with stomach upsets, the doctor refused to sign a death certificate and referred the case to the coroner. Three days later Florence was arrested on suspicion of murder. A search of the house by Maybrick's brothers found quantities of arsenic and the police decided to act. The body of Maybrick was exhumed for analysis and although the examination showed little trace of arsenic, Florence was charged and stood trial at Liverpool Assizes in St George's Hall. She was convicted of murder, despite reasonable doubt, and sentenced to death by hanging. The judge, who was committed to a lunatic asylum two years later, was inconsistent during the trial and there was an outcry on both sides of the Atlantic protesting Florence's innocence.

"Four days before she was due to hang the sentence was overturned. However, she still received a life sentence for attempting to administer arsenic with intent to murder.

"Queen Victoria believed Florence to be guilty and would not allow the sentence to be overturned. Florence was only released after Victoria's death in 1901. She then returned to the states where she wrote a book about her fifteen lost years. She never saw her children again and died in 1941 in Connecticut, a penniless recluse."

"That's so unfair."

"The case came into the limelight again ten years ago when a local man said he'd found Maybrick's diary in which he claimed to be Jack the Ripper. The diary has been discredited but not entirely disproved."

"Wow!'

They sat awhile finishing their drinks and listening to the guttural voices of two elderly men deep in conversation. After several weeks in Liverpool Julia was still getting used to the accent, although she found the sound strangely comforting as if it held the power to transport her back to childhood.

"There is no accent in the world like this one," said Tomasz, reading her thoughts. "Even I can distinguish it from other English accents. It is doomed to stand out. It's like the Scouse voice is always trying to get back to song."

"You are so poetic, Tomasz. Please tell me more about your writing. Why do you do it?"

"I just love words and the way they fit together and I love English, the language of Shakespeare and Dickens. Writing is a compulsion for me; I have to write; perhaps it saves me from madness."

"But don't you think paper books will soon be redundant?"

"No, no. I think people will always want to hold a book, turn its pages, smell the print; turn down the corner of a page."

"But we don't write letters anymore, do we? Everything is done by text and email."

"I still write letters. They are different from emails, altogether."

"How? I can't imagine writing a letter and then having to wait for a response for ages; email is so instant."

"But don't you think that's a bit sad? I still have a letter written by my first girlfriend. I can still smell her perfume on it; feel the pressure she exerted with her pen. I read it a hundred times when I first received it. I felt I was touching something she'd touched. Emails are scentless and so easily deleted."

Julia felt an unexpected twist of jealously as she considered the possibility of a girlfriend. "Yes, but think of all the meaningless words we send. Do they deserve to survive?"

"But you see as a writer I don't think of words like that. I see them as precious; even the bad ones and especially words that tumble out of the human heart when it is in love."

Julia watched Tomasz's mouth struggle to form foreign sounds; the earnestness of his expression as he searched for the right word. It was as if all words hovered before him, waiting to be plucked from the air.

"Tell me about Gdansk, Tomasz. Tell me what happened to you to make you want to leave your home and come to Liverpool."

"Gdansk has always been a nuisance, like Liverpool. It has always backed the wrong side; that's why I feel at home in Liverpool."

"You still haven't answered my question."

"It isn't time for another secret yet. Let's go!" Tomasz was already on his feet, the shadow had settled across his face again.

They walked towards the City Centre. Tomasz pointed out the site of an old Court House on Basnet Street and told Julia about Elizabeth Kirkbride who was tried for the murder of six of her babies whose tiny, decomposing bodies she kept in boxes. They crossed Hanover Street into Bold Street where they finally found crowds of people. They continued to walk until they reached Berry Street where St Luke's, known by locals as the 'Bombed out Church', pierced the skies with its ravaged skeleton. Tomasz led them over smooth cobbles into Pilgrim Street and stopped by The Pilgrim pub; Tomasz walked through a cobbled yard and into the pub. It was now 11.30pm and they were just in time for last orders. They settled with their drinks at a large table. Each table had its own individual Juke Box. Tomasz placed a coin in the slot and a melancholy jazz piece played.

"I have one more murder to tell you about."

"No Tomasz. I don't want to hear about murder; I want to hear about you."

"It is about me, Julia. This is my third secret."

"That sounds ominous." Julia felt a cold claw in her heart. "Are you sure you want to tell me?"

Tomasz nodded. "First let me set the scene. Gdansk has a history of a thousand years, similar to that of Liverpool, but history chose Gdansk as the beginning of the end of the twentieth century. It is of course where the war began but it is the Stocnia Gdansk, the shipyards, that mark the city's place in time; they are where it all happened. There is an ancient crane called Zuraw that sits on the Motlawa River in Gdansk; it looms over the shipyard like some great beast. As a child it both fascinated and terrified me." Tomasz paused and drank down his beer. His expression was intense. "Anyway, after the War and Gdansk's bloody liberation by soviet troops, the Lenin Shipyard became the main hub of the city's workplaces. My father worked for years at the Shipyards; he was a political activist. In 1970, a number of shipyard workers were killed in clashes with the militarised police, causing anger and unrest. Several events led to what began as protests about the inflated price of meat to became a ten million member Solidarity trade union and the shore upon which the wave of the Soviet regime would eventually break."

"It's very hard to imagine. I've never experienced anything like that."

"Conditions were terrible in Poland under communism, Julia but Moscow was unhappy and put pressure on the Polish Government, which it believed was losing control over its workforce. In December 1981, martial war was declared and five thousand Solidarity workers were arrested during the night and imprisoned. My father was one of them.

"Oh my God, that's terrible."

"I remember him not coming home from work and my mother having to explain to us where he was. She was burning with anger about what she saw as his wrongful arrest. I was infected with this anger and with an intense hatred of the system. My father quickly became a heroic and godlike figure to me; someone I wanted to emulate. Censorship was expanded and riot police filled the streets, all strikes were crushed. In October 1982, solidarity was finally banned and there were no more strikes, although it continued as an underground movement.

When Mikhail Gorbachev assumed control of the Soviet Union in 1985, he was forced to initiate a series of reforms which led to the release of many political prisoners, including my father."

"That must have been a happy day for your family."

"He came home a broken man; he looked small and defeated, not the hero I remembered. It was like the best part of him was missing." Tomasz's eyes burned with a fervour that Julia couldn't understand; she had no concept of what he had been through, although she wanted to understand. "Perhaps today we have lost our fighting spirit."

"A lot can be achieved through peaceful protest; you don't have to use physical force. In fact I hate violence; I think it's a sign of weakness. Jerzy Popielusko said those who cannot win through the heart conquer by violence. Ironically he was later murdered."

"Is that the murder you were talking about?"

"No, my murder is much closer to home than that and much more difficult to tell you about. But it is your birthday, Julia… I should save my secret for another time. I didn't mean to bring darkness into this lovely evening."

"I think we're about to be kicked out," said Julia. "Let's walk." They left the pub and continued along Pilgrim Street.

"Tomasz, you can't leave me hanging like this; please tell me your secret."

Tomasz was quiet for several seconds, his head bent and his face drawn in concentration as if battling with his thoughts.

"OK. I told you my father was imprisoned in 1981, when I was six-years-old. Three years later, my anger had grown very strong. I felt impotent watching my mother's misery as she tried to keep things together. My twin, Jakob, was not like me. He was born second and was physically weak, often ill, and a very gentle soul. One freezing February night I shook Jakob awake and we left the house secretly while my mother was sleeping. We went to the shipyards. Riots had been taking place all day and I felt stirred up by it and frustrated that my mother wouldn't allow me to join in. 'You are too young; you might get hurt.' She kept saying. But I didn't feel too young. I desperately wanted to show solidarity with my father and the other prisoners. I had a plan. With Jakob's help I secretly made this banner in our bedroom using an old sheet and felt-tipped pens. I asked Jakob not to tell anyone. I decided I would climb Zuraw and tie the banner to the top to declare Solidarosc. It was a very dangerous venture. I needed Jakob's help to put the banner up and so I forced him to come with me. He cried all the way up Zuraw, sobbed with fear; he was afraid of heights. I goaded him to keep climbing, I called him names and threatened him; it felt like the most important thing in the world to get up to the top, to fly my flag. Jakob pleaded with me to stop but I didn't. He lost his footing and fell to his death."

Julia gasped. "Tomasz!"

"My mother was inconsolable; I had murdered her son."

"But it wasn't murder."

Tomasz stared ahead, his eyes far away. "I became obsessed with how a life can end; one minute there, the next gone. He was my twin, we were connected in some way, yet I led him to his death like a lamb to slaughter. I felt the loss deeply but I couldn't grieve. I felt I was to blame. When my father came out of prison in 1985 he also blamed me. He was very disillusioned; he rejected the docks and opened a bakery. First of all just in our home, the only way he could do it financially. It was like he was in survival mode getting back to basics. He had decided we would never be short of bread again; we would never starve. He had a great need for self-sufficiency after his prison experience. He didn't want to be involved in politics; it had killed his spirit and it had killed his son. The bakery was a success and they were soon able to buy bigger premises with all the modern equipment; for once we were comfortably off. But I felt I could never reach my father or my mother again; they were cut off from me. My father was always too busy with the business and my mother, bizarrely, became obsessed with cosmetic enhancement. She travelled to Warsaw to have Botox; perhaps in an attempt to regain the youth my father had missed and to win him back. She aged considerably after Jakob's death. However, it had the opposite effect. Her face was as lifeless as my father's soul and neither my father nor I could read her.

I became a watchful child; I felt responsible for everything and I was always trying to read my parent's mood. I guess that's why I spied on them. Not because I was a sneaky child but because I wanted to make sure they were OK. Things didn't get better. My father wanted me to work in the business but I had been offered a place at University. We had a terrible row and my mother said things… I could see they would never, ever forgive me for what I had done to Jakob. I went away to Warsaw to study and I have never been back. For a few years I sent the odd letter letting them know I was OK, but that is all."

"But Tomasz, it must be nearly ten years since you've seen your parents. They will be going mad not knowing where you are. I'm sure they will have forgiven you by now; it was a terrible accident."

"Julia," Tomasz stopped walking and turned to face her. His eyes were soft with emotion. "I believe my parents hate me. I don't want to see that look in my mother's eyes ever again."

Julia felt a swift, hot wave of emotion overtake her; it rushed through her body and pressed against her eyes. She felt Tomasz's helplessness, his pain; and there was only one way she could think to offer comfort. She took his hands, pulled him towards her and kissed him softly on the lips. Tomasz returned the kiss more forcefully; holding her face between his hands like a treasure he was unwilling to relinquish. "Julia," he muttered.

She thought she'd only intended a brief kiss but she realised this is what she had wanted all evening.

"I'm sorry," he said, pulling away from her, his eyes dark and fluid, "I've been unfair."

"It's OK; it was nice. Tomasz, I don't know how you can bear it. How can you bear it?"

He smiled. "I've had a long time to learn. Anyway, my walking companion, it's past midnight. Happy Birthday! You still owe me a secret."

She said, "My secret will keep."

CHAPTER 21

Julia knew it would be impossible not to tell Tomasz her true reason for being in Liverpool. He had bared his soul to her and the least she could do was reciprocate. It would be fraudulent not to. She had woken up the day after the walk feeling that a so far undiscovered compartment in her mind had been forced open; it wasn't an unpleasant experience. That night she dreamed of rivers and disconnected murders; she dreamed of Tomasz climbing the crane, of Jakob falling, as if it was her own story to dream about. She had woken up feeling Tomasz's loss as if it was her own.

She thought of the kiss. She was excited by Tomasz; by his difference, his strength, his fragility. Julia wanted him to know that her life wasn't a shallow pool, undisturbed by dark currents or deep-water creatures. Less nobly, she had decided to elicit his help in the search for her father, taking advantage of his feelings for her. She couldn't wait to see him again, but she would have to wait. Tomasz annoyingly refused to use a mobile phone and it was impossible to contact him when he was away from the hostel. She wasn't sure if he was avoiding her or if he was just otherwise occupied. She finally found him writing, alone in one corner of the hostel. He seemed engrossed but looked up as she drew closer and his face broke into an unforced smile. She could tell he was glad to see her.

"Hello stranger. Are you busy?" she asked, suddenly shy in his presence.

"I always have time for you, my walking companion."

"Well, you haven't had much time for me in the past week." She tried to control a demanding note that had entered her voice. His conservative choice of words seemed to deny the kiss.

"Oh, I took on some extra shifts to pay the rent."

"Oh…right. Look I really need to talk…to tell you something…my third secret."

"OK. Shall we go outside? We won't get peace here for long"

They walked to the little garden in the centre of Falkner Square and sat on the parched grass.

"I haven't been totally honest with you about my reasons for being in Liverpool. I have come to do a BA in music and I do want to get to know my place of birth… but there's something else."

Tomasz nodded as if nothing could shock him, nothing would be too difficult for him to hear; it gave Julia confidence to continue.

"I was conceived from an anonymous sperm donor. My mother used a clinic here in Liverpool. I know next to nothing about my father and really have little hope of finding him. But I want to try." Julia stopped herself from saying more. She wanted to gauge Tomasz's response. She thought she saw a slight frown cross his brow.

"How do you propose to do that?"

"I would like you to help me."

"OK. Perhaps you could tell me a bit more about how I could help. This is a new one for me."

Julia lightly touched Tomasz's arm. "You've got the sharp mind of a detective and the imagination of a writer. You must be good at finding things… people."

"That's the nicest thing anyone's ever said to me." Tomasz smiled.

"No need for sarcasm. I know the road where the clinic is… was. I need to see if it's still there; we can come up with a plan to get the records."

"We can, can we? You've obviously been doing a lot of thinking about his."

"I've been thinking about it for years."

"Julia, do you think your records will just be sitting there on a desk in reception; that we will be able to distract the staff with a magic trick and grab them?"

"No, of course not, I just hoped we could try."

"Tell me this, if you manage to find your father what will you do?"

"I don't know. I'll ask him things, about his family... my family. Mostly I just want to see what he's like; if he's like me... if I am like him."

"Is that important?"

"It is to me. I've always felt there's a part of me missing, things I can't make sense of."

"Do these things need making sense of?"

"Yes, they do. They're about identity. I thought you would understand because of your brother." Julia's voice was rising to defensiveness; partly because she'd repeated these arguments a hundred times before but mainly because, in the process of disclosing her plan to Tomasz, it was becoming abundantly clear that what she was proposing, the thing that had thus far only been a fantasy playing in her mind, actually had huge legal and ethical implications.

"Look, Julia, you must understand I have to play devil's advocate, if that is the correct phrase. This is a very big thing you are trying to do. It could open up all sorts of worms."

"A can of worms."

"What?"

"Never mind; look Tomasz, every time I walk down a street in Liverpool, or sit on a bus, I think, that could be my dad over there, or my grandmother, my aunt... even my half-sister or brother. Most people don't have to think like that. I need to know who I am. Everything I am. Tomasz, you told me about your moment in childhood, well my moment was when I was twelve years old and the truth hit me that I was fatherless. I started to feel really angry with my mother; I thought she was selfish to bring me into the world without a father, or any chance of knowing him."

"Whatever my views are of sperm donation, don't be mistaken," Tomasz shifted his seating position, "everyone who has a child, by whatever means, does so for selfish reasons. I can't think of one unselfish reason for having a child. There are enough children in the world, in fact too many. It is the greatest act of narcissism to create something in our own image, for no other reason than to meet our own needs."

"I know, but..."

"I do not want to judge your mother, Julia, or a situation I know nothing about. I am only concerned about you and what effect this might have on you. Of course I am also concerned about myself if I agree to your crazy and very dangerous plan."

"Look Tomasz, I don't want you to do something you don't want to do, but I am going to do this...with or without you."

Tomasz took Julia's hand, which had been absently tearing up tufts of grass and wilting daisies; he pressed his lips to her fingers. "I would rather you do it with me."

*

At the end of September Julia moved out of the hostel and into student halls of residence, next to Greenbank Park. She was glad to have a room of her own again, but missed the hostel with its constant buzz of travellers bringing tales of adventure from around the world. More than this she missed Tomasz, although little had developed since the night of her birthday. A thrilling tension always sizzled between them as they talked or walked, played chess or ate side by side; although they both seemed reluctant to allow it to ignite, perhaps afraid of the consequence of an explosion in such a confined space.

Halls were still quiet with only a trickle of students arriving each day leading up to the start of term. Homesickness reclaimed Julia and she longed to see her mum and friends again. She had agreed to give Tomasz a couple of weeks to think about her proposal and, in the meantime, she tried to avoid visiting the hostel. It was a period of forced reflection for Julia; a state she was unused to. She wandered aimlessly in town, or sat by the little lake in Greenbank Park, attempting to lose herself in books. She considered again whether she really needed to search for her father or whether she had for too long been obsessed with an unrealistic and childish notion. Jack had provided many of the qualities associated with a father: he was caring and playful and he had a wicked sense of humour uncannily in tune with her own, but most importantly he had always been there – for celebrations and commiserations, highs and lows. However, in adolescence, when she found herself brutally awakened, feeling all the pain and beauty of life, she began to question whether she would ever have taken such a special place in Jack's affections if he and Maddie had been able to have children of their own. Was the genetic bond, after all, the most powerful bond of all? This was the question that nagged at her and spurred her on to the search.

It was a soggy Monday morning at the beginning of October when Tomasz suggested they make a trip to Park Road to see if the donor clinic still existed. Julia covered them both with her umbrella as they jumped off the bus at the Dingle end of Park Road. It was a long, wide road with little sense of coherence, as if it had been built and rebuilt over the decades in response to bombs and bulldozers. There was a mess of bingo halls and churches, Job centres and shops. The sky met drab buildings in a relentless sheet of grey. They walked towards the city passing row after row of terraced streets – David Street, Jacob Street, Isaac and Moses Street.

"The Holy land," said Tomasz.

"God, the clinic could be anywhere." Julia felt the

improbability of her goal.

They walked slowly, looking for any signs of a clinic or the previous existence of a clinic. They didn't have a number or a name only that it was on Park Road. They walked the length of the road and found nothing. They decided to walk back again and look for something less obvious. They finally found a narrow building squeezed between a chip shop and a bookie's. They climbed the steps and saw a tiny sign on the doorbell, 'Park Road Clinic', with no indication of what type of clinic it was.

"It doesn't want to be found," said Tomasz."

"It doesn't even look open," said Julia

"Perhaps it would be best if you go to the café back that way while I do some investigation." Tomasz had a narrow, determined expression.

Julia obeyed, finding an empty seat among workmen and people with nowhere better to go. She ordered tea and tried again to lose herself in a book.

Tomasz had spent several hours with Julia discussing possible plans for eliciting information from the clinic. The more they talked the more it became apparent that there were no means other than illegal ones of obtaining the information. Tomasz had tried once more to persuade Julia out of her plan, suggesting other ways of searching for her father on the internet or through support organisations. Julia assured him that she'd spent months looking and knew it was impossible. Eventually Tomasz found himself seduced by Julia's passion. They had come up with plans a, b, and c as well as contingency and last resort plans – they tried to think of every possibility. It was Julia who suggested that Tomasz might have to pose as a sperm donor to really get his foot in the door. Although Tomasz made it clear that he drew the line at actually going through with the procedure.

Tomasz pressed the buzzer at the side of a door that must once have been white. He quickly scanned the entrance hall as he was let in and was glad to see a curled poster showing a baby in the arms of a manically happy and rather dated mother, with the words 'Could you be a donor?' underneath. In fact everything was dated about the clinic, from the threadbare carpets to the drab wallpaper. He was relieved; it gave the place an air of unprofessionalism, which reassured him that there might be a tiny iota of possibility of finding what was needed.

Boredom drew down the face of the young receptionist. Her hair was brassy blond and she was heavily made up as if to compensate for the stark décor of her surroundings. She seemed surprised when Tomasz walked in as if she wasn't used to the intrusion of customers.

"I'm thinking of donating sperm," he smiled, attempting to thaw her, "I wondered what it entails."

"Oh," again she seemed surprised, "You'll need to make an appointment with a consultant to talk more about it." The boredom was hard to shake.

"Can you tell me anything first?" he leaned towards her and whispered, "I'm a bit scared of consultants."

Her face softened and a small smile lifted the corners of her Sienna red lips. "What do you want to know?"

"How long have you worked here…" he glanced at her name label, "Charlene?"

"God about a year," she said, as if it had been an eternity.

"It must get boring."

"It's boring cos hardly anyone comes here anymore."

"Why's that?"

She hesitated and looked along the corridor.

"We're… closing down next year cos of the new regulations."

"What new regulations?"

"The HfEA; all clinics have to be registered. We can't get…we're not registered.

"Oh why?"

He saw her face close down and he realised he'd pushed too

far. “I don’t know, do I? I’m just the receptionist.” She flicked through an appointment book. The pages were startlingly blank.

“Sorry, Charlene, you just seem to know a lot; I was interested. I’m still trying to get used to your English ways.”

“Where are you from?” Her face softened again.

“Poland.”

“Are you skint?”

Tomasz laughed, “What do you mean?”

“I mean, haven’t you got no money; is that why you want to donate sperm?”

He was shocked by her breach in professionalism but grasped at it. “Oh no. I just feel strongly about women who can’t have babies. My sister has been trying for years.”

“Ahhh, that’s awful. Have you got any more questions?”

“Just wondered what you have to do before you can donate.”

“Well you have to go through all these tests… HIV and stuff.”

“Can the child find out who you are when they’re older; I’m really worried about that.”

“No. I think the law is going to change, but not yet.”

“But what if someone broke in here, Charlene, and stole the records.”

“Don’t be daft, we keep our records down in the cellar; they’re all locked up in filing cabinets.”

Tomasz felt his heart sink but he smiled. “So, I’ve got nothing to worry about, then?”

“Since 2001 we’ve been putting everything on computer; we use these codes and stuff so the donor can’t be identified.”

“Oh I see. So it was only if you donated before then that you’d have anything to worry about?”

“Well it’s only since 1991 that there have been proper regulations about sperm donors.”

“So what happened before 1991?”

“I don’t know, do I?” She examined a set of pristine nails, painted the same shade as her lips.

"How do you store all those records, they must go back years?"

"God, you ask a lot of questions, don't you?"

"I'm sorry. I'd rather ask you than some overpaid consultant who just wants my sperm."

Charlene giggled, covering her mouth with a sunbed bronzed hand.

"Look," she glanced along the corridor again, "you might want to wait until we've re-opened under the new regs. We had this inspection last year and we've been told we don't keep our records secure enough… not that it would affect you." She pulled back and adopted a more professional tone. "We've greatly improved our practice."

"So, how long do you keep records?"

"There was no legal requirement to keep records before 1991 because donors were anonymous; most of them were destroyed. Now they're all on this HfEA register."

He imagined Julia's disappointment. Then Charlene leaned forward as if overtaken by a need to confess. He could smell a sweet, sickly perfume that he'd noticed young English girls often wore. "We've got all these boxes down in the cellar full of old files; it's really spooky. I have to go down there on my own sometimes. I hate it."

"Ooh creepy. What's in them?" He could tell Charlene was finally un-tapped; she was spilling out to him, as people often did. Her months of boredom were being unleashed. He felt some guilt at manipulating her like this but he allowed her to continue.

"They should have been chucked out, but apparently the previous manager was a bit of a hoarder, he kept everything, that's why we're in trouble. We've been told we have to log them all onto a computer file and then shred the lot, quickly. They shouldn't even be here and they're not stored securely. It's going to take ages. They go back to the 1970s."

"That's terrible… and they're not even locked up or

anything?" Tomasz leaned closer to Charlene.

"No, some of them have even been chewed by rats… shit… sorry, I mean… it makes my skin crawl. Others were damaged by a flood last year."

"What if someone broke in and stole them… I mean have you even got an alarm on this building?" Tomasz looked around "It looks like it's falling down."

"Yeah, we've got an alarm... its regulations." She sounded momentarily defensive of the organisation that was both her employer and her gaoler. "There isn't one in the cellar though but you'd have to come in the front door to get down there, anyway."

"Look Charlene, you've been really helpful; I have to go to work now." Tomasz pulled his bag over one shoulder. "

Disappointment drew her face down again.

"But first, I need a pee. I'm going to my nightshift and the toilets are disgusting."

"Sure; down the corridor on the right."

Tomasz moved along the corridor, noticing that there were no CCTV cameras. He quickly found the door to the cellar. It had no locks and when he pushed, it easily opened. He continued along the corridor to a door at the end and opened it into a large, messy storeroom. From here the backdoor went out into a high-walled yard. The door was secured by two solid bolts and a Yale lock and the window was barred. He walked with alacrity back to reception.

"Thanks Charlene, I'll think about it and give you a call." He waved. She responded with a small, flirtatious smile.

Tomasz joined Julia in the café and told her what he had found. "You are the luckiest girl alive, Julia. That must be one of the few remaining scenes of malpractice in a country obsessed by regulations. Any other clinic and I would be telling you to give up now."

She was instantly animated. "That's brilliant. You're amazing, to get that much information so quickly…"

"It's a natural talent."

"You're a natural flirt more like." Julia threw her arms around Tomasz and kissed him on the cheek. "This is possible, Tomasz, we can do it, can't we?"

"Hold on, girl. There's a long way to go yet; don't get your hopes up."

"We have to get into that cellar; it sounds like the clinic is falling apart; it can't be that difficult."

"Julia, we're only gong to get one chance at this. If we get it wrong, we're in deep shit. Never mind the fact we might get arrested."

"I know, I know; but at least it seems possible. Please tell me you think it is, Tomasz."

"OK. It might just be possible, but we really need to think this through."

Tomasz returned to the clinic the following week after arranging a meeting with a consultant. He felt unusually nervous as he made his way to a room on the first floor, stopping to chat for a few minutes to a blushing Charlene. He had prepared a convincing story for why he wished to donate, but got the impression that the consultant didn't care much anyway. Blood was taken from his veins by a brisk, friendly nurse and then he was given a clipboard with several sheets of paper to complete. He sat alone in a drab, boxy room feeling that he would one day regret this. Every minute his anxiety increased, a warning to get out, to abandon this mad plan, but the thought of Julia kept him there. They had agreed an elaborate plan; it was a thin plan, full of holes, but after hours of thought they hadn't come up with anything better and had decided to give it a try. Before Tomasz completed the paperwork he sent a text to Julia. 'Come. Five minutes.'

Julia's hand shook uncontrollably as she retrieved the text. She jumped from the chair, knocking the table so that her half finished coffee spilled into a dark pool on the plastic surface. She pulled on her jacket and bag, abandoning the mess, and made her way along Park Road to the clinic.

"Oh my God!" she said aloud as the clinic came into view, "what the hell am I doing?" She looked at her watch and waited for five interminable minutes to pass as a slow drizzle made snakes of her hair. This was stupid, how could it work? The minutes finally elapsed and she buzzed on the door. She entered the building that Tomasz had described with a writer's flair and it struck her forcibly that nearly twenty years earlier her mother had come here, nervous, alone and with a small hope in her heart.

"Can I help you?" Charlene gave a quick glance at the clock above reception. It was four forty-five, nearly home time, but her face still managed a smile, even though it didn't reach her eyes.

"Erm… I wondered if you could help me?" Julia softened her voice. "I wanted…"

At the same moment Tomasz breezed from the back of the clinic.

"All done." He addressed Charlene, ignoring Julia.

"Oh…" Charlene had the expression of someone watching an opportunity pass by. She looked to Julia, unable to disguise her irritation and then back to Tomasz. "Bye, then."

Tomasz waved goodbye. Charlene's eyes reluctantly returned to her unwanted customer.

"Can you give me some information on donor insemination?" Julia was amused to see frustrated desire still in Charlene's eyes.

"Well you're best having a consultation; they can tell you everything you need to know." Charlene was already flicking through the appointments book. "When is the best time for you?"

"How about next Wednesday; three o'clock?"

"No problem. Can I have your name and a contact number?"

Julia supplied a false name and number.

"Oh, do you mind if I use your loo; I'm bursting?"

Charlene looked at the clock again and emitted a sigh. "Along the corridor on the right."

Julia walked along the corridor, controlling her breathing. She continued past the bathroom to the end of the corridor where a door led through into a large storeroom, just as Tomasz had described. So far it was easy; if anyone had been in the storeroom she would just say she'd missed the bathroom. The back door was bolted twice and had a Yale lock. Tomasz had asked her to simply unbolt the door and then to leave as quickly as possible. He would take care of the rest. Julia wriggled and pulled at the bolt for over a minute before it moved across, making a noisy clang in the process. She felt hot and her breathing was rapid. Soon the alarms would be set and doors locked. She looked up to the top bolt, high up on the door, realising that if it was as stiff as the bottom bolt she wouldn't be able to get enough leverage from her current position. She looked around the room, controlling her urge to flee and saw a box in one corner. She pulled it over to the door and stood on it. She began to work the bolt, which was as steadfast as the first, imagining Tomasz waiting impatiently behind the door. The plan had to work before closing time or they were lost. "Come on, come on," she muttered, using every ounce of strength in her body.

"What are you doing?" The voice was deep and foreign. Julia turned sharply and in the process stumbled off the box and sprawled awkwardly on the floor. A large Asian man with folded arms, Julia guessed a consultant, blocked the door. "This is a private area; what are you doing here?"

"Oh God." Julia righted herself and stood up, trying to steady her breathing. She had rehearsed this possibility with Tomasz but now the lines seemed feeble. "I thought I was locked in; I tried the door. I was calling but no-one heard me. I'm sorry."

He looked at the box by the door and back at Julia. "The door isn't locked. Why were you in here in the first place?"

"I was trying to find the toilet. I'm so sorry. I suffer from claustrophobia and I panicked."

"OK, OK." His face softened and he gave a paternalistic smile. "You're alright now. We're closing soon so you need to leave. You wouldn't want to be locked in here all night, would you?" The man took Julia's arm and led her like a wayward child along the corridor, only releasing her as they reached reception. Charlene's smooth forehead was ruffled in puzzlement.

"This young lady managed to lose her way, Charlene. We should order a larger sign for the bathroom door."

"Yes, Mr Muhammad." Charlene took on an acquiescent posture.

Julia was aching to leave the scene of her humiliation and as soon as the door was closed behind her she ran to the alleyway several doors down and followed it to the back of the buildings. "Tomasz," she shouted as soon as she reached the clinic, "abandon, abandon." After a few seconds Tomasz's head appeared over the yard wall; he hauled himself up and dropped with cat-like agility to the ground. He didn't speak but pointed along the alleyway and together they ran to the furthest exit.

CHAPTER 22

In mid-October Julia started her college course. The weather had truly turned and the rain came in sheets, quenching the parks and gardens, cleaning the streets and returning the English temperament to its habitual state of moderation. Julia threw herself into the course, glad to have facilities in which to practice keyboards and something to occupy her mind. As a requirement of the course she soon formed a band with Dan, a guitarist from Kent, Jamaal, a bass player from Manchester and Stephanie, a singer from Auckland. They jammed together, wrote songs, drank and went to gigs in venues across Liverpool. It was a relief to inhabit a relatively normal world again and to forget for a while the aborted foray to the clinic.

Julia felt she at last had a purpose other than the strange disconnected life she'd been living. Compared to Tomasz, her new friends seemed light, shallow even, and it was refreshingly easy. She and Tomasz were still engaged in an intimate dance; only a whisper of air separated them, but they were careful not to breach it by stepping on toes or bumping shoulders. Julia was increasingly frustrated by Tomasz's resistance and decided to pull back for a while and put her energy into the course. She wasn't sure why but she didn't tell the new crowd about Tomasz or about the search for her father and for the first time her life fractured into compartments. To her new friends she was a happy, outgoing and uncomplicated girl from North London. It was only when alone that her thoughts returned to the darker undercurrents of her life. In her heart she hadn't given up the search for her father, despite Tomasz urging her to do so. They had analysed their disastrous attempt, dissected it, put it under a microscope and, after the initial terror and humiliation had subsided, Julia concluded that they had been unlucky and only inches from their goal, while Tomasz concluded that their plan had always been deeply flawed and never likely to work. Julia suggested they try plan 'b' while Tomasz argued they should abandon the madcap scheme altogether.

Tomasz's blood test results came back clear and he was invited back to the clinic to donate sperm. It was at this point, if plan 'a' had been successful, that Tomasz would tell the clinic he'd changed his mind.

"But even if you donate sperm you can still tell them you've changed your mind afterwards; they won't use it." They were in Julia's room sipping vodka and listening to some obscure blues CD Tomasz had picked up second-hand in town.

"No, Julia, I couldn't cope with the thought of sending a child into the world and never knowing who or where they are. You should understand that."

"They're not going to do the thing straight away. Don't they have to process the sperm or something?"

"It's too risky. Don't ask me to do it."

Tomasz's look was pleading and Julia guessed that if she pushed hard enough he would agree but she couldn't do it to him.

"Ok. I'm sorry. I won't ask again."

Tomasz noticed a distance between them after that and Julia visited less often. She said it was because of the mounting assignments at college or band rehearsals or this or that but Tomasz knew she was avoiding him. When he did see her she never mentioned the clinic or showed any resentment towards him for his decision but her mood alternated between taciturn and garrulous as if she was always avoiding the pertinent issue.

The kiss played perilously on Tomasz's mind. He regretted his decision to tell Julia about Jakob's death so soon and thus burden her with this macabre aspect of his life. He was angry with himself, knowing from experience that young women are easily seduced by tragic histories. He had found himself in bed with more than one woman over the years following far less weighty confessions. However, he had discovered with a refreshing certainty when he'd kissed Julia, that he didn't want to seduce this young woman into bed; he wanted much more than that.

He was now torn between two opposing fears: firstly that Julia had only kissed him out of pity and secondly that she had kissed him in preparation for the telling of her own story and to seduce him into helping her with the search. Either way, he felt paralysed. The search had become a convenient decoy and he didn't want it to end. Perhaps the mission was possible after all; perhaps he was being over cautious. After all, what did he have to lose? His life wasn't exactly ablaze with excitement and it would certainly make good material for a book. After two more weeks, he decided to throw caution to the wind. He called Julia to tell her he was willing to give it a try; her joyful response was reward enough.

The following week Tomasz returned to the clinic alone, with a backpack containing warm clothes, food, drink, a book, pen, paper and a few other necessary items.

"You made the decision then?" said Charlene, her face bright with hope.

"Yes, yes; it's all for a good cause."

Then her smile dropped. "Are you going away?" She nodded at the backpack.

"No, I always carry this baby around; I need it for work."

Tomasz had again taken the last appointment of the day and the light was already fading outside. After handing his container to the nurse, he made a quick trip to the bathroom where he removed the cistern lid, pulled out the pin from the ball cock and watched for a few seconds as the cistern filled with water. He then returned to reception, his heart engaged in a mutinous gallop. He knew this part of the plan was weak.

"It's done." He smiled. "Thanks for everything, Charlene.

"No problem." She continued to smile, perhaps hopeful of more communication with Tomasz.

"Oh God, I nearly forgot; there's something wrong with the toilet; you'd better have a look quickly before the whole place is flooded."

"Oh shit, everything's falling apart. I'd better go. See you soon."

Tomasz moved towards the front door and opened it, willing Charlene to leave the reception. She continued to smile and wave coquettishly, so he stepped outside, pulled a small piece of card from his pocket and slipped it between the door-jamb and the lock. He waited for several tortuous seconds and then pushed open the door. To his relief the reception was empty. He quickly headed for the cellar, looking around him before stepping through the door. He gently closed it behind him and descended the steps. He found a hiding place amid tea chests and damp boxes, hoping that nobody had cause to look for files at this time of day.

He only had to wait a short time before he heard voices calling goodbye upstairs and the sounds of footsteps along the hallway. Then, to his horror, the only light, a naked bulb in the centre of the ceiling, went out and he was plunged into darkness. He'd had an irrational fear of the dark since childhood and had been unable to overcome it. He heard the beep of the alarm and the front door slamming shut. He now had no choice but to stay until the following day. Tomasz fumbled in his bag for the powerful torch he used on his night shift. He switched it on and sent the beam around his voluntary cell.

A single wire had been run down into the cellar to supply light. Unfortunately the only switch was at the top of the stairs. Damn it, thought Tomasz, angry with himself for not noticing. But at least Charlene had been right about the alarm.

The cold quickly clung to his skin and started to work its way into his bones. He put on all the clothes he'd brought with him and then got to work. It was as bad as Charlene had described: the smell of damp and rotten paper was oppressive. He didn't relish the idea of spending the night here. He was used to the tedium of night shifts but not in these conditions.

Along two walls stood grey, upright filing cabinets, twelve altogether. Tomasz tried the drawers but as Charlene had said these were locked and the labels on the front informed him they contained the post-1991 files. The floor of the cellar was littered with an array of tea chests and randomly-sized cardboard boxes, which he presumed contained the pre-1991 documents. Some were loose and scattered about the floor – such carelessness, thought Tomasz.

He decided on a system and, hampered by having to hold the torch, started by moving the boxes into a relatively ordered line so that he could work his way through them systematically. The files in the tea chests had fared better than those in the cardboard boxes; some of those in the latter looked more like mush than paper. He was dismayed that many files were illegible and fell apart in his hands; others, as Charlene said, had been chewed by rats. He realised that Julia's records might well be among them. He emptied each container in turn, returning those files to tea chests that were easily eliminated on the basis of date. Files that were strong possibilities based on the information Julia had supplied, he placed into a pile on top of one filing cabinet and those that were less certain into another pile. The smell of tea rose like a ghostly aroma to meet his nostrils and a fine, black dust coated the files at the bottom of the chests.

The earliest records dated back to 1978 and the latest, 1990. The files didn't even make for interesting reading; there was surprisingly little information on each donor and a ridiculously small space for it to be written: a name, a date-of-birth, the date of donation and insemination, and a one line description, which included hair, eye and skin colour, level of educational attainment and interests.

Tomasz was shocked that a father could be selected on such scanty evidence; that something as big as the creation of a child could be treated with such small regard. He thought of his own father and all the qualities that went into making him who he was. He'd never had the chance for higher education but he had a brilliant mind that saw opportunity and took it; that made something out of nothing. He wasn't a particularly handsome man either: of medium height, stocky, with facial features that could be described as asymmetrical, but, even after his imprisonment, his personality was big enough to compensate for his lack of height and physical beauty. Tomasz's mother once told him the story of how she'd had to fight other women off to get to Mr Symansky.

Tomasz worked conscientiously and meticulously for several hours until he had two small piles on top of the filing cabinets and all of Julia's hopes balancing on his shoulders. Every other file had been placed back into containers. He then read through the selected files more carefully, eliminating several more in the process and leaving only three possibilities. He was relieved he had something to take back to Julia, although he was sceptical about her chances of success. He was still uneasy about the search; he felt that some things were better left alone, especially the past.

At nine o'clock Tomasz put the files in his backpack and took out a sleeping bag and a paper bag containing food and drink. He climbed into the sleeping bag, resting his back against a tea chest. He devoured the food and with the prospect of a long night ahead he took out his book and settled back to read. After approximately half-an-hour he thought he noticed the torch beam dimming slightly. He shook the torch and it seemed to respond for several minutes but then the beam flickered again and, like the last hope of a desperate man, it finally died, abandoning him to unremitting darkness. Tomasz shook it again, vigorously, and then removed the batteries and returned them, all to no effect. He grasped around in his bag for spare batteries, something he always carried with him for work, but then he remembered with horror that he'd given his last to a colleague several weeks earlier and hadn't replaced them.

The panic was instant and uncontrollable, clawing away at his rational mind. He stuffed everything back into his backpack and stumbled across the cellar ready to flee at any cost. Halfway up the steps he forced himself to stop and consider the repercussions of his actions. He breathed deeply and after several miserable seconds he made his way back down the steps and across the room. He wasn't sure if he was back in the same spot or whether he had placed himself in some hideous corner, sharing space with rats and spiders. He pulled out his sleeping bag and crawled inside, pulling the fabric up around his head. His disorientation was profound. Fear forced its way from the recesses of childhood, playing havoc with his adult mind. The fear turned to anger. Why was he trying to please Julia like a pathetic dog, putting himself in danger when he had no indication she felt anything for him? He considered himself to be an intelligent man, a thinker, a rationalist, yet he was behaving in a way that contradicted this.

He reached for his bag and felt inside for his hip flask; an eighteenth birthday gift, given to him by his father just before he fled to Warsaw. Rich burgundy leather covered a graceful curve of steel. His father would never be afraid of the dark. How had he managed prison? How the hell had his mind whiled away the minutes and hours, the days and months of that long stretch of time? What nightmares had plagued his nights, what memories had tormented his days? What dark and lonely places had he visited? Tomasz caressed the flask between both hands; finding comfort in the familiar shape; the contrast of the cold steel and warm leather; the simple pattern cut around the solid lid. He placed his mouth on the lid to receive the cold kiss of steel and then removed it, touching his lips to the small opening, feeling the damp of vodka lingering there. He sipped a small amount, feeling it first on the tip and then playing over his whole tongue, hitting the back of his throat and then curling up over the roof of his mouth. He repeated the ritual every few minutes, his senses startlingly alert; he knew sleep was a long way off.

He lay for perhaps an hour like this, although time was already becoming meaningless. How quickly we lose our faculties, he thought. He could hear his own breathing and the occasional rustle of the sleeping bag as he tried to get comfortable. The gap was lengthening between the rumble of cars above and eventually silence was all. The smell of damp grew stronger, filling his sinuses. He could smell other things too: the fur of dogs; the pee of cats; the dung of beetles; the fear of children. Then he heard scratching, the sound he dreaded – the unmistakable claw of rat. He remembered the remnants of food left over from his meal and, fearing the creatures would come to find it, he tore the paper bag from his backpack and threw it across the cellar. He heard the bag drop, then silence. A few seconds or minutes later, the scratching resumed and continued for a long time. Eventually it stopped and silence closed around him. He then wasn't sure which he preferred, the scratch or the silence. At least the noise was a distraction and at least he knew where the bastards were.

Now his mind had little to focus on, except its own contents. He pulled his woollen hat down hard over his head and ears as if to contain his thoughts. He saw himself as a strange animal, a locust in a cocoon afraid to hatch, afraid to be born into the darkness. He thought he could smell coal. It came from another time, when this was a house, with children, afraid of the dark. It wasn't coal; it was tar, no not tar, creosote. It was the creosote on Zuraw, the beast looming over Gdansk shipyard. What was happening to him? He could see Zuraw clearly across the other side of the cellar; he couldn't not see Zuraw. Then he saw small puffs of breath, like spirits, hanging in the darkness. They were coming from Jakob's mouth. He remembered a poem by Ted Hughes, *My breath left tortuous statues in the iron light*. He saw tendrils of mist rising up as Jakob climbed the crane; fear shortening his breath, widening his eyes. "No, please, no please," Jakob pleaded as he climbed after Tomasz; too fearful to go back; too loyal to ask his brother to abort the mission. Jakob fixed his petrified eyes on Tomasz's heels, as he had when following his twin out of the womb.

Zuraw growled, urging Tomasz on; he climbed with a flapping white banner in his hand, 'Solidarnosc'. They had coloured in the lettering with their new felt-tip pens. Tomasz was doing it for his father; for all the shipyard workers. He was brave like his father. Why couldn't Jakob be brave? Then came the cry, the sob and the fall. Tomasz had managed to raise the banner without his brother's help. Jakob was still cowering and gasping below. Tomasz looked up and saw the white banner flapping in the wind. Solidarnosc! Then the cry; the sob; the fall. In his dreams Tomasz had never seen Jakob fall; he dreamed and wrote a thousand alternate endings. Now he saw him twisted and bloody on the floor; the sight he must once have witnessed but hidden from himself for nearly twenty years. Tomasz wept. It was the only way he could describe it, weeping as a sore weeps, without the will of the person involved. He wept for a long time: for Jakob; for his parents; for himself. He felt desperately sad and tired but was unable to find relief in sleep. The impact of sensory deprivation was devastating, playing with the most vulnerable part of his mind, laying him open to every stimulus.

It was Charlene who caught him on the way out, "What are you doing here? You scared me." She looked him up and down, taking in his crumpled appearance and the backpack. Tomasz's brain had slowed down and he searched for his lines.

"I've just come off my nightshift. I've been worried sick all night... about the sperm donation... after the stuff you said, Charlene. I came back this morning to ask if I could change my mind."

"I didn't see you coming in."

"You weren't at the desk... I was looking for you. Sorry, I'm in a mess. I thought you'd understand. He could see she was trying to work it out, like an unwanted puzzle she'd received as a Christmas present.

"You poor thing, you do look a mess. I'm not sure..."

"I've got the money." He pulled cash out of his pocket, "No one will be hurt, I just need to get my sperm back." They both smiled at this.

"OK, just give me a minute." She picked up the phone and dialled a number. "Thanks for letting me know about the toilet by the way... oh yes, Mr Symansky would like to see you. Is that possible? She replaced the handset. "Yes, go up now."

The consultant seemed irritated. Perhaps the sperm had already been promised to some desperate couple. He was relieved to finally escape, dazed and blinking into a striking autumn day in which everything appeared exquisitely alive. Park Road wasn't a beautiful road, but he noticed the texture of bricks, the colour of shop signs, the deep blue of the sky, the shoots of greenery trying to reclaim the land, forcing through concrete. It was like being reborn. He was bewildered that so much had happened to him in a single night, as interminable as that night had seemed.

"God you look awful," Julia said as they sat down on a padded bench in Café Tabac. She studied his face. "You look different, weird. Haven't you shaved? Your eyes look bigger or something." Julia's pupils grew large as she studied his face; how beautiful she was. "Have you got anything?" He could see Julia hadn't slept well either; dark circles ringed her eyes and she seemed agitated.

"I need a pee and a coffee; desperately." He smiled. "The things I do for you, hey?"

"Please Tomasz, what have you got?

"Coffee, please!" He signalled to the waitress as he got up. "And scrambled eggs with chorizo; plenty of toast." He walked to the bathrooms at the back of the café. It felt good to relieve his painfully full bladder. He then looked at his face in the mirror. He was deathly pale but he saw that Julia was right, his eyes looked wider, the lines around them had relaxed; despite his sleepless night, he thought he looked a little more handsome. He washed his face vigorously in cold water and used a paper towel to dry it. He smiled at his reflection.

When he returned coffee had arrived.

"Tomasz Symansky, please, please tell me what you have or I'll die on the spot."

"That'd be a waste of time, after what I've been through. I can't do anything without coffee." He took a large gulp of the hot, black liquid; it tasted wonderful. Julia made a grab for his bag but he was quicker and held on to it.

"OK," he finally relented, "I have something for you, but not much. I can't tell you how bad things were in that rat infested place. Lucky for you. That clinic is going to be closed down. If you'd come next year you would have found nothing."

Julia's eyes widened. "My mum said it was a bit dodgy."

"That's an understatement." Tomasz didn't want to tell Julia about his dark night of the soul; not yet. As time went on he was less certain about what had actually happened to him in the cellar.

"Look Tomasz, I'm really, really grateful for this. I mean it. I will make it up to you one day."

The food arrived and Tomasz forced several forkfuls into his mouth while Julia nibbled at a croissant. He then lifted his bag onto his knee and drew out the three flimsy manila files. Each contained one piece of paper. He laid them sideways on the table so that they could both see them.

"I have only three names, though I swear I looked at every single file in that stinking place. Of course your mother wouldn't have been given names and dates-of-birth, only this little bit of information here." Tomasz pointed to the bottom of the files.

Julia studied the names. "That's him."

"Which one?"

"Him," she pointed impatiently, "Philip Hardy."

"How do you know?"

"My mum said she picked an athlete. It's about the only thing she told me. That's him." Julia's face was flushed.

"He has green eyes but yours are brown." Tomasz didn't need to look to know this.

"Yes, and so are my mum's."

"OK, well don't build up your hopes."

"I won't, but it's a start. I'm going to search today."

"How?"

"Phonebook, Google."

"Do you need me for anything?"

"I think you've done enough, my boy; thank you so much. Go home and take a shower." She pinched her nose.

Back in her room Julia made coffee and then examined the three files: 'Hardy, Philip D.O.B 11 April 1963. Physical Features: Black hair, green eyes. Skin tone: Medium. Height: 6'0. Occupation: Student. Interests: athletics, cars. Sperm donated: 5 November 1983. Used for Insemination on 19th November 1983. Patient ref: 10751'

'Baines, Ronald D.O.B 30 March 1958. Physical features: red hair, blue eyes. Skin tone: Pale. Height: 5' 7; Occupation: unemployed. Interests: none stated. Sperm donated 13 November 1983. Used for insemination 21st November 1983. Patient ref: 10752'

O'Sullivan, Finn. D.O.B 7 July 1964. Physical features: Dark brown hair, brown eyes, skin tone medium. Height: 5'11. Occupation: student. Interests: Music. Sperm donated 10 November 1983. Used for insemination 20th November 1983. Patient ref: 10754'

She liked the name Finn O'Sullivan because of the Celtic connection, which had always held a romantic appeal to Julia. She was also attracted by the reference to music, but she knew that didn't mean Finn O'Sullivan was the one. Her mother had always told her she'd inherited her love of music from her maternal grandmother. Besides, there was no reference to athletics on his record; the one shred of information about her father Julia had clung to from childhood. While her mum hadn't been worried about hair and eye colour or even academic achievement, she had strongly stipulated she wanted a tall man; an athlete, "To compensate for my short legs and hopelessness at sport, which I didn't want to inflict on my offspring."

She moved onto the next donor: Ronald Baines; the name sounded pedestrian and not particularly romantic to Julia, but then, she reasoned, what's in a name? However, he hadn't stated any interests at all, never mind athletics. She couldn't believe her father would be a man without passion for anything. Besides he was only five-foot-seven

Philip Hardy was a good, strong name; solid but with a hint of literary romance about it. Julia was already deciding that Philip Hardy was the one. However, she could hear Tomasz's cautionary voice telling her not to narrow the search too soon, or place all of her hope on one donor.

On a piece of blank paper she wrote in elegant flourishes: Julia Hardy, Julia Baines and Julia O'Sullivan. She stared at the names, as if they were coded messages she could crack if she only persisted long enough. After several minutes she abandoned the paper and took the files down to the common room where there were two computers for student use. The room was empty and she logged onto one of the computers. Firstly she looked up the meaning of each first and last name. Ronald: ruler of the people. Baines: bones, skinny person. Finn: fair. O'Sullivan: dark-eyed. Philip: beloved. Hardy: bold, courageous – as if it could tell her something about the sort of man her father might be? Father, father: she said the word aloud and it sounded strange to her ears; slightly harsh and Germanic, yet with a soft edge, like a feather; a hand stroking a child's hair; a sigh. 'Dad' sounded too familiar; it was someone who called up the stairs to you in the morning. It could be said tenderly, or in the exasperated tones of a teenager.

'Daddy' was more intimate still, perhaps the first word of a babbling child. Daddy: the hero, the playmate; the one who threw you effortlessly into the air and always caught you. To Julia the word 'Daddy' meant a hundred-thousand missed moments.

Julia knew she was avoiding the real search, perhaps afraid of failure or worse, disappointment. She had wanted this for so long but now that it was within her grasp it was a terrifying prospect. She looked up her own name: Julia: usage – 'England, France, Poland, Ancient Rome. Form of Julius and borne by the Emperor of Rome as well as early saints, martyrs and three popes.' Tomasz had been right. Swann: medieval, swan-upper or keeper of swans. Next she entered Tomasz's name. Tomasz: twin. Szymanski: Listener. How strangely apt; it crossed Julia's mind that Tomasz had invented both himself and his story. What did she really know about him? She quickly dismissed the idea and moved on.

Finally, at midday, Julia got down to the real search. She looked up each name on Google, writing down any details that she could find and then she subscribed to a site where she could search the electoral roll and find details on directory enquiries. She recorded all the Hardys, Baines and O'Sullivans who matched the details she already had. By three o'clock she felt weary and confused by the mass of information she had accumulated.

At four o'clock Julia decided Tomasz had slept long enough and she made her way to the hostel with the information she'd gathered. Tomasz was barely awake when she took a strong, black coffee into his dorm.

"Not you again," he said, stretching his arms.

"Get up lazy bones. I need you. I'll be waiting in the kitchen."

Tomasz emerged fifteen minutes later, clutching the coffee cup, his hair in a state of disarray, still damp from the shower and smelling of soap. He sat beside Julia at the table and she told him of her findings, pointing to the copious notes she'd scribbled all over the manila files. Despite his reservations, Tomasz found himself enthused by the intriguing journey. They discussed an action plan which involved calling all the likely phone numbers, with pre-prepared lines depending on the sex and initial response of the person answering. They agreed to start the search with Ronald Baines as Julia believed, much to Tomasz's amusement, that he was the most unlikely candidate because she didn't like the sound of him. She had four possible telephone numbers, but nothing had come up on Google.

Two of the Baines' were dismissed with a few simple questions. Tomasz and Julia were amazed at how much information people were prepared to give over the telephone. The third Baines lived in North Liverpool. A woman answered and Julia quickly handed the phone to Tomasz.

"Hi, is Ronald home?"

"Ronald? Who's asking?" the woman's voice was flat and edged with suspicion. From the tone of her voice Tomasz suspected the man might not be commonly known as Ronald.

"I'm an old friend of Ron's from school; I'm in the area and I'd love to catch up with him."

"You'll find him down the Albion playing bloody pool as usual." The woman seemed to spit the words down the phone and then hung up.

"She's not very happy with him." Tomasz laughed.

They eliminated the fourth and final Baines when they were told he'd just popped out to get his pension. Julia wanted to find the Albion immediately but Tomasz suggested it would be better to wait until she'd received the DNA swabs from the internet company as she might only get one stab at this.

They moved on to Philip Hardy who was listed on the electoral roll, but only until 2001. A Philip Hardy also came up on Google as a member of Wirral Athletics Club and in a local newspaper article for second-place in a cross-country race in Liverpool. However, the race had taken place in 1998. There was nothing after that date on Google or any other site. Tomasz called the one number listed but was told by the current resident that she believed the family had emigrated to Australia leaving no forwarding address. Julia called Wirral Athletics club and the secretary confirmed that Philip Hardy had left the club to live in Australia. She agreed to take Julia's details and pass them on, but she wouldn't give any contact information.

"You'll just have to wait to see if he responds," said Tomasz, trying to ease Julia's frustration.

"But I'm sure it's him."

"Let's concentrate on the third donor first; what do you have on him?"

"I've got six numbers for an F.O'Sullivan, two of them ex-directory and a Finn O'Sullivan came up on Google as a member of a Liverpool band."

"That would fit with the musical interest," said Tomasz.

"Yeah and they've got a gig at the Jacaranda at the end of November."

They worked their way through the available telephone numbers with no positive results. "Looks like he might be ex-directory," said Julia.

"Looks like we're going to a gig at the Jacaranda." said Tomasz.

CHAPTER 23

The Albion was a sprawling pub built in the 1960s. Everything about it was functional. It knew what it was, the Albion. It was a British pub; British being the operative word. The Albion was built to serve the overspill relocated to the north of the city from the bulldozed city centre. Where fields and woods had once provided respite from city life, a forest of bricks and concrete had risen almost overnight. The Albion pub was the hub of this new community. The Albion had been built to serve the working man his beer; an escape from the drudgery of everyday life, but with the rise in unemployment it served a cheap pint to men discarded by the workforce. Inside, the pub was white, male and unlovely. The chairs were cheap and unfussy; the tables had copper tops beaten into dimples that collected ash and beer spills and the carpet was deep red, making the blood and beer spills from Saturday night brawls barely noticeable.

Julia's heart sank as she entered the pub and was assaulted by the smell of stale beer, ash and ingrained dirt. There were three, oversized screens, all showing sport, and positioned so that it was impossible not to have sight of one. Euro pop played from speakers, too low to create a mood but too high to ignore. The music clashed with the racket of flashing and winking one armed bandits. The manager stood behind the bar as if surveying his kingdom, arms folded and a wary expression fixed on his face. A solitary barmaid prowled the tables collecting glasses and ashtrays. She looked as if she could hold her own in any fight.

Her vest top revealed wiry, tattooed arms and bleached hair was scraped back to expose thin cheekbones like steel apple slices beneath her skin.

Julia approached the bar through a fog of cigarette smoke and asked for vodka and cranberry.

"Don't do cranberry, love. I've got blackcurrant juice."

"It's OK. A bottle of Stella will do." Julia had decided to wear heels, jeans and a low-cut top, to help her cause, but she now felt uncomfortably exposed. She looked around for Tomasz, who had entered the bar a few seconds behind as agreed. She spotted him at the back of the pub; he looked out of place; unnervingly foreign.

Once she had a drink in hand Julia turned and scanned the dim interior of the pub. It was Tuesday night, exactly a week after the phone call and the pub was quiet. Julia noticed a table surrounded by men hugging pints. They all looked to be over fifty and she dismissed them. On another table sat two young men of perhaps twenty. The bar was lined by several hardcore older men drinking in comradely silence. So far she'd seen no women, except for the barmaid.

At one side of the pub in a snug, she found two men playing pool. The pool table was well used and marked at the edges by beer rings and dents, perhaps made by crashing bodies. One of the men had a lean, hunted look. His greying hair still had the fading tones of gingery-red and his eyelashes were so pale that his eyes looked naked. His skin was white and dry, emphasising deep lines radiating around the eyes. An unlit cigarette was perched behind his ear and moved in time to the clenching of his jaw as he took his shot. The other man had softer features, with a round, sagging face and a great, apple-shaped belly. His head was shaved clean and a small LFC tattoo was visible on his scalp.

Julia waited for the game to finish and then approached the table.

"Hi guys." Both sets of eyes focused on her chest before her face.

"Hi darling," the lean man said, "What can we do you for?"

"I'm from John Moore's University…"

"Oh shit, a bloody student." A sneer formed on his face.

"Did yer get lost love?" asked the fat man. "Do you need directions back to Bold Street?"

They both laughed at this.

"More like to the other side of Watford Gap by the sound of her accent." Lean man pressed his cue hard into the carpet.

"Hey you, I was born here," said Julia, flicking back her hair.

"Even worse, a posh Scouser;" said lean man scathingly, "but then I like a bit of posh, don't I, Bill?"

The fat man was Bill. Julia mentally eliminated him, leaving the even worse prospect of lean man for a father.

"Aah leave her alone," said fat man. "Can we help you love?"

"I hope so." Julia leaned seductively on the pool table, cringing at her own obviousness. "My Sociology class are carrying out a study on the genetic make-up of Liverpool. I wondered if you two gorgeous guys would like to be part of it."

"Oh God, we're all mongrels here," said fat man, "you'll never sort us out queen; it's like one big pan of scouse." He chuckled.

"You can experiment on me any time you like." Lean man emitted a raucous sound.

Julia smiled, trying to ignore his comments and her growing dislike for him. "I'm covering North Liverpool and people born in the 1950s when there was a lot of change going on in the city; by doing a simple DNA test we can start to get an idea of the genetic makeup of Liverpool. It only takes a few seconds and you might find out something interesting about yourself."

"You can take my DNA now if you like," said lean man, moving his hand towards his flies. "But it'll take more than a few seconds, love. I can go at it all night." His laugh could only be described as depraved.

"Give her a break, mate." A look of disgust crossed fat man's face. "What's the information going to be used for, love?"

"It's all part of the city of culture thing…"

"Oh God, not that crap," lean man sneered; he drew the cigarette from behind his ear and placed it in his mouth; it remained unlit. It jiggled in his lips as he spoke. "They'll build a few posh bars and apartments in the city centre while the rest of the city falls down."

"I know, I know." said Julia, "I don't like what they're doing either, but I just need to get some results so I don't get kicked off the course. And it would be really interesting to find out where everyone comes from."

"As long as we don't get any more bleeding eastern Europeans," said lean man, "the place is already swarming with them."

Julia resisted the urge to turn towards Tomasz.

Round man said, "It sounds interesting. What would we have to do, love?"

Julia desperately needed to engage lean man. She couldn't afford to waste a mouth swab on fat man. "Would you mind telling me your names? I am trying to get a selection of surnames… for cultural interest?"

"I'm Dennis the Menace and he's Gnasher."

Julia felt like a fly and lean man was a small boy pulling off the legs and wings, one by one. There was something cruel rather than playful in his games. She maintained a flirtatious pose, despite her strong urge to smash the beer bottle over his head.

"Very funny; look, if you don't want to play it doesn't matter; there are plenty more fish in the sea." She turned to walk away.

"No, queen, don't go," said fat man. "You're the most interesting, not to mention most gorgeous thing that's walked in here in years. We're dying of boredom."

"And of thirst." Lean man removed the cigarette and drained his glass.

Julia turned back and directed a salacious smile at lean man. "I'll buy you a pint if you agree to do it."

"Now that's more like it," said lean man.

"Ah 'ey, Ronnie, she's a student," said fat man. "She can't afford to be buying pints."

At last a name; Julia's heart plummeted.

"She's probably got more bloody cash than us, Bill."

"OK," she turned to Ronnie, deciding to take a more direct approach and end the unbearable pantomime, "You've got an interesting face; you probably have good genes." He had a face without character or beauty but Julia realised she had to appeal to his ego, rather than his intelligence. She saw a slight softening, a bashful smile. "But maybe you're too young to have been born in the 50s?"

"Nah, he's an old fart like me," Bill laughed. "We went to school together down the road; both born in '58."

Ronnie turned on Bill. "Thanks for giving me age away, mate. I was in with a chance then."

"You're still young," said Julia, staring into a face sagging with inactivity. "You'd be perfect for my study. Red heads are especially interesting. You could have Celtic blood. What's your surname?" She gave him a smile that promised many things.

"Baines; Ronald Baines. Go on then; it can't do no harm." He returned the cigarette to his mouth and lit it with a Swan Vesta. "I still want me pint though."

Julia hastily pulled the swab from her bag before he had chance to change his mind, removed the protective cover and handed it to him. "Just rub it over your cheek for a few seconds."

"Don't be rude… oh you mean this cheek." He opened his mouth to reveal yellowing teeth and inserted the stick, rubbed it along the inside of his cheek and handed it back. Julia replaced the cover and dropped the swab into a plastic bag.

"I'll pop back here in a couple of weeks to let you know the results." She winked.

After buying the men a pint each Julia left the pub followed closely by Tomasz.

She felt woefully deflated. It wasn't so much the man's crudeness that chilled her, as his ordinariness. There were men like Ronald Baines in pubs all over Britain; men with his looks, his attitudes. When she compared him to Jack, he seemed like a different breed.

Tomasz could see the despondency on Julia's face and suggested they go for a drink at one of his favourite pubs, the Atlantic, sitting in decrepit isolation on a windswept stretch of the dock road. They bought drinks and were lucky to find a table in a dark corner. Julia sank into the chair, her eyes swelling with tears.

"This pub reminds me of one I went to in town recently," said Tomasz, attempting to distract her from her disappointment. She nodded absently.

"While I was there this man walks in and orders a glass of Polish vodka. The man sitting next to him says, "That's a coincidence, I too am enjoying Polish vodka. Since I arrived from the old country this is the only bar in which I have found it.' The first man replies, 'Old country, I'm from the old country. Let me buy you a vodka.' As the bartender poured the drinks the second man asks, 'What part of the old country are you from?'

"'Krakow,' replies the first.

"'This is weird, I too am from Krakow. Let's get another shot.'

"The new round arrives and the first man asks, 'So friend, what did you do back in Krakow?'

"'Not much really; I came here right out of high school. I graduated from Lech Walesa Technical Academy in '81.'

"'This is spooky,' replies the first man, 'I too am from Walesa Tech, '81. Let's get another shot.'

"The bartender looks irritated and says, 'Slow down guys, I've gotta make a call.' He calls his wife and tells her that he'll be getting home late. When she asks why he replies, 'The frigging

Liszjewski twins are here again.'"

Julia laughed. "Very funny."

"At least it got you laughing."

"It obviously doesn't take much."

"OK, I've got another one that's a bit more challenging. It's a philosopher joke. Did you hear about the dyslexic agnostic insomniac? He lay awake at night wondering if there really is a dog."

Julia pulled a pained expression.

"OK, OK, I've got a better one than that. A boy is about to go on his first date and is nervous about what to talk about; he asks his father for advice. His father says, 'There are three subjects that always work, my son: food, family and philosophy.'

"That night the boy picks the girl up and takes her to a café in town. After a short time the conversation dries up. The boy remembers his father's advice and asks. 'Do you like chips?' The girl says, 'No' and the silence returns. The boy begins to feel panic and remembers his father's second suggestion. He asks the girl, 'Do you have a brother?' Again the girl says 'No' and stares into her coffee cup. There is an excruciating silence. In desperation the boy remembers his father's third suggested topic of philosophy and decides to play his last card. 'If you had a brother would he like chips?'"

Julia broke into uncontrolled laughter, choking on her drink, so that Tomasz had to pat her on the back.

"It wasn't that funny."

"I – I know. I don't know why I'm laughing really. I'm hysterical." Then she dissolved into tears.

Tomasz placed a protective arm around her. "Look, are you sure you want to do this… if it's upsetting you this much?"

"I'm sorry, I'm fine." Julia pulled a tissue from her bag and wiped her eyes. "It's just the tension; it was so horrible thinking that man might be my father, Tomasz, but I still have to know. It's about my identity."

"Identity is overrated; why don't you find meaning in your own existence."

Julia looked into Tomasz's eyes; anger flashed across her face. "I don't know how you can say that when you've spent your life grieving for your twin."

"That's not about identity; that's about belonging. You don't have to be blood related to belong."

"I'm not sure you believe that Tomasz. Just because you've cut yourself off from your family and make jokes about your own people doesn't mean they're not important to you."

"That's not true. I…"

"I want to go." Julia grabbed her coat and bag and headed for the door.

Tomasz found her sobbing on a desolate piece of wasteland next to the pub. Tomasz folded his arms around her and gently kissed her hair, wanting more than anything to kiss her lips, to take her home and make tender love to her.

"Let's get you back home and I'll make you a nice, English cup of tea."

CHAPTER 24

In the middle of a particularly wet and gloomy November the DNA results came back. Julia was relieved to find that there was no evidence of paternity in Ronald Baines' genetic coding. With the relief came renewed optimism and the certainty that there would be instant recognition and compatibility when she eventually did meet her father. She now focused her attention on the next candidate, Finn O'Sullivan, and his gig at the Jacaranda in two weeks' time. In the meantime she found distraction at college.

Julia was enjoying her new friendships and the opportunity to play with good musicians who pushed her performance to a higher level. She practiced keyboard every day for several hours and the rest of the time was spent in seminars, completing assignments or in practical application. In the evenings she either worked at the bar or went to gigs with friends. Soon the inevitable sexual frissons emerged. It was obvious that both Jamaal and Dan had a crush on her and made overt attempts to please her, while they treated Steph like one of the boys. Julia didn't encourage this situation; she was used to attention from men and often found it irritating. She also enjoyed the banter and camaraderie between the four friends and didn't want to disturb this or alienate Steph.

Steph was a happy-go–lucky girl who never took herself or the world too seriously. She was blond all over and looked like she was used to sitting on boats in shorts and deck shoes. Her skin was clear and brown, except for a few freckles across her nose, her eyes a transparent, sea-blue, her teeth white and her hair a golden tangle. She walked with a purposeful stride that had a boyish quality. She was more comfortable with the behind-the-scenes aspect of the music business but she'd been gifted with a rich, gravelly voice, to which people were compelled to listen and, despite her shyness, she found herself thrust into the limelight. She'd therefore decided to combine a love of travel with a music course in one of the most famous music cities in the world.

Julia suggested to Steph that they have a girl's night out on the town and the following week they hit the narrow strip of Wood Street, crawling through the multitude of pubs, getting giggly on wine. It wasn't long before Julia was attracting attention. Steph commented: "Jeez, you're like a man magnet, Jules." Her voice was devoid of resentment.

"It pisses me off at times," said Julia

"I wouldn't mind a bit of interest. They all treat me like a bloke."

"Oh men are just attracted to the obvious; they just see legs and tits."

"So who are you interested in, hey, Jamaal or Dan? You could take your pick."

"Neither. I just want to be mates with them. I like it that way."

"I know what you mean, but I've got a serious crush on Dan."

"Really!' Julia laughed gleefully.

"Yeah, I might get his attention if he could drag his eyes off you for a minute."

"I'm sorry Steph; it must piss you off."

"Look Jules, I'm not the jealous type. You're gorgeous; I can see why they'd both want you. You're a bit of a mystery too."

"What do you mean?"

"Well tons of blokes look at you but you never seem to notice; you look as if your mind is somewhere else half the time."

This was a shock to Julia; she thought she'd been doing a good job of being present with her college friends.

"We've only been at college a few weeks I'm not going to shag every guy who looks at me. Anyway, I've not long split up with a boyfriend; I'm not ready for another relationship yet."

"OK, none of my business; blokes are nothing but trouble, anyway?"

From time to time Julia longed for deeper waters and thirsted for Tomasz's company. Then she went to the hostel and they played chess, drank vodka and talked. She took for granted that he would be there when she wanted to see him. By now she knew his work shifts, when he slept and the times he liked to write; she hadn't imagined another life for him. She liked to think of him as her beautiful existentialist, heartbreakingly lonely and always waiting for her. One evening, however, she called at the hostel to find that Tomasz was out. The person on reception said he thought Tomasz had gone out with a friend. Julia felt unexpectedly disappointed and jealous of the 'friend'. The fact that Tomasz had one friend now opened up the possibility of a whole life that she knew nothing about; it also meant that his need for her wasn't as great as she had imagined.

*

"The Beatles played one of their first gigs here."

Julia couldn't take in Tomasz's wealth of information; her heart was beating too fast and her mind was a whirlwind of fear. They crossed the bar and went downstairs into the cellar where the stage was set up. There were three bands playing that night but it was only the third band Julia had any interest in. She looked around in a state of terrified elation, thinking that perhaps she was sharing the same air as her father.

It was after eleven when the main band finally climbed onto the stage to set up their instruments and by then Julia was tipsy from drinking too fast. She studied each band member in turn. There was so much activity on stage with sound engineers and band members plugging in instruments and microphones that it was difficult to know who was who, except for the drummer. He had gangling limbs, wild blond hair and prominent teeth and was probably no more than thirty; Julia could find no resemblance. The bass player finally settled to his instrument; he was small and stocky and couldn't have been more than twenty-five years of age; he was also dismissed. The lead singer, who also played rhythm guitar, was now tuning up in front of the microphone. He was tall with mid-brown hair, smattered with grey and had a ravaged, rock star look, although he might only have been in his mid- to late-thirties. Julia thought he was attractive in a younger Mick Jagger sort of way. She couldn't rule him out. The lead guitarist was the most conventionally good looking. He was slim with dark hair and had an engaging face that was already peering out into the crowd. He looked familiar to Julia and she wondered if she had seen him before, perhaps on posters around Liverpool. He only looked to be in his early- to mid-thirties and she thought he was probably too young to be a candidate.

When they struck their first chord Julia dragged Tomasz closer to the stage. "Quite good hey?" she shouted into Tomasz's ear.

He nodded his agreement. "Any idea which one he is?"

"Not sure but perhaps the lead singer. He seems to be the right age. The drummer and bass player don't look right."

Tomasz laughed, "Oh they have to look right now, do they? "

"Well, who do you think it is? Know-it-all."

"Possibly the lead guitarist; he looks a bit like you."

"He's too young, but he's the best looking."

At the end of the gig, Julia braced herself and approached the lead singer, leaving Tomasz to watch disconsolate from the bar.

"Good gig."

"Cheers; it was a good crowd." He had a southern accent.

Julia examined his face and froze as she realised she could be staring into her father's eyes. They were an odd shape, round rather than almond shaped like her own and baggy underneath. His breath smelled sour. She hesitated for too long and he turned to dismantle his equipment. She said in desperation. "Sorry… I just wanted to ask you something." He turned back, frowning as if she was a nuisance.

"My name's Julia Swann; I'm from LIPA." She cringed at her ridiculous words but in the strangeness of the moment she had forgotten everything she'd rehearsed with Tomasz.

He looked amused. "Well, my name is Pete Clarke and I've never been near a bloody music college in my life."

"Pete Clarke? Oh." Her mind rushed to find something else, "I just wondered how you got the gig here… my band are trying to set some up over the next few months."

"Talk to Finn, he does all the donkey work when it comes to getting gigs."

"Which one is Finn?" Julia's heart leapt wildly.

"The geezer with the guitar." He nodded across the stage and then turned his back on her.

Julia turned to Tomasz whose eyes instantly met hers. She pulled a pained expression and shook her head. She then approached the man called Finn. He had finished packing up and was climbing down from the stage.

"Good gig," she repeated.

"Thanks. I enjoyed it." She thought she detected a slight Irish lilt to his voice.

"Some of it reminded me of Echo and the Bunnymen."

He looked surprised. "You know them? You look too young."

"I'm twenty-one. She wasn't sure why she lied. "I've got eclectic taste."

"It's never good to get too narrow." There was a paternal quality to his voice.

"I… I was just talking to Pete. He said you know how to get gigs. I'm in a band."

His eyes now engaged with hers. "Oh, what do you play?"

"Keyboards."

"Brilliant. Just take a demo to the manager. Sometimes you

don't even need that; they'll usually try you out."

"Thanks… can I get you a drink?"

Finn looked thrown, perhaps uncomfortable. "Thanks, but I'm rushing off… up early tomorrow."

"Oh… when's your next gig?"

"January 15th at the Cavern."

"OK, might catch you there."

His smile was uncertain.

Julia returned to the bar, red-faced and humiliated.

"I behaved like a groupie, a flaming groupie. I want to go." She was already moving away from Tomasz towards the door, pulling her coat on as she went. He drained his glass and followed.

"Didn't it go well?"

"I'm stupid and ridiculous… I couldn't think of anything to say to keep his interest."

"You seemed to be doing ok to me."

"He wouldn't accept a drink!"

"You sound as if you're not used to that."

"I'm not."

"He might be married or anything."

This thought hadn't occurred to Julia. She marched towards the bus station pacing out her humiliation in long strides.

"Oh God, I'm so stupid. I should have tried a different approach... he must have thought I was flirting with him. Anyway, I'm pretty sure he's not the Finn O'Sullivan."

"Why not?"

"I think he's too young. Anyway, I'm still convinced Philip Hardy is my father."

"But that's only based on your mother's anecdote about choosing an athlete."

"It's not just an anecdote; it was a definite choice she made."

"OK, well you still need to eliminate the music man from the equation before you go flying off to Australia." They had reached the bus station and stood huddled together in the cold.

"Yeah, well nothing is going to happen until after Christmas." Julia felt tired and defeated. She bit her lip to stop the flow of tears but it was too late.

"Oh darling, it is all too much for you." Tomasz wrapped her in his arms. Julia could smell his scent, strange and familiar, in the warmth of his neck and the cloth of his coat.

"Tomasz, please come back to mine for a drink. I don't want to be alone."

They were silent as the bus traced a route home. They climbed off on Smithdown Road, Julia still leaning into Tomasz, the bitter December wind forcing them even closer together. They climbed the stairs, still as one, separating only as they entered Julia's room. Tomasz stood, polite and still and a little awkward, while Julia put on lamps and placed two glasses side by side on her desk. Without asking, she poured a generous measure of vodka for them both.

"Sit down… take off your coat." She waved vaguely towards the bed.

Tomasz obeyed, perching himself on the edge of the bed.

"I'm sorry," she said, joining him, "I'm just feeling a bit emotional."

"Is it just about what happened tonight?"

"It's that, it's the pressure of college and I really need to sort stuff out with my mum; we haven't spoken in ages. I guess I just need to go home for a couple of weeks."

Tomasz nodded. "I'll miss you."

Julia turned to him and placed one hand over his. She saw desire in his eyes.

"I'll miss you too."

Tomasz took her glass and placed it, along with his, on the desk. He sat down beside her and stroked her face with one hand. He leaned towards her and kissed her gently on her nose and then down to her mouth. Julia pushed him down onto the bed and they lay, the length of their bodies melded together.

PART III

CHAPTER 25

As the train snaked south through the wintry landscape Julia knew she had to sort things out with her mum. It felt unnatural for them not to be on good terms. However, she wasn't ready to tell her about the search; she knew it would create too much anguish. The scenery seemed to be in turmoil along with her mind: trees were bent over by the wind and clouds skated across the sky like Dante-esque souls in torment. Icy rain punished the train windows and hammered on rooftops.

Julia caught the occasional glimpse of celebration: Christmas tree lights performing colourful dances in defiance of the season's deadness and flashing Santas perched on rooftops. She was excited about the prospect of being back in London, seeing her mum, renewing comfortable friendships. She also looked forward to Christmas Eve at Carysfort Road.

The reconciliation between mother and daughter was instant, with hugs, tears and apologies. They didn't talk in detail about their fall out; instead Julia told her mum about college and the new friends she'd made. Beth delighted in her daughter's eagerness and was relieved to see evidence of her happiness.

On Christmas Eve they made the short walk to Carysfort Road, laden with presents. Julia experienced the joy of reunion with the people she loved and the rush of excitement at the sights and smells associated with Christmas, made all the more keen by her absence. Greg and Dave arrived with their newly-placed children, Caitlin and Sam, now aged four and two. Caitlin, the eldest was a sweet but hesitant girl, always watchful and fiercely protective of her little brother. Once they were absorbed in play Greg explained that Caitlin had witnessed horrific domestic violence between her parents and in consequence was anxious and hyper-vigilant. It would take time before she could relinquish her responsibilities and reclaim her childhood.

Jack was on good form playing the host while Maddie was in her element, surrounded by friends. After several glasses of champagne, Julia had to resist the strong urge to tell everyone about her search. It wasn't natural for her to hide important news from those closest to her.

Julia and Beth spent Christmas day quietly together. They ate dinner, watched films on TV and read books curled up on their favourite chairs.

Julia said, "We're like a couple of old spinsters."

"Don't feel you have to stay in with me, love. Go out and enjoy yourself."

"Mum, I am enjoying myself; I've got plenty of time to see my friends over the next two weeks."

The questions sizzled rather than burned in Beth's heart. Despite vowing to herself that she would ask Julia some direct questions over Christmas, she never quite found the right time to do it. She'd been unexpectedly lonely since Julia's departure. She missed coming home to cups of tea and Julia's tales of young life, as well as the opportunity to moan about her day at work. The row had shaken Beth to the core and she couldn't rid herself of the sense of doom that kept her awake at night, along with the hot sweats of menopause.

On Boxing Day they walked on Hampstead Heath with Jack and Maddie, and had lunch at a pub in the village. The remainder of Julia's time was given over to socialising with friends, catching up and comparing notes on their different college experiences.

In the last few days of the holiday, Julia felt the draw of Liverpool like a dark current pulling her back. Tomasz and the search, she realised, were the most pressing and poignant aspects of her present life and both had undercurrents of uncertainty. She missed Tomasz more than she could have imagined, but on their last night together she still sensed resistance in him. They had lain together on the bed and kissed, but nothing more had taken place, despite the desire coursing through their hot blood, beating in their entwined limbs. Tomasz had left at three am with starchy farewells. To Julia it seemed strange and old fashioned; she was eager to get back to Liverpool and confront him about his unnecessary gallantry or whatever it was that prevented him from succumbing to her.

Before she returned, she asked Jack to meet her for a drink at the Rose & Crown. She was anxious about the meeting as she'd decided to confide in him about her search; she was finding the burden of secrecy difficult to bear alone.

"Are you looking forward to getting back to college?" he asked as they sat down.

"Yes." She was relieved to admit it.

"City of Culture, hey? You've chosen a good time to go. When I left, Liverpool was going down the pan."

"Loads of stuff is happening there now; it's got a really exciting vibe."

"It's great having all that independence isn't it? Doing what you need to do without parents looking over your shoulder."

Julia was always impressed by Jack's insightfulness. He had a way of making difficult things easier to say.

"Jack, there's something I need to tell you, but I need you to promise not to tell my mum."

"That's a lot to ask, love." Jack had spent most of his life hiding secrets from the people he loved and he had vowed not to do it again if at all possible.

"I know and I'm sorry but I need your opinion; it will only be for a short time. I'll tell her as soon as I can."

"Oh dear, it sounds ominous; you're not up the duff are you?"

Jack laughed, knowing this was unlikely given what he knew about Julia, besides he already had a good idea what she wanted to tell him.

"Of course not!'

"OK. I'll promise on the condition that you tell your mum as soon as you possibly can."

"I promise." Julia took a slurp of lager. "I've been searching for my biological father." She kept her eyes fixed on Jack's face. His expression barely changed.

"I knew you couldn't not do it – I probably would have done the same in your shoes. How far have you got?"

"I've narrowed it down to two, but I think the most likely candidate has emigrated to Australia."

"Bloody hell, girl, that's quick work. I thought it was meant to be impossible. How did you manage that?"

"With a little help from my friend." Julia told Jack about Tomasz's role in the process.

"Clever but dangerous and highly illegal; you should be very careful."

"What do you think Mum will do?"

"She'll have a bloody fit, you know she will. She's riddled with guilt about everything and she'll find a way of blaming herself; but isn't that what mother's do?"

"But she has to understand why I need to do this." Julia felt her defences rise.

"She might understand, love, but it won't stop her worrying herself to death."

"Oh God, don't say that."

"Look, your mum is responsible for her own feelings; she'll deal with it. You have to do what you need to do. Just be careful, love, feelings have a way of creeping up and taking us by surprise."

"Thanks Jack, but I'm OK."

"Look, love, I think it's important that you understand how

hard your mum has tried to be honest with you over the years. "

"She still chose to use a sperm donor though, didn't she?"

"Yes she did, but she could have lied to you about it; told you she'd had a one night stand or been abandoned by some bastard of a man. She didn't; she took the hard route."

"Look, Jack, I know my mum has always tried to do the best for me but it was like she didn't think of the consequences?"

"Julia, I know you're having a hard time at the moment but remember your mum had difficult choices to make too: I had left her, your grandmother had just died; she was very lonely and wanted a child. Perhaps you can't understand it all right now but you will one day."

"I guess so," Julia dropped her head, ashamed of her harsh words, driven by guilt rather than genuine anger.

"Parents aren't infallible you know; they can make mistakes too." Jack took Julia's hand. "But you're definitely not a mistake. I think of you as my daughter you know. I'll always be here for you."

When Julia left to meet a friend, Jack remained in the Rose & Crown and drank alone, something he rarely did these days. His conversation with Julia had taken him into reflection. He couldn't help comparing himself to Julia at that age and thinking how different things had been for him. He'd had little of her confidence and ease with life, borne out of a solid and open childhood, free from the crippling shame and self-doubt he had endured. Yet he felt sorry for Julia, knowing what a difficult thing identity is and how taken for granted it is by the majority of people. Perhaps that's why he could understand more than Beth why Julia needed to search for her father.

Jack's reflections took him to thoughts of his own father and the fog of silence and miscommunication that had settled between them over the years. He realised it was time to practice what he preached.

CHAPTER 26

"I sometimes think I was born at the wrong time," said Tomasz as they descended the steps into the sticky heat of the Cavern Club. "Although the '50's would have suited me better than the'60's: smoky jazz bars, sleazy detectives…"

"You would have got on well with my grandfather," said Julia absently. She was feeling anxious about seeing Finn O'Sullivan again, although this time she was determined not to humiliate herself or let him get away so easily. They had agreed Tomasz would stay with her this time so that she was less of a threat.

"Good gig," she said, when the set had finished and then realised she'd said the same thing last time.

"Thanks, good to see you again."

"This is Tomasz… my friend."

"Hi Tomasz; do you guys want to join us for a drink when we've finished packing up?"

They sat down and were gradually joined by the band members. They chatted about the gig and generally about music.

"Of course everyone is a musician in Liverpool," said Finn.

"Either that or a footballer," said the drummer.

"Or both," another band member chipped in.

"Well, I've never been much use on a football pitch with this dodgy leg!" Finn tapped his right leg. Julia glanced towards Tomasz.

Tomasz reluctantly left the gathering at midnight to go to work, leaving the steamy warmth of the Cavern for the misty coolness of the dock road. He felt irrationally uneasy about leaving Julia in this man's company. Finn seemed to be a nice guy, but Tomasz could already sense a frisson between them and he didn't like it.

Julia remained with the band for another hour until Finn rose to leave and the other band members followed suit. During this time, she discovered that in his teens Finn had come to Liverpool with his family from Wexford in Ireland and that he had played in bands for many years. He said nothing to suggest he had ever been an athlete and his passion for music was clearly evident. Julia knew this didn't rule him out as her father, but it made it less likely. She also found out that he was indeed married.

"It's been good talking to you," he said. "Good luck with the band." He seemed to choose his words carefully. He held out his hand; Julia took it and felt a shudder running from his arm into hers.

The following evening she spoke to Tomasz. "I just feel drawn to him."

"He's a good looking man, Julia. You have to find a way of doing the DNA test, soon; you can't rule him out yet."

"I will, I will, but I don't want to rush it. I mean I don't want to push him away. He'll think I'm a bit weird if I keep turning up at gigs. Anyway you heard what he said about a dodgy leg; he's obviously not an athlete and I still think he looks too young."

"It might be a recent injury. Anyway, whatever you do, do it soon." Tomasz vocalised this more forcefully than he'd intended. Julia frowned.

"OK Tomasz, I will. As soon as I get a chance. It's not as easy as with Ronald Baines you know. I can't just pull out the DNA swab and stick it in his mouth."

"I'm sure you'll find a way."

Julia decided to give it two weeks before actively seeking Finn out again, although she felt agitated at the thought of waiting for so long and had no idea what her next manoeuvre would be. However, before she had to face this challenge, events conspired to create an opportunity. On a bitterly cold Friday night at the beginning of February, Finn came into Modo.

"What a coincidence," she said, her face instantly flushing.

"So this is what you do in your spare time?" His eyes were playful.

"I have to make money somehow. What can I get you?"

"Four pints of Cain's, please."

"So what are you doing in this neck of the woods?" She felt tongue-tied; everything that came out of her mouth sounded prosaic.

"We've been recording in the studio all day, trying to get an album together." Finn had already told her that he worked as well as recorded in a studio in the city centre; it wouldn't be unusual for the band to come here afterwards.

"Oh I'd love to do some recording."

"Well why don't you pop into the studio one lunch time. I'd be happy to show you around."

Finn rejoined his bandmates in a corner of the bar. Julia's eyes continually found their way to him and she took the opportunity to examine his face. She couldn't shake off the feeling that she'd met him before. He was the best looking of the band members by far: his face was slim; his eyes brown and eager like puppies, exploring every corner of the room. His forehead was wide and smooth and his nose long and slim. Julia particularly liked his mouth, which she decided was an Irish mouth, trembling with words and poetry.

An hour went by before it was Finn's turn to buy another round.

"We're on the shorts now. Four of your cheapest single malts, please. How's it going?"

"Busy as always, but I've got the hang of it now. It took a while."

"I bet. I worked in a bar in Dublin one summer when I was nineteen. God it was crazy. The bar was lined with pints of Guinness at different stages of development. It was so crowded we had to pass them over everyone's heads. I kept spilling the damned stuff everywhere."

"What year was that?" her question was incongruous. Finn picked up on it immediately.

"Are you trying to find out how old I am, you little minx?"

"Just wondered."

"A damn sight older than you, to be sure."

"Go on; how old?"

"How old do you think I am?"

"Ooh, thirty-three, thirty-four."

"That's about right."

"What Thirty-four?"

"Yep. Anyway, have you got any gigs coming up? I'd like to return the favour."

"We're not ready yet, give us another couple of months; I'll let you know."

Julia became aware that Susan was giving her a disapproving look. It was OK to flirt but never to spend too much time with one customer.

The following day, before her afternoon shift, Julia called in at the studio to see Finn. He welcomed her with a broad, slightly embarrassed, grin. Julia greatly enjoyed the lesson in sound engineering as well as Finn's company as they sat side by side at the mixing desk. She thought more than once that this could be her father: his voice, his breath, his skin.When she left Modo after her evening shift she found Finn waiting for her outside. It was two o'clock in the morning and he looked deeply uncomfortable.

"Look, I'm not being weird or anything, I've just finished a gig and I wanted to ask you something."

"OK," said Julia, with a scandalously beating heart, "Shall we walk to the bus stop?"

They cut through backstreets talking about this and that, but as they came to a stop beneath the bright lights of the bus depot, awkwardness settled between them.

"What do you want to ask me, Finn?"

"Why my band? Why me?"

"That's a strange question."

"I know, and I don't know why I'm asking it. I just have this nagging feeling that our first meeting was more than a coincidence."

"I told you I just wanted to get some idea of venues for my band."

"Julia you're at music college; everyone knows how to get a gig in Liverpool." His eyes appealed to her for honesty, but she couldn't give it; she was floundering, trying to figure out the least damaging route to take.

"Look," she turned to him, "I liked your songs and I… I fancied you. I didn't realise you were married; when I did I just enjoyed your company. I'm sorry if I've been a pain."

"Julia, you haven't been a pain. It's just that you… disturb me."

"What do you mean?"

"I can't stop thinking about you, but I can't think about you. I'm married; happily."

"Which bus do you get?" she asked, unable to deal with his words.

"Any seventy-something night bus towards Woolton Village."

Julia knew Woolton was on the outskirts of the city, although she wasn't sure exactly where.

"How about you?"

"I can get the 80 or 86; I'm near Penny Lane." They were both painfully aware of the mundanity of their conversation.

"Look, there's your bus," Finn saved them from more small talk, "you'd better jump on; it's late. He called after her, "I've got another gig at the Jacaranda on Thursday night if you want to come." They gave an awkward wave and Julia jumped on the bus, grateful to be gone. On the way home she mulled over the fragmented conversation, trying to fit Finn's words together into something coherent.

She arrived back at her room and went to the windowsill where a bottle of vodka was chilling; she poured a small measure and sipped it neat; a la Tomasz. It was nearly three and halls were quiet, except for the occasional sound of taxis dropping off clubbers from town. She lay on her bed with the curtains open, the moonlight falling in strips across her body. The light was tinged with blue. She held the clear liquid up so that it glistened in the moonlight. Sleep didn't feel at all close.

She looked around the room that she had now made her own. There was a sculpture, bathed in soft light, a gift from Jack. It was a female figure twisted in either ecstasy or agony; it was hard to tell which. On one wall was one of Maddie's paintings, an abstract with mysterious shapes in deep shades of red and indigo. Julia could see endless images hidden there: faces and flowers, dreamscapes and mythical creatures. Tonight she could see an embrace. On another wall was the Lucian Freud print, *The Hotel Bedroom*. This picture fascinated her. A man, the artist, standing in shadow in the room, the woman, her face ravaged, turned from him. Julia pitied the woman. Her thoughts turned to Finn. She felt a strong desire to see him again, yet his words disturbed her as did her heart's response to them.

The following Tuesday evening Julia visited Tomasz at the hostel. They drank tea by the woodstove, now crackling with heat. Julia still enjoyed visiting this shabby place, seeing new faces hopeful with journeys and adventures.

"Guess who came into the bar on Saturday night?"

"Not Finn O'Sullivan by any chance?"

"You don't sound surprised. Don't you think it's a

coincidence?"

"Why should it be?"

"Well, he's never been there before."

"Liverpool is just a big village, Julia; everyone ends up in the same place." Tomasz could feel the tightness of ungenerosity in his voice. He didn't want to play this game of happy coincidence with Julia. "Anyway, he knew you worked there."

"How did he know?"

"You told him when we were at the Cavern. You said you worked in a bar on Wood Street." He saw Julia visibly deflate.

"Oh. Well I didn't say what bar. Anyway, he can't be my father; he's only thirty-four."

"You seem happy about that."

The truth of this hit Julia for the first time; she felt shame. She realised her response must seem strange to Tomasz when her burning mission for months had been to find her father; she didn't understand it herself.

"I am disappointed but I told you, I'm convinced Philip Hardy is my father."

Tomasz raised his eyebrows. "How do you know he isn't lying?"

"About what?"

"His age; all musicians lie; it's part of the game, isn't it?" There was a hard edge to his voice she'd never heard before; she didn't like what he was implying about Finn and inadvertently about her.

"What's your problem Tomasz?"

"I think you're being naïve, Julia. I really think you must find a way to do this DNA test; it's the only way to rule him out. And then… and then you can start your affair with him." Tomasz jumped up and went to the fridge. He took out the vodka bottle and poured a large glass for himself.

"That's a digusting thing to say... how could you say that?"

Tomasz didn't answer. Julia didn't like this new aspect of his character, although she could recognise the ugliness of jealousy, which she considered to be a forgivable trait. She understood that she would have to be selective in what she told him in future.

Tomasz felt shaken by the conversation and was angry with himself for so visibly displaying his emotions to Julia. He could see the inevitable unfolding of what he'd feared from the first moment he saw Julia and Finn together. He sensed already it would be destructive. Since Christmas he had tormented himself with the thought that he was driving Julia away. It had taken every ounce of his strength to resist making love to her that night in her room, but he felt at the time that it was the right thing to do. She had been upset, she was vulnerable; it wasn't the way he wanted it to happen. Now he doubted his decision.

Julia made more effort than usual to get ready that Thursday night, telling herself it was necessary for eliciting what she needed from Finn O'Sullivan. She put on a sheen of lip gloss, some mascara and a fine spray of ridiculously expensive perfume Greg had brought her back from Paris. She felt guilty as she slipped jeans over silk underwear. She hadn't told Tomasz about the gig and it felt like a betrayal.

To her dismay she bumped into Steph on the way out.

"Ooh, where are you going? You look gorgeous." Steph gave a conspiratorial smile. "Have you got a hot date with some guy I don't know about? I thought you were finishing off your assignment, you naughty girl." Julia felt exposed, as if her intentions were written all over her.

"It's kind of a blind date," she said. "I've been roped into it. I'll tell you all about it tomorrow; I have to go –I'm late."

"All the gory details now, all the gory details."

Julia kept up a fast pace to the bus stop. It began to rain and she pushed up an umbrella, cursing the dampness for frizzing her hair. When she arrived at the Jacaranda the band was already playing their second set. Finn smiled and nodded towards her.

Julia bought herself a vodka and cranberry and stood self-consciously by a wall sipping too quickly while searching the room for people she might know. When the band had finished Finn packed up the gear before coming over to her. He looked anxious.

"Do you mind if we go somewhere else. The lads will get the wrong impression if they see us together." Julia noticed the eyes of the other band members skating towards them. "The Cube is usually open late. Can I meet you there in twenty minutes? I'm sorry, I should have thought it through."

"Sure, that's fine."

Julia imagined he was getting cold feet. She felt young and awkward and imagined Finn laughing with his bandmates; telling them she had a crush; she was a nuisance and he'd sent her packing. She walked aimlessly, anticipating the humiliation of sitting alone, hugging a solitary drink until closing time. She finally found the courage to enter the Cube where she hid in a dark corner. When Finn arrived her anxiety dissolved. He kissed her on the cheek and joined her on her side of the table. Julia had once read that it's easy to tell the people who are faithfully married and those having affairs. The first sit opposite each other, while the latter sit on the same side of the table, hungry for intimacy. The word 'affair' shocked her; it wasn't something she associated with herself.

They remained on safe ground talking about music, and Julia found nothing to convince her that this man was her father, but they were the last to go, reluctant to leave the intimacy they had found. They stood in an alleyway behind the pub, the wind whipping stray papers around their legs.

"Can we hug?" Finn asked

"A non-sexual hug?" said Julia.

They moved together and allowed the full length of their bodies to meet. Julia could feel the hardness in his groin. They laid their cheeks one against the other and then moved their heads around so that their lips momentarily brushed and then they were apart.

"I must go," said Finn, breaking the spell. "Can we meet again, somewhere private? We need to talk about what's happening between us."

"Yes where?" Julia found it difficult to breath.

"How about Sunday at eleven o'clock, Sefton Park?"

"OK, where about?"

"Er… let's say by the statue of Eros?" Finn grinned.

Julia could see both embarrassment and mischief in his eyes.

Julia returned to her room and lay on the bed. She thought about the embrace. It had been one of the most powerful experiences of her life so far. She remembered Finn's smell, the warmth of his skin, the pressure of his body against hers. She re-enacted the embrace over and over again in her mind. Sleep seemed an unnecessary occupation and only came with the dawn. When the alarm woke her she felt exhausted and the doubts crept back into her mind. Not about the embrace, or her feelings for Finn, but about his feelings for her; she imagined he would now be regretting their meeting. What was happening to her? Until a few days ago Tomasz had filled her thoughts and occupied her heart. She believed she had the power to conquer his doubts and demolish his defences. But now a new passion had invaded her heart.

For the next few days, she found it difficult to do ordinary things. Music offered some distraction but only for short periods of time. Even then her mind returned to Finn. A pattern of notes, a scent, a breeze, could take her back to that moment in the alleyway.

Sunday came around all too slowly. The day was cool and a stubborn fog hung like damp sheets over the trees in the park, muffling all sound. The sun was trying to push through with little success. She had trouble locating the statue of Eros and eventually had to ask a passer-by, who told her it had been removed for restoration work years earlier and only the plinth now remained, an ornate bronze fountain standing opposite a crumbling café. He was late; only by fifteen minutes but it was excruciating. She paced around the fountain, looking at her watch every few seconds and turning over every possibility in her mind, usually involving Finn's change of mind.

"I'm so sorry." He arrived from an unexpected direction and she jumped. "Angela left late for church."

Angela. Angela – she didn't want that name to intrude on this day.

"It's OK, I've only just arrived," she lied. "I had trouble finding Eros. He's gone."

"Oh." Finn looked up at the space where Eros had once stood, "I didn't realise. I used to play around here with my mates as a kid."

"Oh, that's a shame."

"Anyway, are you OK?"

"Yes, fine thanks."

This was new to them: the unforgiving flat light, the hush only broken by the harsh call of crows. They were in an amphitheatre, exposed to one another. Their voices seemed to fall like stones between them.

"I can't stay long," he said.

Angela must be the reason; although he didn't say it. Is this how it would be?

"Do you want to walk?"

"Yes, that'd be nice." They strolled in no particular direction, close but not touching, making apologies if they happened to brush shoulders. Julia was aware of Finn's slight limp. They talked about the fog, the cold, the naked trees. Julia began to feel despair. With every step she waited for him to announce his departure. How could he choose this over the comfort of a warm house in Woolton and the easy love of a wife? She stopped very suddenly and turned to him.

"Finn, I need us to talk, properly."

"OK." He looked amused and she was glad to see the sparkle return to his eyes. "Do you fancy a cup of tea, I'm bloody freezing?"

They walked back to the café and ordered a pot of tea. The interior of the café was not conducive to intimacy. Red, plastic tables and chairs stood in stark rows alongside two pool tables. The lighting was harsh and the smell of chip fat invaded every corner of the unlovely space. They were alone except for a plump middle-aged waitress who only had the spectacle of them to feed her interest. They found a corner as far from her imposing eyes as possible and cupped their hands around mugs of tea. Now that they had props they both relaxed a little.

"I must say you suit a red nose." Finn laughed.

Julia slapped his arm. "You can't see the icicles hanging off your chin."

"What are we doing here?" Finn once again brought them to the point. "I didn't ever intend to get into something like this."

"What is it we're in?" she asked.

"I do love my wife, Julia."

"I know you do." She placed her hand on his arm. She felt compassion, but she didn't want to hear those words.

"I know a lot of men say that to sound noble while having an affair; but it's true in my case."

"Is that what we're doing, having an affair?"

His eyes softened and they were hers again. He took her hand. "It doesn't feel like an affair. It feels more than that."

Her heart was malleable in his hands. She knew she should be stopping his words, holding her hands up, screaming him to silence, telling him this can't happen, "you could be my father". But she wanted to hear more of his dangerous, delicious words.

"Julia, since Wednesday night, I haven't been able to stop thinking about you; not for one moment. It feels like lunacy; it's driving me crazy." The waitress walked past their table unnecessarily, checking their half-full cups. They waited for her to return to her counter. "Do you feel the same?"

Julia was struck by the intense vulnerability of this question. A question that must have been asked a billion times throughout history, weighted with longing and despair.

"Yes I do. I can hardly concentrate at college." She saw the power of her words, the joy flood his eyes.

"What the hell do we do about it?" He caressed her hand. He had the same long fingers as hers. "Artists hands," her mum always said, comparing them to her own stubby affairs.

"Look, if this is just too hard for you we don't have to do it." Julia at last felt liberated to say these words, only because she knew he was no longer able to act on them.

The waitress hovered again.

"Look, I probably need to go. Do you want to walk over to my car? At least we'll have some privacy there."

They walked back to the park entrance and climbed into Finn's Peugeot. Julia noticed how he struggled to lift his leg into the seat. He turned the engine on to warm the car.

"What happened to your leg?" She couldn't think of a more subtle way of asking.

"It's a war wound." There was mischief in his eyes.

"No seriously, I want to know."

"I was knocked down by a car."

"That's terrible. How old were you?"

"Oh, I was just a kid."

"Is it hard to talk about?"

"It was pretty traumatic at the time; music saved me from going mad."

"Has music always been your passion?"

"Pretty much...hey, what is this, the Spanish Inquisition? Shut your beautiful mouth and kiss me."

Reassured by his words, Julia moved towards him and at last

the kiss came; imperfect and strange but necessary. I couldn't feel this for my own father, she told herself; I would surely feel repulsion; I would know; I would know.

"You're a witch," he said

As she watched his car move away she felt empty and abandoned. She still had the whole day ahead of her, usually a joy but now a burden. She walked down to the river at Otterspool and stood at the railings, looking into the Mersey. She wanted to see the flow of the river, its perpetual movement. It was only the force of the river that captured the rush of passion in her soul and she knew she'd come to the right place. It didn't matter that the water was grey, that what little she could see of the Wirral through the slowly receding fog was undramatic. She wasn't looking for beauty or drama, there was enough of that in her own heart; she was looking for movement, the flow of life to hurry the drag of time. She stayed there for an hour, walking and then stopping every few minutes to look at the water. She knew that something big was happening to her. It wasn't something that needed to be explained; it was elemental. This was her life in all its precarious beauty; and she had no reason to resist it.

She came to a section of river that reminded her of the walk with Tomasz and inevitably to his words. But she didn't want to go there. She found herself walking back into the city, in the direction of the hostel. She was conscious of her lack of control; that she was being blown by every change of wind. She arrived at the hostel to be told that Tomasz was out. Immediately she felt disappointment. What was he doing? Why wasn't he waiting for her?

By the time she left the hostel, the fog had almost vanished like an old memory; the low winter sun mercilessly burning away the last remnants, revealing a day holding all the promise of spring. She longed for Finn to call; to say he had miraculously found time to spend with her. She walked through the city centre but

Liverpool was deadly quiet on Sundays; it had a Sabbath feel, unlike London, which respected no particular faith or creed. The deserted streets only intensified her sense of abandonment.

With little to occupy her agitated mind Julia returned to her room. The light was already fading and the cold claw of night was beginning to scratch. Her mood fluctuated between dread and elation. She was already losing faith in Finn's words. She put on an old Nirvana CD, trying to find something to resonate with her mood. She looked through her book collection; she wanted to read about love, but it had to be a great love, nothing trivial. She had to go back in time to find what she needed, settling for Tolstoy, and the story of *Anna Karenina*.

Finn texted the following day to say he missed her and would call soon. Julia felt the unpleasantness of waiting, like a child perpetually living on Christmas Eve. For a few days she was fine, the kiss and the text sustained her and she trusted that he would call. By Friday the doubts were once again boiling in her mind, forcing out the coolness of trust and reason. He finally called on Saturday morning and asked if they could meet at the same time, the same place, the following day; she thought his voice sounded strained. Sunday was a very different sort of day with clouds racing across a milky-blue sky and a bitter chill stinging the air. Nevertheless Julia's heart was warmed by the prospect of seeing Finn again. But he arrived with a chilling expression on his face; he took her hands between his.

"I don't know if I can do this, Julia." His words sounded carefully chosen. He looked downcast. What had happened to him in just one week? He told her he was going on holiday with Angela the following day, to the French Alps; he said she should forget him; she was young and should be enjoying life with people her own age. Julia thought he wavered even as he spoke but he finished his speech admirably.

"Has something happened?" She couldn't make sense of the

change in him.

"No, not really. It's just I felt so guilty when I got home to Angela last week."

That name, that name; it slashed her heart. She held back tears, but knew Finn would see the emotion beneath, just as Tomasz had.

"Look. Perhaps if I am away for a couple of weeks it will give me time to think about this. I can't bear the thought of not seeing you… but… I just don't want to hurt her."

"Look," Julia took control. "Let's talk when you're back; I'll understand if you can't do it."

It was better to have a small hope than face the awful prospect of never seeing him again. What she felt for Finn was stronger than anything she'd ever known: she hadn't found her father; she'd found her soul-mate. This is how she explained the overwhelming rush of passion that filled her soul, washing away the comparatively gentle flow of feelings for Tomasz.

*

When Finn returned from the French Alps he was a different man: Julia could see that a switch had been turned on – or perhaps off – in him, and he came to her with a fierce and ardent purpose that was both thrilling and terrifying. Through the days of spring they engaged in an intense affair, meeting at every opportunity, stealing time wherever they could find it. They met in all the dark and seedy pubs of Liverpool where they were unlikely to be seen, and on warmer days, when Finn could manage it, they stole away to the Wirral or Cheshire where they made love in dense coppices or isolated meadows, hidden by trees and wild flowers.

It was an addiction as intense as anything either of them had experienced. Sometimes she would sit in his lap and they would rock, slowly, together, or she would ask him to lie on top of her so that as much of their flesh was in contact as possible. They frequently described to each other their dilemma of wanting to devour each other, to meld atoms, marrow, bone and flesh, as their separation was so painful; yet at the same time to survive so that they could maintain separateness and therefore look upon and love the other. Like many lovers before them, they had a primordial sense of having belonged to one another all their lives, of finding the missing part of themselves. It was generally Julia who described these overwhelming feelings but Finn was quick to agree.

Julia could see that at times Finn found the amount of deceit involved in the affair stressful, especially when he had to lie directly to Angela. He made guilty phone calls, convinced that Angela would hear the lies in his voice and, when he returned home, notice the flush of love on his face, the scent of lust on his skin. But as time went by Julia knew that after only a few hours without her his longing would grow to an unbearable shriek that would obliterate the guilt. She knew this because the same thing happened to her.

CHAPTER 27

Julia hurried alone through Princes Park aware of the fading light and the menacing wind whipping the trees. It was unusually warm for May and this, combined with the strange, lustrous light, was thrilling. She wished Finn was with her now. She wanted him in every moment and the fact he was not there took the joy from things. The thought of seeing him later sent a shudder through her body that felt both spiritual and carnal.

After the first few heady weeks of the affair, when nothing mattered except the uncontaminated pleasure of being with him, Julia was now feeling the true agonies of illicit love, with all of its imposed boundaries. It was not an equal relationship: She had all the time in the world to be with Finn while he had none that wasn't borrowed or stolen. It created imbalance. She felt like a nomad in her own life wandering between hope and despair.

"Do you want coffee?" Tomasz asked.

"Er..." she looked at her watch. "Yeah go on."

"You got somewhere to go?" He already felt the dullness of her impending absence and she had only been there for ten minutes.

"Oh just something with college people." She was shocked at how easily the lies were now flowing. Tomasz didn't even blink. "How's the novel coming on?" she asked, drawing his attention away from the subject.

"I told you, I'm writing short stories at the moment." He was irritated that she hadn't remembered. "They're going pretty well,

I think."

"When can I read something?"

"You don't appear to have a lot of time these days."

"I would make time, Tomasz." She tried to keep the mood light, not wanting a repeat of previous visits when things had become hideously strained.

"So have you done the DNA test yet?" Tomasz couldn't play games; his pressing need was to know what his own future held and as far as he was concerned that depended on the results of the test. Julia was mistress of his agony and his ecstasy.

"I told you, I'm just waiting for the right moment, and anyway they're bloody expensive." She shifted uneasily in her seat.

"It's been months, Julia; when will be the right time?"

"I know he's not my father; it would only be a paper exercise."

"Then do it. He looks like you."

"Rubbish, he looks nothing like me; he's got stubble on his chin."

"Don't joke about it, Julia."

"Well don't be so damned serious all the time."

"It's your life darling." Tomasz jumped up and grabbed the coffee pot, wordlessly offering it to her. She refused with a dismissive wave of her hand.

"Yes Tomasz, it is and I'm kind of sick of your interference."

"Well piss off then silly child." He turned his back on her.

His words were hurtful and she felt tears pushing behind her eyes. She couldn't let him see her cry; it would only compound his view of her as an immature child. Without speaking she stood up, pulled her bag over her shoulder and left the room.

As Julia walked home the rain fell around her like bullets from a metallic sky, stinging her exposed skin. She felt torn by the row with Tomasz; she couldn't seem to make things right. She hadn't been honest with him about the extent of her feelings for Finn and he had no idea they'd been engaged in an affair for nearly three months. But she could tell he sensed something and was deeply concerned. She decided to let things settle for a couple of weeks before seeing Tomasz again. In the meantime she would do the DNA test to put his mind at rest.

Tomasz felt a familiar depression descend on him; it had been gloriously absent from his life for months and its return brought terror to his heart in a way that its constant presence over the years never had. He had been so certain that he'd made progress; that he was at last free of the beast but its prowling return told him his soul was still fragile, that his recovery was an illusion and that nothing was certain. He realised he had placed too much hope in Julia as his light in the darkness and this was unfair to expect of anyone. He longed for the stasis he had experienced prior to her arrival at the hostel, when he had found a kind of contentment in the daily routine of writing, working, sleeping, eating and the other protective mundanities of his life. He knew that his anger towards Julia was unfair; she had made no promises. He was ridiculous.

For the first time in months Tomasz drank beyond his limit and until he was unable to stand straight. He insulted guests at the hostel until the manager told him that unless he went to bed to sleep it off he would have to leave. He did go to bed and fell into a troubled sleep. He awoke late the next day and after two strong coffees he found some clarity in his thinking. He could not bear to completely break the connection with Julia but neither could he continue to see her. He didn't believe she would do the DNA test or that she cared enough about him to listen to his advice; but he couldn't stop caring for her. Once he had decided what he must do there was no turning back. He packed a bag and checked out of the hostel.

*

They had never spent the night together and it had become a burning desire for them both. Not sex, just the intimacy of sleeping side by side. They had to make do with an afternoon nap every now and then, when Finn had a rare few hours free. Julia never slept at these times; she was too excited by Finn's presence, but Finn was a good sleeper, easily lost in a deep, unshakable slumber. Julia would lie with him for a while, study his face, younger in sleep, imagining what it would have been like to know him when he was seven or ten, an adolescent boy or a young man. She was jealous of his past; she wanted it all. Then she would get up and potter about her room for a time until she was even jealous of his sleep and would shake him brutally back to her.

Following a late gig one Thursday night at the end of May, Finn booked the Friday off from the studio and came round to Julia's room at lunchtime. Julia didn't bother going into college; the end of year exams were drawing near and most of her time was spent completing assignments or practicing keyboards. She prepared lunch and opened a bottle of wine. They made love in Julia's narrow bed and then lay with their limbs tangled. Finn, heavy with wine and tiredness, soon drifted off while Julia lay still beside him, enthralled by what she saw as a child-like ability to sleep at the drop of a hat. After a few minutes she untangled herself, pulled a carefully placed DNA test from under the bed and extracted a swab, all the time watching Finn's face. She hadn't been able to think about what she would say if he suddenly woke up and her heart was beating furiously. She lay naked and poised with the swab for some time before his lips parted slightly and she took the opportunity to insert the slim stick into his mouth and rub it gently around his inner cheek. He stirred and she stilled the stick for a few seconds, only moving it again when he settled. She quickly replaced the lid and dropped the swab into a plastic wallet before hiding it under the bed once more.

When Finn left, she repeated the process with a fresh swab on her own cheek, dropping it into the same plastic wallet. She then placed the wallet into an envelope along with a signed document and walked to the post office on Penny Lane. Her hand trembled as it hovered over the post-box, envelope clutched and ready to go. As she allowed the envelope to fall soundlessly into the chasm she felt she was committing an act of betrayal; it had all been too easy.

She didn't hear from Finn for a week after that and she started to believe that he sensed her betrayal. It was unusual for him not to text or call every day, expressing his longing to see her, to make love to her, to be with her. She felt sick with worry, imagining every awful possibility from his physical death to the even worse death of his love. She wondered if Angela had found out about the affair and she felt both excited and worried by this thought. She was tempted to text him, although they had agreed she would only do so in a dire emergency, but she resisted, deciding she would give it a few more days. She distracted herself with coursework and the effortless company of college friends, but this became less effective with each passing day.

True to her decision Julia hadn't been back to the hostel for two weeks and Tomasz hadn't made any attempt to contact her; but now she was eager to tell him she had carried out the DNA test. She missed his friendship and hoped to make things right between them. She was shocked when a member of staff told her Tomasz had checked out of the hostel two weeks earlier and hadn't been back since. She left a message asking him to contact her as soon as he returned and then she walked back through Falkner Square, feeling that a frightening and uncertain shift was taking place in her life.

CHAPTER 28

With the arrival of spring, Finn became aware that Angela, was slowly unfolding, stretching and lifting her head towards the sun. She tentatively reached out towards him and he knew she must have been shaken when he did not instantly reach back.

At the end of May, after a particularly glorious afternoon spent with Julia eating, drinking and lovemaking, he arrived home to be reminded by Angela that it was their wedding anniversary and that she'd booked a meal in their favourite restaurant; Finn was sure her intention was to revive their floundering relationship.

"Finn, you know how much I love you don't you?" she said after dessert.

"Of course I do darling."

"I am sorry I've been so distant."

"Don't apologise; you've been grieving... we both have; it takes time." He held her hand, hoping to still her words, which were just too difficult to hear. But her eyes opened up before him like two black roses and Finn was shaken by the love he saw still buried in the centre. They made love that night with the tenderness that had been so long absent. Finn found this unbearable. He had relied on their distance for the affair with Julia to continue. It would never have started in the first place, he reasoned, if it were not for their awful loss and Angela's unbending grief. He knew that if his relationship with Angela became what it once was, it could not tolerate an affair. Yet, the lovemaking Finn experienced with Julia burned into his soul so that nothing else could compare, not even the tender unions with his wife.

Finn could no longer bear the deceit. He avoided Julia for a week, switching off his mobile phone, as well as his emotions and self-medicating with alcohol to numb the pain. One night, however, he was out with his bandmates following a gig in town when he saw Julia with another man. The jealousy that seared through his heart was instant and merciless. He had to stop himself from running to Julia and flooring the man.

Instead, he watched from a distance feeling impotent, while his lover disappeared into the night. Finn's already shaky resolve completely crumbled and on Sunday morning, nine days after their last union, he called her. However, Julia's trust had been severely tested and she was angry that he had left her for so long in a state of pernicious agony. When he asked if he could see her, she was cool. She told him she'd had a late night clubbing with Dan, her college friend, and that she wanted to "chill" on her own. When he pressed her further she said she had a busy week coming up at college and she suggested they meet the following weekend.

Finn could only think of the man he had seen with Julia, who now had a name, Dan. He was young, handsome and available. Dan could give Julia what he couldn't – time.

By Wednesday Finn could bear it no longer. He'd convinced himself Julia was seeing Dan, and if not Dan then the Polish bloke. Finn had always been jealous of Tomasz, although Julia had tried to convince him that Tomasz was just a good friend.

After rehearsal on Wednesday evening, Finn quickly knocked back a couple of pints with his bandmates and then made his excuses. He bought a bottle of wine from an off-licence on Smithdown Road and made his way to Julia's halls. Standing beneath her window he called her on his mobile. There was no answer. He then asked for her at reception but was told she was out. Where the hell was she at this time of night? He could only think that she was out with Dan and this thought incited him to anger. He did what he had never done before and used the key Julia had given him on his birthday, wrapped in an inordinate amount of purple tissue paper, to let himself in. Frank, the security guard, was in the lobby but he was now familiar with Finn's visits and didn't ask questions. They made small waves to each other as Finn passed. On his way up to her room Finn noticed mail in Julia's pigeon-hole. This upset him further as it seemed she hadn't been home all day. He grabbed the bundle as he passed.

The corridors and stairways, usually alive with the thud of music and student laughter, were now almost deserted and he was overtaken with a new fear that she'd gone home to London for the summer without telling him. He was relieved when he let himself into her room to see an unwashed coffee cup and clothes strewn across the bed. He threw the mail onto her paper-cluttered desk and lay down on crumpled bed sheets. He opened the wine with the corkscrew on Julia's bedside table and poured himself a large glass. He loved this room – the posters on the wall, the carefree mess of student life – it was brimming with youthful optimism and was the scene of the sweet, illicit love that had filled the empty corners of his life for over three months.

He buried his face in the scents of her pillow, willing her to come home. "I love you my darling," he muttered, "everything will be alright if you just come home to me now." He filled his glass again and felt the red poison intoxicate his mind. The thought struck him that she might not come home at all that night and if she didn't he would go insane. In his agitation he jumped from the bed and fell back down immediately when dizziness overtook him. He hadn't eaten well for days and the alcohol moved quickly through his blood. He waited until the dizziness subsided and then slowly stood and walked over to her few shelves, and browsed through the CD collection.

His attention was drawn to her small desk and with the permissiveness of passion he searched without shame through the drawers. Among piles of revision notes and bank statements he was surprised to find a sheet of paper covered with his signature.

On closer inspection he realised they had been copied from an original, over and over again, and that by the end of the page they were pretty convincing. He smiled at this endearing obsession in his beloved. She was always saying strange and lovely things, like how she wanted to possess him, to know him at every age of his life. She was such a thinker; it was hard to keep up with her at times.

With tears pushing the back of his eyes he returned to the bed and gulped down another glass of wine, trying to still the anxiety that was rising to fever pitch. It was now two in the morning and she still wasn't home.

From the bed his eyes scanned the corners of her room; the room that contained all the objects of her life. He remembered a time when he could barely fill a room with his own possessions and now he'd accumulated enough clutter to fill a three-bed house; so many unnecessary things. His eyes fell on the pile of mail scattered on top of the desk. He jumped up again and gathered the envelopes in his hands, examining each in turn. Two of the letters had London postmarks: one, a red envelope with fancy hand writing on the front, looked as though it might be from a female friend. He had an overwhelming desire to open it; perhaps Julia had confided in this friend. He boiled the kettle and eased it open over the gush of steam. It wasn't as easy as he'd thought, especially when drunk, and he tore the envelope. Inside was an invitation to a friend's birthday party in Soho on 6th August. There was a little hand written note:

Hi Jules,

We're all missing you. Hope you're having fun in little old Liverpool. Can't wait to see you and catch up on all the goss. Here's to long summer days (and long summer snogs I hope).

Carrie x

Everything was a threat. There was no stopping him now; he

opened another letter containing information about upcoming events at the Playhouse. It only highlighted the things he'd never been able to do with her; the things she could do with other men. He didn't bother with the music magazine that lay exposed under a plastic wrapping, but he opened the official letter with the London postmark.

It was difficult to make out what it was about. At the top it said *Test Report* and underneath, *Results of DNA Analysis*. There was a case number and the name of the company, *London DNA Services*, and then Julia's name as the client. Beneath that it said *Motherless Paternity Test* and the date of receipt of the items: *15th May 2004*. A confusing list of numbers and codes swam before his eyes and then he focused on his own name: *alleged father, Finn O'Sullivan*. With a dry mouth he continued to read.

Explanation of the motherless paternity test: When the mother is unavailable for paternity testing, a Motherless Paternity Test is conducted to prove that a man is or is not the biological father of another person.

This was followed by more numbers and Xs and Ys in various columns, headed *child* and *alleged father*.

There was then a sentence that filled him with horror: *Interpretation: Based on the DNA analysis, the alleged father (Finn O'Sullivan) IS NOT EXCLUDED AS THE BIOLOGICAL Father of the child (Julia Swann) Our opinion of PROBABILITY OF PATERNITY is based on the above noted consistencies. The term consistent means the band sizes of the tested alleged father match the corresponding band sizes present in the child.* The letter was approved by *Dr K Greene (Molecular geneticist)* and *Dr Mohammed Hussein (DNA Analyst)*.

There were various FAQ's: *What does: 'NOT EXCLUDED as the biological father' mean. It means that the tested man (alleged father) has the DNA profile (bands) expected of the biological father. Hence the result is consistent with the fact that the tested man (alleged father) is the biological father of the child. What does*

'PROBABILITY OF PATERNITY' mean? This is the percentage likelihood that a man with the genetic markers (alleles) of the alleged father is the biological father of the child as compared to an untested and unrelated man of the same ethnic origin.

The meaning finally forced its way into Finn's alcohol addled brain and he fell onto the bed groaning and clutching the paper. He tried to fight his way through the haze to make sense of what he'd just read. His thoughts flew to their first meeting; her questions; the recognition; his gut feeling that she had engineered the meeting. Everything slotted together into hideous sense. But why in God's name had she started the affair? In a sickening plunge Julia descended from angel to demon. Finn jumped from the bed and threw up in the sink. He rinsed his face and swallowed mouthfuls of water, then, as his mind screamed into lucidity, he flew to her desk again. He had seen her passport when searching through the drawers but he'd only looked at the photograph, taking a moment to admire the beauty that was his. This time he looked at the date-of-birth, 1st September 1984. She wasn't yet twenty-years-old. She had deceived him from the start. Then he remembered his own lie. But it was an innocent lie compared to hers. He studied the photograph again. Did he now see a demonic glint in the eyes he had adored? Was that serene smile in fact the leer of a mad woman? His daughter? His daughter. He lay on the bed thinking and trembling and thinking; trying to find alternative explanations for the madness. His thoughts eventually turned to Angela.

There had never been a question of whether they should be together, and although he'd indulged in a string of relationships before he met Angela, he hadn't felt he was giving anything up when he surrendered his heart. She was a calm and certain person with clear plans for the future – she would finish her degree, complete her legal training, marry, work for five years and then have children – two. She would remain involved in a little legal work, to keep her finger in the pie, until she returned to her career only once the children were safely in school. Finn loved her certainty. He believed Angela led him in the right direction; prevented him from making impulsive decisions.

Like his father Finn had discovered a talent for athletics at an early age. He had been the best athlete in his school in Wexford, winning numerous medals at sports days. He moved to Liverpool with his parents in 1976, at the age of twelve, when his father was offered a job at Ford's. While Finn faced initial bullying because of his accent, he was resilient and likable. He excelled at sports and used this as well as his humour to win over his peers. His father urged him to join Liverpool Harriers, hoping Finn would achieve what he was never able to. However, in the bigger pond of club athletics Finn realised that his talent might not be as great as he and his father had initially hoped.

When Finn was fifteen, a school friend invited him to Eric's, 'the coolest club in Liverpool'. Eric's had come up with an innovative scheme to allow under eighteen's to see top bands by introducing alcohol-free matinee performances. They saw Teardrop Explodes and Echo and the Bunnymen; Finn felt intensely excited and was inspired by Will Sergeant's guitar playing. From that point on he spent any spare cash he had on records; music took over from athletics as his obsession.

Nevertheless, as he moved through sixth-form College and into his first year at Liverpool University Finn continued to dedicate himself to athletics. He lived a sober life mainly socialising with other athletes, avoiding too many drunken nights and competing most weekends. However, he was increasingly aware he was now a small fish and that he had to work harder than other athletes to achieve success. With the many temptations on offer at university he was losing interest in the rigors of the athletic lifestyle; at times he hated it.

One October night at the beginning of his second year at University, Finn was hit by a car while out running. The bones of his lower right leg were shattered and he was unable to walk without crutches for several months, never mind run. Mixed with his devastation about the damage to his physical appearance and the frustration about his lack of mobility, he also felt a guilty modicum of relief. He had an excellent excuse not to train or compete again, without the need to disappoint anyone. Unable to do much for himself during the long process of recovery he moved back to live with his parent's, who were now ensconced in leafy Cheshire. They showered him with care, trying to compensate for the despair they imagined he must be feeling at the tragic end to his athletics career. When Finn returned to halls two months later he was relieved to escape what he felt was the undeserved pity of his parents. However, still unable to easily get around Finn was soon bored. It was a friend who suggested he take up a musical instrument to pass the time.

On one of his many visits to the hospital for check-ups, Finn saw a leaflet in the waiting room asking for sperm donors, for a small financial reward. Not thinking too much about what it meant and desperate for cash, he struggled on his crutches against an obstinate November wind to the clinic on Park Road. The blushing nurse asked him a lot of questions, including why he was on crutches. He told her he'd been a promising athlete but could no long run due to an accident, adding, "But don't write that down; I'd rather you say I was a musician."

He became a character around the campus, hopping around on crutches, guitar flung over one shoulder, drowning his sorrows at the bar. He felt the sweet tragedy of his life and realised what a powerful aphrodisiac this was to women. In a short space of time he went from clean-cut athlete to long-haired musician. Angela fell for this persona and eventually the man beneath. They met at a party on the last day of term; they kissed and danced all night and, when Angela returned to her family home in the South East of England, he thought of her longingly all through the summer break. When they met again in September they knew they wanted to be together.

They married in a registry office in May 1986, the same year that Angela moved into her first law firm. After graduating Finn trained as a sound engineer and after a year on the dole he found work as a technician in a recording studio in town. When Angela was twenty-nine, they tried for a baby but this didn't go to plan; she had three miscarriages over four years. Finally, after numerous tests and five years she became pregnant again. With careful monitoring and bed-rest she carried the baby to twenty-eight weeks. However, she suffered massive internal bleeding and the baby boy was delivered by caesarean and kept in an incubator. They called him Richard after Finn's father. But after ten weeks he gave up his struggle. They stood over him in the hospital room, stroked his tiny hands and watched him die. Angela was told she might have difficulty conceiving again.

Two years later Finn began to see some light, but his wife was still lost to grief and was unable to return to work. Finn didn't know how to help Angela – she had always been the strong one in the relationship. It was at this time that Angela started to attend church in Woolton; it was another part of her life from which Finn felt excluded.

They lived in a state of fragile harmony. At first Finn desperately tried to recreate their former closeness with exotic holidays and romantic dinners, but after another year of frustrated effort he gave up, feeling angry with Angela for abandoning him. It was at that point he met the beautiful young woman in the cellar bar.

Her substantiveness was shocking when he'd been living with a shadow for so long. Now he knew her substance was the same as his own; exactly his own.

Finn felt the full horror of his situation; it weighed down every inch of his body. He fell from the bed and stumbled from the room. He felt grateful to see a black cab outside. He jumped in and sank heavily into the back seat.

CHAPTER 29

Julia had worked in the library with Steph until late to complete her final assignment and then they'd sidled into town to celebrate the end of term with Dan and Jamaal and some other students. The celebrations had been spoilt for Julia because of her aching heart and she now had to decide whether to remain in Liverpool for a few more weeks or return to London for the summer. She was tempted to punish Finn by leaving for London immediately, but she knew in her heart that she couldn't leave the place where he lived and moved and had his being.

She sensed something was wrong even before she saw the rumpled bed and mess of papers scattered about the floor. The rank smell of vomit lingered in the room and she noticed the empty wine bottle on the bedside table. Her first thought was that she'd been burgled, although there was no evidence of it at the door or window. She picked up the party invite from Carrie. Why had it been opened? She gathered the opened mail from the floor trying to make sense of what had taken place. It was then that she found the letter from London DNA Services. The disintegration of her psyche began almost immediately.

"No," she said aloud "No, no, no."

She lay on the bed curled into a foetal position, hugging her knees. Her mind flew to Finn, wanting his comfort; she realised the anomaly of this and groaned. Her mind couldn't coalesce the man who was her lover with the man who was her father. Each time she realised they were one and the same, her mind skated away in another direction. After moments of agonised thought she picked up her mobile and called Finn; it went straight to voicemail but she didn't leave a message. She tried many times through the rest of that interminable night, but was unable to reach him. Finally at eight o'clock in the morning she left a message, "Please call me." She drank vodka to ease the unremitting pain in her heart, but the pain defied the alcohol, rising like a discordant note again and again.

All that day Julia stayed in her room, ignoring phone calls from anyone who wasn't Finn, and Finn didn't call. By the end of the day, and after reading the test results a hundred times, she had convinced herself that they were wrong. Phrases like 'Probability of paternity' and 'Is not excluded' were not certain enough for her. She had to see Finn to convince him the results were wrong.

It wasn't until early evening that he called.

He said. "We have to talk." His voice was barely audible.

They met by the plinth, which they still referred to as Eros, now mocked by his absence. Finn couldn't look her in the eyes.

"What's wrong with you?" His voice was strangled. "You must have known."

"I really didn't think it could be you." She tried to explain as calmly as she could what had happened, the sequence of events, all the time aware of the implausibility of her own story. He shook his head, his mouth agape as if he couldn't comprehend, as if she was using a foreign language.

"How could you let it happen, Julia? You must be crazy. It's horrendous."

"Perhaps the test was wrong; it's only…."

Now he did look into her eyes; in disbelief. "Julia, you have to wake up to what is going on. This is real. I am your… father." He sounded as if he might choke on the word.

Julia felt uprooted; tears spilled from her eyes. Finn hesitated momentarily, looking as though he might go to her, but then he seemed to shake away any urge to compassion. Julia took a step towards him. He backed away; recoiled; lifted his hands as if to shield himself from danger.

"Look. Don't contact me again." His voice was raised in anger, although it sounded false to Julia. "I don't want to see you. It's best."

"Please, Finn; we love each other." She knew her words were lunacy.

He looked at her again, incredulous. "You must be insane. You've ruined my life." His voice was quiet now and this was more frightening to Julia than the shouting. He turned from her and walked away.

She screamed after him, "And you're responsible for mine."

He left her standing alone under the statue-less plinth. She felt bewildered; incapacitated. She fell to the ground and sobbed.

"Are you OK?" A young couple hovered above her, holding hands. "Can we help?"

"Thank you… I'm OK."

"Are you sure?"

"Yes. I've just had bad news. I'm… going home."

The look of concern remained on their faces as they left her.

Halls were mercifully deserted; nearly all the students had left for the summer. Julia returned to her room and lay on the bed. The light soon faded from a day that had never really brightened. All objects in the room lost definition as the colour leaked from them, leaving a blanched, insipid version of themselves. Julia felt objectified, with no more substance than the curtains or desk, the bed or the books on the shelf; she felt she was seeing the real state of things. The Lucian Freud was disappearing into murky grey and the artist now looked sinister standing in the shadows by the window with the austere Parisian architecture outside. The woman lay in rumpled sheets, her face ravaged, her expression desperate. Julia no longer pitied her; she could fully identify with this woman's despair. As she stared the painting faded, faded, faded, each figure disappearing into blackness.

She was woken by a noise outside. It was three a.m. and soft orange light from a street-lamp spilled through the window. She heard a group of revellers, their voices loud in drunken inhibition. Their shouts were accompanied by the ragged sound of barking. She went to the window and was about to pull the curtains across when she noticed a dark figure standing on the opposite side of the road. It was a man but the light was still too poor to see much and his face was obscured by the rim of a hat. She thought it might be Finn and she considered running down to him but then the figure turned abruptly and marched away.

She drew the curtains and switched on a lamp. She made herself tea, which she sipped absently, still disorientated with the weight of a profound sleep. She slept for several more hours. It was as if her mind and body were shutting down; sleep was a gift, an escape from horror. When she woke at eight, denial had once again set in. She showered and dressed and made her way to Wood Street for her evening shift at the bar. Susan looked at her more closely than usual.

"Are you OK; you look weird?"

"I'm fine," said Julia, "I just have a stomach ache."

"Have you been partying with your friends again?" The tone wasn't unfriendly but there was admonishment in Susan's question.

Julia smiled, grateful for the lead. "OK, I admit it; I have. I handed in my last assignment on Wednesday; been celebrating ever since."

"OK, well get to work. We've got a party in here tonight and Debbie's rung in sick. I need all hands on deck." Julia worked harder than ever, anticipating every job, working quickly and efficiently. The effort was exhausting and she fell into bed at three, sleeping solidly until one o'clock the following afternoon. In a daze she made her way to the bar for the afternoon followed by the evening shift.

Much of Sunday was lost to a torpid sleep and she awoke feeling unrefreshed and with a slow gnawing pain; her stomach had been so knotted, she had hardly eaten for days. She showered and dressed with the intention of first strolling through Greenbank Park to clear her head and then buying provisions. But when she stepped outside she was startled to discover a day exploding into summer. She could hardly bear to breath in: the smell of fresh air made her think of him, the seductive sweetness of mowed grass was him; the scent of roses and wallflowers was the aroma of their love: every new bud, tree's sap, dew drop, quality of light, semi-tone of nature, gnats breath, leaf's whisper, cat's cry, all and everything was him.

She quickly left the park and headed for the safety of shops, dragging items indiscriminately from shelves, paying for them and retreating to her room. She ate bread, cheese and olives and read the newspaper, somehow occupying the empty corners of the day. Always her mind was turning, turning; trying to make sense of the nightmare in which she found herself. She wanted to do the test again, use a different company. If only he would agree. He must surely see the impossibility of such a passion existing between flesh and blood. She ventured down to the TV lounge, clutching her mobile phone, in case, in case. She sat in the dark, watching TV until midnight, staring, but not seeing.

The following morning she woke with a strong resolve. She must see him. As she sipped coffee she arrived at a plan; it was a plan hatched from the lunacy of grief. She pulled all of her clothes from the wardrobe and laid them out in a colourful fan on the bed. She chose an outfit she'd bought for a wedding several years earlier but never worn since. She put it on and then tied her hair up in a tight knot on top of her head. She applied heavy make-up and slipped on a pair of heels. Finally she placed a pair of large, sunglasses on her head. She looked in the mirror and was pleased with the result; she looked like a sales rep or a beautician.

She left halls, pulled the sunglasses over her eyes and headed purposefully for the studio on Parr Street.

Julia knew that Finn left the studio most lunchtimes for fresh air and a bite to eat. She waited in the shadows of a doorway opposite for what seemed an eternity, unable to move for fear of missing him. She was heartened by the thought that his devastation had kept him from work but then he appeared with a colleague. His dark head lifted briefly towards her so that she saw a quick flash of his capricious eyes.

The brief glimpse of him only made the longing worse; she didn't know how he could be going about his business so nonchalantly when she was crumbling.

There was a thundery quality to the light. She walked home past the skeletal remains of the bombed out church. She was a stalker; there was no other word for it. Looking upwards, the sky seemed impenetrable, like hammered metal; she felt it might close in on her, fall and crush her along with this fragile city. She suddenly had a sense that she was being followed; she quickly turned, looking all around her, but there was no-one about.

Despite Julia's resolve not to repeat her humiliating actions, she did so two days later. This time she followed at a safe distance. He was alone and seemed to walk with no clear plan or purpose. She thought he looked older and in the exposing sunlight she noticed grey peppering his hair and a thickness setting in around his waist. She thought he must be suffering too and she pitied him.

Back at halls that evening she tried to practice keyboards but had little motivation and instead she read, flitting butterfly-like between the pages of novels, searching for something to make sense of things. She called her mum to say she would stay in Liverpool a little while longer to play some gigs with the band.

She ignored the disappointment in her mum's voice.

The following day she ventured along Allerton Road browsing in charity shops and to her delight she even found a cheap blond wig. That night, wearing one of the outfits, she followed Finn home to Woolton on the bus. She sat where she could see him and she studied the movements of his head as he turned to glance out of the window. She thought she would cut off her own hand to know what was in his mind.

He jumped off the bus on the elegant tree-lined boulevard of Menlove Avenue and walked into Woolton Village. Julia followed. The older houses of the village were mainly built of red sandstone but Finn turned into a road of modern, brick-built semis with small front gardens. At last, she saw where he disappeared to when he left her. She watched the sun drop behind his house and the flickering on of electric lights. She imagined his life inside the rooms of the house, carrying out the sacred rites of married life.

She returned to halls shocked by how far she had gone. In a sudden reaction, she stuffed the newly acquired clothes and accessories into a black bin bag and tied a tight double knot. The following day, with the freshness of self-disgust still in her heart she went out to visit some of the museums and art galleries in the city centre, dumping the bag in the large communal bins on the way out. She avoided the studio and returned to halls at five to get ready for her evening shift at the bar.

"Are you sure you're Ok?" Susan asked, scrutinising Julia's face, "You look as if you've lost weight and you're very pale."

"I'm fine; just a bit tired." Julia was actually in a buoyant mood. She felt high after the purging ritual; certain she must be on the road to recovery.

"I'll probably go back to London next week," she told Susan at the end of the shift.

"That's OK; it's quiet with the students gone, but can you let me know for definite tomorrow?"

Julia didn't sleep well that night. She became fixated on the clothes in the bin. In the terrifying loneliness of the night, they took on gargantuan significance. At five, she pulled clothes over her nightwear and went down to the bin storage. With great difficulty she toppled the large bin and extracted the bag, which was now covered in stinking slops. She carried it up to her room, tore it open like a wild cat and emptied the clothes into a pile on the floor. She scrunched up the shredded bag and threw it into the bin. Then she switched off the lights and fell back into a relieved sleep.

The weekend passed in a blur of work and sleep. On Monday Julia returned to Woolton Village in disguise, telling herself it was part of the grieving process, a way of coming to terms with things.

She stood at some distance from the house. In the daylight she could see the details of the manicured garden lined with chrysanthemums and yellow tea roses. She waited for some time before her rival stepped gazelle-like from the house. She was petite and elegant with a straight-backed walk and a graceful turn of head. She wore white-cotton pants, a navy blue t-shirt, a white silk scarf and black ballet pumps. Julia guessed the clothes were expensive. Her hair was cut in a short, sensible style but with French flair. She only caught a brief glimpse of a small oval face before Angela turned and walked towards the village centre. She wasn't what Julia had imagined. She had the assurance and sophistication of a thirty-something woman, at home in her skin, but with none of the dowdiness that can come with middle age. Angela's reality had been brutally stamped out as a prerequisite for the affair but now she moved before Julia, terrifyingly substantial.

Julia followed Angela onto the main street and watched her go in and out of the grocer's and the fishmonger's. Eventually, Angela entered a café and Julia followed. The decor was flowery with little white lace-draped tables baring identical stainless steel condiment sets and tiny white vases of artificial flowers. There were a couple of elderly ladies at one table and a man reading a paper at another. Julia positioned herself where she could see Angela's face, bathed in sunlight from the window. The sun exposed the truth: fine lines and dark circles framed eyes that were pink and puffy. She's been crying, was Julia's first thought and, then, with a leap of the heart, she knows the truth. After several minutes a woman entered the café; she had a pinched expression. Angela greeted her warmly with a kiss to the cheek. They ordered food and then fell into easy conversation, speaking quietly so that Julia could barely hear.

"Are you OK?" the woman asked. "You look terrible."

Angela smiled weakly. "You know, as well as can be expected."

"What happened?"

Angela leaned in towards the friend and spoke in a hushed tone that was inaudible to Julia; the rest of the conversation was lost to her. However, the few words she heard as well as Angela's expressions confirmed to her that things were not well. She carried this small hope for the next seven days, resisting the urge to follow either Finn or his wife. She took as many shifts in the bar as Susan could give her, covering staff holidays and sick leave. Between shifts she collapsed into bed grateful for the torpid sleep that overwhelmed her.

Sunday was her day off and with too much distended time on her hands she succumbed again to her compulsion. She took the bus to Woolton Village and waited by the lych gate at St Peter's church. Angela appeared ten minutes before the start of the service and didn't immediately enter the church but instead wandered around the grounds, stopping occasionally to read inscriptions carved on gravestones. She came to a halt by a white headstone on the outer edge of the churchyard, where the newer graves were laid. Above the stone was a small cherub, head bowed towards the earth and flowers clutched to its rounded belly. Julia watched spellbound from the camouflage of a Yew Tree as Angela placed her hand on the cherub's head and traced her fingers over its unmalleable curls, across its snub nose and rosebud mouth. Angela's mouth moved silently, whispering secret words. She crouched on her haunches in front of the grave, still whispering. Finally she moved her slender hand to her mouth and kissed it; she then transported the kiss to the stony mouth of the cherub.

After several seconds Angela stood up straight, took a final look at the grave and then walked purposefully towards the church. Julia followed. The bells were beckoning worshippers to prayer and once inside organ music serenaded their steps. Angels and demons soared on windows made kaleidoscopic by the sun and the smell of incense perfumed the air. Julia chose an empty pew at the back of the church intending to leave before the start of the service so she could examine the grave that had occupied Angela.

Suddenly Angela turned and her gaze seemed to fall directly onto Julia; her face was dappled with blue and red light. Julia instinctively slid lower into the pew, hoping to become invisible. Angela's face broke into a smile, transforming it from attractive to something closer to beauty. It was shocking. A man walked down the aisle and Julia realised he was the cause of the transfiguration. It was Finn. He sat beside his wife, turning to kiss her on the head with the most exquisite tenderness. Julia couldn't bear to watch and with legs buckling beneath her she left the church and the village.

CHAPTER 30

Weekend revellers were in high spirits and one young man, belonging to a particularly rowdy stag party, took a fancy to Julia. This wasn't unusual in itself but the more inebriated he became the more persistent he was, until at closing time he attempted to grab Julia and kiss her. She had hold of a barely touched glass of red wine and without hesitation she threw it at the man. He batted the glass away and a messy arc of red liquid covered them both. Julia unleashed her emotions onto him, screaming into his face. The man sobered up amazingly quickly and appeared terrified. Susan quickly intervened, telling Julia to wait in the back of the bar while she dealt with the situation. Julia sat on a stool shaking while Susan's uncompromising voice could be heard warning the man not to treat her staff like that and expelling him from the premises.

When the bar was empty and the doors locked, Susan came through to the back.

"Look, I only live across the road, come and soak that shirt in water before it's too late."

Julia followed Susan like a broken child, too weary to protest. She followed her onto Seel Street and into one of the Urban Splash apartments that had sprung up around the city in recent years. Inside, the décor was modern and bright. Susan seemed more vulnerable, less certain outside the environment of the bar.

"Sorry, I've got nothing in the fridge; I'm not very good at the food and hospitality thing. I've got loads of wine though?"

They sat on a beige sofa drinking white wine, while Julia's shirt soaked in a bowl of soapy water. She wore one of Susan's tops.

"Not a bad fit," said Susan. "We must be close in size on top. It's just my bum that's twice the size of your skinny ass." They laughed.

"I like your clothes, you always look cool," said Julia, feeling the awkwardness of their situation.

"So, which part of London are you from?"

"Stoke Newington; in the north. But I was born in Liverpool."

"You're joking; you're so posh."

"Well, we left when I was less than two. How about you; where are your family?"

"My parents live in Aigburth. I've got one brother; he lives in Manchester."

"Only one?"

"Yes. Do your parents live in Stoke Newington?"

Julia had the sense that Susan was happier when asking rather than answering questions.

"My mum does."

"Where's your dad?"

Julia controlled the desire to spill her story to Susan, but Susan noticed the hesitation. "What's the matter; what have I said?"

"Nothing."

"I'm sorry; I was being nosey."

For the first time Julia saw the guard lower in Susan's eyes and vulnerability show through.

"I came to Liverpool to see if I could find out anything about my father…my mother used a sperm donor twenty years ago. That's what's been freaking me out."

"My God girl, now I understand what's going on."

"What do you mean?"

"I knew something was odd about you."

"Oh thanks."

"No, what I mean is I recognised a kindred spirit, though it took me a while. At first I thought you were just a southern princess."

"Again thanks."

"Sorry, I'm being blunt. I was adopted."

"Oh, When?"

"I was a baby; I have no memory of my birth parents but I always felt this hole in my life."

"Oh my God; have you traced your mum and dad?"

"No." Susan's face seemed to snap shut. "They're not my mum and dad; I've got parents and I'm very happy with them."

"But aren't you curious to know?"

"No. You don't have the right to call yourself a mother just because you give birth to a child or a father just because you provide sperm. If you can't take responsibility don't have a child; simple."

"But they might have had their reasons."

"I've only recently read my adoption file and that's as far as it goes. I just wanted information." Susan folded her arms across her chest. "So," she said focusing on Julia, "have you found out anything about your father? I didn't think it was possible."

"Not much…it's complicated." Julia wasn't ready to tell Susan more. "Did you find anything interesting on your file?"

"You don't give up do you?' Susan grabbed the wine bottle and re-filled their glasses.

"I found out that my mother's name is Lisha; my grandmother, Kathleen, was a white-Irish woman and my grandfather, Adika, was a West African seaman who sailed into Liverpool from Ghana, with a cargo of bloody palm oil."

"Well that's already a lot more than I know about my father."

"It said in the letter that Lisha grew up around Toxteth; she struggled with being 'half caste,' that's the term she used, and she changed her name to Lisa to try to fit in. She met my dad in 1966; he was an American serviceman. When she got pregnant with me he dumped her and buggered off back to Alabama. She gave me up for adoption and followed him there."

"She was very young to bring up a baby."

"She should have thought about that before she shagged him. Anyway, she said she was doing the best thing for me. She was happy when the social worker told her I was going to a white couple in the posh part of Liverpool."

"Your parents are white?"

"Yes; she obviously didn't have a clue what that would be like for me."

"What was it like?"

"I always felt loved by my parents; they couldn't have done more for me and for the first twelve years of my life I didn't have the language to describe the difference I felt as the only black child in the neighbourhood. It was only when the Toxteth Riots hit the news in 1981 that I heard the word racism for the first time and realised that's what had been happening to me. I put my head down and worked twice as hard as all my friends at school, but I still couldn't shake off this feeling I had."

"What feeling?"

"A kind of…emptiness or abandonment. Anyway I went to uni and qualified as a psychologist."

"My God, Susan, I didn't know that."

"Not many people do. I even started to train as a therapist and that was when things got really weird. God, have you seen the time. I need to get to bed. You can sleep in the spare room."

Julia lay in soap-scented sheets thinking about Susan's story and how they had more in common than she could ever have imagined. 'These holes in our lives,' she thought. 'Why do they matter so much, these holes?' Susan suddenly made sense and she wished she'd confided in her about Finn. There was no one else to talk to and Julia knew she was dangerously close to meltdown. The incident in the bar had shown her that much.

Sunday was Susan's day off and she invited Julia to stay for brunch.

"Do you think identity is important?" Julia asked over scrambled egg.

"Woah girl, that's a bit heavy for this time in the morning." Susan laughed.

"Sorry, I know it is, but I can't stop thinking about the stuff you were talking about last night. Most of my black friends have a really strong sense of identity. I've never had that."

"Well I didn't until I was at least twenty-five. I was totally fucked-up. Probably still am. Identity isn't just knowing stuff about yourself or your family; it's something about how you are...reconciled with yourself."

"But how did you get to that point."

"Well I started this training in therapy. I suddenly had all this time to think. I was reading all these books on black identity and stuff. I couldn't cope with it and so I ran. I left the course and opened the bar."

"But what about the training? I think you'd make a really good therapist... now that I know you better."

"And realise I'm not such a hard faced cow after all?"

"No... I mean."

"Don't worry, that's what everyone thinks when they first meet me. You never know, I might go back to it one day. Anyway, enough about me, Miss Avoidance, tell me what's going on for you."

Julia finally had a chance to tell her story, unburdening herself to Susan. She told her about Tomasz and Ronald Baines and finally about Finn. Susan tentatively placed her hand on Julia's arm. The touch was like the turn of a key, the opening of a lid and there was nothing now that could keep her quiet.

"Susan, I'm not convinced Finn is my father. Isn't it too weird to have such strong feelings for your own flesh and blood?"

"Look, I don't want to freak you out, Julia, but when I went to see my file the social worker told me about this thing called GSA,

Genetic Sexual Attraction. She said if I decided to trace my birth family I should be aware of it. It sounds uncannily like what you've experienced."

"What is it?"

"From what I remember, she said it can happen to people who were separated from their family at a young age. Usually these natural barriers are built up, which means we don't fancy our brothers and sisters or our parents, but if kids are separated from their family early on these barriers don't develop. The social worker said that if adopted people meet again in adulthood they can sometimes feel this overwhelming attraction, even stronger than the attraction between non-related people. It's to do with stuff like pheromones and genetics and being attracted to people who look like us. I can't remember much; you should read up on it."

Julia was silenced. Her mind was in a frenzy trying to piece together the now glaringly obvious signs: the recognition on first meeting Finn; the overpowering attraction that had flushed out all rational thought and consumed her. She remembered Tomasz's warnings, his conviction that she and Finn looked alike. With a cold certainty she knew that Finn was her father. She felt the blood drain from her face and a dizzying nausea overtake her.

Susan's eyes widened. "I'm sorry; I'm such an insensitive cow. It doesn't always happen. I don't know if it would happen at all with a sperm donor."

"You were right to tell me, Susan. It's confirmed what I already knew. Finn is my father. Oh God. What have I done?" Julia fell forward, cradling her head in her hands.

Susan moved tentatively towards her and placed an arm around Julia's shoulders. "You have to stay away from him, hon, it's the only way. Why don't you go back home… to your mum. You really need her now. Does she know any of this?"

Julia shook her head.

"Go home; she'll understand."

Julia left Susan's apartment feeling like an empty husk. Susan had made it clear that she could call anytime if she needed to talk and must only come into work when she was ready. Julia knew Susan was right; she must contact her mum; tell her everything. Back in her room she pulled a backpack and a small case from her wardrobe and, with a feeling close to optimism, she stuffed in her few belongings. But as the hours passed and her little room was stripped bare, her heart betrayed her. She had to see Finn one last time; she had to tell him about GSA; he had a right to know. This feeling grew stronger with every minute until she finally gave into it. She picked up her mobile phone and sent him a text.

*

Finn didn't have a clue how he'd managed to get back home from Julia's place that terrible night three weeks earlier. As the taxi bumped and swayed along Menlove Avenue he'd felt weak and nauseous, ignoring the driver's chat, in an attempt to control his desire to heave. When he arrived home Angela was still up. This was unusual. He'd imagined sneaking into a dark and quiet house, gathering his thoughts before facing her in the morning. He ran to the bathroom and retched. Angela rubbed his back and spoke soothing words, and it was too much for him. He moved into the bedroom and fell onto the bed, now sobbing. He then found himself telling her everything, hoping she would take pity, but Angela seemed to grow smaller as he spoke. He saw the hurt he was causing, but his need to confess felt greater than his need to protect Angela.

They talked for hours about what had happened, what had gone wrong between them and about Finn's deceit. Angela absorbed the information and turned it over slowly in her mind. Then she told Finn she would stay with her parents in Surrey for a couple of weeks and would decide what she wanted to do. Finn's heart plummeted, but he knew that this is how Angela worked: she wouldn't be rushed. She said she understood that Finn might want to speak to Julia "one last time," to tie up loose ends.

Angela left for Surrey the following evening and only then did Finn contact Julia to arrange a meeting in the Park. He stole himself against her damning beauty, resisting the urge to take her in his arms and pretend, like her, that this wasn't happening. He swayed between horror and compassion but the horror won.

For the next two weeks he went about his business at the studio, hardly aware of what he was doing. Horror and despair opened and gaped before him at every turn; every thought went back to what had happened, what might have happened, until he felt sick with the effort of suppressing his thoughts. He convinced himself that he had in fact ended the affair before he found the letter in Julia's room; that he had only ever wanted things to be back to normal with Angela. And he waited for Angela to decide his fate.

After two weeks Angela returned, composed and decided. She had done a lot of thinking, weighed everything up. All things considered, she'd decided she couldn't throw her marriage away. She loved Finn and knew he loved her. As much as anything he had been a victim of circumstances, and she could therefore forgive him. However, there were conditions: he mustn't see Julia again. While she could acknowledge that Julia was his offspring and he might need to have limited contact in the future, it was crucial there be a cooling off period and that any future meetings, for the purposes of information sharing, should take place in a supervised setting. If he met her in any other circumstance it would be end of their marriage. Finn readily agreed to all of these conditions, grateful beyond words for Angela's clear thinking. For days he followed her around like an insecure child, looking for approval, waiting to do her bidding.

It was only on Sunday morning when Angela left for church, that Finn was shocked to find his thoughts return to Julia. He worried, feeling he had been too harsh at the final meeting; she was so young. He tried to substitute paternal feelings for uncomfortable sexual stirrings; he paced about the house like a caged bear. Finally, he grabbed his car keys, making a hasty decision to join Angela at church, hoping it would somehow purify him and strengthen his resolve. The sound of the music, the sight of her face illuminated, immediately lifted his spirits. He felt a reassuring surge of love for her. He was grateful beyond words for her forgiveness. After church they went out for Sunday lunch and she told him in a calm voice that she had spent time at the grave before the church service and had finally been able to say goodbye to their baby, to Richard. Now she felt she could move on, not forget but move on; they could move on together. They squeezed each other's hand frequently over lunch.

As the days went by and Finn relaxed in the knowledge that his marriage was safe, his gratitude towards Angela was superseded by irritation. He felt she was dictating what he should do without really taking responsibility for her part in the difficulties that had arisen in their marriage. He chose to interpret her composure as smugness and he told himself that she had always tried to exert control over his life in very subtle ways.

He worried about Julia and the state in which he had left her; he wished he could see her one last time to really know that she was alright, to end things properly; but Angela's ultimatum rang in his ears. When he received the text from Julia the following Sunday morning, just after Angela left for church, 'Please meet me one last time. Need to talk,' he erased it immediately, but he couldn't erase it from his mind. He thought Angela was being unreasonable and worked himself up into resentment before replying to the text, 'Eros. Twenty minutes.' Angela was usually at church for about two hours. If he got a move on he could spend nearly an hour with Julia. He grabbed his car keys and flew out of the house, leaving his mobile phone on the hall table.

CHAPTER 31

Julia called Susan later that night, hardly able to talk for sobbing. Her meeting with Finn had been traumatic. They had both deceived themselves into thinking it was about closure, but their hearts were unable yet to close and seeing each other was unbearable. They had clung to one another, breathing in elemental scents but avoiding a kiss or any contact that was too intimate. It was a desperate, useless exercise, leaving them both wrung out and defeated. They realised immediately that their situation was impossible and that all they could do was somehow get over this.

As they held each other in the car, rain falling like tears down the windscreen, Julia explained to Finn what Susan had told her about GSA and it made sense of things for him. They couldn't be father and daughter and certainly not lovers or even friends; there was no relationship for them. This was the inconsoling truth. Julia saw the resolve in Finn's face and it shattered her. They parted in despair.

Susan ordered Julia to come round to the flat immediately; Julia had barely stepped through the door when she crumpled at Susan's feet, the weight of the past weeks finally toppling her.

"Oh hon." Susan helped her up and led her to a kitchen chair. "What is it? What's happened?"

"Susan, I haven't told my mum; I meant to but everything has gone crazy again." She told Susan about the meeting with Finn, her inability to let go. "I know it's insane but I still love him; I still want to be with him. It's not like he's my father in the real sense of the word, is he?" Julia's look was pleading. Susan wasn't seduced by it.

"Julia, he is your father in the only sense that matters. Have you really thought about the implications of continuing with this?"

"I love him so much; I can't let him go." Julia felt this with such force that she stood up, agitated by the conviction and paced about Susan's kitchen.

"OK. OK. Sit down. You have to calm down and think this through. I'm going to get you a brandy." Susan returned and forced a glass into Julia's hand.

"Get some of that down your throat. Now listen. Finn is your father. Genetically, biologically, in every way he is your flesh and blood. You cannot legally be with him and you could never, ever have kids together. Do you understand that?"

Julia nodded.

"You are under a spell, Julia, the spell of genetic sexual attraction and you have to break it…"

"How… how the hell do I break it?"

"I don't know but you have to. Nothing good can come from this, believe me."

Julia's eyes flew to Susan's. "How can love not be a good thing? I bet hardly anyone feels what we feel for each other, not in a whole lifetime. I don't care if we can't have kids. I have to be with him." Her voice was now defiant.

"You are delusional, girl, you can't see clearly; it's like a bloody drug. Anyway, it sounds to me as if Finn wants to put an end to this; it's you who won't let him."

"No," Julia wailed, "that's not true; he's just in shock. He won't be able to stay away from me. I know it; he loves me too much. I saw it in his eyes."

Susan grabbed Julia's hands and jogged her, trying to bring her agitated gaze back. "Julia, Julia, listen to me. You have to let him go. You have to get a train back to London. You have to tell your mum everything. How about this for a deal: if you still feel the same in a month's time then come back and do what you have to do, but please at least try."

At last Julia heard Susan's wisdom.

Julia returned to her room and this time she booked a one-way train to London, leaving the following lunchtime. She once again packed her bags and placed them by the door. Then she drank vodka until she sank into oblivion.

*

She was asleep when the police banged on her door. She awoke, feeling groggy and disorientated. She was tempted not to answer, thinking it was the concierge, but then it crossed her mind it might be Finn. The knocking was persistent and Julia finally struggled out of bed to open the door. They spoke kindly, the male officer more than the female, but they didn't give her a choice. At first she thought it was a mistake. It was only when they said they wanted to question her on suspicion of incest that the truth hit home. The word 'incest' was like a bee sting. Julia had never thought of this word in relation to her passion for Finn. She found herself shaking; the shake took over her legs, making it difficult to stand up straight. The policeman steadied her.

"You have to come to the station."

She thought first of Finn, then of her mother and then her thoughts flew back to Finn, hoping she might see him in the police station. She was horrified by herself.

It was her first time inside a police station and she was led into the back by the policeman who made friendly exchanges with colleagues. He took her into a small room where three orange, plastic chairs were pushed neatly under a brown, melamine table. A jug of water, a glass and a tape recorder sat on top. The building didn't seem to fit her crime. Incest sounded Victorian: sordid and shameful; it spoke of the gallows, of dis-inheritance and depravity. They explained her rights. Julia refused a solicitor, believing that her explanation would suffice. Then the interview commenced.

The officers were mainly interested in sex, or the many euphemisms they used for it – intercourse; consummation;

penetration. They wanted to know if it had taken place, how many times and had she consented. She tried to explain as truthfully as possible what had happened but they looked disbelieving; she realised this was because it was unbelievable. They asked her the same question disguised in many forms until she felt frayed. She didn't lie, she admitted that she and Finn had made love many times, but she wanted them to understand how she felt; she wanted them to understand the madness of love and how it distorts everything. But they couldn't seem to grasp it; their looks were blank as if she was speaking another language, as if everything wasn't, after all, only about love.

"Have you spoken to Finn; he'll confirm what happened?" she asked several times.

"We will be interviewing Mr O'Sullivan," they eventually answered.

Julia realised that the police officers were out of their depth. They knew this young woman before them was an unlikely villain but they still had to play the part. They understood better theft and assault, drug dealing and prostitution.

It suddenly struck Julia that Finn would get the harder time: they wanted to see her as a victim; a young woman betrayed, seduced, while they would treat Finn as the villain, the middle-aged pervert, preying on a vulnerable woman barely into adulthood.

"It was my fault," she said, and then repeated it so there was no room for misunderstanding. "I knew there was a chance he was my father but I didn't tell him. He's totally innocent. As soon as he knew, as soon as we both knew, it stopped. There was no more sex. He doesn't even want to see me again. Our only real crime was betrayal. We had an affair. Is there a charge for that?"

Her voice was rising to the thin edge of hysteria. A large part of her wanted to give in to it. Perhaps if she screamed and just kept screaming, fell to the floor, stared at the ceiling with eyes fixed, perhaps then the questions would stop; perhaps they would admit her to an asylum, where she could lie still in a white bed, within white walls, made numb by white pills. Sanity depends largely on a narrowness of vision, she had once read. Perhaps if she kept her vision small she wouldn't lose her mind.

The police officers, sensing an imminent breakdown, decided to end the interview. Hysteria was too big and uncomfortable an emotion for this ten-by-ten room.

"We will contact you shortly. Just make sure you're reachable at all times. Perhaps you should call someone… your mum or a friend; and get yourself some legal representation as soon as possible."

Julia stepped out into the incongruous sunlight feeling as empty as a shell washed up on a beach. She had been forced open and a pearl torn from her for scrutiny. The verdict was the pearl was false, a good fake. Her love for Finn was in fact an overwhelming compulsion brought about by a genetic phenomenon; a demon disguised as love. All of this, she concluded, was punishment for her greedy and obsessive need for a father.

When Julia arrived back at halls, five hours after leaving that morning, her mum and Jack were waiting. They were the people she needed to see, Julia realised. They led her to her room and she sobbed into her mother's arms. Beth didn't say anything for a while. She had seen the look on her face; *wretched* was the word that came to mind. Eventually Julia came to a stop like a car running out of gas. She laughed a little and wiped her drenched face.

"Cup of tea?" Jack asked, smiling and bringing normality.

"How did you get here so quickly? Who told you?" Julia sat on the edge of her bed while Beth and Jack sat on the only chairs in the room. They sipped tea.

"That's the strange thing, love. I received an anonymous phone call. It was a man. He said, 'Julia is in trouble.' He told me briefly what had happened." Beth's face crumpled. "We left immediately."

"Who was he?" Julia knew it must be Finn but wondered how he had managed to get hold of her mum's number.

"He wouldn't say."

"Did he have an accent?"

"Sort of, but I have the feeling he was disguising his voice. Was it him?" Beth asked. "*That man*." There was venom in her words.

"I guess so."

"It's a bit late for him to be taking responsibility now, isn't it?" A rare show of anger flashed across Beth's face.

"Mum, it isn't like that."

"Sweetheart, I'm sorry, but I don't understand. How could this have happened without me knowing? How long has it been going on?"

"Only since January; I first met him last year…"

"Last year; so you were seeing him when you came home at Christmas?"

Julia's eyes met Jack's and guilt flashed between them.

"Not like that. I'd met him a few times but only in a crowd. Nothing had happened then."

"And what has happened now?" Beth's voice was small and tight.

"Everything that could happen." Julia had no energy to soften the truth.

"Oh my God! I just don't understand. He must be nearly 40… he's your… oh my God. I should have stopped you coming here."

"Mum," Julia took her mother's small, shaking hand, "you couldn't have stopped me and I didn't know he was my father when it started."

"You didn't know… but how… you're going to have to explain. It's too much."

Over the next hour Julia told her mum the story, including her conversation about GSA. "I'm convinced that's what it is."

Beth let out exclamations at various points and squeezed tears back into her eyes. She saw it as the consequence of her choice; the force majeure she'd set in motion twenty years earlier. She took the full brunt of its catastrophe, choosing to see her daughter as a victim.

They came to a point where hunger and fatigue were more pressing than their need to resolve everything and they ventured to an Italian restaurant on Allerton Road. Jack and Julia talked about innocuous subjects but Beth was silent, moving her food about her plate.

"So what happens now?" Jack asked after dinner.

"I don't know." Julia spoke softly. "The police might need to interview me again."

"You need a solicitor," said Jack. "Do you know the legal position?"

"I think we're accused of incest; but it is up to the Crown Prosecution Service to decide whether to prosecute. I wasn't really listening at the end."

Jack's heart went out to Julia. He remembered his own arrest years earlier; his horror at being handcuffed and taken into a cell and the feelings of guilt and self-loathing that had stayed with him for years.

"Do you still love him?" Beth lifted her head as if surfacing from deep waters.

Julia hesitated only for a second. "Yes I do. But I'm not going to see him again. I had already decided that before the police came. I just… I just need time to get over him."

"Are they going to question him?" Beth asked. "He's the one they should be arresting."

Jack rested his hand on Beth's. "Of course they'll question him love. We just have to leave it to the police now."

"Mum, you told me he was an athlete; that's why you chose him; but it didn't say that on his details."

Beth paled. "The nurse told me he was an athlete… I don't

think it was written on his details… it was a long time ago. She said he was handsome and that he was… or had been an athlete… I'm not sure."

"But why didn't you tell me that? I asked you to tell me everything."

"I told you everything I thought was important. I'm sorry."

"It's all water under the bridge now," said Jack seeing the panic and despair brewing in Beth's eyes. "No one could have predicted this."

Jack and Beth booked into a hotel near the Albert Dock. They suggested Julia stay there too but she insisted she wanted to be in her own room. They agreed to meet early the following morning to see a solicitor on Dale Street.

The solicitor looked as baffled as the police. She'd had to do some research to find a test case before they'd arrived and said it appeared from similar cases that if they could convince police the relationship was over, they might get off with a caution.

"The relationship is over," said Julia flatly.

"It might help that he's married and seems intent on staying with his wife," said the solicitor. "In some cases the incestuous couple are determined to stay together."

"So there are other cases like this?" asked Jack.

"A few; usually brothers and sisters separated at birth by adoption. Some have received custodial sentences but only because they have persisted in a physical relationship involving penetrative sex; some have even had children together."

"Prison seems very harsh," said Jack.

The solicitor shrugged. "As I said, incestuous couples do not usually receive a custodial sentence these days, if they can prove they don't intend to continue sexual relations."

"That can't be easy to prove."

"No."

"What about the Crown Prosecution?" asked Beth. "What do

they do?"

"The job of Crown Prosecution is to make sure the right person is prosecuted for the right offence and that all relevant facts are considered. They must be satisfied that there is enough evidence to provide a realistic prospect of conviction."

"And how long will they take to decide?" asked Julia

"It's hard to say. It depends on how busy they are, but hopefully no more than a few weeks."

"A few weeks!" Julia already anticipated the agony of waiting. "What do I do in the meantime?"

"I'm afraid you will just have to be patient... and stay away from the other suspect."

"His name is Finn." Julia looked into the solicitor's eyes. They were unblinking.

"I want to know who called the police," said Julia, her face set in a thunderous expression as they left the solicitor's office. "It was over between us; there was no need for the police to get involved."

"I want to see him," said Beth, ignoring Julia's comment. "I'm so bloody angry. I want to know what was going on inside his stupid, stupid head."

Julia turned sharply. "Mum, please don't do that."

Beth looked at her daughter with a steeled expression. "I'm sorry love but I have to. Your future is on the line and it's about time I took some action."

Julia could see her mum was unshakable in this decision and she glimpsed an opportunity to keep a link to Finn, no matter how tenuous. "OK." She said handing over her mobile. "But try to find out who called the police and please don't lose it with him; he honestly didn't know."

To Beth's surprise, Finn immediately agreed to see her that afternoon.

"I have to do this alone," she told Jack when he offered to accompany her.

Jack drove Julia into Cheshire for lunch. They stopped in a village and drove to an old pub called the Ring O'Bells, huddled under the gentle curve of Overton Hill. Inside, the pub was surprisingly untouched by modernisation with uneven walls and floors, low beamed ceilings, a collection of old brasses and a clutter of pictures from different eras. It was a good place to forget for a while. They sat by an unlit coal fire with half pints of real ale.

Jack distracted Julia, as he had in her childhood, with stories of old Stoke Newington and how it had changed. He then told her about his recent trip with Maddie to South America where she had shown him where she'd lived and found inspiration for her paintings. He then moved onto Greg and Dave's parenting adventures. Julia was grateful, although her mind was never far from the visit her mother was making that afternoon.

Beth was shocked by his likeness to Julia; she hadn't prepared herself for this and was baffled that neither of them had seen it. She could fully understand her daughter's attraction to him; he was a very handsome man and his gentle Irish voice was seductive. The house was stylishly decorated but it appeared that Finn had neglected it since his wife's departure. The curtains were half-drawn and several used cups and plates were abandoned across furniture, as if there had been a death. Finn wasn't alone; a tall, elderly man was moving around the room, pulling back curtains and clearing dishes into the kitchen.

"Hello, I'm Richard, Finn's father." He held out his hand to Beth. "Please, have a seat."

"Thanks, I'm Beth."

Finn asked, "Is it OK if my dad stays with us?"

"Of course." Beth kept her face fixed as she sat in an armchair; Finn sat at one end of the sofa. Richard left the room and then returned with a tray of tea and biscuits.

"Please help yourself." He sat in an upright chair slightly away from them.

Beth turned to Finn. He was having difficulty looking her in the eye. His head was slightly bowed and his neck had flushed scarlet. Beth found it difficult to conjure up anger.

"I'm sorry," he said. This was a trigger.

"Why did you do it? She's so young; you should have known better."

He didn't try to defend himself. "I know; I'm so sorry."

"Do you know the damage you've done?"

"I'm very aware of it; my wife has left me…"

"To Julia." Beth's voice rose to an unknown level. "The harm to Julia, my daughter."

Finn's eyes finally locked with hers and Beth could see torment. "Of course I do. I've thought about little else."

"Who told the police?"

"Angela, my wife… I arranged to meet Julia one last time. Angela found my mobile with the text message. I was stupid. She had already told me she would leave me if I saw Julia again. She said she did it to save me from a worse fate."

"So why did you see Julia again?"

"I wanted to know she was OK. It felt unfinished… she's my daughter."

Beth suddenly felt the unlikely truth that this man was the father of her child. She felt mildly embarrassed, as if sex had actually taken place between them. He looked so young; she could see how Julia could have convinced herself he wasn't her father. But the likeness…

"At least you bothered to ring me, to let me know she'd been arrested." She couldn't help easing his discomfort.

"I'm sorry, I don't understand?"

"Your call; but why disguise your voice?"

"What call?"

"It wasn't you? She could see it wasn't by his blank stare. She would have to deal with that later. "So, do you want to stay with your wife?"

His eyes liquefied. “Yes, I do. But it’s too late. I’ve blown it.”

“We don’t know that.” Richard spoke for the first time; he had a stronger accent than his son’s. “She’s gone to her mother’s in Surrey for a few weeks; I’m sure she’ll come round. They have a lot of history you know.” His eyes met Beth’s, parent to parent.

Beth noticed how striking Richard was: tall and athletic, probably about sixty with pure white hair and a healthy glow. His presence was strong and reassuring. He wore a tenacious but kind expression. She turned back to Finn.

“And how are you and Julia going to stay away from each other? You’ll have to, you know.”

“I know. We have to be rational; understand what happened to us. I think it might be easier for me; I know what I want now.”

“I hope you don’t mind my interference.” Richard spoke again. “I know this is awful for you Beth…for all of us, and it could take some time to get sorted. You might think it presumptuous of me but you and Julia are welcome to stay with me in Cheshire. Julia and Finn need some distance from each other but the police won’t want Julia to wander too far until it’s sorted. I don’t like to think of you wasting your money on some impersonal hotel.”

“Oh no… really, we’re fine.” Beth was thrown by this generous offer. “My sister lives on the Wirral. I was thinking of asking her if we could stay.” In truth, Beth had considered this possibility but quickly dismissed it. She hadn’t even told Maria she was in Liverpool; she couldn’t bring herself to discuss the exquisitely painful details of Julia’s situation with anyone else, even her own sister.

“Well, have a think about it. The offer remains open. I have plenty of space and, as strange as it sounds, I am family.” Lines radiated from Richard’s eyes and she saw humour behind his stern veneer.

“Ok, I’ll think about it; thanks again.” Beth gathered her belongings, feeling there was nothing more to say. “I’m sorry about the tea and biscuits.” The tray was untouched.

"At least let me give you a lift; I need to be getting home, anyway."

Beth accepted the lift in Richard's old BMW. They made small talk for most of the short journey. Beth was struck by the changes that had taken place in Liverpool since she'd left. She was glad. In one sense she'd turned her back on her place of birth but it didn't mean she no longer loved the city or wanted the best for it.

Richard pulled up outside the hotel.

"I'm so sorry for all you've been through, Beth. My son is a little hot headed and bloody stupid at times, but he's a good man."

"He's not the only one to blame for this mess."

"I hope you're not blaming yourself, young lady."

Beth couldn't help laughing; she felt as old as the hills.

"I wasn't even young when I made the decision to use a donor; I can't blame it on youth." Then she cried.

"Now now, you mustn't do this to yourself." Richard patted her arm, "None of us can see the future… thank God. Look, please think about my offer; it'll do you both good to have a bit of country air."

"I just don't think it would be good for Julia to be surrounded by memories of Finn. It might make her want him back even more."

"Actually, I was thinking it might have the opposite effect; I'm a bit of a schemer, you know." Richard chuckled. He pulled a mobile phone from his jacket pocket, "Look, here's my number; Finn and Angela bought me this damned thing last Christmas. Now what's my number?" Richard fiddled with the phone.

Beth was flustered as she jumped out of the car and entered the hotel lobby.

"You look odd," said Jack, who was standing in reception.

"Oh, what are you doing here?"

"Erm I'm staying here; is that OK?

"I mean, I thought you'd be out somewhere."

"I was waiting for you to ring me so I could pick you up from

Woolton, as we agreed."

"Oh sorry Jack, Finn's dad gave me a lift."

"OK. Drink. Bar. Tell me all?"

They sat in the ubiquitous hotel bar sipping their drinks; Beth filled Jack in on her visit.

"God, you're just too nice, Beth Swann. I thought you'd gone on the warpath and you end up forgiving him and accepting a lift from his dad. What are you like?"

"I haven't exactly forgiven him and I'm still angry, but I could see his point of view."

"You can always see everyone's point of view, Beth. Anyway, are you convinced it's over between them?"

"I'm convinced he wants it to be over."

"I'm not so sure about Julia," said Jack.

"What do you mean?"

"She isn't going to get over him quickly."

"I wish we could take her back to London with us," said Beth.

"She has to stick around until the police decide what to do. But I agree she needs some distance from the situation."

"That's what Richard said."

"Who?"

"Finn's Dad, Richard; he's invited me and Julia to stay with him in Cheshire; until things are sorted."

"I can see his point. Why don't you give it a go? It will cost you a packet to stay in this place."

"You know I'm hopeless at staying with people and I'm not sure it would be good for Julia. Anyway, what will you do?"

"I can look after myself. I was thinking about making a visit to my old man; it's about time. Then, if you no longer need me, I might surprise Maddie by going back early."

"You can't stay away from her even for a week, you old romantic fool."

"Hey, less of the old," Jack grinned.

Julia was surprisingly keen on the idea of staying with Finn's father. "I've got to get away from Liverpool for a while; it's driving me insane." She didn't add that she liked the idea of sleeping where Finn had once slept, inhabiting the same space. Over dinner she drank in her mum's account of the visit to Woolton.

"Finn said it wasn't him who called to let me know you'd been arrested. Isn't that strange?" They were all baffled by this, not least of all Julia. They could only conclude that it had been Frank, the concierge. He had let the police into the building and probably seen Julia leave in the police car, although he hadn't said anything subsequently.

The following day Julia went into town to let Susan know what had happened. The bar was quiet and Susan invited Julia to stay for a drink. She was sympathetic as well as shocked by what had taken place.

"Our conversation helped me to reach some decisions of my own," said Susan, looking almost shy. "I met with the social worker to ask about meeting my birth mother."

"Wow, that's a big step."

"Well I think I'm going to write first; she might be a nutter or something."

"Look. I want to thank you for all your support." said Julia. "I might not have listened very well at the time but it really helped me to sort my head out. I hope we can stay in touch."

"You'd better believe it girl. When I make a friend I don't let them go that easily. I want to hear how everything turns out."

Julia went on to Bold Street to buy some supplies before the move to Cheshire later that day. It was as she came out of a pharmacy that she thought she saw Tomasz retreating through the crowds. She pushed her way through dozens of shoppers, calling his name, but after several minutes of searching she lost sight of him.

CHAPTER 32

The vision of Tomasz stayed with Julia as Richard's car crossed Runcorn Bridge into Cheshire. She stared out of the window watching the pale-green girders of the bridge flash by like prison bars. Her mum had introduced her to Richard only half-an-hour before and she was still trying to absorb the fact that he was her grandfather; Finn's father. This bizarre reality, combined with the sighting of Tomasz, left her reeling.

Richard and her mum chatted about this and that in the front while she sat like a sulky adolescent in the back. As much as she loved rural scenery, for Julia true beauty lay in the city: in its neon lights and ambitious towers, its slices of greenery all the more precious for being hemmed in by urban landscape. Liverpool had been the playground of her passion and it was still dizzying with its memories. Yet she knew she would probably have to leave it behind, along with Finn and Tomasz, and everything else she had known there.

Silence closed around them as they pulled into Richard's drive and the only sounds they could hear as they climbed out were of gravel under their feet, birdsong and the distant hum of a lawnmower. The house was built of large slabs of red, Cheshire sandstone, covered in part by honeysuckle and wisteria. But the overwhelming scents were of cut grass and wallflowers, two of the sweetest, most evocative smells on earth to Beth.

Julia was more interested in the inside of the house, for this had been Finn's home in adolescence. Between these walls he had eaten, slept and thrown his schoolbag to the floor. Inside, silence reigned. Even the ticking of the clock had a subdued quality.

Julia scanned the hall for signs of his presence and was greeted by a large photograph of Finn and Angela, looking the picture of marital bliss. Finn had his arm around Angela's shoulder and she was laughing as if he had tickled her or told her a joke just before the shot was taken. There was nothing to suggest a rift between these two. Julia realised how difficult the weeks ahead would be.

Beth saw the kind of house she had always longed for. It had been lovingly lived-in and was even a little tatty in places, but it possessed great harmony of dimension and a beauty and charm that her own home sadly lacked. The house had been decorated with great care by Mrs O'Sullivan, Richard explained, and hadn't been changed since she had died ten years earlier. They were shown into the lounge, where bookshelves lined the alcoves on either side of a real fireplace. Beth's eyes were drawn to a photograph of Richard, presumably with his wife. Richard looked much younger than now and his hair was almost black. The woman was small and slightly plump but she had a face that shone with rosy warmth.

"Let me take your bags," said Richard. "I'll show you to your rooms. You can freshen up while I stick the kettle on."

They were each shown to a bedroom, decorated heavily with floral prints. The rooms spoke of loss and Beth felt sad for Richard.

"Do you fancy a stroll?" Richard asked after they'd finished tea. "I usually walk by the river in the evening."

"That'd be lovely," said Beth.

"Do you mind if I don't?" said Julia, "I'm feeling a bit tired."

"You do exactly as you like, darling." Richard cleared the teacups. "Help yourself to anything and don't be afraid to have a nose around."

Julia watched her mum and Richard crunch along the drive. She thought how bizarre it was that her mother and her grandfather were walking side by side as if it had never been any different. Once alone, Julia took Richard up on his offer and had another look around the house. She thought she might feel something, perhaps vibes from the past; evidence of Finn's existence here. She went into the dining room, which didn't look as if it was very often used. There was a highly polished dark wood dining table and six upholstered chairs. A sturdy Welsh dresser stood along one wall and a cupboard door had been left open a tantalising six inches. Julia pulled it wider. The smell of lavender hit her forcefully; it was the smell of her grandmother. The cupboard was full of Irish lace tablecloths and mats that she imagined Richard couldn't bear to give away, even though he would never use them.

There was also a stack of photograph albums and with a thrill Julia pulled them out. She sat on the floor next to the dresser and looked through them one by one, starting with what looked to be the oldest album, covered in cracked brown leather with the words *Our Photographs* etched in gold on front. The pictures were black and white, mainly holiday snaps of Richard and his wife. There were captions mentioning various places in Ireland and less frequently abroad.

Polaroid shots were introduced in the next album, the colours now faded into an orange wash. 1964 introduced the first photograph of Finn, a tiny baby held in the arms of a proud mother. They were in Ireland outside a low level house. Various characters appeared, all of them a mystery to Julia. There were shots of Finn's first Holy Communion, birthday parties, holidays, trips to Blackpool. It had all taken place before Julia had even been dreamt of. Then Finn on sports day, running, jumping, holding trophies with an audacious grin. In the next one, Finn in a running vest and shorts standing with a group of men, all holding medals. This wasn't school sports day, this was a serious competition. An inscription under the photograph informed her that the team had won second place in a four hundred meter relay in Manchester. It was 1981. Julia felt sick. He'd never mentioned this. Why? In fact, he told her he'd had the accident when he was "just a kid". She studied the photograph more closely. He must have been about eighteen or nineteen; the same age as she was now. Perhaps to a man nearing forty, an eighteen-year-old was still a kid. If only she'd pushed the point at the time; she had been so stupid.

With trepidation she continued to turn the pages. There he was at his graduation. A label told her it was September 1984, the month and year of her birth. This was a shock. He stood in his gown, grinning; college friends milled around him, hair sticking out beneath mortarboards placed at rebellious angles. Standing next to Finn was the young Angela. She had been a very pretty young woman. Her figure had been fuller then and her face open with optimism.

As she progressed through the years, an almost undetectable shift took place in Julia; she was no longer looking at pictures of her lover in all of his delightful poses; she was looking at her absent father. Her mother had been living in Liverpool at the time, bursting with pregnancy, while Finn looked carefree, totally unaware that his daughter was about to enter the world. The thought crossed her mind that their worlds were never meant to meet; she had ripped through time, creating chaos.

However, the next page produced the greatest shock of all, causing Julia to gasp and drop the album. She quickly scooped it back up and brought it close to her vision so that she knew she wasn't mistaken. In every shot Angela was heavily pregnant; Finn invariably had his arms placed protectively around her shoulder and they carried all the hope of parenthood in their faces. He had another child; how could he have kept this from her? Everything in her wanted to snap shut the album, protect herself from what the following pages might bring, but she was compelled to witness the unravelling tale. The next page told a very different story: Angela had lost weight, an enormous amount of weight. Her eyes looked blank and her smile was thin. Finn looked bewildered. He still had his arm around his wife but there seemed little connection between them. There was no baby. Julia turned page after page but there was no evidence of a child. At first Julia wondered if they had given the baby up for adoption but then she remembered the scene in the graveyard and understanding dawned on her.

The final photographs, most of which were loose in the back of the album, spoke of loss. Richard was without his wife; Angela and Finn without their baby. Julia felt overwhelmed by sadness; for the first time she had a deep sense of the pain she had caused. She returned the albums to the dresser and went to her room where she lay, startled by the pain and responsibility of adulthood. She finally drifted into a light sleep into which the noises of the day frequently intruded through her open window: birds; lawnmowers, voices. Laughter downstairs finally brought her to, but she stayed in bed until her mum knocked an hour later to tell her dinner was ready.

Beth felt an incongruous lightness of spirit after the walk with Richard. They had strolled along the River Weaver with the sun low and the sky red-streaked; the water seemed to flow liquid-copper beside them as Richard talked in mellifluous tones about the various birds they saw, telling her their names and habits, as if they were old friends. At every moment Beth had a sense of something, a kind of *déjà vu*; a feeling she couldn't quite put her finger on.

The following day Richard suggested they go to Beeston Market and Julia agreed to accompany them. The sadness of the previous evening still lingered and she didn't want to be alone. Richard was good company and at various points in the day it crossed Julia's mind that he was actually more intelligent than his son. Deep conversation had never been a feature of her affair with Finn; but her physical need of him had been so urgent that it consumed their time together so that nothing else mattered. She had occasionally tried to engage him in deeper topics but after a short time he would make a joke or pull her towards him for a kiss. She noticed how easily her mum and Richard were now chatting, moving between current affairs and the state of the world, to trying to recall the name of some actor they both liked back in the sixties. They stopped for lunch in a pub near Beeston and then visited a candle factory. Julia suspected they were in collusion, distracting her like a child with scented candles and ice cream.

That evening Julia became obsessed with thoughts of Tomasz, wondering if it had really been him she had seen on Bold Street and, if so, why he hadn't tried to contact her. She felt hurt by his sudden disappearance. She also wondered if Tomasz had informed her mum of the arrest; but it didn't really make sense.

"Mum, can you tell me anything else about the guy who called? You said he had an accent and I assumed it was Irish; do you think it could have been Polish?"

"I suppose so. As I said, it sounded disguised but when I think about it it could have been Eastern European. Why? Do you think you know who it was?"

"I'm thinking it must have been my friend, Tomasz, but he disappeared a few weeks. It doesn't really matter." Julia had a plan. She was growing restless in Cheshire and decided that at the next opportunity she would go to the hostel and see if Tomasz had returned.

"There are a few things I'd like to do in Liverpool. I think I'll go tomorrow."

"Things like what?" Beth sat up straight; her expression perturbed.

"I want to see if Tomasz is back."

Beth looked suspicious. "Is it really necessary?"

"Mum, don't worry. I'm not going to do anything stupid."

"I would just feel better if you avoided Liverpool for a while."

Richard, perhaps sensing a dispute, said, "Look, I was thinking I might pop in on Finn tomorrow, see how he's doing. I could drop you off at the hostel and pick you up on the way back."

Beth relaxed into the sofa, glancing at Richard with gratitude.

The following day, Richard dropped Julia in Falkner Square. She pushed open the front door of the hostel, with a feeling of hopefulness that had been absent for some time.

"Hi stranger," a familiar face greeted her.

Julia was relieved to find that the often-pedantic manager was out and instead Matt, a young and very laid-back Australian traveller, had been left in charge.

"Hi Matt. How's it going?"

"Crazy, but cool." He had his feet up on a chair and his hands rested behind his head. "How about you?"

"Cool thanks. I'm wondering if my friend Tomasz has been back; we keep missing each other."

"'Fraid you've missed him again. He came back for a few days and then left again."

Julia felt like crying with frustration but she kept her cool. "Did he say if he'd be back again?"

"No, but he left some of his stuff so I guess he will at some point."

They chatted for a while and as they did Julia formed an idea.

"I've just thought, Matt," she said. "I think I might have left a coat here. Can I have a look upstairs?"

People often left bags and other belongings at the hostel when they went off travelling. Staff kept them in a tiny room on the first floor. The arrangement was casual, covered by a notice that read, *Leave belongings at your own risk. We cannot be responsible for missing items*.

"Sure, here's the key, go have a look." He handed a large chub key to Julia. She went up to the first floor and unlocked a door to a small room, piled high with backpacks, sleeping bags, tents and other items. She moved bags around and shifted shoes and then saw Tomasz's small day pack. She felt the thrill of discovering buried treasure.

Inside she found a red jumper that he'd often worn in the winter. She automatically lifted it to her nose and inhaled. She pulled out a Ben Webster CD, a book of short stories by Chekhov, in Russian; a notebook, a pencil and a half bottle of vodka. She laughed with delight; the contents of the bag just about summed Tomasz up. There was also a wad of loose A4 paper, slightly crumpled. The title page read *Stalking Angels and other Short Stories by Tomasz Symansky*. This was a real find. "I'm sorry Tomasz," she said aloud. "You owe me this." She slipped the manuscript into her bag and then tore a page from the notebook and scribbled a note in pencil.

Tomasz,

Sorry for stealing your stories. You have taught me the art of detection and now I have turned villain. Forgive me. Please contact me when you're back. I miss you.

Julia x

The manuscript seemed to vibrate and burn with energy on the journey back to Cheshire. She waited until her mum and Richard left for their evening stroll and then she moved into the garden and sat on the bench in the sunlight. She took the manuscript out of her bag, carefully, as if it was a rare text. She opened it at the beginning and turned the pages over to get an idea of the content. There were seven short stories, all containing the same detective, Pete Rourke. She returned to the beginning and began to read.

*

"Do you think she's OK?" Beth asked Richard. The evening was once again infused with a kind of magic.

"She seemed fine on the way back; quite chatty in fact. I think the photos might have helped."

"What photos?"

"I was a bit sneaky and left the photo albums where I thought she'd probably find them. She asked me a few questions about them in the car today and I got the feeling they'd been a bit of a...what is it young people say... a wake up call."

"You really are quite canny, aren't you Richard. Thanks for caring so much."

"She's a lovely girl, Beth. She's like you."

"Oh, do you think so? I've always thought she must be more like... like her father. She's beautiful."

"And so are you, but I meant she's like you in personality."

"Oh, I see." Beth blushed again. "Richard," she hesitated. "I haven't asked you yet what your views are on... well on how Julia was conceived. I really thought it would be impossible to find her biological father, you know."

"You couldn't have known what the world would be like in the twenty-first century, Beth; it would have seemed like science fiction. You did the very best for Julia."

"But you still haven't told me what you think of me using a donor."

"Look, I didn't have to face the choices you faced. Maeve and I...well we had our son and then Maeve couldn't seem to have any more children. But you see we just had to accept it. There were no other choices open to us then: no IVF, no miracles of science. Perhaps it made the whole thing easier. We were sad that we couldn't have a brother or sister for Finn but we accepted it. At least we'd been blessed with one child. Look," Richard stopped walking and turned to Beth, "I don't judge you at all if that's what you think. If I'm honest I did feel angry when Finn first told me he'd donated sperm; he can be very impulsive. But when I thought more about it I realised it could be a real gift, giving someone a chance to have a child. Who's to say what's right or wrong?"

"I guess so, but I just feel responsible for all this pain. It's like

I opened a Pandora's Box. God, I'm the last person to open a bloody Pandora's Box."

Richard laughed.

"What?"

"You analyse too much, Beth. Perhaps you just have to accept what's done is done. Anyway, remember hope was also unleashed from Pandora's Box, not just evil."

"I would do anything to stop Julia feeling this pain; you must feel the same about Finn."

"I learned a long time ago that you can't stop your offspring going through pain. They scatter rocks in their own path and then they have to walk on them… like we did. There's no way round it. We can only be there to pick the stones out of their feet… if they want us to."

When they returned from the walk Julia was preparing dinner and seemed unusually cheerful. This is a healing house, thought Beth. It is full of soothing energy. They chatted with some normality over dinner and then Julia said she was going to her room to read. Once in bed, she pulled the manuscript from under her pillow with a feeling of great excitement. She had enjoyed Tomasz's first short story, written in a faux 1950s American detective style and was eager to read another. She turned the pages, deciding which to read next, examining the titles to help her decide. She came to the seventh and final story, called *Stalking Angels*. It was shorter than the others, perhaps unfinished, and she was intrigued by the title. Then she saw it, written in barely legible scrawl beneath the title: *For JS, my troubled Angel.* It was dedicated to her; she was sure of it. She fell back into the pillow and began to read.

CHAPTER 33

Stalking Angels by Tomasz Symanzky
For JS, my troubled Angel

I

Liverpool sips at a river the colour of tea while the evening crowns her with a tangerine sky. She looks sad, this queen; all her best bits are huddled at the front like a B-movie actress pushing up her drooping breasts; she is trying to distract you from her sagging arse. She has some spirit this chick and despite her shabby exterior she has a heart of gold. She can sing too, boy can she sing; she even dances if you ask her nicely, although her high kicks don't quite cut the mustard these days. She has taken some stick lately; it must be hard after the praise they used to lavish upon her. Not just for her looks, of course; she had talent too, real talent and plenty of rich suitors. Sure, some of them were a bit dodgy earning their bucks by foul means, making a name for themselves off the back of her legendary fame. But there were the genuine types too, hard grafters who helped to build her reputation, spread her name around the world (Although she sometimes had to spread her legs.) She was an international star for a while, the 'centre of the universe', as some famous geezer once said. But her looks faded and she insisted on singing the same old songs until no one wanted to listen. She couldn't compete with the bright young things. When she fell, boy did she fall hard; she still has a few scars to show for it. Fickle business this: they praise you one minute; turn on you like a pack of dogs the next. All was lost, or so it seemed, but now there's a chance her star will rise again. The money is flooding in from across Europe; all eyes are turned on her. Now she can afford the facelift she's wanted so badly, maybe a boob-job too. It might not stretch to an arselift but then that doesn't matter; no-one need see her arse.

II

I tripped off the ferry with a thin straggle of passengers. My heartbeat was allegro, my paws as damp as a weekend in Widnes. I'd been staying across the water in the quiet end of town; the quiet end of a quiet town. I'd stupidly thought a mile-width of muddy water would make me forget her. It didn't. It made me want her more. The sky looked hard, the rain fell hard and I didn't know where to begin. East sounded good so I headed east. Who am I kidding; I headed straight for her apartment, like a dog on heat. I headed for Gambier Terrace, a seedy stretch of town huddled beneath the wagging finger of the Cathedral. The rain was driving straight at me; it soaked through my blue jeans, stung my thighs; it dripped down the collar of my jacket and filled my boots. I wasn't dressed for this weather. At least I'd worn my trusty Fedora, a disguise and some protection from the rain. I stood for an hour outside her digs, under an excuse for a tree, dodging shafts of freezing rain and wondering what it was all about. Then she flew down the steps, pushing up a red umbrella, with a smile as broad as Princes Avenue and I knew what it was all about. She didn't see me. Not that she was looking. She was blind to me. I was a colour she couldn't see. Anyway, I didn't want to be seen. Old Socrates gave us the caution, As wolves love lambs, so lovers love their loves. *Perhaps she feared my rapacious hunger. I was devastated by her disinterest so I decided to disappear. I became private detective to my own case, trying to solve the crimes of my heart.*

I'm one of those vile men who live off the back of other people's fears; I lurk in dark corners to incriminate those seeking illicit pleasures. But she was the detective in our relationship always looking for clues. She laughed when she discovered my penchant for chess. She said, 'Let's play strip chess, to make it more interesting.' I said 'OK'. We removed an item of clothing for every piece lost. For the first three games she played in a state of Botticelli undress; by the fourth game it was I who lay naked like a child. I remember there was a full moon that night; we could see it through the window as we played.

'I can see the moon in your eyes,' she said with that smile.

'I can see your eyes in the moon,' I responded, knowing that these two statements about summed up our relationship. She was my Belle Dame Sans Merci. *I lost her, though she was never mine to lose. She fell fatally in love with another man; a love always destined to destroy. All I could do was watch from a distance and hope to rescue her if she only once asked.*

III

Tonight, dressed in red, she is going out to kill. She is flushed with the full beauty of youth, with a purpose that has nothing to do with me. She collects the stares of men like butterflies in a jar: blue, yellow; red, purple; she is saving them to admire when she is old. By then they will be dust; they live only in response to her beauty. Drawing closer, her lips are too red, as if she has already killed. Perhaps she has. I can see the dark sheen of satiation in her eyes; she is blind to everything; everything that isn't him. Her strides are long, they carve out her purpose, cutting away all that has gone before, tearing up the past; making confetti of her story. Forward is the only way to go, dragging the past behind her like an unwilling child. She opens doors even if they lead to eternal voids. Don't you know my love you should never open the door to the least of evils, for many other greater ones lurk outside. I cannot follow. I will not follow her there. I have no choice but to follow. I cannot leave her here. Her purpose necessitates the ruthless obliteration of others: the other woman; me; those who care about her. I see her run to him whenever he calls. There is little left of her; it has all been surrendered to this passion. In love, they say, we find part of ourselves but perhaps we only buried that part in the first place because it caused us too much pain.

IV

I watch her disintegrate; first with love and then with the loss of love. I see her change from girl to woman; from woman to demon; from demon to child. I see her empty out and crumble. I follow and I watch. My heart crumbles along with hers. I love you. You walk up Bold Street into the gloom outside the city lights. You pass the bombed out Church, abandoned in its glory of devastation, forcing its jagged remains into unbreachable skies. You are returning from your humiliation. You have become what I am and you are wilting from the shock of it. Yet you do it again, like a wolf licking a knife over and over, slowly draining its own blood. Can you not see he is no match for you? He slopes through the streets; his yoke is weak. You walk behind, blinded by the sun; you only see his silhouette, not his substance, like the exaggerated image on a movie screen. You create him in your own image; he will not stand the test of time. You walk straight and superior, your eyes keenly intelligent but you are so blind.

V

We are all fragile: we are damaged goods. The first air we breathe is filthy; then follows hunger, shit; wind, vomit, the unanswered cry; teeth ripping through flesh; the loneliness of the cot, the stench of neglect. We are riddled with invisible cracks and given the right set of circumstances we can all be broken. The knowledge of what you discovered split you in two.

I had to go to Manchester on another case; a man suspected by his wife of having an affair. I stay in a cheap hotel near Piccadilly and for three days I follow the rounded shoulders of this grey man through the streets of an unfamiliar city. It turns out he isn't having an affair; he just walks for hours on his own after work, repeating the same route over and over again. His face is unreadable until he nears home and then it landslides into dread. I almost wish he was having an affair. His wife seems disappointed when I hand her the report and with a smouldering look she asks me to stay for a drink. I decline the invitation; I have to get back to you.

I knew it wouldn't be enough for you to follow him; you had to know about her. She's an attractive woman, his wife, God's messenger. She looked like a nice person too. You saw that, didn't you? You could hardly bear it. What could be more devastating to a lover than the niceness of a wife? Believe me, I have talked to enough desperate lovers to know. You knew you could compete with her beauty and win hands down. You could have demolished her if it came to a test of intellect or wit, but niceness, I'm afraid there was no contest and you knew it. In demonic disguise you wait outside an ordinary house, extraordinary with your flowing gowns and yellow hair, my lily white Lilith, talons red and heart set on destruction.

I will never forget that scene in the churchyard. You walked through the lych gate, twenty paces behind her. You watched as she moved; a ghost among the dead. You stood behind a Yew Tree watching her. I stood behind a gravestone watching you. The sun made a halo of your hair. She went to a grave guarded by a fat cherub and stroked its unyielding limbs. Her thin hand moved to the face and traced every curve and hollow with her fingers; you watched her tears, puzzled, as if watching an obscure play. You followed her into the church and sat in the shadows at the back. You once told me you don't feel at home in sacred places; you are a fallen Angel, my love. I watched you as you watched her as she watched Christ on that cross. He didn't budge an inch to help any of us.

VI

You are Ardhanarishvara, male and female. You stand face to face, beneath the empty space where love once lived, two halves

of Lord Shiva. You peer into a tarnished mirror, yet neither of you can see that it is yourself looking back. You are made of the same stuff and are torn asunder by this reality. He steps back from you, almost reels; his face is horror. Yours is denial. He must know. Therefore you must know. But still you walk towards destruction.
VII
I stand beneath her window chained to her. I am filled with the dreadful thought that her mind cannot bear this reality; that she will take the easy way out. I will her to work through the suffering instead, to know the rooms of her own country before crossing that threshold. Her window captures my imagination like a vent into heaven. I ignore the drunken insults of boys; the bark of an old dog. I am rewarded with a glimpse of her. She is still here.
VIII
Her sins have found her out and I watch, impotent, as she is taken away, her eyes dark pools of fear in a bloodless face. I am so close to running to her then, dragging her from her captors; taking her away with me, but I realise I cannot save her. You are lost. When you return much later your face is ravaged; it is pulled out of shape to fit the grief in your heart. I have done what I can to help and now I must go. This is a case I cannot solve…

Julia placed the manuscript on the bed and laid her head back into the pillow, ravaged by what she had read. Despite the poetic licence, there was no doubt Tomasz must have followed her for several weeks. She didn't feel angry or afraid; she felt elated. Tomasz wasn't her stalker; he was her guardian angel. What she'd read wasn't a story; it was the most beautiful love letter she had ever received.

CHAPTER 34

Jack caught up with his sisters over lunch and then, for the first time in a year, he visited his father. The relationship had always been strained. Jack imagined that his old man could never shake off the image of his son stealing underwear from washing lines or forgive him for his botched suicide attempt. Jack didn't blame him for this but he wished his dad had at least tried to understand something of the turmoil he had endured as a young man. The last meeting had been particularly fraught. It was a family wedding and it seemed to Jack that his father used the occasion to humiliate him in front of Maddie. He controlled his anger but had vowed not to put himself through it again. It was Maddie who persuaded him to "let it go" and not waste in resentment the few remaining years he might have with his father.

Fifteen years earlier Dan had re-married a small, frilly woman called Jean who had moved into Jack's childhood home. She fussed around Dan like a broody hen and Jack found it difficult to see this fussing woman in his mother's place, although he was glad that his father had found companionship, and perhaps even love. Jack suggested they go out for a pint, fully expecting Jean to tag along as usual but to Jack's surprise his dad picked up his coat from a hook in the narrow hall and told Jean they'd be back for dinner. Jack realised It was the first time they had ever been for a pint together, just the two of them.

They sat on bar stools drinking Guinness. Dan was now seventy-five but looked older, small and frail with legs struggling to reach the ground. Jack remembered him as a big man. He told his father about his teaching job and how much he enjoyed working with young people. In the absence of Jean's nervous chatter Jack encouraged his dad to talk about himself.

"I still miss your mum, you know. Jean's a good woman but she will never replace Iris." He looked straight ahead at the iridescent bottles hanging upside down above the bar. "I was a right bastard, son, I never treated her right and I've regretted it every day since. I wasn't a great dad either." It wasn't exactly an apology and Dan still hadn't looked his son in the eye but it was all Jack needed.

After a short silence, Jack guided the conversation to safer ground, for his father's sake, and they fell into an hour of recounting stories about Iris and the sweet and often funny things she'd done. They found themselves laughing aloud. Dan tentatively patted his son on the back, something else he rarely did, perhaps for fear of catching something.

It was his dad who suggested a second pint and they moved on to talk about recent changes in Liverpool with its City of Culture status. This led them to Anfield and the easy topic of their football team. Then they realised it was late and Jean would have dinner ready, so they knocked back their pints and left the pub. They felt pleased that time had flown rather than dragged its heels between them as it usually did. They walked home in an elevated mood; the things they had talked about were far outweighed by the things they hadn't, but it was enough; it was a start.

Jack left his dad's house that evening with a sense that he'd tightened a loose thread flapping around in his life for too long. Now he couldn't wait to get home to Stoke Newington and to Maddie. Back at the hotel he watched a chatshow and part of a meandering thriller before trying to get to sleep. However, he was constantly woken by the banging of doors and the internal groans and creaks that seemed a feature of all hotels. At three-thirty he finally gave up, deciding to check out and start his journey home. He imagined slipping into bed beside Maddie in the morning, breathing in her scent.

His spirit lifted as he joined the M6. He turned on the radio and sang along, feeling sizzlingly awake. Past Birmingham a slow drizzle fell but it didn't dampen his mood. Tired of the radio he put on a Radiohead CD, moving his head, watching the windscreen wipers keep time to the music: no regrets and no surprises. The rain laced the windows, forming a fragile protection. What a mess Julia had got herself into; she might have been his own flesh and blood they were so alike. Jealousy forced its way to the surface again. Recent events had reminded him that Julia wasn't and never would be his daughter. He felt sadness and an uncomfortable anger towards the man who had fathered but never appreciated his own child.

The rain came down in torrents, battering the windscreen. Jack switched the wipers to the highest speed and turned his lights to full beam; he pulled into the inside lane, leaning forward slightly to see ahead more clearly. The road and sky merged into one grey, sodden sheet; everything turned to liquid. There was still relatively little traffic, a few cars trying to beat the rushhour, like himself, and trucks going about their business.

As he joined the M1 a large truck thundered past at great speed, ox-blood red and glistening with rain. It pulled in front of him. Jack kept a steady speed, while the rain punished the road and the windscreen. The back of the truck was tall and intimidating with no company name or advertising slogan to break the red wall. He didn't trust it; the brake lights flickered on and off and it moved erratically across lanes. Jack signalled to overtake and moved into the middle lane, hoping to put some distance between them. The trees and fields blurred into one, bleeding colour like a child's painting. As he drew level with the truck a huge wave of spray smashed into his windscreen and he was momentarily blinded. He managed to keep the car steady, knowing not to brake sharply in such treacherous conditions, but, to his horror, the truck started to move into the middle lane, either not seeing him or not caring. Jack flashed his lights and sounded the horn, but it was clear the driver wasn't going to delay his manoeuvre.

"Shit," Jack said aloud, quickly realising his predicament. He couldn't get past the truck; the only option was to brake. With a quick glance in the mirror he pumped the brake a few times hoping it would be enough to get him out of trouble, but it had absolutely no effect. The car assumed a life of its own, gliding above the road, at the mercy of physics, ploughing ever closer to the side of the truck. He had no choice but to swerve into the outside lane and towards the central barrier, knowing this was the worst thing he could do; he was aquaplaning out of control.

He clipped something, perhaps the central barrier and in panic pulled sharply on the handbrake, sending the car into a spin. He thought, I'm a hazard, a death machine, killing people with every spin: children, young couples, holiday-makers. The blood-red truck moved into the distance, oblivious to his plight. Then he hit something else, this time with more force than before, and the car was instantly flipped over onto its roof, turning and spinning, turning and spinning; he was on some sadistic fairground ride that was never going to end. Bizarrely he could still hear Radiohead, *No Surprises*, as if it was always meant to be the theme tune to his death. The car turned in time to the music over and over, round and round. It was too cruel that Maddie would lose two people she loved in the same way. How would she manage her grief? He felt the purest love for her, an exquisite love, free from lust or jealousy; selfishness or condition. Was he still alive or had he crossed through a door into death? *I know death hath ten thousand several doors for men to take their exits*. How on earth had he remembered this? It was Webster, *The Duchess of Malfi*. He had learned it for his English exam, thirty-four years earlier.

He was startled by the lucidity of his thoughts; as if his mind had been yanked open, spilling its contents to make him light for death. He had escaped death once before; it had to come sometime. He begged for a few more years, now that he had learned the secret of life. Julia is young; she'll survive my death; she'll only have fond memories, but she'll never know the whole truth of who I am. I wish I'd known my mother better; perhaps I'll see her again in the dark unknown after death. I am a small boy, scared and alone, seven-years-old and lying in a bundle of my sister's dresses. Three-years-old and holding my mother's nylon petticoat beneath her dress. Standing in a local corner shop. The shopkeeper is a big man with a loud voice; Jack has always been scared of him but he is comforted by the silky-soft material attached to his mother's warm body. He's in his mother's arms, a baby; looking up into her face; sinking into the unfathomable love of her eyes.

Surely this isn't a real memory; there is forgiveness in her eyes; there's nothing to forgive. He is in the womb, a tiny curled foetus, unfolding by the minute; neither male nor female; perfectly both. The female is at the centre, like the stone in the middle of the peach, the rock that holds us together. The face of *Mona Lisa* hovers before him in her infinite mystery; the face separates and becomes all the women he has ever loved staring down at him. Maddie stands above him, crying through a smile; there is Gloria and Beth and Julia and, look, there's Anna. The smell of petrol forces its way in; there's a bright flare of light and the sear of heat on skin. Then he is flying through the air; weightless, he imagines leaving his body and the world behind.

CHAPTER 35

"The rain was heavy last night," said Beth as they sat down to breakfast.

"Yeah," said Julia, "it kept me awake, and when I did sleep I had really weird dreams." She didn't tell them she'd dreamt about Tomasz and Zuraw again. This time she was climbing Zuraw after Tomasz, trying to tell him something, but he couldn't hear; he was racing away from her. He was carrying a large banner and across it were the words, 'Know the rooms of your own country', written in thick swathes of blood. She awoke with a sense that she was losing something important.

It was as they were finishing breakfast that the police called Julia on her mobile, asking her to come into the station.

"We have some news from Crown Prosecution."

Richard called Finn who informed him that he had also been asked to go in. It was agreed that Richard would drive Julia and Beth to the station and wait for his son outside, to avoid any awkward meetings.

A policeman informed Julia that Crown Prosecution didn't consider there to be enough evidence to make a case, but if evidence of 'ongoing sexual relations' was produced they would have to reconsider. This was a huge relief to them all and Julia realised she was now free: she could leave Liverpool at any time; there was nothing to stop her. She was surprised by her lack of desire to run to Finn, even though he was only within a few feet of her.

Julia and Beth went to a café in Blackburn place to celebrate over lunch, while Richard stayed with Finn, who, in Angela's absence, was in no mood to celebrate.

From the café Julia called Jack on his mobile to give him the good news, but his phone was dead.

"That's weird; there's no tone on his mobile, no voicemail or anything."

"Call the hotel," suggested Beth, "he might still be in his room."

Julia called reception to be told Jack had checked out in the early hours of that morning.

Beth laughed. "I knew he wouldn't be able to stay away from Maddie for much longer. Try the home number."

Maddie answered and Julia shared the good news with her.

"That's great," said Maddie, "I'm so pleased it's over. Is Jack there; I've been trying to call him for ages?"

"Oh, we thought he'd be with you. As far as we know he left Liverpool early this morning to get back. He wanted to surprise you."

There was silence at the other end of the phone. Then a quivering voice. "I sensed something in the early hours. I knew it wasn't right."

"Maddie." said Julia, "I'm sure it's OK. He might have stopped off somewhere to sleep… or maybe he's taken it slowly. It was pouring down last night."

"I know," said Maddie, her voice now flat and certain. "I'll contact you later. I have to make some calls."

"Oh God, Mum, Jack isn't home yet. Maddie sounded really worried."

"But we don't know when he set off. I'm sure he'll be OK."

"You didn't hear her voice Mum; she sounded as if she knew something. Oh God! I couldn't bear it if anything happened to Jack."

Back at Richard's house they drank tea with anxious sips; mobile's switched on and few words exchanged. At some point Julia's phone rang, causing them to jump from their seats.

"You answer please, Mum." said Julia, handing the phone to Beth. She sat forward clutching the arms of the chair while Beth emitted small 'yes's' and 'no's' and 'Oh Gods!' Julia had never seen a face drain of colour so quickly.

Beth put the phone down and looked at them, wide-eyed. "Jack has been involved in an accident. It's very serious. We need to get back."

Within two hours they were on a train at Lime Street Station, waving goodbye to Richard. They held hands, side-by-side, occasionally giving each other reassurances, but mainly staring, but not seeing, the passing scenery. They got out at Milton Keynes and took a cab to the hospital where Jack had been admitted. They found Maddie wringing her hands in the waiting room. They hugged her silently and then found a quiet corner in which to huddle together.

Maddie spoke in short monotone sentences, barely able to organise her thoughts. "They couldn't identify him. The car burst into flames but somehow he was thrown clear. He had no ID on him. He always empties his pockets when he's driving. He puts everything into the glove compartment – keys, mobile, wallet – and it was all destroyed. They didn't know who he was. They were just waiting for someone to call. When I did they told me…"

"How is he, Maddie?" Beth placed a firm hand on Maddie's arm and tried to focus her panicked mind, "Have they told you how he is?"

"There's lots of damage and blood loss, he's in surgery… ruptured spleen; lungs; broken bones. They couldn't tell me if he'd live." It was now that Maddie broke down and Beth and Julia took her hands, one each. "My mother couldn't survive it, why should Jack?"

"Jack is younger, Maddie, he's strong." She knew this wasn't necessarily logical but it was all she could think to say.

After some painfully distended time, a nurse found them and ushered Maddie through into a corridor, while Beth and Julia remained in the waiting room.

"Mum, I love Jack so much. He's like my dad. I don't want to lose him."

"I know love. I know."

After another interminable wait Maddie returned. Her face was unreadable. "He's still sedated so I couldn't speak to him. They said they've managed to stem the flow of blood. It looks as if he'll make a recovery… from the accident, anyway." Maddie didn't look appropriately relieved.

"What do you mean? What's wrong Maddie?" asked Julia.

"They scanned every inch of his body when they were assessing his injuries and they found something that shouldn't be there."

"What?"

"A tumour… on his liver. They can't operate because of its position. They'll have to start chemotherapy as soon as he's stable."

Beth and Julia returned to London the following day after booking into a hotel with Maddie for the night. Jack would have to stay in Milton Keynes until he was in a stable enough condition to be moved; he would then begin a course of chemotherapy in London. Beth and Julia agreed to return in a couple of days to visit Jack and bring more clothes and toiletries for Maddie, unless Jack's condition deteriorated, in which case they would return immediately. Back in Stoke Newington, they began the heart-rending task of calling all the people who knew Jack and Maddie to inform them of the accident. When they had finished they sat back exhausted.

"Poor Maddie." They repeated at various points. "She loves

him so much."

"Mum, do you think he'll be OK?"

"Love, he's in a bad way. He has to recover from his injuries and then fight the cancer. It's a lot to ask, but if anyone can do it Jack can. I still think we have to prepare ourselves for the worst."

Julia sobbed; Beth knew that all the woes of the past months were being released in one gigantic wave of emotion. She led her daughter to the sofa, covered her with a soft blanket, which had been dragged out of a pine chest many times over the years for childhood illness and upset. She boiled eggs, mashed them up, smothered them in butter and sprinkled them with salt and pepper. She made toast and tea and brought them to her daughter on a tray. Then they sat together in the lounge watching a black-and-white movie. Beth felt a sense of usefulness; she could still provide for her daughter's needs.

The following day they returned to Milton Keynes with a small suitcase of Maddie's belongings. Jack was still heavily sedated and the sight of him wired up with drips and monitoring equipment was shocking. The visit was short and Julia and Beth returned to London, leaving an anxious and increasingly weary Maddie to keep the vigil.

This is how the weeks of August passed. Each time they visited, Jack had made small but significant improvements but still he lay sedated and helpless. He spent his birthday in hospital. Julia's own birthday a week later was a low-key affair. She met up with a few friends but didn't feel much like celebrating. She was in a reflective mood, hardly able to believe all that had happened in the two years since her 18th birthday celebrations. She had been a child then, she thought, a naïve and silly child. Now at twenty she felt like a woman.

Once the imminent danger of losing Jack had passed, Julia began to think again about all that had happened in Liverpool. Sometimes it was a strange and distant dream; at other times her life in Liverpool seemed startlingly real, more real than the undefined greyness of her current existence, always waiting for news of Jack's progress, worrying about her future. Mostly she felt numb, and this was a blessing.

After long discussions with her mum Julia had decided to put her studies on hold for a year. LIPA had agreed to defer the BA; she'd done well in her first year exams and had the option of returning next year if she wished, or alternatively to transfer to a London college. Julia found a sales assistant job in a music shop on Denmark Street to tide her over while she considered her options.

Seeing that her daughter was ravaged by the events of the past months, Beth suggested they have a weekend break; not too far away so that they could return quickly if necessary. Beth felt she too needed a break from the endless trips to the hospital, the fighting through traffic and the smell of sickness. She didn't really care where they went as long as it was away.

"Gdansk," said Julia without hesitation.

"Gdansk, why ever would you want to go there? I was thinking more of Paris or Rome; somewhere beautiful and cultured."

"It's supposed to be… interesting."

Beth sighed. "Why do I always feel you have a plan brewing, my dear?"

Beth missed Richard more than she'd expected. She imagined him walking by the river or sitting in his garden in the evening sun; she missed his company as well as the tranquil beauty of Cheshire. She had been trying for weeks to pinpoint the feeling she'd had while living there. One grey September day when struggling for a seat on the 73 bus, it dawned on her that the life Richard had was the life she had been longing for since childhood. The words of a poem she'd read many years earlier came to mind, *I have a life I long to meet, without which life my life is incomplete*. But in the same moment she pinned the feeling down she also realised that she would never have the actuality; it was a butterfly dream.

Richard called Beth once a week to see how they were holding up. At the end of September he called to let her know that Angela and Finn had decided to get back together after discovering Angela was pregnant. They discussed how best to give this news to Julia. Beth dreaded disturbing her daughter's fragile peace and was tempted to hold off for a few weeks, but in the end decided to bite the bullet, reasoning that it might be another nail in the coffin for Julia's obsession with Finn.

Julia said nothing for a few seconds and then: "God, it will be my half brother or sister; how weird!" She didn't mention it again for a few days. She absorbed the information, allowed it to settle and then assessed its affect on her emotions. She concluded that more than anything she felt the horror of what might have been for her and what might never have been for Angela. She felt a penetrating sadness that she still couldn't shake off, but she didn't feel overwhelming jealousy or anger or painful longing for Finn; somehow these emotions had been stamped out. Nature's healing had begun; little green shoots pushing through scorched earth. It was how it should be.

If she was totally honest, she knew that her feelings for Finn were miraculously on the wane, while her feelings for Tomasz were waxing brightly in her heart. She didn't confide this phenomenon in anyone for fear they see it as a weakness in her character; she even questioned her own integrity. But the more she thought about it the more she understood that the gentle swell of feelings for Tomasz had begun in her heart long before the wave of passion for Finn had crashed over her, washing everything else out of its path. Now that the wave was ebbing she found evidence of her feelings for Tomasz still there, like a half-completed pattern of shells left on a beach. She couldn't think of a way of explaining it to anyone.

CHAPTER 36

"I want to go to the docks; to the maritime museum. There's this crane, Zuraw, it's mediaeval and supposed to be really interesting."

Beth looked puzzled by her daughter's sudden enthusiasm for museums; they had barely touched down in Gdansk after an early flight from Stansted.

"OK. Shall we get a drink first?"

They unpacked their small bags and then wandered into the city centre. The late September day was unusually warm, with only a few small, white clouds skating across the sky. They found a café in a square and sat outside with coffee and pastries. Beth felt light-headed with tiredness while Julia appeared excited, even agitated.

"This is great, isn't it, Mum?"

"It's nicer than I thought, and quiet," said Beth. "So come on, love, tell me about this Tomasz. I know this trip is really about him."

Julia was momentarily silenced by her mother's directness, but she wanted to be honest, after the months of deceit, and so she told her all about Tomasz: their friendship; his support during the search; his concern about her relationship with Finn; and his pleas for her to do the DNA test. She told her about Tomasz's sudden disappearance and the discovery of his short stories. She only omitted a few small details – mainly those that might put Tomasz in a bad light.

"You certainly live an interesting life, love. Are you sure he's sane?"

Julia laughed. "He's completely sane, Mum. I think."

"So it was Tomasz who called me that day?"

"It must have been. I'd really like to find out where he is. I miss his… friendship."

Beth gave her daughter a scrutinising look but didn't push the subject. "The most important thing at the moment is that you recover from your experiences in Liverpool. Don't get yourself too emotionally fraught, love."

"I won't Mum. I am already feeling much better, but Tomasz's friendship is important to me."

"Are you hoping to find him here?"

"No." Julia's tone was adamant, but her face told a different story. "I doubt he'll be here, anyway. It's just that he described this place to me. I really wanted to see it."

Beth wasn't convinced but didn't press further.

After coffee they headed for the Motwala River and the maritime museum. Julia's heart thrilled as she stared up at Zuraw. It was as wonderful and terrible as she had imagined. Jakob had hurtled to his death on this very spot; the horror of it froze in her heart. She understood why it would be difficult for Tomasz to return to this place.

After spending time in the museum and then strolling along the river, they wandered back to the hotel for a few hours rest. They returned to the old town for dinner that evening and were able to sit out in last vestiges of summer warmth.

"Mum, this is so lovely," said Julia. "We haven't done anything like this for ages."

Beth soon felt giddy with the wine and was overtaken by a sudden rush of love for her daughter. "I know love. It feels really good. I worried that we'd grown apart."

"Never Mum; you're my best friend." Julia squeezed her mum's hand.

The following day they looked around the historic centre of Gdansk. Julia couldn't help but scan the crowds for Tomasz's face and peer into the many bakeries they passed, imagining that each one might be Tomasz's childhood home. She had a nagging urge to meet his parents, to tell them not to worry about their son or blame him for Jakob's death. When Beth returned to the hotel for an afternoon rest, Julia said she'd like to continue exploring the city alone. She retraced her steps, returning to each bakery she'd seen en route.

"Do the Symanskys own this bakery?" she asked. She was met by blank stares or apologetic negatives from those who could speak English. By five o'clock she felt weary and was nurturing tiny seeds of doubt about Tomasz's story. Defeated, she decided to return to the hotel. On her way she saw a young, bright girl walking towards her and felt an impulse to ask her the same question.

"They own the bakery on Poznan Road," the girl answered in clear, fluent English, "you must go left and then second right."

Julia felt intensely nervous as she walked the short distance to a road she had somehow missed. She hesitantly pushed open the bakery door and was met by the face of a young assistant peering over a counter piled high with powdery bread rolls, cakes and startlingly white meringues.

"Is this the Symansky bakery?" Julia asked.

"Who's asking?" a voice came from the back of the shop, and then a man appeared, rubbing powdery hands on a striped apron. He was small and stocky with a strong-featured face. He was by no means classically attractive but his eyes were bright and inquisitive and humour played behind them; he smiled. Julia had a sudden image of him naked and covered in flour; she quickly shook it away.

"Oh, I'm sorry to disturb you. It's just… it's just I'm a friend of Tomasz's." The man's eyes narrowed and his smile dimmed but didn't disappear altogether.

"I see. Well then you must come in." His English was hesitant but good.

"Oh no, I really don't want to bother you..."

"Please, come through. My wife will want to meet you." His tone was insistent.

Julia followed the broad shoulders of Mr Symansky through to the back of the bakery, suddenly regretting her impulsivity and wondering what on earth she would say to these people. They walked past stainless steel ovens, cooking implements and clean-scrubbed wooden work surfaces. She followed him up a set of narrow stairs to a living area. As he reached the door to a room, Mr Symansky shouted something out in Polish. Julia could make out Tomasz's name. She was led into a cosy lounge with a clutter of furniture in clashing, earthy fabrics. Julia thought how different it was to a typically English home. An exceptionally attractive woman stood in the centre of the room, wringing and twisting her hands. Her wide eyes blinked and darted over Julia, but apart from these agitated movements there was a strangely still quality to this woman; she stood quite rigid and her face was smooth and inexpressive; in fact her eyes seemed to be making up for the inactivity, as if trying to escape from the rigid prison of her face. Julia had the sense she was seeing characters from a book, coming alive before her eyes.

"Hello." Mrs Symansky spoke hesitantly. "You are a friend with Tomasz." Her English wasn't as good as her husbands. Julia shook a cool hand.

"I was just visiting Gdansk and I thought I'd pop in to say hello."

Mrs Symansky looked to her husband who translated the words.

"Sit, sit." Mr Symansky gestured towards a straight-backed chair with a dull yellow and green nylon-stretch cover. "You would like a drink? We have a very good apple juice."

"That sounds lovely."

He again spoke to his wife who immediately left the room.

"We have not seen Tomasz for a very long time. His mother misses him."

"He is well… he is writing a lot." Julia was unsure what she should say. She felt again the inappropriateness of her visit.

"Writing, writing that is all he does. There is a good business waiting for him here if he will just come home." Mr Symansky waved his hands around the room indicating the extent of the business waiting to be claimed.

"So when did you last see my son?"

This was the question Julia dreaded.

"Apple." Mrs Symansky returned with a tray bearing three tall glasses. She smiled but only her mouth moved.

Julia took a glass and sipped the sharp, fresh juice, a welcome relief to her dry mouth. "Mmm."

Mrs Symansky said something to her husband in Polish; he turned to Julia "When did you last see Tomasz?" This question had to be answered.

Julia hesitated. "Well, actually, I haven't seen him for a few weeks. I wondered if he'd come here?"

Mr Symansky's face dropped into disappointment or perhaps anger; it suddenly looked ravaged and Julia imagined she was seeing the impact of prison. She felt shame at having meddled, bringing more pain to this wounded family.

"But I know he was recently in Liverpool," she added with forced brightness. "I called to the hostel where he was staying; he was definitely there only a couple of weeks ago. I'm sure he'll be back."

Mrs Symansky turned to her husband and a look passed between them. Then she walked, straight backed, to a dark wood sideboard and pulled open a drawer. She pushed her hand to the back and pulled out a bulky envelope. She held it to her chest as if reluctant to part with it and then handed it to Julia, giving a quick nod to her husband.

"My wife would like you to deliver this to the place where our son will be. She wrote it a long time ago, after Tomasz left, but we have not heard from him for many years now. She had given up hope of ever finding him."

"But I don't know if I will see him again –"

"Please, just leave it in a place where he might go. At least we have hope. We have forgiven him and we hope he can forgive us."

"Forgive you?"

"We never told him that we didn't blame him. He will know what we mean."

Mr Symansky escorted Julia to the door and then spoke in hushed tones, nodding up to the ceiling, "She's breaking her heart without him."

Julia walked back into the evening sun, clutching the letter to her heart, but her heart was shadowed by the image of Tomasz's bereft parents: all that impossible sadness concentrated in his mother's eyes. But at least there was hope and at least she could now do something for Tomasz. She was realising more and more clearly that she'd only ever taken from Tomasz, that she'd betrayed his friendship abhorrently, ignoring his feelings completely. She hoped it wasn't too late.

Over dinner Julia made a decision to tell her mum the full story of Jakob's death and Tomasz's estrangement from his family, finishing with an account of her visit to his parents that day. She saw a measure of disapproval in her mum's eyes.

"Oh Julia, this man means a great deal to you, doesn't he?"

Julia stared into her risotto. "I just want to make things right."

The day after their return to London Julia placed the letter from the Symanskys in a large envelope addressed to the hostel, along with a brief note urging the hostel manager to keep the letter safe in case Tomasz returned. With a thrill she posted it.

CHAPTER 37

Jack lay alone in the king-size bed where he and Maddie had slept each night, side-by-side. He looked through the window at treetops, piercing the stars. He loved the little square of outdoor life he could see from there; the changing artwork of the days and nights, framed by a sash window. He had never really cared if the sky was heavy with cloud, frozen white; flat and grey; deep azure or impenetrable black. What mattered was that he saw it all with the woman he loved. He didn't want to die; he didn't want to miss a single day with her; yet he knew this place could be his deathbed; the small square of sky his final view.

Maddie had arranged the room with flowers and cards from well-wishers, including several from his students. It was only now that he really saw how much he was liked.

He lay under white, Egyptian cotton sheets, his face made luminous by the light from the window. He wore a dark, silk gown the colour of the midnight sky. It was an Art Noveau number Maddie had picked up from a vintage shop in Hampstead, simple in design, except for some pleated detail around the neckline. He felt calm and happy, although he knew it was probably the morphine maintaining him in this state. His skin was pale and transparent and he had no hair anywhere on his body: He was as smooth as a baby; as smooth as a woman.

"After all these years of trying to persuade you not to shave your legs," Maddie joked, "and the whole bloody lot falls out." Jack's body hair had been one aspect of his masculinity Maddie had found difficult to concede; she loved the dark tangle of hair on his legs and forearms; he had only shaved them a couple of times for special occasions and Jack had reassured her he didn't want it gone permanently.

Maddie still felt a quiver of shock every time she walked into the sick room. Not so much at the vision of Jack stripped bare, but because of his strange beauty that took her breath away. His eyes were huge, mercurial pools standing alone in an island of bleached skin, drawing her in with hypnotic lure. His startling radiance seemed to come from within and this troubled Maddie deeply. She feared he was making a transition into death.

It was nearly four months since the accident, which had now become a marker for everything: BA and AA. After two months in hospital most of Jack's injuries were healing well and despite still being in a lot of pain he was able to get out of bed for short periods each day. He had been allowed home with strict instructions and a comprehensive package of nursing care, only returning to the hospital to initiate a new treatment cycle. Doctors told him, with a dry laugh, that he had been lucky; the tumour had been discovered early because of the accident, as a result they had been able to start chemotherapy and the prognosis was better – not good but better. Indeed Jack felt lucky. Every minute he had AA was a gift.

When Julia, Beth and Greg had come to visit earlier that day Jack hadn't covered the silk gown. He had discussed this with Maddie, told her he didn't want to lie about himself anymore. In the privacy of his own mind he thought that if he was going to die he wanted everyone he cared about to know who he really was: both Jack and Anna. Maddie had agreed to speak to visitors beforehand, to prepare them for his 'appearance'.

Julia had come in, eyes wide, fearful. "Your hair!" she said, fighting back tears. She kissed him on the cheek and then sat on the edge of the bed. Beth and Greg held back a little, but Jack could see the naked shock in Beth's eyes. He marvelled at how much he saw in this new enlightened state. He could peer into a person's soul, and how beautiful it was. If only he could convey to people just how astonishing the human soul is beneath its fragile case. Maddie's soul was especially beautiful; it was so full of love it made him want to weep. He had always been jealous of the female soul but now he could see that all souls are made of the same substance. It's the physical packaging – barbed hormones, tough muscles and flesh; the cage of bones and wire-mesh of sinews – that betrays the soul's true tenderness. He knew rationally that it was only the morphine giving him these wonderful insights but he didn't care – he also knew that in some sense he was seeing the truth

"I like your gown," Julia finally said after the usual sickbed small talk.

"Thanks, Maddie chose it; she has a good eye."

"She should paint you; you look like something by Toulouse Lautrec."

"Thanks a lot. Are you saying I look like a lady of the night?"

"No, just very *fin de siècle*," Julia laughed. "So, did everyone know that my dad was a trannie apart from me?"

Jack's eyes were fluid. "You called me Dad."

"Yes, well, you're the closest thing I've got."

"Again, thanks."

"I only found out by accident," said Greg, moving closer to the bed.

"You look beautiful," said Beth in a quiet voice and they all turned to look at her.

"Thanks love."

As he stared at the stars that night Jack felt relief and gratitude at how bravely the people he loved had accepted him. He knew it was only the beginning; that not everyone would be so magnanimous; but being honest was like breathing out after holding his breath for a very long time. He had nothing left to hide. Now he could concentrate on staying alive.

Julia was deeply upset after the visit and sobbed for a long time in her mother's arms.

"Was it a shock to see him... like that?" Beth asked hesitantly.

"He looked like he was going to float away, Mum, like he's going to... die. I can't stand it."

"It's OK love; it's just the effect of the drugs." Beth remembered her father having a similar appearance prior to death, though she didn't say this to Julia. "What about the... cross-dressing?" Beth asked after a few minutes and when Julia had quietened down.

"Weird," she said. "But not shocking."

*

Christmas was fast approaching and everyone was making plans for how to spend it. One Friday evening in early December, Richard called Beth to ask if she and Julia would consider making a trip to Liverpool before Christmas.

"Finn and Angela wondered if it isn't time we all meet and do a bit of talking."

"Oh!" This was a shock to Beth. She had imagined this scene would never have to take place. "What would be the purpose of that?"

"Perhaps several things," said Richard, who had obviously given it a lot of thought. "It would be a way of establishing what sort of relationship, if any, Julia and her father will have in the future," Richard was choosing his words carefully. "It will give Julia the opportunity to ask her father any questions she might have; it will give Angela the opportunity to face her fears and it will give me the chance to see you and Julia again.'

"I can see it might be useful," said Beth, cheered by Richard's words; she had grown fond of him in recent weeks, "but I'm concerned it will set Julia back again. She's doing so well."

"Well, why don't you ask her? If she doesn't want it to happen then it isn't going to."

Later that evening Beth told Julia about her conversation with Richard.

"I'm not sure if I can face it, Mum. I'm not sure if I can face Angela. I feel so guilty about what I did."

"Perhaps it will give you chance to tell her that."

"I'll think about it."

That night Julia lay awake with restless thoughts pacing about her mind. She felt like a child recovering from a nasty fall off a bicycle. She knew the best advice was to get back on as soon as possible, but she still felt the rawness of her wounds. Going back was a good idea on many levels; she felt the tug of the thread connecting her to Liverpool, reminding her that she hadn't yet moved on and her life in London felt temporary, like being in limbo. She was always waiting for news about Jack; most of her friends had returned to University and she felt dissatisfied with her job as a sales assistant. She'd thought about writing to Angela many times, to tell her she was sorry, but she just didn't know how to do it without sounding false. And then there was the matter of Tomasz, who she was unable to forget. The idea of calling at the hostel, one last time, had its appeal.

Her feelings were complex but there was something exciting about taking positive action at last, to release her from this strangely suspended state.

The following morning at breakfast, when mother and daughter sat at the table, Julia shared her thoughts.

"OK," Beth said in an even voice. "I'll let Richard know and he can make arrangements."

Beth called Richard as soon as Julia had left for her Saturday shift in Denmark Street. He sounded pleased and said he would get back to her with some possible dates. Two hours later he called with a date in two weeks time, a Saturday. Beth told Julia that evening.

"That should be fine. I am supposed to go to a gig with Josh that night but it's not important."

Josh was an old friend of Julia's who had recently shown romantic interest. Beth had encouraged the friendship on the grounds that he was a nice, straightforward boy and the same age as Julia.

"Oh that's a shame… if you're sure."

"Yeah, yeah. I can see Josh anytime. Shall we book tickets now?" Julia was already pulling the laptop towards her and with a few efficient jabs at the keyboard the train tickets were booked. Beth felt a quiet elation.

Two weeks later they boarded a train to Liverpool. Richard picked them up at Lime Street Station and they made the familiar journey to his house in Cheshire. The scene was very different this time, with trees stripped bare and the night frozen and black. The Cheshire air was sweet and pure after breathing clammy lung-fulls of London air and Beth inhaled deeply. The trellis on the side of Richard's house was now bare and the naked vines were skeletal hands climbing the wall. To Beth the scene was just as beautiful as in the ripeness of summer.

"I've made you a bit of supper; I don't know if you're hungry… you're probably tired. I'll take your bags up… I've arranged for us to go to Finn and Angela's at eleven tomorrow, if that's OK."

"Are we going to their house?" Julia was a little alarmed by this information; she'd imagined a neutral venue.

"Angela has been advised to rest as much as possible; because of previous complications."

"Oh, I see. That's fine," said Julia, submitting to her penance.

They were quiet as they drove to Woolton the following day. Julia's mouth was dry and she felt sick in the pit of her stomach. The village was decorated with Christmas lights and a tastefully dressed tree. Shop windows bulged with all kinds of seasonal goods. Julia felt a return of shame as she saw the streets where she had stalked Angela months earlier. She had told no one of this shameful activity. Only Tomasz kept her secret as she kept his; they were partners in crime.

To Julia's shock, Angela opened the door, bursting with pregnancy. Julia could see the partial return of the woman in the photograph, rounded and hopeful, although telltale signs of worry were now permanently etched around her eyes. Angela's look was wary and her body was rigid, as if she was steeling herself for the meeting. Finn looked uncomfortable, not knowing whether to stand or sit and ending up perched on the arm of the sofa until Angela returned with a tray of drinks. She placed them on a coffee table and then lowered herself into the sofa; with gratitude Finn slipped down beside her. To everyone's relief Richard took control, acting as a kind of chair of the meeting. He introduced possible topics and then only intervened if the meeting fell into an uncomfortable silence. Beth took on a similar, though less involved, role.

On the whole it was a successful meeting. Angela was gracious, opening the way for Julia to apologise, although the coolness in her demeanour never thawed. She said she understood what had happened. She wanted Julia to know that she was happy for an exchange of information to continue, even an occasional visit, although she wasn't sure if she could handle Julia and her husband meeting alone, just yet. She needed calm and certainty over the coming months. As the meeting progressed, Julia gained the distinct impression that it had largely been Angela's idea. She'd had to see, with her womanly intuition, whether Julia was a threat to her happiness. When she felt somewhat reassured, she relaxed into a posture of confident wife and hostess.

It was only towards the end of the meeting that Finn and Julia managed a furtive glance towards one another. Julia now saw a rather hunched and emotionally weak man, who had fallen victim to a mid-life crisis as much as genetic impulses.

At many points in the meeting he looked as if he was about to grab hold of his wife's hand, or even rest his head like a child on the comforting bump of her belly. Julia saw that Angela was the stronger of the two, the rock of the relationship. She felt she was seeing him objectively for the first time and could coldly list in her mind the things she liked about him and the things she didn't. She marvelled at the extent of her former blindness and felt startled by the staggering depth of the feelings she'd had for this man. Yet she was also struggling to see him as a father and she concluded that he would probably always remain an unclassifiable aspect of her life.

She wondered how Finn now viewed her, whether he felt the same sense of having escaped. He did, in fact, but for different reasons. He now saw a beautiful, insouciant and slightly scary young woman sitting before him. He saw that, once the passion had worn thin, he could never have satisfied her intelligent and inquisitive mind. He still felt a nagging attraction towards her but only as he might feel an embarrassing lust towards the daughter of a friend.

At the end of the meeting Finn handed Julia an envelope. "It's a family tree with a few interesting facts and photos," he muttered.

"Thanks, that's great. I look forward to seeing it."

"If you need anything more, just let me know. My email address is in there." They fell into awkwardness and this seemed an appropriate place to end the meeting. They rose from their seats and Angela told Finn to get coats. While they waited Julia looked into Angela's eyes.

"I would really like to know how everything goes… with the baby." She nodded towards Angela's bump.

"I will let you know. Good luck with everything."

They drove back to Cheshire with a sense of relief bordering on elation.

"How about lunch in a country pub?" Richard suggested. He drove to a quaint place in Little Budworth with an open fire roaring at one end and the quiet murmur of conversation. They discussed how the meeting had gone and they all agreed it had been a good idea and very productive. After they had eaten, Julia took out the O'Sullivan family tree. Richard added clarity to a few points and told Julia stories about the antics of her ancestors.

"They were a lively lot," he chuckled.

The following day, before catching the train back to London, Richard dropped Julia off in the city centre while he and Beth went to the Albert Dock for lunch. Julia headed for Wood Street where she'd arranged a quick drink with Susan.

Afterwards, Julia headed for the hostel. When she pushed open the front door she saw a stranger in reception and her heart sank.

"Is Matt around?" she asked.

"Matt? I think the guy left to go travelling a few weeks ago; I'm new." He had an accent that sounded Scandinavian.

"I used to stay here. I had a friend… a Polish guy called Tomasz. I just wondered if he'd been back."

"Was he the writer? I've heard about him."

"Yes. Has he been back?"

"Yes," the man nodded slowly. "I think he did come back recently but then he left again."

"Oh." Julia felt the heavy drag of disappointment. "Do you know if Dave gave him the letter I sent?"

"Hang on. Let me ask Dave." The guy disappeared for a few minutes and returned, holding something in his hand.

"What is your name?"

"Julia. Julia Swann."

"Well, then this is for you, Julia Swann." He handed her a slim, white envelope with her name, c/o the hostel, written on the front. "Dave said he gave your letter to Tomasz weeks ago; soon after that he left."

"Thank you so much." She clutched the letter to her breast.

Despite the coldness of the day Julia immediately made for a bench in the little garden at the centre of Falkner Square. She instinctively lifted the envelope to her nose and breathed in deeply;

she could have sworn the smell of fresh bread infused the paper.

She remembered Tomasz' words about the beauty of handwritten letters and his sensory delight in revisiting the letter from his first girlfriend. This raised the possibility that Tomasz had found a girl who deserved his love more than her. She could hardly bear to open the letter, fearing what it might tell her. She sat staring at it for several minutes, passing it from hand to hand and turning it over and over. Eventually she succumbed to its lure and tore it open. Inside was a photograph of a stone Angel. It was quite magnificent, with its gown sweeping over a graceful form; one hand on its heart, the other hanging by its side. The Angel's head was bowed in apparent contemplation and its unusually elaborate wings filled the frame. The Angel had turned mossy green in places and ivy climbed up its torso and curled around its neck. Visible behind the statue was an ivy-clad tree, through which glinted a low evening sun. Julia turned the photograph over. On the back there was a riddle:

Near Frankenstein's line
Nevermore Raven perches
Where Pilgrim meets Friday
Poetess and two churches
In New Campo Santo
Dissenting 'til death
Remember, Father of Hymnody
Breathed his last breath
And here I will linger
When day meets twelfth night
Where Brook flows to Elm Tree
This Angel takes flight
My hope is too fragile
So please, love, be kind
For love's the noblest frailty
Of the mind.

This was all. Her mind flew into panic. She was due to meet her mum at Lime Street Station in an hour, yet Tomasz could be somewhere in this city; waiting. Why couldn't he just use a mobile phone like a normal person or at least tell her in plain English where he would be? She studied the picture again. What on earth was he trying to tell her?

On impulse she ran to Catharine Street and flagged down a black cab. "St Peter's Church, Woolton Village, please." After what seemed an interminable time she jumped out next to the church, asking the cab driver to wait. She ran through the lych gate into the graveyard and walked briskly between the graves. It was immediately clear that the mossy Angel in the picture was unlikely to be at home in this manicured setting. Even so, she hurried around the perimeters, dismissing each grave as she went. She halted to look at the grave Angela had stopped by, where Richard, her half-brother, was buried. Then she ran back to the cab.

On the journey to Lime Street she examined the postcard again, back and front, but she realised the riddle would need more than a few minutes to solve. She studied the front of the envelope and her heart leapt when she realised Tomasz had posted it from Gdansk.

She arrived at the station with five minutes to spare. Her mum stood on the concourse with Richard, an anxious expression on her face.

"Sorry," Julia said as she ran, breathless, towards them, "I got caught up in stuff."

They said goodbye to Richard and found their seats; soon the train pulled away. "Mum, why don't we invite Richard to stay for Christmas?"

"Oh, I hadn't thought about it, love."

"I'd like to get to know him better; he is my grandfather. Anyway, you seem to get on really well with him."

Beth looked out of the window at the retreating sweep of Lime Street Station. "I'll have a think about it."

CHAPTER 38

The following day was Monday and Julia's day off. After her mum left for work she made a cafetiere of coffee and studied the riddle once again, examining every detail of the photograph for clues. "I'm hopeless at riddles," she muttered, "why did you set me a riddle, Tomasz?" She switched on the internet and searched through every cemetery in Liverpool, hoping to find one that could possibly accommodate such an Angel. Liverpool had many cemeteries but the online photographs available showed row after and row of orderly graves and no sign of vine-tangled Angels. She realised she might have to explore further afield. She googled graveyards in Gdansk and found several references to 'The Cemetery of the lost Cemeteries', a memorial dedicated to the citizens of Gdansk who had been buried in one of the twenty-seven graveyards that were either destroyed in WWII or purposefully bulldozed at the end of the war.

After several hours, Julia felt frustrated and her mind was bent over with words and images. She called Maddie, who invited her round to Carysfort Road. Snowflakes were falling as she made her way there. They hardly looked as if they could survive the crash to earth.

"How's Jack?" she asked as soon as Maddie opened the door.

"Come and see for yourself." Maddie led her upstairs and into the attic room. Jack was sitting on a stool, working some clay. Julia could see flecks of snow beginning to lace the glass of the skylight. A pale slant of light fell across Jack's face. His head was still bare but there was some colour in his cheeks.

"Wow Jack, you look well."

Jack looked up. "Hi love, I feel well, thanks."

"He seems to be responding to treatment." said Maddie, "but we go back to hospital after Christmas for tests. I'll get us some drinks."

Julia threw her arms around Jack. She felt his still shrunken frame beneath baggy clothes. "I'm so glad."

"To what do we owe this pleasure?" Jack waved his clay-covered hand in the air.

"Are you any good at solving riddles?"

"I can't solve the riddle of my own life, never mind anyone else's."

Julia handed Jack the postcard, which he held between two clay-free fingertips.

"Very mysterious; what's this about?"

"Oh it's a long story. My friend Tomasz sent it to me. I think it might lead me to him; if I can solve the flaming thing."

"Very interesting: angels, poets, graveyards, death. Is he a cheerful soul, your friend?

Julia gave a wry smile.

"I'm sorry, love, my brain isn't very focused at the moment. I could give you some wacky insights if you like but I'm not sure they'd be much help. Ask Maddie."

"Are you talking about me?" a tray appeared through a hole in the floor. Julia ran to take it. "Have a look at this Mads; it's your kind of thing," said Jack

Maddie sat on a stool and examined the riddle; her clear green eyes scanned each line.

"Umm; very interesting: poets, angels, death..."

"Yeah, yeah," Jack chipped in, "Tell us something we don't know."

"God, I think I preferred you when you were all ethereal and compliant." Maddie slapped Jack on the arm. "I know Campo

Santo means sacred ground in Spanish."

"I think it's a cemetery somewhere," said Julia, "because of the picture of the Angel on the front."

Maddie turned it over. "Oh yes, that figures. But you need to know where it is?"

"Yes."

"It's quite an elaborate angel; almost like a fairy with those detailed wings and the cap on its head. It's not typical of angels in Western Christian art. Sorry I'm not being very helpful. It could be Spanish, though it reminds me of stuff I saw in Lachaise Cemetery in Paris."

"God, maybe, he's leading me to Paris; does he think I've got time to swan around the world looking for him?"

"Romantic though," said Maddie, smiling at Julia.

Julia felt herself redden; she spoke quickly, "Anything else you can think of?"

Maddie turned the photograph over and examined the riddle again, "Well, twelfth night could be a reference to Shakespeare or it might just mean the actual twelfth night, on 5th January."

"Really!" Julia was excited. "That could be when I'm supposed to meet him."

"I'll copy it down and have a good look later," said Maddie.

"You should ask your mum," Jack suggested as Julia was leaving. "She reads more than anyone I know and she was always good at *The Times* crosswords and stuff like that."

"Oh yes, before I forget," said Maddie, handing the postcard back to Julia, "I'm inviting a few people over as usual on Christmas Eve if you and your mum are around and as long as Jack is well enough..."

"I will be," said Jack, already returning to his sculpture.

The snowfall was heavy during the night and surprised everyone in the morning with its glaring audacity. Julia dragged her mum into Clissold Park, "Before it's ruined." They completed a quick circuit past the birdhouse, the café, around the tennis courts and back. Julia was satisfied.

"I have to get to work now love," Beth protested.

"Will you look at the riddle with me tonight, please?"

The past few days had been busy with Christmas shopping and hectic work schedules. Neither Julia nor her mum had had chance to look at the riddle, although it was never far from Julia's mind. Beth was particularly agitated after Richard had agreed to stay for Christmas. She had lost the knack of entertaining and was in an anxious flutter about getting everything right.

"Yes, I promise."

After dinner that night Beth pulled her reading glasses on and studied the riddle with her eyebrows drawn together in concentration. She frequently scribbled notes on a piece of paper. Julia listened to her mother's mutterings with one ear while the other ear was attached to her ipod. After an hour Beth said, "OK, I think I've deciphered some of it, but why don't we work together. If you get on the internet, I'll tell you what to look up."

Julia tore out the headphones, jumped up and sat next to her mum on the sofa with the laptop on her knee.

"What have you got?"

"I'll start with the bits I'm more sure about: Pilgrim probably refers to *Pilgrim's Progress* by John Bunyan and Friday might be Man Friday from *Robinson Crusoe*, by Daniel Defoe, but I don't know where the two authors met or if they ever did, and I don't know if it means 'meeting' in the sense of dates, places or ideas? Now I know Daniel Defoe lived in Stoke Newington for a time… But I'm not sure about Bunyan."

"OK, I'll look him up." Julia made some confident taps on the keyboard.

"John Bunyan… blah blah… oh wait a minute, there is a connection to Stoke Newington; he stayed here for a while. Maybe Tomasz is here, in Stoke Newington… the Angel might be in

Abney Cemetery."

"Hold your horses, love, Abney is a big place; let's do a bit more work before you go rushing off into the night. *Father of Hymnody*," Beth ran her index finger along the line, "I think that could be Charles Wesley. He wrote tons of hymns; we used to sing them in the Brownies before I got kicked out for being a Catholic. But as far as I know the Wesley's never lived in Stoke Newington."

"What does *Dissenting 'til death* mean?"

"I'm not sure. I think Dissenters are the same as non-conformists. The Wesley's were non-conformists and I think I remember reading that John Bunyan was imprisoned for his non-conformist beliefs."

"OK, let me check. Gosh this is sooo exciting. Yes, John Bunyan was imprisoned for preaching without a licence; he was baptised in the river Ooze. Does that make him a Dissenter?"

"I should think. What about Defoe?"

"Wait a minute… yes, Defoe was a non-conformist too. There was a Dissenting Academy in Stoke Newington. Perhaps that's the connection. Let me Google all three names and see what comes up… Defoe, Bunyan and Wesley. Ooo! There's a place called Bunhill Fields in Islington. It says Bunhill comes from Bone Hill. It has been a burial site for a thousand years… blah, blah. Yes, here we are: Bunhill Fields was a Dissenter's graveyard. Bunyan and Defoe were buried there as well as Suzanna Wesley, the mother of John and Charles. You were right, Mum." Julia almost knocked the computer off her lap in her excitement. "It is Charles Wesley. Tomasz's Angel must be in Bunhill Cemetery. I'm going there tomorrow."

"OK, but shall we look at a bit more; it might help you locate the Angel."

"Yes, go on; this is addictive."

Beth returned the glasses to her nose. "What about *Where Brook flows to Elm Tree*?"

"I was wondering about that. Perhaps there's a brook in Bunhills, but I can't find any reference to it on the Bunhill site."

"Perhaps you'll find that out when you're there. OK, I'm not sure what *Frankenstein's line* means but Mary Shelly was the author of Frankenstein; and I think she was born somewhere in North London."

"All those years of burying your head in books wasn't wasted after all." Julia tapped the keyboard. "OK, Mary Shelley was born in London, the daughter of Mary Wollstonecraft, an eighteenth-century writer, philosopher and feminist who wrote *Maria, or the Wrongs of Women*, in which she asserted that women had strong sexual desires and that it was degrading and immoral to pretend otherwise. This work damned Mary in the eyes of critics throughout the following century; poor woman. She died ten days after her daughter was born. Some think the loss of her mother brought about Mary Shelley's obsession with bringing the dead to life; hence Frankenstein."

"So you could say Frankenstein had a direct lineage to Mary Wollstonecraft's death," said Beth.

"Oh listen to this, Mum, Mary Wollstonecraft was a non-conformist too and she was involved in the Unitarian Chapel on Newington Green, but I can't find a reference to where she was buried."

"Your friend is leading us on a merry little dance, isn't he?"

"He's a bit of a Dissenter too; though not in the religious sense."

"I am looking forward to meeting this man," said Beth. "OK, one more line then I have to go to bed; I'm exhausted. *Nevermore Raven* I think refers to a poem, *The Raven*, by Edgar Allen Poe. I think he had some connection to Stoke Newington too."

"What does *Nevermore* mean?"

"It's a very dark poem. One night a raven visits a man who is heartbroken at the loss of his lover; the man keeps asking the raven questions but to every question the raven only replies

'Nevermore.' The man slowly goes insane. On that cheerful note I'm going to bed." Beth rose from the sofa. "Don't stay up too late; we have a busy day tomorrow."

The next day the snow lost its battle against the sun and an unusually warm southerly wind. Julia had never worked on Christmas Eve before and it felt strange to her, as if another part of childhood was losing ground.

As soon as she was let out of work Julia headed for Bunhill Fields, through heavy Christmas Eve traffic. To her disappointment, a notice informed her that the graveyard had closed at four and wouldn't be opening again until 29th December. She walked around the circumference of the burial site and peered through forbidding gothic railings, but it was too dark to see far and her view was largely obscured by trees.

Richard arrived at seven-thirty. They had a glass of wine together and then they walked over to Carysfort Road, where Julia had already absconded. Carysfort Road looked the picture of Christmas cheer with flickering candles, a sparkling tree and bunches of holly, heavy with blood-red berries. Jack stood beside the crackling fire, one elbow resting on the mantelpiece and a glass of ruby wine in his hand. He wore jeans and a cable-knit jumper and looked the picture of the gentleman host. As people arrived he offered drinks while Maddie brought in plates of food.

Maddie had limited the invites to close friends so that it wasn't too taxing for Jack. Greg and Dave had already planned to spend Christmas in Spain with their adopted children, but Pat made an appearance. She had now retired and was fulfilling her dream of planning small gardens for space-starved Londoners. Kate, now in her thirties, didn't come; she had climbed the ladder of a successful advertising company. "Her life's a whirl of non-stop social events," Pat told them with barely disguised pride.

There were a couple of notable absences from the soiree:

friends who, it seemed, hadn't been able to accept Jack's revelations and others who, although they didn't say it in so many words, always seemed to have prior engagements. Jack and Maddie had been wounded by this, but were reconciling themselves to the inevitable fall-out.

By eleven Jack was flagging and at midnight he fell asleep on the sofa. Maddie saw the guests out, inviting them over for dinner on New Year's Day.

"Jack insisted," she said. "It's like he's making up for lost time."

Christmas dinner was a quiet affair. Richard didn't comment on Beth's brick-like Christmas cake or lumpy brandy custard; there were enough alternatives to compensate for the few disasters as well as enough to feed them all for a week.

"I think I've overdone it a bit," said Beth, surveying the mass of deserts and cakes spread across work surfaces; her panic buying now seemed ridiculously over the top.

"Better too much than too little," said Richard, kindly

After lunch Julia met up with friends in the Red Lion. Josh was attentive, manoeuvring himself into positions that maximised his physical contact with her. The more attention he gave her, the more Julia realised she wasn't in the least attracted to him and she found creative ways to extricate herself from his company.

She was aware of small cracks opening up in old friendships; already she seemed to have little in common with certain friends outside the uniting interest of school or adolescent pursuits. She thought she could predict those who would be lifelong friends and those who would soon be relegated to childhood memory. She found herself comparing her male friends, including Josh, to Tomasz and they were often found wanting. She longed to get back to the riddle; it connected her to Tomasz, transporting her into his curious mind.

Boxing Day started bright with a brisk, cool breeze.

"We're going for a walk on Hampstead Heath," said Beth after breakfast, "do you want to come?"

"No, I want to chill out today, play keyboards; watch trash on TV."

But after they'd left Julia found she couldn't concentrate on her scales or settle to watch TV and eventually she returned to the riddle. She browsed all the sites that made reference to Bunhill Fields and was pleased to discover it had once been known as 'The Campo Santo of the Dissenter'. This convinced her further that this was the place she would find Tomasz on Twelfth Night.

The following day Beth and Richard went to visit museums while Julia walked to Abney Cemetery, first sending a text to her mum, 'Gone looking for angels'. The sun was struggling to burn through the strands of mist hanging like lost spirits over Sycamore, Poplar and mature Willow trees. She strolled along the main paths looking for any sign of the Angel, in case Bunhills turned out to be a false lead. There were many angels lining her path, most dappled with lichen, victims of vines and creepers, but none looked exactly like Tomasz's Angel. After several minutes of exploration she heard a noise behind her; she turned sharply to see a dark shape move in the undergrowth. She suddenly felt vulnerable and was aware of her solitude. It crossed her mind that Tomasz was here, perhaps living rough among the gothic ruins of graves and monuments. But then a man stumbled from the undergrowth and reeled onto the path, almost falling to the ground at her feet. She gasped, but quickly assessed that the man, who clung for dear life to a can of Special Brew, was hopelessly drunk and unlikely to attack her, or succeed if he tried. However, the encounter shook her and Julia decided to return another day.

The following day Beth saw Richard off from Euston Station and despite being glad to have her home back, she felt an inexplicable sadness. Richard had become a true friend, and, apart from Sasha who she still saw occasionally, Beth realised he was one of the few friends who was truly her own.

CHAPTER 39

Julia finished work too late to get to Bunhill Fields that day; in fact it wasn't until New Years Eve, when staff were let out early, that she had her first opportunity to explore the graveyard. It was an entirely different sort of place to Abney: It had been well maintained and was used by city workers as a place to lunch. There was a grassy area and numerous park benches provided for eating or simply reflecting; and even on this cool December day, suit-clad workers consumed sandwiches and soup among the graves and oaks of the ancient burial site. Julia's heart was beating fiercely as she walked the straight paths of this tranquil setting. She read on an information board that victims of the plague had been buried here, piled one on top of the other. Dissenters had later been laid on top of their corpses. It was unconsecrated ground and therefore known as a burial site rather than a cemetery.

Despite the quantity of people buried there over the years, it was a compact area and after wandering for only a short time it became apparent to Julia that not only was there no brook, but neither were there any angels. The graves and family tombs were mostly simple and unadorned as befitted the non-conformist life. Julia felt the slow drag of disappointment and wondered where she could go from there. It crossed her mind that Tomasz had made a mistake when designing the riddle, making it impossible to solve. This thought sent a thrill of panic through her heart. She couldn't imagine never seeing him again, or bear him thinking she didn't care. She left the graveyard and made her way to local shops where, with lethargy taking hold of her, she bought last minute items for the party that night.

When she arrived home laden with bags of shopping, she felt despondent. "It isn't Bunhill Fields, Mum; there aren't any angels there."

"Never mind, love, there's plenty of time. I'm sure we can work it out." Beth glanced at her watch. "You'd better think about getting ready for your party."

Julia enjoyed the party more than she'd anticipated. After a couple of drinks, her despondency lifted and she threw herself into the action. Just before midnight someone passed around champagne and, when Josh ran to her side with a hopeful expression, she allowed him a long, slow kiss to the chime of Big Ben. They danced until three and then caught the night bus home together, saying goodnight at Julia's door.

She slept until midday, waking to the smell of coffee and fried eggs and the haunting sound of Joni Mitchell. Without the inhibiting effect of alcohol, guilt and regret made an uncomfortable appearance.

"I thought I'd better invade your senses," said Beth as Julia dragged herself into the kitchen, a sloppy dressing gown pulled around her. "We're going to Jack and Maddie's in a couple of hours."

"Oh yeah, I forgot."

"Do you want eggs and coffee?"

"Yes please, Mum, I'm starving. Oh God, I kissed Josh last night."

"Why did you do that? I didn't think you liked him."

"I was drunk. It seemed the right thing to do at the time. Now it's going to be way harder to tell him I'm not interested."

"Well you never do things by halves, do you love? The words 'tangled web' and 'weave' come to mind."

Jack was playing backgammon with Greg while Dave was in the kitchen preparing food with Maddie. Caitlin and Sam were battling with a jigsaw puzzle on the floor. Caitlin gave a wary look when Beth and Julia entered the room, like a small lioness protecting her cub. She had only met them a couple of times and wouldn't yet allow them a place in her world. Conversely, Sam ran to them, eager to engage. Beth settled in a chair by the fire while Julia gently offered help with the jigsaw. Without eye contact, Caitlin gave a small nod of assent.

At three they sat down to eat. Dave was trying out several new recipes and there were sighs of pleasure as the guests tasted each new dish. Julia was glad to see that Jack was getting better by the day: he seemed less ethereal and more earthbound. After dinner, Julia and Greg cleared the dishes and chatted in the kitchen over soapsuds.

"I believe you've had a riddle from lover boy. Have you solved it yet?"

"Hey, he's not my lover boy and no I haven't solved it yet."

"Can I have a look later? I'm crap at riddles but I love the romance of it all."

"Sure, any help is appreciated. How's it been with the kids? They seem happy."

"We've had our ups and downs. They're still quite insecure. Caitlin started school in September and she really freaked out."

"Is that usual with adopted children?"

"Apparently. We've read a whole library of books about it but it's still hard to deal with when it's actually happening. Sam is much more settled, probably because he was younger when he came to us. He didn't witness as much crap. She's like a mini-mummy at times. We're trying to help her just be a child again. Anyway, we love them to bits."

"What's it like being a house husband?"

"Oh, I love it most of the time; it's like discovering a whole new world. I go to all these parent and toddler groups and gossip about clothes for hours."

"You're so gay."

Greg laughed. "I'll probably start some part-time work once Sam has settled in nursery. I do think my brain's getting a bit mushy."

"Hey, less talk and more work you two." Maddie whipped Greg on the bottom with a tea towel.

"And here's Aunt Maddie," said Greg. "The kids absolutely adore her; she can do no wrong."

Julia noticed the pleasure infuse Maddie's face. "It's because they know I'm a soft touch."

"Hey, Mads, have you got a copy of that riddle? I want to see it."

"Oh yes; we've worked out a few more lines but we didn't get very far; we've been too busy. It's in there; you go and have a look while I make coffee."

Greg and Julia sat on the sofa staring at the riddle, while Beth commented from a distance.

"For a start Charles Wesley isn't the *Father of Hymnody*," said Greg.

"Who is then?"

"Isaac Watts."

"Who's he?" asked Julia.

"Are you sure?" said Beth. "I was certain it was Charles Wesley."

"How on earth did you know that?" asked Maddie as she brought in a tray of coffee.

"Hey, I don't tell too many people about my sordid past but I'm actually the son of a preacher man. I was brought up in a non-conformist household and I know for a fact that Isaac Watts and not Charles Wesley was the *Father of Hymnody*."

"Oh dear, that could change everything," said Beth.

"I think Isaac Watts had some connection with this area," said Maddie. "I seem to remember reading it somewhere."

"His name does sound familiar, now you mention it," said Julia. "I'm sure his grave was in Bunhill Fields."

"But there aren't any angels in Bunhill," said Beth.

"Why does Tomasz have to be so bloody cryptic?" said Julia. "It's driving me insane. I only have four days left to work it out."

"Perhaps he needs to know you really want to see him," said Maddie, "enough to bother working it all out."

"We'd better get the kids home to bed," said Greg, rising from the sofa. "We'll pay for this in the morning." There were loud protests from the siblings as games were packed away, coats put on and they were bundled into the car.

"Good luck with the search," Greg shouted as they pulled away.

On the evening of the third of January, Beth and Julia once again found time to sit down together to work on the riddle, armed with the new information supplied by Greg.

"OK, let's be systematic," said Beth. "First of all check if Isaac Watts is the *Father of Hymnody* as Greg said."

Julia tapped the keyboard. "Yes, here it is. Wikipedia says Isaac Watts is known as the father of English Hymnody and he's buried in Bunhill Fields; there's a picture of his grave."

"OK, so that doesn't change much; let's look at another line."

Julia read, "*Poetess 'twixt two churches*. I was assuming the two churches were the Wesleyan chapel and maybe the Quaker meeting place by Bunhill Fields. William Blake is buried in Bunhill but I haven't found any reference to a poetess."

"I still have the feeling it's somewhere closer to home," said Beth. "Most of the other writers had connections to Stoke Newington."

"Do you know of any poetesses who lived in Stoke Newington?"

"I have a feeling there was one but I can't remember her name."

"OK, female poets; Stoke Newington… blah, blah. Here's one: Anna Laetitia Barbauld, 1743 – 1825; she was a prominent eighteenth-century poet, essayist, and children's author. She lived in Stoke Newington from 1803."

"Anything else?"

"It says Barbauld's literary career ended abruptly in 1812 with the publication of her poem *Eighteen Hundred and Eleven*, which criticised Britain's participation in the Napoleonic Wars. She argued that the British Empire was waning and the American empire was waxing, and that Britain would become nothing but an empty ruin. Listen to this:

And think'st thou, Britain, still to sit at ease,
An island Queen amidst thy subject sea…
So sing thy flatterers; but, Britain, know,
Thou who hast shared the guilt must share the woe.
Nor distant is the hour; low murmurs spread,
And whispered fears, creating what they dread;
Ruin, as with an earthquake shock, is here

"Scarily accurate, hey? She sounds a bit like Tomasz with all her doom and gloom. Anyway, she published nothing else in her lifetime."

"Does it say where she was buried?"

"It says her husband took over the chapel in Newington Green – another Dissenter – but he went mad and one day chased her around the house with a knife. She jumped out of the window to escape. He later drowned himself in the New River. Anna died in 1825 and… Mum, Mum… she was buried in the family vault in St Mary's Church. I can't believe I haven't even looked there. Shall we go now?" It wasn't a question; Julia was already placing the laptop to one side.

"I've walked past there a thousand times," said Beth, "and I really don't remember seeing any angels. Anyway, it's too dark, love, we won't see anything." Beth knew her protests were to no avail.

"We'll take torches; it isn't very big. Come on, Mum, it'll be fun."

"What about the rest of the riddle."

"We'll look at that when we get back."

They found a torch and put on coats and gloves. The wind had changed to easterly and it attacked any exposed skin with bitter stabs.

"What I do for you; you're mad, daughter," said Beth, pulling her coat tightly around her.

They wandered down the little path running alongside St Mary's Old Church.

"Wait here a minute, Mum, I'm going to climb over and explore at the back of the church."

"Are you sure you should be…"

Julia was already over the railings, disappearing among the dark silhouettes of graves. Beth saw erratic arcs of torchlight and then she was left in darkness. Five minutes later, Julia returned, casting the torch beam into the skies as she climbed over the railings. "No angels here; another false lead."

"I didn't think so. Now can we please go home for a hot cup of tea?"

"What if Tomasz got his facts wrong, Mum?" said Julia, back in the warmth of the flat. "I might never find him."

"He writes detective stories doesn't he? Surely he'd check out his facts. Anyway, let's carry on." Beth placed the glasses on her nose and looked with librarian efficiency at the riddle. "We've established that Tomasz will be waiting in the mysterious location on the 5th January, Twelfth Night." Beth took a sip of steaming tea.

"Yes, in two days' time."

"At what time?"

"When day meets night; in other words at dusk, I think. I looked it up; the sun sets at six minutes past four on the fifth."

"So you won't have long before it goes dark."

"No, and I don't fancy hanging around in a graveyard."

Beth lowered the riddle to her lap and sought Julia's eyes. "Are you sure you want to do this, love? You don't have to be there you know. Perhaps it's too soon."

Julia contemplated her mother's words for several seconds.

"Mum, I have to do this. I have to see Tomasz again. There was something… special between us."

"OK. Let's come back to this with a fresh mind tomorrow."

The following evening Julia met Josh for a drink to tell him she didn't want a relationship, only friendship. Anger flared in Josh's eyes and he accused Julia of leading him on with the kiss. Julia defended her position, saying she had been drunk, that she had never given him any encouragement before New Year's Eve and that he practically forced himself upon her. After further heated exchanges, Josh stormed out of the pub leaving Julia with a half glass of wine and a prickly sense of guilt. She drank the wine and made her way home.

"How did it go?" Beth was washing dishes in the kitchen.

"Terrible. He was really angry. I don't think he'll want anything to do with me again. God Mum, why do I mess everything up?" Julia crumpled into a chair.

"I'm sure he'll get over it love. It was only a drunken kiss. His pride is hurt."

"I must be really stupid. I don't think of the consequences of anything I do. I hurtle from one disaster to another. I can't even solve a stupid riddle."

"It's a good job you've got a brilliant mum then, isn't it?"

Julia's head shot up. "You've worked it out?"

"It was going round and round in my head last night in bed and then I had a flash of inspiration in work today."

"Tell me, tell me." Julia looked eagerly into her mother's face.

"Well, we didn't take enough notice of the details; we were too caught up in the bigger picture."

"What do you mean?"

"Well," Beth dried her hands, sat opposite Julia and pulled the riddle across the table towards her. "It says:

Remember, Father of Hymnody

*Breathed his last breat*h."

"Isn't it Isaac Watts after all?"

"Yes it is, but it's not Bunhill Fields."

"But that's where Isaac Watts is buried."

"But that's not where he breathed his last breath. You don't breathe once you're dead."

"Of course, you genius. Where did he die?"

"The site of New Campo Santo."

"That's Bunhill Fields."

"No, again it's in the detail. Bunhill Fields closed for burials in 1854, after that the *New* Campo Santo was opened and became the main burial ground for Dissenters."

"Mum, just tell me where it is; I can't bear it anymore."

"OK. I've been doing a bit of Googling myself. Isaac Watts spent the last years of his life living in Abney House with Lady Mary Abney, the widow of Sir Thomas Abney, who was once Lord Mayor of London."

"Where?"

"It no longer exists; it's been demolished..."

"But..."

"It says, *Remember*, *Father of Hymnology*. As a crossword fanatic I should have taken notice of the word, *Remember*. There's a memorial to Isaac Watts on the site of Abney House."

"Which is where?"

"The *New* Campo Santo."

"Mum, for God's sake, where is it?"

Beth smiled. "Abney Cemetery."

"Oh my God, right on our doorstep."

"Well, we kind of got sidetracked, didn't we? And I didn't help by leading you up the garden path with Charles Wesley. But no harm done, it's not too late."

"So Tomasz's Angel takes flight in Abney cemetery tomorrow at sunset. But how do we find the right angel?"

"I think there might be a clue in the last two lines.

Love's the noblest frailty

Of the mind

"They're from a poem by Dryden, but I can't find any connection between Dryden and Stoke Newington and he wasn't buried in Abney Cemetery."

Julia yawned. "I think I'm too tired to look at any more tonight."

"Let's sleep on it sweet daughter."

CHAPTER 40

5th January came shrouded in thick fog, the likes of which was now seldom seen in London. Julia couldn't see to the bottom of the tiny garden and her heart sank. She'd been awake early, eager to get to Abney Cemetery and identify the Angel. She had taken the day off work, while her mum wasn't back in the office until the following Monday.

"Mum, how am I going to find the Angel or Tomasz in this?"

"Oh dear," said Beth peering out of the window, "it might lift in a couple of hours."

"I'm sure the gods are against me."

Beth laughed. "Why have you gone all Shakespearian?"

"Because I feel all Shakespearian; I feel like a tragedy."

"Poor love. Lets wait for a couple of hours and then I'll come with you."

At ten-thirty there was no sign of the fog lifting but Julia persuaded her mum to go to the cemetery anyway.

"I'm telling you," said Beth, with rare forcefulness, as they entered the cemetery grounds, "you're not coming here at dusk if it's like this. I'll lock you in your room if I have to."

Julia laughed. "There's no lock on my door, Mum, and, anyway, I'll climb out of my window; I've done it before."

"You what…?"

"Only joking; don't worry, I won't be coming here if it's like this. Tomasz will just have to find me."

"It really is a very beautiful place," said Beth, as they traced the network of tangled paths overarched with dark branches made sinister by swathes of fog. The air was thick and acrid and the harsh call of crows seemed to hang intimately close to them in the unusual stillness of the city air. Julia had downloaded a map of the cemetery and it showed an asymmetrical petal-like pattern of paths with the centre housing the chapel and Isaac Watt's memorial. However, the map wasn't detailed and proved to be of little use. Instead they tried to carve a systematic route through the disorientating shroud of fog, walking first around the whole perimeter of the graveyard and then around each petal. However, they could see that many graves stretched back beyond the paths, lost to thorns and foliage and that it would be impossible to locate all the angels in these inhospitable conditions.

"I really don't think Tomasz would expect you to go deep into the undergrowth; wouldn't he choose somewhere safe and obvious?"

"He's a crime writer, Mum; he would want to keep me guessing to the end."

After walking for over an hour they became hopelessly disorientated and took a further half-hour to find their way out of the Cemetery onto Church Street, by which time they were cold and hungry. They returned home for lunch, despondent.

"I'm going to kill him if I ever find him." Julia hugged a cup of hot soup with numb hands.

"Why would he choose that particular angel? Out of all the angels, why that one?" said Beth, who was now completely captivated by the solving of the riddle.

"I don't know, perhaps he liked it."

"But that's not how a detective's mind works, is it? Remember I'm a big fan of detective novels, everything is there for a reason; every character; every stone; every name."

"Every name." Julia sat up. "What about Dryden? The whole riddle led us to that quote from Dryden – *Love's the noblest frailty of the mind*. Let's do a name search on the Abney Cemetery site."

"But John Dryden isn't buried there; he's in Westminster Abbey."

"It doesn't matter. Perhaps it's just a way of identifying the Angel; the meeting place."

"It's a long shot but give it a try."

Julia tapped the keyboard. "OK, there are thirteen Dryden's buried in Abney, all with section references. I'll mark them with crosses on the map; it will narrow our search, although it could still take ages; there are loads of graves in each section."

"What about *Where Brook flows to Elm Tree, this Angel takes flight*. It's the only line we haven't worked out; I'm pretty sure there isn't a brook in Abney, but there are plenty of Elms. Do you think it means anything?"

"Hang on," said Julia. She examined the map closely. "Yes, I thought so; the writing is very feint but I can just about see each path has a name: Oak, Hawthorne, Elm. And there's Brook. Mum; one of the crosses falls on the intersection of Brook and Elm. This must be it."

Beth jumped up and looked out the window. "The sun's trying to come out. You still have… forty minutes to find your angel. Do you want me to come with you?"

"No Mum; I have to do this on my own. If he isn't there on the dot of sunset I promise I'll leave."

By the time Julia reached Abney Park the sun had succeeded in burning away the fog to reveal a clear, milky-blue sky. But the day was rapidly growing colder and misty breaths curled above her head like ghostly tendrils. Julia walked quickly, pulling her coat tighter around her. She felt inordinately nervous as she entered the cemetery gates, realising that within the hour she might once again see Tomasz. Now that it was a real possibility she wasn't quite sure what she would do. This was new territory for them both.

Even with the reference, it took some time to find the Angel; it was smaller than she'd imagined but nevertheless quite beautiful. She pulled the photograph from her pocket and held it up to compare the two; they were identical. The light was fading fast and she switched on her torch, aiming the beam along paths and into dense undergrowth for signs of Tomasz, or less desirable apparitions, but there was nothing. She bent down to read the inscription: *In loving memory of Thomas Dryden, beloved husband of Jessie, who passed away on November 29th 1914 aged 36.*

The bells of St Mary's struck four.

"OK Tomasz, you have six minutes to get here and then I swear on your Polish arse I'm going to leave." She stooped lower to take a closer look at the inscription, most of which was covered by undergrowth. She pushed back brambles and nettles and focused the torch on the plinth to try to read moss-ravaged words carved nearly a century earlier. At the very bottom, barely legible, was engraved: *Know most of the rooms of thy native country before thou goest over the threshold thereof. (Thomas Fuller 1608–61)*

A shiver went down her spine.

"You look so beautiful in the setting sun."

Julia jumped up to see Tomasz standing behind her.

"How long have you been watching?"

"Long enough."

Epilogue

People don't walk in straight lines; they make patterns – curves, zigzags, messy diagonals, great flourishes, tight circles. This thought turned around in Beth's mind as she sat on the little bench underneath the window. .If she could see the pattern her life was now making she thought it would look quite beautiful and, above all, simple. This was the sunniest spot on a June morning and peaceful too, except for the chatter of birds, the hum of lawnmowers and the buzz of bees collecting pollen from rock roses and foxgloves. The day was heavy with honeysuckle, wallflowers and lemon balm releasing their scent into the air. If she breathed really deeply, she thought she could just about catch the salty odour of the not too distant sea. She felt a little emotional.

A butterfly flew across her path and skittered about buddleia and red valerian; it was a Common Blue. She was beginning to learn the names of a small section of the plethora of wildlife to be found. Common Blue, it looked anything but common. It didn't stay still for long; it flitted from plant to plant, landing on a spray of white clover in the grass before dancing into the air and perching on the arm of the bench. Beth noticed that the wings were edged with back and white and that close up the colour was a startling, iridescent lilac. The wings closed, touching over its body to reveal a greyish, ground underneath and then it slowly opened again to display its unashamed beauty. She only had a few seconds to take this all in before the ephemeral creature was gone.

Beth gazed along the gravel path, curving gently past the front of the house. For the first time she noticed, with an unexpected glee, that it was not only made up of a colourful mix of pebbles but also a variety of small, broken shells. She removed her sandals and allowed her feet to nestle in the sun-warmed mass. She closed her eyes and imagined herself on one of the cherished beaches of childhood.

The sound of a car horn shook her back to reality. She brushed pebbles from the soles of her feet, slipped her shoes back on and adjusted her cardigan; then she ran along the drive to the gate.

"It's a lovely day." Richard smiled through an open car window. "Are you still up for a spin to Liverpool?"

"Ooh yes; but...can we go by ferry? I haven't done it for years."

"If you like; we've got plenty of time."

Liverpool's waterfront gleamed with post-millennium audacity: skyscrapers, shopping centres and state of the art stadiums gathered, jauntily, around older, more conservative relatives, pushing closer to the river, higher into the sky.

"It looks hopeful, doesn't it?" said Richard.

"Yes," said Beth, "I'm glad."

They strolled around the deck to look back to where the Wirral and North Wales sparkled like an emerald in the sun.

"So how are you coping with retirement in Cheshire?" Richard asked.

"I miss Julia like mad, but I love it."

"It must be a tad dull after the bright lights of London. It's a quiet life, really."

Beth turned to Richard, "Say that again, please."

"What? … It's a quiet life?" They were leaning on the railings, side by side, their arms meeting in a comfortable and barely noticeable brush.

"Yes, that."